D1194055

The Lübecker

M. J. JOSEPH

the Peppertree Press

Sarasota, Florida

*This is a work of fiction. Resemblance of the characters presented
herein to persons living or dead is purely coincidental.*

Copyright © M.J. Joseph, 2018

All rights reserved. Published by the Peppertree Press, LLC.
The Peppertree Press and associated logos are trademarks
of the Peppertree Press, LLC.

No part of this publication may be reproduced, stored in a retrieval system,
transmitted in any form or by any means, electronic, mechanical, photocopying,
recording, or otherwise, without prior written permission of the publisher and
author/illustrator. Graphic design by Rebecca Barbier.

For information regarding permission,
call 941-922-2662 or contact us at our website:
www.peppertreepublishing.com or write to:
the Peppertree Press, LLC.
Attention: Publisher
1269 First Street, Suite 7
Sarasota, Florida 34236

ISBN: 978-1-61493-524-7

Library of Congress Number: 2017909546

Printed January 2018

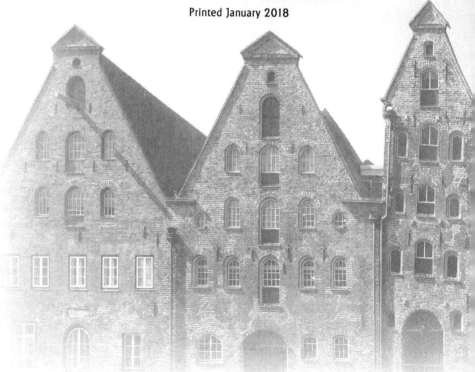

For Terry

1

Dr. Tomaso Bettoli looked down at Dr. Sam Yoffey, who was sitting on a blackened, scarred hickory stump, picking with the edge of his thumb at the black shell of a nut, exploring grooves where the nut's skin had lifted away. The stump had been created some years, ago, after a squall had moved in from the Bay over the Bluffs and blown the tree down. Men had hacked at the stump for a while, trying to shape it into something flattened, and their axe bites had left their straight and wedged marks. There were trees everywhere: hickory, oak, magnolia, all hung with moss swaying in the light breeze stirring from the Bay, below.

"Sam, you can't save them all; premature births are all too common, here on the Hill. The women don't let anyone know they're in trouble until it's too late. Some are afraid of their husbands, some rely on midwives. Who, knows." said Bettoli.

Dr. Bettoli was from New Jersey, and having served his commitment with the Navy, left his last station in the adjoining town to serve as a physician in the town across the Bayou from the Hill. He was only able to visit patients on the Hill once a week—far too seldom. He had let it be known through medical schools that he was looking for a partner and one day, Samuel Yoffey, late of South Carolina, had arrived at his door. Yoffey had worn the same clothes he was wearing today: khaki pants, white cotton shirt with two chest pockets, and cowhide brogans—all items procured from his father's dry goods and surplus store.

"I'll leave you, now. Maybe old Jones still has my boat unrented." And so, Bettoli left the tired, sad young man muttering to himself to walk down the Hill to the boathouse and hopefully, rent a boat to row back to town, to rest in his house atop Town Hill.

"It's 1886; might as well be 1786, as far as these poor women are concerned." Yoffey said. He looked out over the Bay, silver and calm with sea birds wandering from the Hill's shore out to the white sand island, the spit that enfolded the harbor. He lifted himself from the stump. It had been a long night, and the peace he'd enjoyed with the hickory nut was to be left behind for a while. He walked back to the little cottage, passing unwashed children of all ages, a parade of dirty bare feet, and mostly blond and light-eyed heads.

As he entered the house, he went into the mournful room and accepted the small bundle from Sister John. The nurse had worked with him several times, but neither Yoffey, nor the nurse had been able to accustom themselves to such scenes. Yoffey moved the bundle to his left arm and said to the Sister, "I'll take it to the Esther, if you'll see to the girl, please."

The Esther was the Hill's infirmary, hospital, and late-morning gathering place for the Hill's women, who sat in the most comfortable crux of its low stone wall to gossip and complain and keep account of their neighbors. The Esther House had been founded by Miss Esther Cord, a well-to-do spinster who had lived out her days in a tall, wooden mansion next door, the daughter of a timber magnate who had appeared on the Hill in the 1830's, the scion of an old, Mississippi plantation family.

Esther Cord inherited the white, columned house and a fortune that she devoted to establishing a hospital for the residents of the Hill with a group of nuns she had invited from across the South, most of whom had walked away from disparate orders to serve more of mankind and less of the Church. These women had kept their distinct habits, and somehow had captured the support of the nearest Catholic priest, who was careful never to mention the ladies of the Esther to his superiors.

Sam bent his back forward to stretch in the early day and cool air, quiet except for locust with their insistent buzz along the Bayou as the sun rose higher into a clear sky. Sam left a couple of hours after the rosy shafts of the dawn had begun to reach over the east bluffs and fall down the great hill that defined the community, bringing the season's heat through the trees to meet the Bayou's interminable humidity.

The young doctor left the small shotgun house, meeting no one except one or two of the girl's worried women relatives, some holding hands, some holding their sides or pulling and twisting stringy hair. All the men were in the Bay or the Gulf. A sandy path paved with magnolia leaves, each side lined with large white chunks of marble, all growing green with age, led away from the small house. The pervasive beards of Spanish moss hung slightly angled from the live oak branches tangled over the ill-defined yards that neighbored the sad home. Yoffey followed the dirt road along the Bay heights and decided to detour and trudge down the narrow trail dividing the native tangle of dewberry vines, yaupons, and false rosemary. As the trail began to rise, he came to the long thicket of palmettos which, as he'd learned as a boy in South Carolina, harbored rattlesnakes. The palmettos led up the hill, and he rejoined the road as it curved and straightened into a wide, dirt lane that led to the Esther Sisters, as they had become known to the tiny community.

The hospital had been established after the Civil War and the number of sisters varied according to a management Yoffey didn't attempt to understand. The "Mother" was always glad to see him, notwithstanding the news he brought or the time of day he appeared. As he walked up the concrete steps onto the porch, he noticed that the painted boards were wearing and flecked, but clean as always, the wood declining under the feet that trod them and the sisters' application of rough brooms and potent mops. He nodded to the thin black boy who rose to open the black screen door. As he entered the reception room, he was met by a new face fixed into a coif and veil and an old-fashioned, dampened bandeau. Her eyes shone light, brilliant gray, and she stood before the young man as an apparition of the type of Rococo light he'd seen in museums, a kind of beauty he could not recall encountering amongst the living.

As he opened his mouth to speak, Mother appeared, shook her head, and unclasping her hands, held them out to take the bundle. "This is two, this week, doctor."

"Yes, Mother, birth mortality is so common on the Hill," Yoffey said. "The womenfolk run themselves to death, trying to earn extra money across the Bayou, and the men are never around, until after dark. It's hard to know an ailing woman by the light of a kerosene lantern and then, after pulling up oysters or mackerel all day, trying to look at them through eyes half drunk or half asleep. I am a twenty-six year old doctor, I do not want to keep delivering these premature and stillborn babies, Mother. I suppose that I'm just tired."

Tears welled up behind Yoffe's spectacles, over his soft brown eyes. His ample mustache was damp, and the curls of his black hair, loosed by the removal of his hat, had spilled over his forehead. He bowed, walked out onto the porch and sat down at the left edge, knocking his heels against the brick that lined the bottom and hid the cool and dusty underside of the building. He allowed a few of his tears to fall and took out his plain, white handkerchief, to wipe them away and blow his nose.

The sisters were busy, as always, working the grounds' verdant collection of flower bushes, hedges, and grass, as well as cleaning, and more cleaning of the stone fountain with its Virgin standing, hands clasped. Other nuns walked their patients around an elliptical stone path that circled the building or pushed them in wooden wheelchairs, silently cutting through the usually indifferent and voluble gaggle of women who had found the perimeter wall's ideal corner. Behind Yoffey, a steady influx of maids with food from the richer families mixed with the sick and the dying to enter the front door and leave their offerings. Occasional cackles and southern articulations of *uh-huh* or *uh-uh* or *ah-ha* of ladies filled the air as visiting Esther Foundation members came and went, most hailing from across the Bayou and town.

Presently, the young sister he'd encountered came out of the building and offered him a cup of strong, black coffee. Yoffey accepted it and ashamed of his tears, whispered, "Thank you, Sister."

She stood behind him for a few minutes,until he seemed calmed, and then sat down next to him. Her bright eyes and full lips were the only things he noticed and pulled his mind away from his amassed grief and into her presence. She offered her hand, a defiant gesture that would never have been allowed by her original order and introduced herself as Sister James.

Yoffey accepted her hard and callused hand and said, "I'm Sam Yoffey. You'll have to get used to me. I'm the only doctor practicing east of the Bayou. Your physician on the Hill, ma'am."

"Dr. Yoffey, that's a beautiful accent you have. South Carolina? I believe that I've heard it at the abbey, where I trained."

"Yes, ma'am, born and bred, except for some training in Paris."

The two young people sat quietly. Sam sipped his coffee, trying to revive his spirits and alertness, and Sister James watched the activities of the other nuns about the hospital grounds and the antics of the poor Hill women, who occasionally rose from the wall to bring to life an absent member of their tribe with comical, idiomatic wiggles and other more lively gestures. "Where do you maintain an office, Doctor?" the young nun asked. "Do you live on the Hill, or in town?"

"I work out of my home, on the highway, just through those trees. It's just a small house. Not much to come home to, but I bought it with money I earned in Charleston and some help from my folks."

"I must get back to work, Doctor; I will see you again." Sister James rose quickly and her heavy, black heels knocked loudly across the wooden porch, but were somewhat softer as she went inside, the door opened again by the black boy. He sat back down onto the unbending boards, leaned back against the white, lap-staked wall, and seemed almost asleep. But with his down-cast gaze and heavy eyelids, it was impossible to tell until someone approached the screen doors.

Yoffey left the Sisters of Esther and walked east around the point where the streets met, doubled-back, turning west where First Street met Second Street, and ambled the short distance to his home. It was a small, tan stucco house with a neat yard of various types of trimmed grasses, surrounded by a white picket fence. The small sign on the right porch pillar read: Dr. Samuel Yoffey M.D. Against the doorframe rested a somewhat tarnished, gold-plated mezuzah, which the doctor instinctively patted as he pulled open the screen door and entered the front room. The mezuzah was a gift from the rabbi he'd grown up under, a very old and dark man, a descendant of the Brazilian Sephardi who had traveled north with the traders and arrived hundreds of years ago in Charleston. On the office desk, under his rusting grapeshot paperweight, Sam found several hand-scrawled messages, most asking for appointments and stating when the patient would return for an answer. Sam sat down, sorted the messages, and attempted to distribute the appointments according to the patient's scheduled return, finding only one or two conflicts. This was a daily routine for the doctor. He picked up the grapeshot and wondered: Spanish or English?

Sam unlocked the inner door to his parlor and found one of only three pieces of personal furniture: a long, dark chaise. He hung his hat on the fancy end-post and taking off his spectacles, laid them on his chest after he'd lain down and begun to rest. He was of average height, with well-developed legs and a robust chest. He was black-hairy, and where the sun usually struck him, darkly tanned, but otherwise pale. His hair was usually unfashionably long due to demands on his time but mostly because of his dislike of using the services of the Hill's barber.

Most of the people on the Hill thought Sam was Greek—one of the many ethnicities attracted to the greater community of the Bay and its adjacent community where Yoffey practiced. Even the barber thought he was Greek, giving himself free reign to express his outrage that Jews and niggers were allowed in Florida. The barber was a tiresome, dour man, whose clientele were mostly the poor fishermen of the Hill who frequented his shop to get a shave and a haircut, but mostly to stock up on his various offerings of chewing tobacco and snuff.

Sam slept undisturbed until four, when his maid arrived to clean and prepare dinner. She was a large, black woman of eighteen named Gomey Luke and usually brought her son, Temple, to help. Temple was a large boy, only four or five, and given to periods of extraordinary indolence. The doctor would often be distracted from examining a patient by Gomey's high voice filling the small house with a variation of "Temple, you 'bout wulfless!" Gomey had her ways also. During his first year in the Village, Sam had found that she grew more and more agitated as dusk approached, and as the days become shorter into the fall and winter, she would arrive at his place earlier and earlier.

One day, Sam asked her why she just didn't come at four o'clock every day, as he had asked, and Gomey replied, "Boss, colored people ain't gonna be caught on the Hill after dark, you ought to know that!" That being understood, Sam walked down to Jones' Boathouse Crabs and Bait and asked old Jones to send him a reliable bayman.

The next day, a spry young man of eighteen or so arrived at four o'clock. The boy still had pimples and wore a relatively clean, white cowboy hat. He had long legs that exceeded the length of the faded dungarees he wore and a clean, stiff work shirt favored by people of his kind. A Florida coast accent betrayed him as a bayman's son, with perhaps enough literacy to get him through the life he expected to lead. When Sam stood up behind his reception desk, he said, "I'm Dr. Yoffey, what can I do for you, young man?"

The boy replied, "Well, I reckon it's what I can do for you now, Doc. Old Jones sent me." The boy shifted his weight from one foot to the other and cocked back his head. He was unusually clean for a person of this community—fingernails white, wearing recently laundered clothes.

Sam looked him up and down and decided that the boy could handle himself in a scrape, given his height and attitude, and so asked, "Do you own your own boat? Do you hate colored folks?"

"Well, Doc," addressing the last question first, "I ain't gonna bed down with one, but no, they don't bother me. I didn't come from the Town. I grew up in the Bay, where it's just work and minding your own business. I have a boat."

"What's your name, son?"

"Well, I got a kind of a Yankee name—at least that's what my friends say. It's Willard Wentworth. Everybody calls me Willard. My old pappy was named Millard. He died when I was four from something that hit him at Petersburg. My mammy is still living, though, and takes in washing and on Friday, helps old Jones clean fish."

Sam told Willard to sit down. "I have a colored maid who is afraid to be up here on the Hill after dark. Now, I don't want her here until four and her duties will keep her until after dark during the late fall and winter. I need a white man to escort, to take this woman back across the Bayou after dark. I'll give you a nickel a trip. I'll keep you working throughout the year—light or night. You'll have to come up here to get her."

"Deal, Doc. I'll take care of it, and if white folks give me a hard time, I'll handle. Most folks around know better than to mess with me."

"Just what I want to hear, Willard. Here's a nickel, in advance."

"Thank you, Doc. I'm your man. Where'd you find that grapeshot?"

"One of my patients brought it to me. He said he found it one day when he was digging out a root at the Esther.

"English, I reckon, Doc."

"See you tomorrow, Willard, at four."

Gomey agreed to the plan, and as the years went on, she became somewhat haughty about the fact that she was escorted every day by a white man. Temple became somewhat relaxed around white people, although segregation would keep him and his succeeding generations down for another hundred years. Willard and Temple became friends and it was not unusual to see them coming up the Hill with Gomey with Willard's arm around Temple and Temple wearing a pair of Willard's salt-stiffened, old shoes.

Sister John continued working with Sam for a few more months on the Hill, then one day as Sam was on his way to the Esther, he found the old nun lying in a patch of deep, green grass, just up the street from the hospital. She was clutching her cross, but a few ants were crawling about her face and rigor mortis had begun. He ran to the Esther and got a rickety gurney and the black boy at the door, and they brought the body back to the hospital and Sister John's companions. He stood over the body as Mother brought in the death certificate for him to sign, and brushed away the ant that he'd missed when he was wiping her face, as she lay in the grass. The Sisters gathered around the body and Sam, nodding to Mother, left them in peace and to their grief.

Sister James began working with Sam. In the week following Sister

John's death, the young nun would usually walk to the doctor's door and give him a note on Esther stationary, signed by Mother Simon Mark. Usually, the note portended a birth with a woman's name and address, but sometimes it held details of a chronically-ill member of the village, usually a diabetic or heart patient. Sometimes an injury would enter the endless stream of Esther requests and Sam would become somewhat excited by the challenge. He would usually have to negotiate a fee from the patients, but occasionally Sister James brought one or two silver dollars from the hospital taken in from the numerous churches, even Protestant churches across the Bayou, that seemed to stand on each street corner of the town.

In late March of 1888, Sister James appeared at Sam's door with a note from the Mother, asking for assistance with a young man who had been involved in a boat accident. The day had been blustery, with heavy clouds of blowing rain. The patient had rowed out to the family fishing smack to check the anchorage across the Bay and found himself boarding a swaying and rocking boat with an unsecured boom swinging wildly. The sail was slightly unfurled and moved the long boom with unbelievable rapidity. The man's younger brother eventually rowed out to help but found his brother unconscious and bleeding from the head with an apparent broken arm and severely cut leg. The brothers made it back to the bluff steps, but several neighbors had to be enlisted to bring the injured man to a waiting wagon through the squall that had finally loosed upon the Hill. The wagon took the wet, cold and battered man, now wailing with pain and fear, to the Esther.

Sister James came out to meet the wagon under the building's portico and ran back in, immediately asking Mother Simon to examine the patient. Mother Simon didn't have to see the man. His screams of agony were enough for her to instruct Sister James to go to Doctor Yoffey's office and bring him back at once with her to the Esther. Sister James ran out, past the wagon, just in front of a group of soaked nuns and attendants delegated to bring the injured man inside to a waiting bed. She was almost blinded by the rain, her heavy black shoes full of water by the time she had gotten to a swamped Second Street and turned the corner towards Sam's office. She slogged her way along the muddy furrowed road, stepping up onto the shoulder bank to avoid the occasional automobile, or much more often, a wagon. Several date palm fronds leaning out along the road slapped her as she sidled her way along the bank and her skin grew colder and colder as the relentless rain saturated her habit and eventually, her underwear. She stopped, removed her plain shoes, and rubbed the tender spots the stiff leather had left on the sides and heels of her feet. She jumped back into the outer rut of the road and began running again, barefoot, trying to make up the lost time, finally coming to the white picket fence in front of Sam's office. She hopped over the fence in her mud-stained clothes, ran down the concrete walkway, and up onto the porch. She opened the front door.

Sam sat humming the "Star-Spangled Banner," sorting papers at the reception desk. He looked up to see the barefoot young woman with clinging black clothes and limp coif and veil. Sister James' shining gray eyes held his attention, and he realized in that instant what he'd never dared admit to himself. He had fallen in love with this nun. He hurried around the desk and grasped the nun's shoulders. "Why in the world are you out in this weather, Sister? Stay right there. I'll be right back."

Sam ran to his parlor door and unlocked it. He found a quilt one of his patients had used to pay him with and returned to Sister James, wrapping her into the warmth of the heavy patchwork of cotton, holding her in his arms for a moment, perhaps too long. "Here, Sister, let me get you something warm to drink," Sam said.

"We don't have time, Doctor. We have to get to the Esther to attend an injured man."

"Give me an idea of the extent of the injuries, Sister."

"Cuts to the head and leg, I think, broken arm, maybe a concussion."

Sam went into his private quarters and found an old army poncho and the extra pair of high boots he'd bought from his father's surplus and retrieved his raincoat and an umbrella. He placed the poncho over the nun and pulled socks onto her feet and slipped them into the high boots. They left the office and walked along the banked roadside with Sister James holding onto Sam and managed to avoid most of the swamped roadway to the hospital. They climbed the wet steps behind the old wagon that had delivered the injured man and went inside, leaving the poncho and umbrella on the porch. They were met by the sounds of the man still howling with pain and encountered the gang of nuns and attendants who had brought the patient inside and were removing his clothes.

Sam shooed most of them away and told Sister James to put some dry clothes on and return as soon as possible. The poor patient was near shock, and after Sam had quickly assessed his injuries he injected him with morphine. In time, the injured man calmed down and began a rambling description of what had happened to him, mixed with a somewhat lewd fantasy about Lulu, who later was revealed to be one of his cousins. Sam sewed up the man's deeper cuts, set his broken arm and after Sister James returned, asked her to wrap the wounds. The man's head moved freely, and he remained conscious, despite the morphine. There didn't seem to be anything that time would not heal, but Sam could not bring himself to leave. He finally noticed that Sister James had not put on a coif and veil and was startled to see the damp, short, light brown hair spiked up away from her face.

Mother Simon walked into the room and looked at the two young people sitting beside each other. Sam was cradling his chin in his palms, elbows planted on his knees, leaning over the drowsy patient, and Sister James sat bolt upright in a dry habit, but with only wool socks covering her feet.

"How is the patient, Doctor?" Mother asked.

Sam jumped to his feet at once, startled out of his reverie and the warmth he knowingly shared with his assistant. Sister James stood up, also, flashing her bright eyes at the young doctor, as Mother spoke.

"And, Sister, why aren't you wearing shoes and all of your habit?"

Sam spoke first, "The patient has suffered several deep lacerations and a nasty contusion to the head. I've decided to stay and observe.

Shock could become a problem, and I may have to administer more morphine, Mother Simon."

"And the shoes, coif and veil, Sister?"

"My shoes were soaked when I went to alert the doctor, Mother. I have them drying by the kitchen stove. I forgot my veil, Mother Simon, in trying to assist."

"There is a reason God has us cover our heads, Sister James. Please remember that only Our Lord demands fidelity to your vows." As the Mother left the room, she muttered to herself, "I've lost another Sister, I fear."

Sam and Dr. Bettoli continued their partnership and the Hill, it seemed to Sam, grudgingly, began to benefit from their efforts. Bettoli was less and less a presence, as his own Town practice grew and Sam's competence expanded on the Hill. Sister James was absent for many months. Mother Simon assigned a new nun, Sister John Peter, to assist him on Esther missions. The broken bones and lacerations the baymen brought to him and the pregnant women, who had finally begun to visit his office for examinations, kept him busy, but he thought constantly of Sister James. He would not pursue questions concerning her absence with Mother Simon, but he looked for Sister James when he was required at the Esther. Sister John Peter did mention, one day, when Sam seemed particularly gloomy, that Sister James had been reassigned to the Mobile, Alabama Arch Diocese. He thought, "So, that's where that lovely accent came from", which made him more lovelorn.

Early in the spring of 1889, Sam invited the Town's new Reform Rabbi to dinner. By then, Sam had purchased a new home near the shores of the Bayou with money his parents had sent him, which allowed him to keep his own boat to use as a ferry. Rabbi Michael Fischer had been in Town for nearly a year and this was his first visit across the Bayou to see the only Jew living on the Hill. The Rabbi was short, rotund, and had wavy red hair that he parted high up on his head to conceal his receding hairline. He wore a kippah, though he knew that Reform Jews had exempted themselves from head coverings since the movement arrived from Germany twenty or thirty years before. He had heard about Dr. Yoffey from some of his congregation, those who had received the doctor into their community and used his services, but the Rabbi had never met him. All Rabbi Fischer knew about Sam was that he'd been raised in Charleston by parents who had been prominent members of the Charleston Honorable Society. He himself had been associated with the beginnings of the various social organizations of New York that were espousing Jewish assimilation, although he came from a relatively poor background and wondered just how much the Jewish groups springing up in north and south Manhattan really had in common.

Willard arrived in his blue boat at a dock on the west shore of the Bayou to collect the Rabbi at five. He asked for a payment of five cents, which the Rabbi had assumed Sam, as host, would have paid. Fischer silently gave Willard the five cents and Willard rowed him over to Sam's new dock, which was longer, sturdier, and fixed on heavier creosoted posts than old Jones' dock located a couple of hundred yards north. Willard looked curiously at Fischer and wondered if the kippah was some kind of Jewish device used against sunburn or bald spots. The crossing took five minutes and five words from Willard: "Let me help you out." Fischer took Willard's hand and was pulled from the boat onto the dock and pointed in the direction of the house.

Temple, peeking around the blinds, yelled, "Mama, mama, that company's here!"

"Hush up, now Temple. Get on back outside," Gomey told him.

Sam, hearing Temple, pulled on his formal coat and walked out to meet the Rabbi on the stone walkway leading to the house. "Rabbi Fischer, I've heard such good things about you. Welcome."

"Well, doctor, I've heard very little about you except that you never socialize with our community," said Fischer.

"That's true, and I regret being unable to mix with the Town's gentry, Rabbi, but being the only physician on this side of the Bayou, I stay rather busy."

"Can't afford a nickel?"

"I'm afraid, to purify an old saying, it's a case of bringing Moses to the mountain! Anyway, Willard gets a nickel out of me nearly every day."

The two men shook hands, and Sam asked the Rabbi how he found North Florida, proceeding to rib him about being the first and only "Yankee Rabbi" to visit the Hill. He showed Fischer around his gardens and allowed the smell of fried chicken and greens, with the ham bones removed, of course, to drift around them.

As Sam was showing and describing a particular camellia he was proud of breeding, Sister James came around the corner of the house with a small folio of documents sent from the Esther. "I'm so sorry for disturbing you, doctor, but I saw Temple, and he told me to find you here," said Sister James.

"Why, that's fine, that is just fine, Sister! You've returned to us! I hope Mobile was fulfilling. May I introduce to you the first Yankee Rabbi to visit the Hill? This is Rabbi Michael Fischer, late of New York, or some place north of our humble region."

"How do you do, Sister? The doctor kind of lays it on thickly, doesn't he?" said Rabbi Fischer.

The sister curtseyed and lifting her bright, shining eyes, said, "You'll have to forgive the good doctor. He's just trying to get even for our losses during the War of Northern Aggression, Rabbi." The girl smiled, batted her lashes, and instantly had the Rabbi imagining the young woman in a camisole, much to his discomfort. Her lilting Mobile accent, the perfection of her facial structure, and the suggestion of a slim figure under the black habit, were more than the Rabbi's imagination could redirect.

Sam had asked Mother Simon to send over all of the recent death certificates that needed his signature, and had had Gomey fry an extra chicken and cook an extra-large pot of greens. On cue, Temple came out to them carrying a basket containing the food.

Sam said, "Sister, we have over-prepared, so young Temple here is going to accompany you back to Esther House with this little bit of food for you and the other Sisters."

"My goodness, Dr. Yoffey, that's very kind of you! Bless your heart!" said Sister James.

And with that, Temple looked up at her with his broad, toothy smile and led the way back to the hospital. Sister James looked back and smiled again, fixing the Rabbi's attention in the way a wife, had the rabbi been married, would certainly have noticed.

Sam led the Rabbi into the house and sat him at the dining table. Gomey brought the food out and Willard, who had changed into footman's attire, served the food according to Sam's training. The Rabbi, whose family had emigrated from Germany a generation ago, had grown up poor and, sponsored, entered a local yeshiva, learning a narrow, Jewish, etiquette. Fischer found that this presentation was as entertaining as the Jewish households across the Bayou had offered during his recruitment to the Town's synagogue.

Sam poured the French wine. "Rabbi, please let us know if there is anything we can get for you."

"I don't know, with Willard serving, he'd probably demand payment for any extra requests, Doctor."

Shall we have a toast?" Sam and the Rabbi raised their glasses, and Sam said, "To this momentous visit by our blessed Rabbi! May he preside over a harmonious community and find beauty amongst its inhabitants!" They drank deeply. "Now, Rabbi, we have fresh gumbo as our soup this evening, and our entrée will consist of fried chicken, done according to a little recipe I picked up in Paris."

The Rabbi had consumed another rather large glass of wine, quickly refilled by Willard, and after the main course, felt himself sated. "This has been wonderful, Doctor, just wonderful. May I offer a toast, also?"

"Why, of course, Rabbi, please do!"

"To the great traditions of the South."

"Hear, hear, the great traditions of the South!" Sam lifted his glass with one hand and smoothed back his black locks with the other.

After the meal and the toasts, the men repaired to the smoking room as Sam enjoyed calling the front parlor. Their cigars lit, brandies in hand, the gentlemen began to talk about the only other subject in their present alcohol-infused universe—women.

"I believe it's going to be a Southern girl, for me, Doctor," the Rabbi said.

"Call me Sam, please. Rabbi, there's a quality about Southern women that us lucky few men get to appreciate. These are the daughters of Helen, of Aphrodite, Athena—the products of generations of good healthy breeding! You get yourself assimilated, Rabbi, and maybe you'll be able to recognize the goddess standing near you."

"I couldn't agree, more, Sam. Call me Mike, by the way."

"Well, Mike, allow me to tell you first, I'm going to marry that Sister James. You can put that in your pipe and smoke it, my broad-minded friend. I'll expect you to perform the ceremony."

"Gladly, Sam, just name the date. What about her religious vows? I would have to insist that she convert first."

"Well, if that won't get your doyens talking, I don't know what will, Mike!"

"You want doyens, Sam, you should see what I had to put up with up North!"

"Ah, hell, women are the same everywhere, in some ways. Except for my Sister James, of course."

"Of course. You better be glad that I'm a man of God, or I'd be leaving the Torah behind to get near that nun. By God."

"Michael, I believe you've about had all the liquor you need, my boy."

"Listen Sam, you wouldn't believe what those *sheina Meidelen* like to do with yeshiva students! By God, they'll curl your *payot*!"

"You're going to bring down the Big Y on yourself."

"Well, maybe I should shut up. Anyway, I should forget that *shiksa* of yours."

"*Shiksa!* I'll teach your Yankee ass to speak respectfully about southern women, Jew or gentile, you *Shiker!*" Sam reached over to the man of God and knocked him off of his chair, initiating a spilling of wine, the pulling of shirt collars, the swinging fists and repeated tripping, until Sam found himself testing the window's copper screen with his head until the rabbi got tired of trying to put the doctor through it.

Temple, peeking around the door and seeing Sam and Michael at each other, ran back to Gomey. "Mamma, them white folks is trying to kill each other!"

"Well, child, that's white folks."

2

It was a spring Saturday in 1894 in the Hanseatic city of Lübeck. David Rosenberg jumped the three slate steps down to the narrow sidewalk and skipped across the cobblestones of *Engelsgrube* to the wider, opposite walk. His mother's words as she saw him to the door, called after him as he flew out the stone-cased doorway, set amongst the ocher accented and rust brickwork. "Don't cause your aunt to bury you in a heap of garden stones, you little teaser!" He looked back at their home and felt an impish delight as he contrasted his family's new house with the whitewashed and ornamented wall of the neighboring house rising up to his left, just beyond the black iron gate closed against the dark and dank cobblestone passage that separated the homes.

The street was busy. Hansom drivers were easing their steeds around tight corners against the guttered fall of the crowned streets, and household servants were moving both ways, enjoying their half-days off duty. He looked back down to *An der Untertrave*, the street along the harbor, and counted six ship's masts rising from the *Holstenhafen*, then turned left toward the single spire of the Church of St. James, an enormous barb rising above the buildings, in partial shadow, before him. Lübeck was mild and bright, the late winter fog finally lifted and the boy's tread sure on the unusually dry stone pavement. He ran past the house fronts, most of which reached well into the sky with crow-stepped or sloped brick gables, always playing in the boy's imagination as sails, like those he watched coming down the Trave and furled on the ships lying-to in the *Holstenhafen* and the other harbor, the *Hansahafen*. He crossed *Breitestrasse*, the north-south thoroughfare running in front of St. James's, the seafarers' church, and skipped along the church's south wall, past the memorials built into the bricks, dedicated to men, all Lübeckers, resting in the cold, hidden, depths of the ocean that had offered them livelihood and adventure. He always wondered if perhaps his father, whose wealth had depended on the comings and goings of ships, had known any of the drowned sailors, like the Schenck brothers and the eight members of the Herwig family, there inscribed. Passing the church, he crossed *Königstrasse* and ran into the warren of *gänge*, the maze of carefully-tended alleys stitching the busy streets and, by their closeness, binding the residents of the old town to a convention of courtesy and very competitive fastidiousness. The code of tidiness, like the fortunes of many of the families inhabiting the dwellings among the innumerable twists and turns of the passageways, had prevailed like the chill of the harbor's waters for centuries.

The boy was excited, and catching his wavy reflection in the windows of the houses and shops, he tried self-consciously to keep a smile away from his lips. He clutched the note in his pocket from his *Tante* Kathe; his aunt had invited him to visit her at his grandparents' home. Kathe was finally making good her promise to visit in the spring. She was his mother's younger sister, a true Kahn-Matthäus, tall and blond, with many friends and, for David, a fellow conspirator against the machinations of the adult world. His mother called her *Athena*, as she spent so much of the year in Greece. He loved her and told his mother that he wanted to marry his *Tante* Kathe as soon as he became a man, which he declared to her, was only four years away. His mother told him that at sixteen, he might be too old for his aunt and screamed with laughter. That made no sense to him, but he delighted in his mother's, at least to him, incomprehensible joke, certain that the humor was dispensed from an exuberant and loving heart. Another true Kahn-Matthäus, his mother.

The journey to his grandparents' home from his own was taken with steps long-practiced by the boy. His life thrived between his parents' and grandparents' houses, between the women who filled them with life; they had been the stones bearing him through the travails of youth. But these walks to the Matthäus house, accompanied by his growing years, had begun turning David's thoughts to his absent relatives, his father's, the Rosenberg's. He had begun to consider the bits of information that had fallen to him about his father's family and had grown unhappy that he could not fill out a satisfying sketch of the other parts of his heritage, just as he remembered how the construction of his new home a few years ago had challenged his imagination, with beams and rafters jutting bare and useless from the completed side of the house. He had not met his other grandparents until he was eight, and would never see them again, both now dead. His father rarely mentioned his family in David's presence, and when he did so, it was usually only in reference to the family's sugar refining business. His only household reminder was a small candleholder his father called a menorah that had appeared a year ago on his father's writing desk.

He knew of an uncle, whom he understood to be older than his father and who lived in Klein-Wanzleben, where the company's offices were located. Although his father did not seem to be involved with the Rosenberg business, David knew from his mother that his father shared ownership of the sugar company with his uncle and that his father owned a shipping company separately there in Lübeck called the Sachenzucker Exports Company and took sugar refined in his family's factory in Saxony-Anhalt into his warehouses for shipment around the Baltic and beyond. Indeed, David often visited his father's office near their home on the west side of the *Altstadt*, the Old Town, and considered the building and the adjoining warehouses part of his provenance.

David raced on, hopping low walls, shortcutting the walkways, and sweeping over and through the efforts of fussy resident gardeners. He overtook several people, his sudden appearance startling and staggering elderly walkers, and more than once causing real annoyance to strolling adults where paths crossed. The morning light was parsed unevenly among the dwellings, the houses' density and heights determining the fall of golden rays upon the network of alleys, ceding most of the ground to deep shadows. As David raced on, sweat began to bead on his forehead and his light wool coat was becoming damp and burdensome with his exertion. The temptation to shed it was only overcome by his fear that someone would report his slackness to his grandmother, or worse, his mother. One's dress was to be correct, especially when in public. He decided to slow to a walk as he approached the crowds beginning to appear near shopping areas just off his grandparents' street.

He finally reached his grandparents' home at 3 *Hundesstrasse* and stepped under the stone arch and into the courtyard among delicate linden trees and budding lilies. The house's entryway was supported by ornate and volute pillars and capped above the lintel with curving stone, swept up into a smaller arch. A bronze plaque read: *Matthäus 1823*.

Thoughts of Kathe flooded the boy's mind as he came near the door. He remembered her last parting from him. The winter sun's light shone through the waves of her blond hair, affecting a halo that had dulled when she put on her fur hat. She wore an enormous fur coat. How would she look today? He opened the door and rushed by Lotte, the middle-aged housekeeper, and ran into his grandparent's parlor shouting, "I'm here, I'm here!" At once, Kathe appeared behind him and pinched his side, which caused him to give a loud "aawk!" The boy jumped and turned to her, startled, arms opened, but he screamed as he looked into a ghoulish, Greek mask his aunt had used to cover her face. Kathe wrestled him to the floor and tickled him mercilessly, laughing at his cries and resisting his twists and kicks.

His grandmother, Elisabeth Kahn-Matthäus, ran into the room and shouted, "That's right; hold that little criminal down, and I'll fetch *Polizeidirektor* Klinsmann! Lotte! Tell Gottfried to go to the *Bahnpolizei* at once! We have a very dangerous man in our house!" and then, "Gottfried! We don't have time for the police! Bring me a knife!"

This brought a loud wail from the writhing boy.

Finally, Kathe relented and got to her feet, pulling the boy up with her. The women were possessed by mirth and the boy brushed away tears of laughter as he continued to giggle. Kathe held him away from her and looking him up and down proclaimed, "*Mutti*, David has grown so! What have you been feeding him?"

"You'll need to ask his mother that question; he never visits his lonely old *Oma*."

"Not true! I do, I do, every afternoon, after *gymnasium!*"

"What is this noise?" David's grandfather said as he entered the parlor. Bernhard Gerfried Matthäus was a man of medium height, balding, with a slight stoop. He wore a magnificent moustache, still matched in color to his fringe of brown hair. He looked out upon the world above frameless spectacles perched mid-nose with kind blue eyes.

"*Oma* and *Tante* Kathe were torturing me!" David shouted.

"In all my fifty-four years I have never witnessed such a cruel scene! Did *Oma* threaten to cut off your spigot again?"

"Yes! But I fought her off, *Opa!*"

Bernhard looked at his grandson and thought, "So like these women."

Indeed, David was almost the image of his aunt. Slim, with finely formed limbs and blond hair, only his dark brown eyes announced him as his father's son. Bernhard asked David if his father was still away in Saxony gathering sugar beets.

"Yes, *Opa*, but he's expected home tomorrow."

"Well, you tell your dear father that I'm looking forward to seeing him next week." David would not forget to give his father his grandfather's message, as it seemed to him that the two men rarely spent time in each other's company. This, as the boy would learn as a man, was not actually true. His dearest male family members held twice weekly luncheon meetings where, as David would discover, business affairs and matters concerning his future were discussed. As quickly as he had appeared, Bernhard quietly slipped out of the room and left the boy to the attentions of the women.

"Mother told me that you were going to bury me in a heap of pebbles, *Tante!*" said David, looking straight into Kathe's eyes.

"I have heard that you have been boring old Lotte with your stories, little *Hermes*. We want her stay with us, you know," said Kathe.

"No, you cruel Athena!" David shouted, proudly shaking his head side-to-side and revealing *his* interest in Greek mythology.

"Well, I suppose there will be no need for pebbles, today, but don't forget, I'm *Tante Athena!*"

"*Oma*, I'm very hungry" David said as he heard Lotte rattling dishes in the dining room.

"Then, we must feed the little god," said Elisabeth.

"I'm not little, *Oma!*"

Dinner was finally served and the boy showed an enormous appetite, causing his grandmother to exclaim, "He eats like a beggar!"

Soon he was up and running around the table to Kathe, he began pulling on her arms, saying "Get up *Tante*, get up! It's time to go!" Kathe casually rose, and looking David in the eye, strode past him to her room.

They had left the Matthäus house at noon, and as soon as they were outside, David grasped her hand and led the way toward *Königstrasse*. As soon as they had left, the neighborhood could hear cries of "Slow down, David!" echoing through the streets as the boy pulled his aunt along the *Hundesstrasse*.

Kathe had declined her father's offer of the hansom, wishing to stroll the short distance to her sister's home and was surprised when David asked her to go to the *Katharineum*, the *gymnasium* occupying the old Franciscan monastery adjacent to St. Catherine's church. "I want you to see my roses and my rooms at the school, *Tante*." Though the monks were long forgotten, the buildings had been home to schoolboys for centuries. They walked west, and when they approached the east end of the *gymnasium*, David led Kathe through the narrow gang behind the school buildings. As they approached the rising church walls, David pulled Kathe toward three rose bushes tucked near the corner of the south transept. "I have named these bushes, *Tante* Kathe, *Oma* Elisabeth and Mama Gabriele."

Kathe walked to the roses and asked, "Which is mine?"

David said, "Yours has red roses, *Oma* has pink and Mama's roses are white." David took out a pocketknife and leaned down to cut the stem of a Kathe rose. He proudly presented the flower.

Kathe inhaled the scent of the flower. "David, did you know that when Roman mothers and fathers had secrets to tell, they would place a red rose on the door of their rooms to tell others to stay away?"

"Do you have secrets, *Tante* Kathe? I have. There is a secret concerning my roses!"

"And do you wish to share this secret?"

"My secret, *Tante*, is that these roses came from the old Jewish cemetery in Moisling."

"Why did you visit the Jewish cemetery, David? And who are you to take roses that were planted to honor the memories of those buried, there?"

David blushed. "*Tante*, I was forced to go there by Schneiderlin and Grow, the nastiest boys in the entire school. They wanted to show me where they planned to bury me after torturing me! They called me and father Christ-killing Jews! They said that the cemetery was the only place for Jews."

"But David, you are not Jewish, you have never lived in Moisling, and your father was baptized into the Christian faith. Those boys are wrong; they do not understand that for you to be considered a Jewish person, you'd have to become a member of that faith! Since your mother is Christian, you are not Jewish. Your father's heritage no longer applies to his religious faith. He is a Christian."

David knew from his grandfather Matthäus that over the centuries, few Jews had been allowed to live in the Old Town. Bernd had always delighted in conversing with his grandson about the city's history and, of course, his family's immemorial role in the course and progress of his birthplace. This was how David had first learned of the Jewish cemetery and the fact that David's Matthäus and Kahn ancestors had various dealings with the community's resident Jews. In fact, David's parents had never hidden his father's heritage and had taken the trouble to expose the boy to Jewish customs and holidays, all presented as part and parcel of the necessity of the Old Testament to the exegesis of Christianity.

"I understand, *Tante*, but the roses were growing everywhere, even covering the graves and tombstones. I thought the bushes made the cemetery ugly, and I became afraid."

"Why were you afraid, David?"

"I imagined the roses choking the people lying buried there!"

Kathe looked intently at her nephew and pulled the child to her. Her thoughts moved away from the scene to a time and place that twisted and bound the strengths of her mind and heart. She recovered herself and said, "David, you shall have no more trouble with those cruel boys."

"But they really *believe* that I am a Jew and should be killed!"

"Let's speak no more of it. Thank you for showing me my red roses, darling boy." Kathe made a mental note to mention David's dreadful experience to Bernd, who she knew would speak to the school's director about the behavior of Herr Schneiderlin and Herr Grow. Like all Matthäus's and Kahns would have expected, Kathe *knew* that something would be done.

David led Kathe into the open yard behind the school and pointed out the rooms where he spent his school days. He described his teachers and his studies and a galaxy of friends who shared his time at the gymnasium. He told Kathe of the retired soldier who occasionally gave special lectures during history class. The elderly man had been a Lübecker, who left his independent, native city to attend the Prussian War Academy in Berlin. Although he was commissioned before its founding, his service helped fulfill the commitment of the then named North German Confederation to the German Empire in the days before Germany became largely unified. The boys listened to him describe his rise through the ranks, his duties as a general, and his Franco-Prussian War experiences, especially his posting at Versailles during the siege of Paris. His stories of the careers of a few of his fellow soldiers, some well-known to most of his countrymen, always ended with his deep voice demanding, "God keep the *Kaiser!*" David's uncle, General *Graf* Siegfried von Petersruhe, Kathe's husband, was always mentioned.

"Shall I tell you another secret, *Tante*?" asked David.

"Is your secret ready to be told, David? Does it *need* to be told, darling?" replied Kathe, with some unease.

"Only to you, *Tante*."

"Then tell me."

"I am going to apply to the Prussian War Academy, *Tante*. I want to be a soldier like *Onkle* Sigi."

"But David, what will your father do if you become a soldier? Why not follow him into business?" Kathe asked. "My Sigi is a noble and was required by his family and ruler to be a soldier, my darling."

"*Herr* Schlarp will be there to help father."

"But *Herr* Schlarp is older than your father! He'll probably retire long before your *Papa*!"

The boy stood quietly for a few moments. He gazed absently at the old school building before him and finally said, "I will not follow my father; it is my duty to help protect my family, *Tante*. All of my life, I've heard stories of Napoleon's occupation of Lübeck and other places: I will fight against Napoleons! "

"But your Papa will need to you to help him manage the company, *schatzi!*

The boy is too young for these plans, thought Kathe. "David, you must build upon your heritage; your father and grandfather belong to Lübeck! Your ancestors' names have been part of the city's life for hundreds of years! Traders, lawyers, men of commerce that make the city strong and independent. Your blood *is* Lübeck!" The thought of losing David to vulgar, militarist Prussia was abhorrent to Kathe. It was true that Lübeck could never be her life, now, but it was home, in spite of her own restless history. Unlike David, his aunt knew a great deal about her heritage: there were no mysterious gaps, no questions about either side of her family. She was a product of the Kahn and Matthäus families, names familiar through the ages as Ältermänner, or elders, of the merchant league of northern German cities that once made Lübeck its center. Nearly all the males, like her father and grandfathers, were lawyers and she inherited their facility for studiousness, far exceeding the requirements and expectations of her tutors.

Prussia was alien to Kathe, to be avoided, full of crass and intimidating philistines. She had hoped to see David growing into a scholar and businessman like his father and her own forebears. Her path into adulthood could not have taken her in a more dissimilar direction than the future the boy was proposing for himself. When she was sixteen, she began living in Tübingen, in the company of *Frau* Schmitt, her chaperone, once her mother's maid, auditing a curriculum of classical languages at the city's great university and, as she once put it to her mother a few years later, "studying the ancients to avoid the twin ruts of most German society—God and snobbery."

Her mother, recalling Grimm's tale, *Frau Trude*, had thrown back her head and said with feigned indignation, "It gives such a bright light!"

This brought Kathe's response, "*Mutti*, I haven't seen any black or green or red men or devils in Tübingen!" inspiring laughter between them. The easy banter of the two women had always brought on a period of homesickness after she took leave of her mother.

Kathe was deeply attached to her loving and patient parents, but even before the university, she had defied the ciphers of her family's class by becoming involved at fourteen with an intense and charismatic pastor, a man who had become nearly obsessed with her. She had wanted to deepen her religious commitment and had thrown herself into the strictures of the pastor's teachings, withdrawing from her friends and becoming a laconic and brooding presence in her home. Her mother wept and her father brooded at the changes this experience had wrought upon their daughter; this was not the gregarious and happy girl they had reared. All of this ended one evening when they were alone, after the pastor's attentions drifted beyond the ambit of Kathe's spiritual needs to the pastor's rush at her with an entangling embrace as he wrestled to kiss her neck and face. Kathe withdrew from his pleading, rough advances and the next day went to her father's office and begged Bernhard to contact a family friend to obtain permission to pursue studies in Tübingen.

Throughout her time at the university, living independently and feeling as if she was recovering from a period of morbid illness, she began to lose the sense of taboo her upbringing had instilled or, even, an inclination to explain herself. Her mother and father had regained the daughter they knew as a happy and lively person, but lost her daily presence. Though they had expected learned men to be drawn to her, they worried that if their conventions and fears weighed too strongly, they might lose her again, perhaps forever, and so supported her determined movement through a life dominated by intellectual curiosity, or as some of her friends, mainly male, concluded, *compulsion* to take them on intellectually.

Over the last few years, Kathe's life had moved from Tübingen to Zurich, where she attended the university and although her academic emphasis had been working in philology and ancient Greek, she took her degree in philosophy. She had frequently journeyed to Greece and Italy to work excavations and assist philologists, sometimes only as an amanuensis or custodial clerk. In the beginning, when a chaperone was still required, she sometimes managed, with a little bribe, to free herself for a day or so and found uninhibited companionship among the "diggers" and scholars working in the inspiration of their remote and ancient locations. Strong friendships developed, and she occasionally encouraged her male and female colleagues' eager and expectant hands to know her a bit, but she had not given over her virginity, and gently brushed aside the challenges, especially of the young men who fell in love with her. She had enjoyed sharing her body, and learned to find resolution with them, but it was a limitless intellectual embrace that she most asked for and offered, to the disappointment of a procession of her fellow scholars. But unknown to anyone, she felt compelled to preserve these moments, to prolong the after-image by using a simple code to record observations about these encounters and what they had triggered in her and her partners. Their names, their eye and hair colors, their vocal habits, and their scents became part of her note headings. The notebook, reading like an ancient text, full of epithets and coded location names, was precious to her. She wanted to remember these times, relive them, and compare her life against them through the years. Six years ago however, there arrived in her life two people, a male and a female academic colleague, and three years ago, a warm, older man, who came to be the culminant tenants of these remembrances, offering all she wanted. She closed her notebook and, now she had come back to Lübeck to share the odd joy that her marriage to Sigi, the general, had brought her.

David and Kathe left the gymnasium grounds, slipping through the narrow ally back onto *Hundesstrasse.* Turning right toward *Königstrasse,* they could see standing slightly to the southwest yet another standard of Christian Lübeck, *Marienkirche,* St. Mary's Church. The old gothic structure soared above all of the buildings in the Old Town, its brick buttresses rising out of the chapels built into the church's north and south aspects, like arms pushing up from the earth. The bells of the mighty church were the grandest in the city.

"David, what do you imagine when you see St. Mary's? I imagine a giant insect! Look at the buttresses, don't they look like legs?"

St. Mary's had been the Matthäus family's church for hundreds of years, the place of David's baptism. His grandparents, mother and he attended through the *Briefkapelle,* the Epistle Chapel, located on the side of the south tower, opposite the town hall. Kathe had abruptly ceased attending services there before she left Lübeck. David's father, though it was never discussed, had only been in the building once.

"Yes, *Tante,* I can see that, but please do not tell mother. Since you stopped going to St. Mary's, did you stop believing that God exists, that the stories of the Bible are only tales like the Greek stories? *Will you go to hell?*"

"I don't believe that church can help *me* with ideas concerning a God," said Kathe with authority, but she couldn't help fearing that her sister would be indignant if she knew of her directness in answering David.

"Some of my friends say that God does not exist anymore, that churches are God's gravestones. I'm afraid that because I listen to this kind of talk, and that because I would rather read the Greek stories than the Bible, I might go to hell. Why does God give us a choice, if he created us? Schneiderlin told me that my father and I are going to burn in eternal hell anyway, because Papa is a *Jew!* Why didn't God make all of us Christian? Is life just a worry about hell?" said David.

Kathe took David's face in her hands and said, "I believe that most people are born in goodness, and your father is very good.

I believe that young minds are half full of what they've been told to believe about God and half full of desires and whims that they have been told are evil and selfish. David, perhaps God set limits upon himself to give us a chance to do the things that would make *him* complete in our minds. He allows us to make choices and the church helps people know which choices would be most helpful to God. In guiding people, perhaps the Bible and the church use hell to frighten people into at least behaving themselves and, perhaps, into making the choices that are helpful to God. If you simply live life with compassion for others, it will lift your mind above worries about heaven and hell."

The pair turned up *Königstrasse*, eventually crossing the street behind St. James' to begin retracing David's steps. David began to see the tops of the ships' masts as they emerged from the narrowest run of *Engelsgrube*, the English street. He also noticed men touching their hats to Kathe and women smiling their appreciation of her beauty as they walked towards David's home. Kathe's cream-colored dress shone brightly in the sunshine, the style accentuating her bosom and, like all of the other passing women, distorting her rump, giving her natural gait a slight sway. This was not her preference in style, but she knew that her mother adored the dress and Elisabeth had been pleased to present it to her. Wearing it was an undemanding kindness, considering the challenges she had thrown up to her family. She was afraid, however, that she had presented her family yet another challenge with her response to David's fears. She considered what she had said and knew that she had not faithfully conveyed her beliefs into the words she offered him. But how to do it after years of thought and rigorous study? How would she refine the banquet of learning that had been hers into a mere child's portion? The words, the *poetry* required, eluded her, perhaps because she feared venturing too far with her sister's son, perhaps because for Kathe *all* is to be doubted, and that, for most people, was not a conclusion they would choose to live by.

David was pleased that Kathe had not dismissed his questions or mocked his fears. The serious moments did not give way to pensiveness; he was as happy as ever to be at his aunt's side and his thoughts gathered away from the destiny of sinners and took up some of the usual imperatives of his life. Hunger won out, and he thought about the afternoon meal after his nose detected *Rübenmalheur,* a sausage-laden stew the family cook served every Saturday without fail. Ships' masts began to appear taller, rising from the *Holstenhafen,* and he could hear the sound of a brass ensemble playing in the small park near the *Drehbrücke,* the new swing bridge, echoing through the street. Once again, he took Kathe's hand and pulled her into a quicker pace, as they began passing the last of the houses leading to his own. They had to stop abruptly at the numerous alleys spilling onto the street to allow people to emerge and board their carriages or step ahead of them onto the sidewalk. The pair recognized most of those encountered, and David's excitement was replaced with impatience as greetings were exchanged and small conversations initiated, especially between the ladies. David did meet *Herr* Schlarp, however, who invited him to visit the main sugar warehouse later that afternoon.

David's friends knew that he would be missing from their group from 1:30 until 3:00 on this and every Saturday afternoon and so organized their activities accordingly. If he went to the warehouse, he would miss them altogether this day, but an invitation from *Herr* Schlarp was not to be missed. The boys would normally meet at the north end of Old Town along the river, near the construction site of the new lift-bridge being built over the Elbe-Lübeck canal. The group would watch masons bricking the neo-gothic shapes of bridge towers at each bank of the waterway and the workmen in the smithing shed, robust and husky individuals pounding into shape smaller steel components of the bridge. The noise increased when drays heaped with materials arrived and shouting began between the drivers and the workmen—arguments about which cart to unload first, how many men were needed, and how much time could be allowed in transferring the freight to the site. The boys laughed continuously at the scatological bent of the workmen's swearing and the unrelenting complaining of the drivers sitting atop their wagons watching the unloading and handling of their consignments. The construction of the bridge had consumed half of David's life; it seemed that it would never end. But its completion was an article of faith amongst the boys because of the decision they had taken together the year before to place a memento of a lost friend within the tower on the Old Town side. The boy they mourned had drowned two years ago trying to swim to the Old Wall peninsula in the turbid Trave near this site where the river splits around Old Town. Each Saturday, the boy whose turn it had been to keep the memento would bring the object, a statuette of the Kaiser, to the gathering in the event an opportunity might present itself to secrete the little memorial into the building. David would risk missing the operation today, but trusted his friends to forbear leaving him out if circumstances offered them the chance to execute their mission. He had been the one the boy's mother had chosen to give the statuette, and it had been his idea to give it up to the group's wish to pay tribute to their friend.

Finally, David and his aunt arrived at the Rosenberg house, set apart from its neighbors by four massive ground floor windows. The door was set within an extended portico, which rose away from the house to enclose a stairwell within. Cream-tinted granite cladding faced the huge double-doors and the familiar reddish and orange brick completed the stairwell extrusion and the crow-stepped gable, a concession to traditional Lübeck architecture. The house, built in 1886, replaced two homes lost to fire a year earlier and was half again larger than the other houses on *Engelsgrube*, indeed larger than most of the private homes in the city. The new house incorporated a spacious conservatory into the rear third of the bottom floor, enclosing an area devoted to David's mother's use as a showcase for flowers cultivated in her small greenhouse outside. David used the lion's head knocker to bring the housekeeper to the door and stepped back as the door opened to allow Kathe to lead him into the house.

The housekeeper, Brigitte, smiled her greeting and curtseyed, pulling the door against her body as the pair entered. She helped

David pull his sailor's tunic over his head, taking it and Kathe's light shawl, as they paused in the wide foyer. David was allowed to wear a loose, white cotton shirt at home, a casualness his father insisted upon for the boy's comfort. This belied the family's rather formal decorum, but neither parent wanted a sweaty child in the house. Brigitte hurried David out of the room, fussing at his tousled hair.

"Gabi, what a beautiful dress!" said Kathe, as her sister approached from the drawing room. "You look splendid, as always."

"Says the modern Salome to an ancient Bathsheba!" replied Gabriele Dagmar Rosenberg *nee* Kahn-Matthäus.

The sisters embraced and stood looking at one another for a few moments. Gabi Rosenberg was a woman of twenty-eight years, like Kathe tall and slim, but with straight light hair naturally streaked with several blond shades. Her nose was straight, her skin as taut as a doll's face. She offered the innate geniality common to her family. "How is the saintly Mother Elisabeth, this day?"

"I don't think she's giving up on producing another John the Baptist. Papa is wearing *that grin*!"

"The *sleeping late* grin, ah yes!" said Gabi.

Gabi led her sister into the conservatory and seated her near one of the banks of flowers occupying space along the curving windows. "My son has been asking about you daily."

"He is growing into a sensitive young man. The sugar baron's sweet heir."

"You know, Papa calls Jürgen the *Zuckersheisser*!"

"Father thinks he's L'Arronge, with his dramatics, but mother is worse. Where did these people come from?"

"Jürgen says they should go on stage together!"

"God help us."

"Jürgen is in Saxony, I hear."

"Returning tomorrow. He went down to speak with his brother about an accident at the refinery. He's worried about conditions there; things have changed since their father died." Gabi said.

"I know it is presumptuous to ask, but is Heinrich neglecting the company again?"

"Speaking of L'Arronge, he's become a *Leopold,* I'm afraid."

"Well, don't forget that Leopold redeems himself in the end." said Kathe.

Gabi sat silent for a moment, and then said, "I believe that Jürgen will ask Heinrich to buy his part of the company. Jürgen told me that other companies, good, reliable, companies, have approached Heinrich about handling their exports. As long as Heinrich is involved with anything Sachenzucker, Jürgen will be worried."

3

Willard stood at the base of the dock with his arms folded, brow furrowed, and mouth set into a frown. He looked at Sam and said, "Ten cents, Doc."

Sam replied, "Ten cents, hell! What's gotten into you, Willard? You trying to get rich with this ferry service?"

"That rate is only for Rabbi Fischer."

"Why are you picking on the Rabbi? I know he's tight, but he *does* pay!"

"He called me a *hayseed!* I've never hoed a row in my life, Doc; I'm a Bayman, period. That boat ain't no farm, and I'm not about to take myself up in the country to raise no cotton." Willard knocked back his immaculate cowboy hat a few degrees beyond his forehead.

"Now Willard, damn it, he didn't call you a *hayseed*, he called you a *Hasid*. He was referring to a particular type of person who wears fringes exposed from under their coats. He just noticed that you had your shirttail hanging out under your pea coat. He didn't intend any offense, I promise."

"Well, I guess you Israelites have your own ways, but it's still ten cents."

"Seven."

"I'll think about it, Doc." Willard turned and walked long strides to the end of the dock and left in his blue boat.

Sam turned around also, and shaking his head, walked up the sandy bank and across the dirt lane to his home's walkway. He was still muttering to himself as he approached the screen door, noticing Gomey cleaning the horizontal wood slats of the hanging porch swing with particular vigor. "Gomey, are we expecting company, this afternoon?"

"Well, how should I know, Doc? You the society director around here. I just cleans what needs cleaning and this swing right here needs cleaning."

Sam knew something was afoot; Gomey didn't just put that kind of elbow grease into something unless there was urgency. This being a Thursday, he knew things were due to begin slowing down domestically, and seeing Gomey in Monday form inspired questions in the doctor's mind. He was constantly amused by his servant and her boy and couldn't imagine getting through the kind of life he'd chosen here on the Hill without them, but they were somewhat predictable, he thought.

That day, he had found himself with a relatively quiet afternoon; no babies ready to be born, nothing from Esther House, and just two appointments, the last of which didn't appear at the little office. So he took himself home from the office on Second Street and decided to take a nap, until Temple tapped him on the foot as he was drifting into unconsciousness and strange dreams on the parlor couch. "Willard say he needs to talk to you, Doc."

There was Willard, insulted and indignant, like Achilles brooding, standing on the dock, arms folded, legs fixed wide apart, and ready to take a stand. *Hayseed.* Good God. A precious afternoon of rest, ruined. He couldn't really blame Willard; he'd grown up in the Bay and that was all he knew. Farming, to Willard's mind, was anathema to his kind and to believe he was being called a hayseed, especially by a *Yankee*, was very low indeed. Sam would spar with him some more on the ferrying rate and a plan to do so was taking shape in his mind.

"Gomey!"

"Yes, sir, Doc? What you needs, now?"

"What's for dinner?"

"Oysters that I got fresh off the fish wagon this morning. I was the first one at him, after he blew his conch horn. Big oysters. Took Temple two hours to shuck them all."

"Do we have enough to send a dozen to Mother Simon?"

"Sure do, Doc. I had her on my mind when I picked them out of the ice. Got a whole potato sack shucked."

"Have Temple run up there and let her know that we'll be sending her some this evening. Ask him to look around for Sister James, also."

Okay, Doc." Gomey had already done all of this, arranging for Sister James to come to the house to get the oysters after 4:00.

At about 4:30, Sister James knocked on the front door of Sam's residence. Gomey greeted her, pushing her farther back on the porch with the screen door and inviting her to sit down on the swing. "I've just about got those oysters ready, Sister. Please wait out here, 'cause the house is so hot, and all." Gomey went inside and found Sam in his study and told him to go keep Sister James company out on the porch. Sam pushed his desk chair back, knocking it to the floor, and rushed out of the room without saying a word.

Gomey thought, uh huh.

Sam stepped out of the house and turned to find Sister James seated in the center of the porch swing. She had been rocking, and as Sam looked at her, she had the soles of her shoes extended out, away from her outstretched legs. She quickly pulled her legs back in and placed her feet back onto the bricks, pulling the hem of her habit down as far as possible, halting the motion of the swing. She said, "I'm here to receive some fried oysters from Miss Gomey, Doctor."

"Well, how are my friends at the Esther, Sister?"

"Everyone is fine. Things have been quiet for a while, God be thanked."

"Sister, may I sit with you?"

"Of course, Doctor."

Sam sat down gingerly, watching the slightly rusted chains hanging above, trying carefully not to tip the swing abruptly. He was dressed, as usual, in khaki pants and a white shirt, but also wore a fine brown sweater with a white wool scarf hanging loosely around his neck. He was quiet for a moment and then said, "Sister, caring for sick people is most fulfilling. I believe that God has given me this mission in life and my life here on the Hill has been most rewarding. Although there are days when I face tragedy and bereavement, I wonder if I was meant to face these things alone, as unbearable as they can seem to a man. I do apologize for being so forward, Sister, but when I have had a particularly trying day, I find myself thinking of you. I can *only* think of you. At my darkest moments, I find comfort in imagining what life would be like to share all of my joys and trials with a woman like you. I know that we were born into different traditions, but I think of you the way I believe God determined a man should think of a woman, and I forget that you have forsaken the world and, to my deep disappointment, the possibility of a man, of me as perhaps a companion to you." Sam ran his fingers through his dark hair, pulling his locks away from his forehead and looked deeply into Sister James' eyes. He instinctively took her hand and pressed it to his lips.

Gomey's heavy tread approached through the house, and Sam released Sister James' hand and sat upright, turning his body away from the nun. He didn't want to embarrass Sister James, and he certainly didn't want Gomey to witness such a delicate moment of candor between them. This was academic, as Temple, placed by Gomey, had been watching from deep within the azalea hedge along the far side of the porch and would report the entire scene to her later.

"Why, here we are, Sister. There's oysters for the Mother and a cake for you to share with the other Sisters," said Gomey, smiling. "I always love seeing my Sister James coming around to our lonesome place here on the Bayou! Helps cheer up old Doc here, always moping round like he do."

"Thank you, Miss Gomey; I hope to be coming more often." Turning her head and looking intently into Sam's eyes, Sister James said, "I'll be off now. Thank you all so much! I declare, Mother will be so pleased!" The nun rose, accepting Gomey's basket, and escorted down the steps by Sam, started her walk back to the *Esther*.

"Come in, now, Doc, dinner's on the table. Shame a man has to eat by hisself," said Gomey, shaking her head.

Sam did as told and climbed the steps solemnly and stepped into the house as Gomey held the screen door. She followed Sam inside and as he sat to his dinner, and brought out the doctor's precious sweet ice tea, made from the brand his mother still used in South

Carolina. Sam thought about what he said to Sister James and hung his head. How could he expect her to give up her life, to love *him*? But, he thought, here was one of the most beautiful women he'd ever seen, whose presence pleased and upset him, the thought of whom wrested him from daily cares and burnished his image of womanhood. There were other women, but they would all suffer from comparison, he feared, and he would ignore them all by just throwing himself into his profession. Now, he was beginning to pity himself, and he felt ashamed and silly. He began to eat and tried desperately to think of other things.

"Gomey, when Willard comes to get you, tonight, I'll have a note for you to deliver to Rabbi Fischer." After Sam finished eating, he went to his desk and wrote:

Dr. Samuel Yoffey
4 March 1892
Rabbi Michael Fischer

Mike,

Willard believes that you insulted him by calling him a Hasid. I would be, frankly, but Willard misunderstood you. He thought you were calling him a HAYSEED. To reconcile the perceived offense, he is doubling your ferry rates to ten cents. I tried to correct the misapprehension and even offered him seven cents, but I don't know if he'll take it.
I want you to bring that beautiful new Polish girl over to the Hill. Just get her in the boat with Willard and let her sit near him and you two come and have Sunday dinner with me. And don't let those damn Baptists get you hung up as a church guest this time, for God's sake. Tell the girl to smile at Willard on the way over, also.

Yours,
Sam

In due time, Willard appeared and escorted Gomey and Temple to his boat. He rowed them across the Bayou gloaming and helped them out at the Town landing. Willard tied up and walked with them to the top of the Town Hill and saw them to the street where they would catch the trolley for home. Later, Gomey sent Temple around to the Rabbi's residence, behind the synagogue, to deliver Sam's note.

Mike told Temple to wait, while he composed a reply.

Rabbi Michael Fischer
4 March 1892
Dr. Samuel Yoffey

Dear Sam:

What is a HAYSEED? Anyway, I'll ask Miss Yablonsky to accompany me to Sunday dinner, although I must question if this gives an appearance of prostituting a member of my congregation. Stop swearing about the Baptists, damn it.

Yours,
Mike

The next day, Friday, Sam went to his office early, as was his custom, to complete paperwork and answer any pending correspondence. He caught a ride with his neighbor old Jones, sitting uncomfortably beside the weathered old salt on the buckboard of his old boat wagon. Jones hauled boats for fishermen across the Hill to the east side of the peninsula, where he backed the wagon and slid the boats down a steep, sandy bluff. The boats always came to rest against a pile of discarded ties that ran for a quarter mile along the railroad tracks. Some of the boats, understandably, had blunted prows and some had misspelled obscenities painted along the hulls directed to the attention of railroad engineers. One read: "Stoke the wife, I'm tired." Another: "Keep going, she's on my hook." Sam jumped off in front of his office, yelling thanks to Jones, and began his day as the wagon bumped along toward the Bayside.

No babies were ready for his attentions, so Sam spent the day receiving patients. He had six scheduled and two sent over from the Esther. All were routine: sprains, shortness of breath, lacerations, and two children—a brother and sister—with lima beans stuffed up their noses. One patient sent over from the little hospital, a woman of twenty-eight who lived with her husband and three children on the northeast section of the Hill, came in to be examined for a stomach complaint. After Sam completed his examination, he accompanied her back to the Esther, instructing the sisters to prepare the woman for immediate surgery. He called Tom Bettoli for assistance and waited for him to arrive.

The surgery revealed that the woman was terminally ill with intestinal cancer. There was nothing the doctors could do and Sam asked the nuns to keep the woman comfortable with morphine. The hospital staff was able to contact the husband, a fisherman, later that evening and explained his wife's condition. Sam agonized over the thought that an earlier diagnosis might have saved the woman, but Dr. Bettoli assured him that the woman probably had just begun to experience symptoms. Sister James had been shaken by the outcome, thinking that the poor woman had been in the prime of her life with three children to watch grow up. The nun withdrew and wept alone on the front porch for a few minutes until she was able to compose herself enough to assist with cleaning the operating room. She watched Sam as Bettoli counseled him and felt his extreme disappointment with his attempt to help the dying woman. Sam washed and changed back into his office clothes. Taking a cup of coffee with Mother Simon and Dr. Bettoli, he began to revive his spirits and decided that he should go home.

The day was late and the Esther's driver took the doctor home in the covered wagon that served as an ambulance. Gomey was waiting for him and knew that things had not gone well that day. The black boy at the front door had advised Temple, who had stopped by the Esther having been looking for stray chickens around the Hill, that the doctor looked sad and to be sure to tell Gomey. He duly did, holding a chicken by the neck in each hand. Sam entered his house, sat on the parlor couch and lay back. He'd taken his straw hat off, which he'd worn in recognition of an unusually warm March day, and rested it on a dining room chair. He looked up, stretching his neck and closing his eyes.

"Ain't no napping time, Doc. You needs to get on up and wash for dinner. I gots something special for you, tonight," said Gomey. "You is having gumbo, and it's full of big shrimp I got off the wagon this morning. I got chickens for that special Sunday dinner you got planning for Rabbi Mike, too."

"When did I mention Sunday dinner, Gomey?" Sam slowly opened his eyes and set his hands to push himself away from the seat.

"Why, it must have been Rabbi said something, Doc."

"I'm thinking of inviting Willard, also."

"Doc, I knows you likes that boy, but he's just a scallywag what needs to stay out in the Bayou where he belongs. Just let Temple take him a mess of fried oysters. That'll make him smile."

"Just how many bags of oysters did you buy from the wagon, Gomey?"

"I told you two, Doc."

"No, ma'am, you said one."

"If you'd been listening, Doc, instead of daydreaming about pretty girls, you would have heard me say that Temple had shucked one bag."

"What makes you think that I daydream about pretty girls, Gomey?"

"Doc, is you or is you not a man in his prime? Ought to be looking for a wife, what you needs to be worrying about. There was a real smart-looking girl come around today from the Baptist church over in town trying sell me some kind of coonass cakes. She was looking to raise money for the church. Said they was having a lecture series, whatever that is."

"Lecture series, hell. I hope you didn't buy anything."

"No, sir. I knows you about half-Catholic and gives all you can to the Esther."

"Gomey, you have any more of that sweet tea, or are you just going to let my glass become superfluous to the evening meal?"

"There he go, talking fancy, down to the poor help, again. Purfalus, now that would make a good baby name, anyhow." Gomey went into the kitchen and brought a pitcher of sweet tea and sat it before Sam. She reached down, picked up a glass, and filled it with a flourish. "Now, then, got rid of old 'Purfalus.' You know, Doc, I think we ought to name that old tom what comes around at night, Purfalus. Any cat would be proud to have that name. Maybe I should have been an animal doctor, Doc, with an imagination like that. Might have found you a horse girl by now and had a mess of black-headed babies running around for old Gomey to chase after. Well, I reckon you'll settle on some sweet girl with a fancy Mobile, Alabama accent from a good, rich, Catholic family."

"Gomey, please, take Willard some fried oysters."

"Already have, Doc."

"What?"

"Already did, Doc. While you was going on about this and that, I had Temple run him down a dozen, or so."

"Or so?"

"Well, that boy has to eat, Doc. He ain't purfalus to the evening meal, usually."

"Gomey, isn't it time you went home?"

"I'm gone, Doc, soon as you gets through and I washes the dishes. You don't have to get yourself in a mood, anyway."

Friday came and went, and Sam spent his Saturday looking in on patients at the Esther. He had lunch with Mother Simon and spent the afternoon fishing off of his dock. Old Jones came over, and they talked about starting a motorized ferry service.

"Could get us a one-lunger, Doc. Somebody would have to learn how to work on it. Hell, Willard could do it. Pass me back that jar, there, Doc," said Jones. Jones had gotten Sam started with chewing tobacco and moonshine, and Sam always looked forward to spending his Saturday afternoons with the old pirate, as Jones was known around the Hill. "Here, Doc, try a plug of this. Came from Mobile. A young feller comes over to visit with his sister at the Mercy, one of them nuns, and brings me bag every couple of weeks. If you like it, I'll tell him to bring me a couple of bags. Has some special name for it, which I forget right now. Real friendly feller with some education from the sound of that accent. Mobile, sure enough."

Sunday morning, after early services at the A.M.E., Gomey and Temple appeared in the house to prepare Sunday dinner. Gomey was still humming hymns and Temple climbed and ran and hollered like a wild boy set free from some form of cruel bondage. As she opened Sam's bedroom curtains Gomey said, "Doc, 'bout time you got up. You Israelites always taking your time like old Moses. Forty years, it took him to find the Promised Land. Well, I reckon it'll take you forty years to find a wife the way you're going, and like poor old Moses, you'll miss the Promised Land too. At least in that department, if you knows what I means."

"Gomey, the coffee brewed, yet?" asked Sam, yawning and running his hands through his tangle of black hair.

"Doc, do you smell any coffee brewing? Just because you and old Jones gets into some shine on Saturdays and you can't crawl out until 9:00 on Sunday morning, ain't going to make me get that coffee under your nose right when I wakes your shaggy self up on Sunday mornings. Go on, get yourself a bath! Moaning round here like some Bayou scallywag. The Lord strike me dead, but I wish I could lay around until 9:00 on Sundays. But I hears His call and I'll be skinned if I'm going to turn heathen like some folks I know," said Gomey.

Sam slinked off to the bathroom and shaved clean and showered leisurely, now that he had had a gas water heater installed. He looked at himself in the mirror after wiping away the condensation and saw that his eyes were not as bloodshot as he thought they would be, but he certainly needed a haircut, a chore he'd forgotten again yesterday.

After breakfast, Sam went behind Gomey to see that the house was in order and found he had only to organize and put away his medical literature and wash out the spittoon, which Gomey usually cleaned. Finally, the smell of fried chicken and turnip greens pervaded the house and Sam relaxed, waiting for Mike and Miss Yablonsky, whose smile he hoped had softened Willard's heart back to seven cents a trip.

At 1:00 p.m., Willard appeared at the porch, opening the screen door for Miss Yablonsky and Rabbi Fischer. He was smiling, and when Sam went to pay him, Willard waved him off, saying, "I'll make this one on the house since you sent me that dozen fried oysters the other night. We'll just keep it at a nickel, Doc. The one rate makes it easier to cipher." Willard left and found Temple merging with him as he walked toward the dock. He handed Willard a chicken leg, matching the one he had been enthusiastically gnawing. Temple elbowed Willard and whispered, "She fine, Willard. Rabbi got him something for dessert!"

Inside, Sam greeted his guest with enthusiasm saying, "Rabbi, the congregation just gets more beautiful," while looking at Miss Yablonsky. "Ma'am, I hope you had a comfortable passage across the Bayou; please make yourself at home." Sam winked at Mike and after seating them in the parlor, excused himself to survey the dinner table one last time. Gomey stuck her head out of the kitchen and gave Sam a questionable look and disappeared again. Dinner was being served. Sam walked back into the parlor and saw before him Rabbi Mike, Miss Yablonsky, and, to his shock, Sister James. Miss Yablonsky sauntered over to Sam and put her arm through his and with an excruciating Lower East Side, New York accent said, "Doctor Yoffey, I didn't realize you had acquaintances outside of the faith."

Sister James stood stock still, slightly blushing, which to a Mobile girl was horrifying and said, "Doctor Yoffey, I won't disturb you any longer, I just wanted to return these platters and the basket we borrowed last week. Mother Simon sends her best regards and thanks." She looked at Sam with blazing eyes and a slight jutting of her lower lip and went out of the room.

Sam felt his mood plunge, and leaving his guests, he followed Sister James to the end of the front walk. Using both hands, he pulled her back to him and leaned his head down and whispered, "Miss Yablonsky and I are not involved romantically, Sister. Look at me, please."

Sister James turned in Sam's embrace and met his gaze.

Sam said, "Marry me, Sister James."

4

The polished gravestones reflected Jürgen Rosenberg's movement up the low hill. The grounds of the cemetery in Hildesheim were turning from winter brown to green, and the linden trees were showing leaf-buds above their knaggy trucks as a few small birds played among them. The trees' grasping gnarls had held the soil still for the many generations buried and those destined to rest there. As Jürgen walked, he remembered a phrase from his youthful Torah lessons: *Olam ha-Zeh*—the world of falsehood—the tuition one must pay for the Messianic bliss to come. He breathed the air of his parents' and brother's sinful, suffering world, pitying them, and felt sorrow for their acceptance of the ancient teachings that guided them. He was grateful for his health and the joys of this life. He accepted the suffering and the pleasure life's passage held for him. *Olam ha-ba*—the world is simply here, he thought, and there is nothing to be done about it. He thought of another phrase he'd heard from his sister-in-law: *We are only in our bliss when we are in greatest danger.*

Near the top of the low hill he arrived at the graves of his parents, and looking at each flat headstone's Jewish calendar dates, thought how meaningless the numbers would be to his own wife and son, to nearly all of his friends and acquaintances. Nathan Amos Rosenberg, Miriam Wolfssohn Rosenberg, the names inscribed in handsome, flowing script, were strangely alien to him, names representing their and his own past lives, for years now, little associated with his life, the deaths worked out of the patterns of his day-to-day existence. Standing before their graves, he knew that time had not allowed the difficult memories of his relationship with his parents, especially his mother, to be softened by singular, contented moments remembered from his early childhood before his apostasy.

The subsequent years had brought nothing but greater strain and fewer and fewer visits, even as they had bound their businesses together. Nothing had been redeemed for Jürgen, except the quiet assurance that his father had loved him in defiance of his mother's unalterable bitterness toward him, the prodigal son. No judgment or wish to shun his presence came from Nathan. Jürgen asked himself, perhaps for the thousandth time, how he could be so utterly unlike his parents, especially his mother, as to defy comparison. But yet, a close look revealed Jürgen's physical similarities. He possessed his father's impressive height; large, hazel eyes; thick, straight walnut brown hair, combed-back from a widow's peak. And from his mother, he had inherited a prominent, slightly hooked nose, strong jaw, small ears, and slim frame.

Jürgen, standing alone on the graveyard hill, recalled his mother moving toward his father's open grave, his father's brothers, bearing her between them. His brother Heinrich followed as they walked up the hill, dodging the gravestones of the Jewish Cemetery. The woman would not look at Jürgen. Her steady hands dabbed a handkerchief to her eyes, but her flushed face was unbowed and her mouth set, a thin banner of inexorable determination to bend her world away from the dead man lying within the beautiful box she approached. She had pulled her arms away from his uncles, gently, and nodded to them to sit with her as Heinrich, his father's designated *Kaddishshel*, began to recite the mourners' *Kaddish* prayer. *Yitgadal ve-yitkadash, Shmei rabbah*—may his name be magnified and holy—all for the glory of the master of the universe, the first step in pushing the mourners beyond their grief. While the casket was lowered into the earth, Jürgen had thought only of his father as his relatives had eyed him with scowling features or simply indifferently. Heinrich, weeping openly, tossed in the first soil, followed by Nathan's brothers and a close friend. His mother, standing erect and unmovable, eventually swept her hand over the grave, then bending down to grasp a tea cup of black earth, she cast the soil into the gaping lesion amongst the indifferent poplars offering only their shadows. Heinrich's two sons, standing petulant and bored with their mother Greta, shifted and fidgeted, lightly pulling at their mother's arms, not asking to leave the solemn scene, but merely seeking the reassurance of her presence.

Jürgen looked at the gravestones closely, the edges nearly hidden under the thin, sprouting grass, stepped onto the small mound that separated his parents' final rest, and remembered his last conversation with Nathan. "My son, we two are like opposing peaks: we dominate our separate lives, but our love for each other flows into valleys as common soil. Let us not forget. Let us stand in our heights and watch the play of our differences worry others. You are my dear son, and that is all that your life has awakened in me. Forgive your mother and brother. They will always be bound, as if by a strangling *tefillin*, held in the throes of our religion's ancient conventions. I forgive them."

Jürgen's eyes filled, but he did not weep for his father. He knew that Nathan had admired his decision to leave the family's sugar company to found his own firm and pursue the export trade, and his father's words of encouragement and small loans were, in the beginning, the only factors sustaining him as he pushed the limits of his credit and nerve. But the mighty mountain of his father's unmixed love had been replaced by the image of his relatives sitting on the low stools, tearing their cloths, and comforting each other, but most importantly, daring not to mention the name Jürgen.

When Jürgen wrote to his family a few years before his father's death to announce his engagement to Gabriele and his decision to convert to his fiancée's family's faith, his mother had sent the letter back to him in pieces. Heinrich traveled to Lübeck and delivered articles saved from Jürgen's youth and the message that he was dead to his family. He quoted only his mother's words of recrimination, not mentioning their father in any context. Heinrich allowed that as their business contracts could not be easily duplicated elsewhere, the family would not work to break them. They would continue to send their sugar to Sachenzucker Exports for delivery.

A year after his father's burial, Jürgen had attended his mother's funeral in the same reticent manner, stopping outside the knot of relatives and watching as her body was delivered to the earth. He remembered that there had been no acknowledgements of his presence, and he had not tried to make himself available to his family and former friends. As the casket was lowered, he had turned and walked back to his carriage and departed directly to Lübeck. He left the space between his parent's graves and found a small, clean stone bench and sat down. His mind could not stop remembering, and he allowed himself the precious time to ignore the worries of his present business life and the dread of the long, uncomfortable journey back to Lübeck to continue to think of his family. He recalled his last visit with his parents, two years before his father's death, when they had traveled to Lübeck, their only visit to his home and the only occasion when David was presented to his grandparents. His mother had come with great reluctance, but his father had demanded that she accompany him. Nathan Rosenberg was not a cruel man, but he knew his status and reminded Miriam of hers in the starkest terms. She obeyed, and the Rosenbergs of Hildesheim met the Rosenbergs of Lübeck on a Wednesday evening in 1892.

The housekeeper had shown Nathan and Miriam into the anteroom off the library, and Gabi Rosenberg welcomed her in-laws, shaking their hands and inviting them to follow her into the large, book-lined space behind her. On cue, the housekeeper, Brigitte, had brought David to Gabi, who carried the boy across the room to meet his grandparents. Nathan rose and met her halfway, holding out his hands to take the boy into his arms and saying, "It is an honor to meet you, *Herr* Rosenberg." Miriam remained seated, her jaw set and her eyes cast down. Nathan doted on the child for a few moments, then swung around to his wife and offered the boy. Miriam rose, moved her hands down her dress and with noticeable hesitancy reached for David who asked her, as she took him into her arms, "Shall I call you Grandmamma?" Miriam's head snapped back and she gave the child a fierce look before turning her face toward her husband. David struggled out of her arms and ran back to his mother. Gabi's face revealed nothing, and she rang a small bell to summon Brigitte who arrived within seconds. "Brigitte, we shall have coffee, now," commanded Gabi.

The housekeeper left the room and very soon, a kitchen maid delivered the coffee service into the library. "*Herr* Rosenberg, may I serve you coffee?" Gabi asked.

"Yes, please, my dear, and you may serve *Frau* Rosenberg also," replied Nathan.

Jürgen had been standing in an adjacent hallway as Gabi had insisted, because she had wanted to confront her in-laws alone. He was immensely proud of the way she seemed to manage herself, and after coffee had been served, he walked into the library. The room was empty of people, but he glimpsed his wife in the adjoining conservatory bowing down to pick up a small lily growing in an ornate pot with one hand, balancing her coffee cup with the other. He entered the windowed room and stepping from behind his wife, offered his hand to his father. Nathan embraced his son and both men were interrupted by the jumping presence of David, demanding that his father pick him up. Jürgen tenderly embraced his son and pulled his father toward him, asking a waiting photographer to enter the room and capture the scene. The flash went off, and as Jürgen's eyes adjusted, he saw his mother looking at him. "Mother," he said.

David jumped down and shouted, "Papa, this is my grandmamma!" He ran to Miriam, grasping her hand and led her to Jürgen.

Jürgen said, "Mother, a room has been prepared for your comfort. Our housekeeper will show you the way and will alert you before dinner is served." Dismissed, to father and son's satisfaction, Miriam disappeared, leaving David.

Picking the boy up again, Nathan took his daughter-in-law's hand and said, "Jürgen, you have a wonderful family. You have done well for yourself, and this you have done without me. I cannot change your mother and brother, but as the head of our family, I honor you and your family and will keep this visit in my heart forever."

Jürgen's memories of his last meeting with his father seemed to melt away the dissociation between Nathan's stone and the man, giving the son the succor his heart had long sought, and as he gazed upon his father's name, he quietly celebrated the man who, like a benign eclipse, had kept him moving into light. Jürgen had not been able to accept the fact of his father's removal from the world or that Nathan's death was absolute, irreversible, until that moment. He was glad that his father had not insisted that he yield to his mother's demands for attention and religious fealty that had ultimately bound his poor brother. He thought of Heinrich, arranging every movement and thought of his life around Miriam, moved, like a celestial body in illogical epicycles around a great star, to justify its predictable path.

Jürgen's thoughts were interrupted by the sound of someone approaching from the street. The tread was unhurried but seemed to be moving toward him.

A voice called, "*Herr* Rosenberg?" A small man, wearing an embroidered *kippah* presented himself. "I am Rabbi Leo Graetz." Jürgen stood up and nodding a greeting, shook the man's hand. The rabbi wore a long, black coat and black gloves, in spite of the morning's moderate temperature. He was holding a small book, which he absentmindedly slipped into a coat pocket. He was rather stocky, with a neatly trimmed gray beard, fleshy red lips, and, behind round spectacles, smiling gray eyes. "I lead the Reform Temple, Herr Rosenberg."

"*Gut Shabbos*, Rabbi Graetz. I believe that you must have me mistaken for my brother, Heinrich," said Jürgen.

"*Gut Shabbos, Herr* Rosenberg, but you are mistaken, my dear man, it is you, Jürgen Rosenberg, I seek. Your brother told me that I might be able to find you here, although he made a point to observe that he would be surprised that you would take the trouble."

"My brother and I are not close. How can I help you, Rabbi?"

"*Herr* Rosenberg, some years ago, your father, may he be at peace, was kind enough to assist my congregation by extending to us a loan. He did this, despite opposition from his own *schul* and, I might add, your mother and brother."

"I am aware of the loan. Again, how can I help you?"

"*Herr* Rosenberg, we have sought to repay the loan during the last several years, but your brother has refused to acknowledge the debt. His lawyer, *Herr* von Strumond, has told me that Heinrich regards the loan as contributing to apostasy and that you, an apostate, should be the Rosenberg I consult concerning the repayment of the loan."

"Rabbi, unless a legal instrument has been prepared giving me authority to act on the loan, I am afraid that I cannot help you."

"Your brother has prepared the necessary authorization, expensing this to us, I might add. Could you, perhaps, accompany me to settle the matter this morning? I have warned *Herr* Strumond, whom you know, of course, of this possibility. He has agreed to meet us at my temple at 10:00."

Jürgen looked at the rabbi and replied, "Even you Reform Jews know better than to transact business on *Shabbos*, I would have thought. I don't detect an *eruv* behind you, Rabbi, so perhaps you would be good enough to accompany me in my carriage."

"*Herr* Rosenberg, you haven't forgotten all of your training, I must say."

The two men walked down to the waiting carriage, and Jürgen gave directions to his driver, Petersen. Jürgen was silent, obviously deep in thought, and the little Rabbi made no attempt at conversation. As the carriage reached the temple, Jürgen said, "I understand that a head covering is unnecessary in a Reform temple."

"That is correct, *Herr* Rosenberg, but I encourage it notwithstanding. I, too, was brought up in a Conservative *schul* and some things have remained important to me. I *wish* to be identified as Jewish, even as I comprehend assimilation to be an answer for us in this society."

Jürgen placed his hand upon the rabbi and said, "I pray that this will come to pass, someday. An answer for the Jews."

Jürgen followed the rabbi into his office where the lawyer, Strumond, was waiting. "Ah, my dear Jürgen, it is very good to see you, again. How are you?" he asked.

"Very well, *mein Herr*, very well. I commend you for continuing to tread the tightrope dividing my family. I hope Heinrich has been civil."

"Not civil, but *tolerable,* and most importantly, a prompt remitter!" Albert von Strumond was a gentile, like many of the professionals Jürgen's father retained or employed. Jürgen had discussed his plan to leave his father's firm with Strumond before announcing it to his parents. In representing his interests in the establishment of formal contacts with Nathan's company and others, Strumond had advised retaining the services of a particular law firm known to him in Lübeck: that of Bernhard Gerfried Matthäus.

The documents were presented, and Jürgen signed his name where indicated but asked Strumond to prepare a document on the spot, allowing Jürgen to forgive the loan to the temple. Strumond asked for a sheet of paper without letterhead, and wrote out the agreement. Jürgen reviewed the document, signed it, and handed it to Graetz, who said, "This is most unexpected, gentlemen!"

The business concluded, the congregation richer and the rabbi formulating his next sermon based on the day's events, Jürgen was ready to take his leave. As he shook hands with the two men, he noticed a vivid painting of an Orthodox rabbi carrying a Torah scroll hanging behind Graetz's desk and a small daguerreotype of a man wearing a Prussian uniform resting on the top shelf of an open cabinet to his right. The daguerreotype's silver frame held a smaller silver frame that held a German Cross, joined to a circle containing a depiction of a red eagle. "My grandfather, Captain David Graetz, taken in Frankfurt, where he helped break up the revolutionaries," explained the rabbi.

"How did your grandfather find the army life?" asked Jürgen.

"He was comfortable as a soldier, though he resented the discrimination pervading the ranks, especially, the higher ranks. He found himself passed over for promotion in favor of gentiles junior to him quite often."

"And, unlike me, he chose not to become baptized to help achieve his goals?"

"He never considered converting and even served on the board of the yeshiva I attended in Potsdam," said Graetz.

"Tell me, Rabbi Graetz, if you don't mind, why did you become associated with the Reform Movement?"

"I simply grew tired of being tangled in *mitzvoth* so removed from modern life that striving to observe most of them did nothing to strengthen my faith. And, frankly, I believe it is man's salvation to *wrestle* with the world and God to find some reconciliation with human suffering and mortality. Wearing fringes to remind me of the laws regarding lust did nothing to impart faith to me in the laws themselves regarding lust. Not wearing linen and wool together does nothing to help me believe that the Divine is relevant to man's experience. And who, in this age, would use a millstone as security for a loan? To revisit our business here, *Herr* Rosenberg, I am afraid that your brother's attitude toward the loan your father made to us seems as silly as the *mitzvoth* not to paint portraits or sculpt images of human beings. After all, your father charged no interest as demanded by *his* Judaism."

"Gentlemen, though I find your learned exchanges concerning the Rabbi's faith intriguing, I must take my leave now, so that I may answer to a higher power: Frau von Strumond. Thank you, and again Jürgen, how wonderful it was to see you." said Strumond.

"I must be off also, gentlemen." Jürgen left the little rabbi and instructed his driver to return him to the Celle train station, where he had been met the evening before. The cabriolet bucked forward, and the men started along the brick road leading out of Hildesheim, into countryside so familiar to Jürgen. The delay caused by his visit with Graetz would probably force him to overnight in Celle, but the rough forty-mile ride would certainly not encourage further travel in any event. He didn't reconsider altering his plans to get back to Lübeck quicker. This was a journey in the open air though the landscape of his youth he had wanted to make for some years. At least he would have more time to consider his meeting with Heinrich yesterday, the reason for his trip.

Jürgen considered his talk with his brother conclusive to their business relationship. It was to Jürgen, in spite of his dislike of his brother, curiously saddening. Heinrich had refused to meet Jürgen at his home and only agreed to a brief conference in von Strumond's offices. The lawyer had been away on business and Heinrich had bullied his way through the firm's clerks to find an empty office. Letters had been exchanged between each brother's representatives, and a purchase agreement for Jürgen's holdings in the sugar business had been produced some weeks in advance. Jürgen had not dared to hope that a reconciliation with his brother could be established, but simply wished to establish enough of a rapport so that the two men could deal directly with each other concerning the small matters that would invariably arise between them. Their father was gone and they could mediate their small differences without incurring unnecessary costs, if only Heinrich would treat him as a business associate and not the modern incarnation of a less learned Elisha ben Avuyah!

The sale of Jürgen's Sachenzucker holdings, the family's sugar company, had come about as a result of his concerns regarding the future of the company. Of the several problems troubling Jürgen, two had finally persuaded him to liquidate his shares of the company. The first problem was presented by Heinrich's decision to relocate the company's headquarters to Klein Wanzleben, some eighty miles from Hildesheim where Sachenzucker had been founded by their grandfather. The company's own sugar beet fields had been located north and east of the Hildesheim refinery, but a substantial number of contract farmers were located close by in the west. Dealing with the western farmers would become less personal, and the small margin their deliveries provided would become vulnerable to poaching from other sugar producers willing to invest the time and energy to develop relationships with them. Maintaining the contacts with the western farmers that had so carefully been nurtured by the Rosenbergs would be very difficult from the new center.

Jürgen had always feared, whether Sachenzucker moved or stayed in Hildesheim, Heinrich was not the man his father had been and would ignore the farmers. Further, investing in new offices would not keep the company from falling behind technologically or improve labor relations or working conditions. When Heinrich revealed his intention to move the central offices away from the refinery, Jürgen began consulting his father-in-law about selling his interests in the company. After convincing Bernd that he would not be dissuaded, Bernd duly contacted von Strumond and negotiations commenced. Ten days later, Bernd met with Jürgen and argued strenuously against the terms Heinrich had set. Jürgen asked only for a few modifications and instructed Bernd to proceed. Thus, the resulting sale patently favored Heinrich. Jürgen agreed to accept 60% of the discounted proceeds in cash, with the balance structured in annual payments over ten years. He told his father-in-law, he felt in his heart that, at best, he would receive only about 75% of the ultimate selling price and, perhaps, another 5% from what he felt an inevitability—the liquidation of his brother's entire holdings due to what would, in seven or eight years, be forced on Sachenzucker due to a worming, predictable mismanagement.

The carriage clattered along the narrow road, putting up dust and startling birds resting in heather. Jürgen removed his hat and found the warmth of the late morning sun on his thick hair soothing. He had always enjoyed the scenes of the ineluctable routines of bucolic life—cowherds moving their charges along a worn trail, the work of tillermen curling up the earth, the sowing of seed, and the clang and ring of milk urns being moved about dairy sheds. The smells of hay and manure of cattle and pigs, the smell of a turned field or wet pastures, these smells comforted him. He recalled spending summer afternoons at the farm of a gentile friend watching his father bring calves to the bottle and the comical movements of the man bracing his legs, one against the flank of the animal, one against the low fence on the open side of the shed, while the calf walked sideways and twisted its head within the unforgiving hook of the farmer's arm. Milk would be everywhere, drenching the farmer's overalls, pouring off of his face and cap and soaking the animal's head, its wide nostrils pulling the liquid into its face. Jürgen admired these families who only wished for routine, but whose lives were pushed about by the unconquerable changes of weather and the bygone indifference of armies trooping through their lands, their livelihoods. That men and women would rise before dawn, muster their children to their tasks, and work the earth and raise their animals for so little, perhaps asked too much of them. These people, to Jürgen, who suffered spring frosts, summer droughts, blight and disease, seemed the apotheosis of human endurance.

The travelers passed a stand of maidenhair trees leading them into a small forest of black poplars, large-leafed limes, and beeches. The stench of the maidenhair trees followed them some distance into the wood and brought Jürgen out of his reverie. The air grew cooler and the sun ran its shafts through the trees only occasionally. He became restless, finding the drive savaging his lower back, and when Petersen asked to stop to relieve himself, a stab of impatience scattered his thoughts and he had to recover himself to politely respond. He realized that his legs could benefit from a stretch and, with the driver, stepped down to the dusty roadway. He could hear the call of a cuckoo, perhaps seeking another bird's nest in which to abandon its eggs and in the distance beyond the trees and the maddening calls of a black swirl of starlings making for Denmark. He walked ahead of the carriage and found a dim trail angling gradually down the side of the steep hill that fell away from the roadbed. He also needed relief, he realized, and followed the dim trail farther and farther down. As he stopped to urinate, he noticed the top of a ruined brick wall, black with mildew and topped with streams of green slime infesting the remaining mortar, halted intermittently by a series of remaining bricks. As Jürgen looked more carefully, he could see the top third of an old abandoned millwheel rising above the wall at some distance, the useless machine tilted and deprived of many of its paddles, the remaining of which stood out rotting and scarcely connecting the wheel's sides. His curiosity moved him farther down the path, and holding a limb, he slid down to a bed of soft white sand near the tilted ruins of an old millhouse, its bricks forming a half wall with the remaining piled against it, rising out of the missing riverbed's sand. As his shoes touched the sand, he heard a small gasp and turned his head just beyond the millhouse to glimpse a flash of pale, bare skin as someone disappeared into the wood beyond the remaining dip of a small, nearly still, creek. As he kept turning his gaze, he found a young woman, perhaps seventeen or eighteen years old, trying to hide her nudity by rising to her knees and pulling the garment that had been her bedding up to her breasts. Jürgen was stunned from seeing only the third nude female body he had ever beheld. He asked,

"Are you alright, *Fraulein*?"

"Please, *mein Herr*, leave me," she pleaded.

Perhaps with the certain knowledge that they were alone, he fixed his gaze upon the girl. His eyes followed the line of her frame from her bare shoulders to the projection of her nude, round buttocks resting on her ankles.

After a long moment, she said, "Please?"

Jürgen finally remembered himself, and his genteel instincts turned him away from the scene.

He walked back toward the embankment of the ancient stream and caught the limbs of a shrub to haul himself back into the forest and climb the hill. As his right foot reached the top, the shrub gave way, pulling from the earth and sending Jürgen falling backwards, arms flailing, his hands grasping at air, and finally, the back of his skull found one of the many rocks that had rested where it was left by human intention or indifferent nature. His body slumped down, crumbling in a finely dressed heap.

The girl heard his head hit the rock and dropping her rags, ran to him fully nude, as his body made a last concession to his position and dropped his legs to the side. She straightened him, and cradling his head, said, "*Mein Herr, mein Herr!*"

Jürgen could hear, but the girl's voice sounded far away. His last ember of consciousness was fading and he could dimly discern the girl's chest dissolving into a flush, and finally, only her hovering, over-large, and swaying, pink nipples. He reached up to her and whispered, "Graetz."

Above them, a voice called, *Herr* Rosenberg! *Herr* Rosenberg!"

The girl called out, "Here, *mein Herr*; he is here!" She ran back to her clothes and pulled them over her head quickly. She saw Petersen descending the hillside, ran back to the embankment under him, and calling him down, led him to Jürgen.

The young driver jumped from atop the embankment into the nearby ruin's scent of mildew and was shocked to see his master lying unconscious in the sand. He frantically moved his hands up and down his face and knelt before Jürgen to try to detect breathing. He placed his ear to the older man's chest, and after several seconds, said, "He's alive! Please help me carry him up to the carriage."

"Please, *mein Herr*, the only thing he said was, 'Graetz.'"

Petersen and the girl managed to get Jürgen up the hill and into the carriage, and the boy whipped the horse around back toward Hildesheim. The young woman stood in the middle of the ancient roadway, pulling back her long, tangled blonde hair, and her breasts began to quiver as she gave herself to sobbing. Finally, finding a lone, fallen tree trunk to sit down upon at the edge of the forest, she buried her face in her hands.

The injured man lay across the seat, his body bouncing and his loose limbs bobbing as the carriage rolled across the road. At one point, Jürgen fell headfirst onto the floorboard where he remained nearly still, rocking back and forth against the back of the driver's seat. Just before dusk, the carriage entered the town, Petersen dragging its wheels across the slick pavement of stone and brick and stopping at the temple. He ran inside, and finding only an elderly woman sweeping, asked her directions to the rabbi's home. He jumped down the building's steps and took the reins again, hastening the exhausted horse forward to a house several hundred feet down the street. He bounded up the steps and pounded upon the doors several times.

A woman opened the door and Petersen breathlessly explained his situation. The woman nodded, shut the door, and sought the rabbi. He came to the door, listened to Petersen tell his story, and ran down to the street to examine Jürgen. He called back to his wife, who was standing in the doorway, shocked at the scene. She ran to her husband and he said to her, "Please call Strumond and make an inquiry at the *schul* for *Doktor* Stein!"

Jürgen was carried into the rabbi's home and placed on a bed in a spare bedroom. He mumbled unintelligibly for an hour or more, saliva running from his mouth and soaking the pillow under him. At last, Strumond arrived and left to send a message to Bernd, passing *Doktor* Stein on the front steps as he left the house.

Bernd received the telegram at 9:00 that evening. He immediately went to Gabi and Jürgen's home and informed her as to what had happened. He suggested spending the rest of the night preparing for the journey to Hildesheim. Gabi made arrangements for David to stay with his grandmother while she and Bernd were away, and finally, at 4:00 a.m., was able to get a few hours of worried sleep before they had to catch the train.

The day's traveling was grueling to father and daughter. Gabi tried to bear up well, but broke down in spite of her best efforts to remain calm. Bernd did what he could, trying not to dwell upon the possibility of losing his dear son-in-law. He realized that Jürgen had been one of the very few men he had ever unreservedly trusted. Along with Dieter Schlarp and Hugh Twinge, Jürgen was his closest friend. May God help my grandson, he thought. The train pulled into the station where father and daughter were met by Strumond.

Gabi's hand instinctively covered her mouth as she entered the bright bedroom and saw the still, silent form lying under white sheets before her. *Frau* Graetz steadied Gabi as she took in the scene. She knew her husband Jürgen Rosenberg as the embodiment of élan and purposeful movement, but he was silent and pale, still and prone on a bed with a bandage wrapped completely around his head concealing his eyes. A faint pink stain could be seen spread faintly to one side of the bandage, touching the pillow supporting him, and his brown hair rose into a blossom, spilling toward the top of the heavy gauze wrap. The room was lightly scented with fresh cornflowers that sat in a squat, blackband ironstone vase, resting on a bureau opposite the injured man. The room's solitary window was slightly opened and allowed an insignificant breeze to push and pull the shears between the plain, gray linen curtains.

"Has he regained consciousness, at all?" asked Gabi.

"This has been his condition since young Petersen brought him here, *Frau* Rosenberg," said Rabbi Graetz. "The physician has advised that he not be moved until he should awaken. We have only noticed a slight, intermittent tremble of his left hand's fingers."

"Why was he brought to your home, *Herr* Graetz?" asked Gabi.

"Young Peterson told me that the only word *Herr* Rosenberg uttered when he found him was my name, and he thought *Herr*

Rosenberg wanted to be brought to me. I have no idea why he should seek me out in particular, but I am honored to be of support."

"I am so grateful for your assistance," said Gabi looking at the Rabbi and his wife.

"Again, we are honored to help. My wife contacted *Herr* Strumond, while I settled *Herr* Rosenberg."

"*Herr* Strumond was kind enough to telegram last night, but as you can see, my father insisted that we wait until first light to make the journey to you."

Bernhard Matthäus stepped forward and offered his hand to each of the Graetz's and said, "Allow me to say how very grateful I am to you, Rabbi and *Frau* Graetz. My son-in-law is a fine man and we shall pray for his recovery. May I ask, will the physician call again this evening?"

Rabbi Graetz replied, "*Herr Doktor* Rolf Stein will return soon. He is not a member of my temple congregation, so I know little of him, but I understand that he studied his art in Vienna, *Herr* Matthäus. I believe that *Herr* Strumond concurred with my decision to enlist the services of this physician."

"Strumond did mention in his telegram that our dear Jürgen was being attended by a physician of outstanding reputation. May we know what, if anything, *Doktor* Stein has said about how long Jürgen may be in this state, Rabbi?"

"We know *Herr* Rosenberg's condition is terribly shocking, *Herr* Matthäus, but *Doktor* Stein assured us that his heart and breathing are very strong and that we must wait for nature to offer healing. He has every hope that *Herr* Rosenberg will awaken in his own time. Please, *Frau* Rosenberg and *Herr* Matthäus, we have arranged chairs for you on either side of the bed. Please sit and make yourselves comfortable and allow us to answer to your needs," said *Frau* Graetz.

Gabi and her father took a seat and nodded thanks to *Frau* Graetz. Gabi dabbed at her eyes with a handkerchief she pulled from the sleeve of her dark blue dress and reached for Jürgen's hand after noticing it slightly twitching. She had never seen her husband so inert, even when she had watched him sleep, so it seemed to her unworldly.

Her own mind had become leaden during the journey from Lübeck, and she bowed her head, surrendering to the one, overwhelming concern: how could she live without Jürgen? Her chest heaved with frequent sighs, and her legs both trembled beneath her skirt, occasionally lifting her heels and knocking them back to the floor with a loud clack. She began to think of Jürgen's reason for journeying to Hildesheim and the specter of her brother-in-law's dour face entered her fretful thoughts—Heinrich, the wretch, the unloving, unforgiving brother of her dear husband.

Rabbi Graetz had quietly left the father and daughter to the ministrations of his wife, a deeply caring and sensitive woman. *Frau* Graetz was the perfect companion to a man of the rabbi's vocation and responsibilities, and he left the small group with no concerns that the needs of their guests would be ignored. As he walked to his study, he considered how much Germany had changed for Jews during the course of the last fifty years, but remembering Heinrich Rosenberg's bitter words concerning his brother's apostasy, Graetz couldn't help wondering how Rosenberg had managed to sever his religious ties so completely and married into such, as he was given to understand by Strumond, an influential gentile family. He hoped the answers to this question did not lie simply in self-serving ambition or, perhaps more elementally, in the extraordinary beauty of *Frau* Gabi Rosenberg. Cynical considerations were anathema to his status as a religious leader, but he was as modern a man as the unconscious merchant lying in his guest bedroom, and he knew those disparaging motives would not have been easily dismissed by those of the world Rosenberg had entered. How many times will he hear Goethe quoted concerning this incident? Graetz asked himself.

Rabbi Graetz entered his modest study and stood for a moment, looking past the flowered motifs of the wallpaper and through the room's two open windows at the small enclosure that housed the family's *mikva* near the family's washhouse. Though he used the bath daily, and he regarded it as a vestige of his youth and his father's predictable, conservative life, it brought him a few minutes of

solitude and calm. He sat down to his well-organized desk and decided to open a copy of the *Tanakh,* one sent to him from a wealthy
Berlin widow he had comforted during her husband's final days. He
would look for portions to be read from the *Torah* scroll during next
Shabbos services and think about his accompanying sermon. But he
could not separate his congregational life from the suffering of the
strangers in his own home. As he began to read, his housekeeper,
Frau Wax, appeared and announced the arrival of *Doktor* Stein. He
placed the ribbon to mark his place in the book and rose to follow
Frau Wax through the house to the front parlor.

"Good evening, *Doktor* Stein; thank you for coming."

"Yes, please allow me to examine your houseguest," said the dour
man of medicine.

"Through here, if you recall, *Herr* Doktor," said Graetz.

Herr Doctor Rolf Stein wore a plain, black *Kappel,* misaligned
to the right side of his skull below which very slight carrot-colored
side-curls could be discerned hanging loosely away from his face,
almost hiding his ears. He was tall with deep-set black eyes and a
fixed, unexpressive mien. To Graetz, Stein was clearly uncomfortable
in his presence, and his impulse since meeting Stein was to try to put
the man at ease.

Graetz stopped abruptly and turned about to Stein, who was following and said, "*Herr Doktor,* I'm told that you studied in Vienna.
Were you also uncomfortable with liberal Jews there?"

Doktor Stein sucked breath through his slightly bared teeth, and
with a rapid whisper replied, "Sir, I do not appreciate the practices of
Jews such as I've seen in this household. Without your *Kappel,* you
may as well be a *goy!* Your own wife wears her hair uncovered in the
presence of strangers, and you *harbor a heretic!* Yes, I know who the
patient is: his story is quite well known in my *schul,* as perhaps you
can imagine."

"We will not agree upon religious practice, *Doktor,* but I pray
that you keep the tenets of your profession foremost in mind when
you treat *Herr* Rosenberg. Be warned: the patient's *Goyische,* as you
would have it, wife and father-in-law are with him. Remember, even

though *Herr* Strumond approved your assistance, I chose to allow you to care for this man because of your reputation as a physician, not as a Jew."

Stein instinctively put his hand to the side of his face and raked his fingers through his red beard. His set jaw relaxed somewhat, and he nodded Graetz forward. The two men moved down the hallway and entered the bedroom. *Frau* Graetz sat opposite the foot of the bed, and Stein heard Gabi speaking in low tones, describing David. Bernhard rose and nodded his head, accepting *Doktor* Stein's offered hand. Stein nodded toward Gabi and turned slightly to acknowledge *Frau* Graetz. The light had changed in the room, showing Jürgen's features more distinctly and drawing the physician's attention to the man's right hand twitching sporadically at his side. Stein stood still, taking in his patient, waiting, and giving the body before him a few moments to reveal something new, something unobserved during his first visit. At length, Stein sat in the chair proffered by Bernhard and opened his medical bag to find the instruments necessary for the examination.

As Stein moved Jürgen's head forward to inspect the dressing, a low moan issued from Jürgen's lips. "Pain," said Stein to Gabi, "a good sign." Finally, the doctor said to the wife and father-in-law, "*Herr* Rosenberg must not be moved for some time to come. He has a broken right clavicle, some bruised ribs, I suspect, and a profound injury to the head. *Frau* Rosenberg, I would suggest that you retain a nurse for his care; this I can assist you with. The next day or two will determine if *Herr* Rosenberg will recover. I will return in the morning."

The doctor gathered his instruments and placed them in his bag, and bowing to the patient's family members, left the room with the Rabbi. He walked somewhat briskly, his heels pounding the wooden flooring loudly, and over a shoulder, bid Graetz good evening. He let himself out of the front door and made for his automobile.

Frau Graetz walked up and patted her husband on the back, saying, "Do not fret, my modern Elisha, my apostate without side curls or *tzitzit* fringes. Come, let us look in on *Herr* Rosenberg."

Graetz looked at his wife, a woman slightly taller than himself and said, "Thank God for you, my dear."

Bernhard rose as the Graetz's entered the room and said, "I'm glad you've come, my dear friends. May I speak with the Rabbi, perhaps in his study?"

"Of course, *Herr* Matthäus. My dear wife, would you keep *Frau* Rosenberg company? Please follow me, *Herr* Matthäus," said Graetz. He led the way out of the room to his study and indicated a chair. Bernhard sat down into the large, aging but comfortable chair of wool and silk. It had a tapestry set into a light green background that depicted laden grape vines running from the seat and flourishing up the back and surrounded by burnished mahogany and supported by bowed legs finishing in the same wood and dull, gunmetal claw feet. "How may I assist, *Herr* Matthäus?" asked Graetz.

"Rabbi, my daughter has insisted that Jürgen be moved to local apartments when he seems strong enough to unsettle. She asks that you provide a list of hotels and landlords who might be able to accommodate or recommend a place for her. Neither she, nor I, wish to inconvenience your family any longer than is necessary. I must admit, however, that she is being, perhaps, somewhat impetuous and should let these next critical days pass here, imposing, I am afraid, further upon your gracious hospitality. I, sadly, must return to Lübeck, tonight," said Bernhard.

"My dear *Herr* Matthäus, your daughter and son-in-law are welcome here. With the nurse being provided by *Doktor* Stein, we will manage quite well. I agree, based on the doctor's observations, that *Herr* Rosenberg should not be moved soon. My wife and I are at your service and hope that you and *Frau* Rosenberg will allow us to continue to provide what we can for your comfort," responded Graetz.

"You are most generous, Rabbi. *Frau* Graetz has been a wonderful companion for Gabi and with the addition of a nurse, I truly hope that your wife's burdens, so generously born on our behalf, will ease. Tell me, Rabbi, if you care to speak about it, to a gentile's eyes there seems to be a very noticeable difference between you and *Doktor* Stein. When Jürgen came to us, he was much like you, although without the head covering. As a member of your faith's clergy, I would have expected your demeanor to have been more severe, more apparently religious, as it were. *Doktor* Stein's appearance seems to have you less so, to this uninformed member of another faith."

"*Herr* Matthäus, you are most observant. The *Herr Doktor* and I differ dramatically, as I gather *Herr* Rosenberg does with his brother, on matters of religion. The *Doktor* follows a more conservative approach to our faith, observing more rules, or what we call *mitzvoth*, and, for instance, is compelled to utilize certain habits of appearance to remind himself of them. Members of my branch of the faith have more freedom to choose what, amongst the many, many, strictures, set down for us, imparts the most meaning and contribution to our religious lives. We have much less desire to be seen as separate, as apart, from the majority of people we encounter each day. I see *Herr* Rosenberg's conversion to your faith as an act that, whatever his reasons, was correct for *him*, and do not condemn him for it. *Doktor Stein* sees only apostasy and betrayal. We all deal with good and evil, the fear of death, and suffering in our own way, and it is my prayer that all of us be respected for the faith we choose to assist us through life. I do not condemn *Doktor* Stein, as he does me, because I understand him and his fellows, but I do wish that more tolerance would emerge from the conservative corners of Judaism."

"Well, Rabbi, thank you for educating me. Now, how can I help you?"

"*Herr* Matthäus, we only wish for the pleasure of your company, again, very soon, under more auspicious circumstances. Please let me know when you wish to leave, and I will have you driven to the train station."

5

The Saturday afternoon meal had been heavy as always, and David felt slow and sleepy as he rose from the table. He had told his *Oma* that he had received an invitation from *Herr* Schlarp asking him to visit his office that afternoon, something not unexpected by Elisabeth as Schlarp's invitations were arranged by Jürgen Rosenberg and noted in Gabriele's household schedule. Jürgen had wanted David to become more familiar with his company, and he wanted his employees to become used to seeing David on the premises. David stretched and hung his eight-year-old head, looking sidelong at his grandmother before breaking into a broad smile. He went around the table, kissed her, and announced, "I'm off to the office!"

Elisabeth had wondered what to do with the boy this day. His father was away, perhaps watching the poor child's prospects expire as Jürgen and Heinrich dissolved their partnership. When David came to table, she said, "You so remind me of your dear *Opa*, such sweetness and purpose. Did I ever tell you that he wore a pocket watch when he was eight? Your great-grandparents called him the *Bürgermeister*!" Elisabeth thought of her beloved husband, and was proud to realize that she still harbored the schoolgirl desires that her husband had quickly indulged after their marriage some thirty years ago.

David called out goodbye as he and Brigitte left the house. Brigitte accompanied David to the end of *Engelsgrube*, where he turned left onto the sidewalk along *An Der Untertrave* and began walking south toward Sachenzucker Exports. He walked parallel to the *Holstenhafen* harbor, its quay crowded with ships lying bow to stern, almost touching. He carried on his shoulder the rucksack his grandfather had given him on his last birthday, the waxed cotton bag cool and clammy to his touch. It contained a light coat and a jar of his grandmother's pear relish for *Herr* Schlarp. He made his way along the building fronts, past the small pavilion where the town's brass band had played earlier in the day, and stopped to watch a street laborer emerging from a narrow *gänge*, carrying a large sack on his back and pushing a cart piled with crates of herbs. The worker turned left and pushed ahead of the boy toward *Fischergrube*, and David took in the aromatic wake of the cart as he matched steps with the man and followed. He did not notice Brigitte, trailing a short distance behind, nearly overtaking him when he stopped as the cart appeared, her thoughts adrift in memories of her own walks along the harbor. The herb man guided his cart to the boarded entrance of an old, empty warehouse after crossing *Clemensstrasse* and stopped, dropping his sack. David could see that the man was young but very tired as he held a spoke of one of the cart's wheels and lowered himself carefully onto the building's stoop. The man looked up the street with wide, staring eyes and found David standing a few feet from him. The man held up a hand with splayed fingers and began contorting his mouth as if to form words. There was only silence, but the man's face looked desperate, pleading. As he looked at David, his expression slowly changed, and he began to relax. He dropped his hand and slumped into the doorframe, closing his eyes. David moved sideways looking at the man and passed the quiet figure and his cart unafraid but puzzled. Was the man afraid? The man was clearly troubled, but should his behavior mean something? The boy looked back and could see the man through the gap between the cart and the building, his head hung forward and his cap pulled up as he leaned into the doorjamb. The cart man's eyes were open again, and his mouth agape. David could no longer smell the herbs.

Brigitte waited until the boy resumed his walk before stirring. She had watched David and the carter and found the scene moving. The poor, silent creature seemed to ask David for something and in silence, the boy seemed to give it. She kept her eyes on the boy as they continued along the lively road, busy with merchant's carriages, buggies and trade wagons. A ship's chandler was taking in and spilling captains and mates and ordinary seamen. The sidewalk was crowded with the seafarers, and Brigitte worried that David might get knocked down and trampled underfoot. The boy wisely moved toward the building and waited for a lull in the traffic, eventually falling in behind a group of men all emitting puffs of pipe smoke and carrying a long crate. Straw dropped from the gaps in the crate's slats, and the smell of gun oil blended with the aroma of the men's burning tobacco.

A man shouting, "Hold it, there!" hurried past David and the men stepped off the curb, motioning to stop the traffic. The man in charge, David thought to be a First Mate, waved impatiently at the traffic with one hand and at the seamen with the other, yelling for his men to "Come along, damn you!"

As David stood in front of Three Voices Bakery and watched the sailors cross the *An Der Untertrave*, an obese man sidled through the sidewalk throng and pushed against him, turning him sideways. The huge man, obviously a baker, wore an apron the size of a ship's banner smudged with marzipan and jellied fruit. David turned about to see his friend, Sebastian Kringle, looking down at him. The baker's beard was black and shiny but streaked with white flour, and his eyes were bloodshot from the marathon of work through the previous night, preparing for the Saturday and Sunday demand. David and his father made weekly visits to his bakery to pick up two hundred loaves of bread for the Sachenzucker workers, which Jürgen Rosenberg bartered for generously with sugar. Together, Jürgen and his son would give the workers their loaves at the end of Saturday, a workday demanding only one shift. Today had been different with Jürgen away. The bread had been delivered to Sachenzucker by one of Sebastian's employees.

"Good afternoon, young Rosenberg," said Sebastian. "On your way to the office?"

"Good afternoon, *Herr* Kringle. I *am* going to the office," said David.

David was amazed by the man's size. Even his hands were huge, each as big as a person's head, thought David. He noticed that *Herr* Kringle seemed to be anchored in place as he spoke, leaning toward and then away from him, his arms never still as he talked with the boy. The huge man's baker's hat seemed to be a steeple to David, so very tall with a rim that had a large, round stain centered at his forehead and light smudges of his trade all along the side of the fitted band.

"The bread has been delivered—"

Suddenly, David felt his neck flung back and a part of a hard loaf of stale bread clipping his shoulder as Kringle picked the boy up and moved him behind his huge frame.

Women's shouts of "too much, Kringle; three liars; and *schwindler!*" accompanied more hurled hunks of stale bread and handfuls of black river muck. The sidewalk crowd seemed to howl as one as several pedestrians were pelted while *Polizistin* whistles began sounding. There was a scramble as the angry pack of women ran through the soiled townsfolk and disappeared into a narrow lane between Three Voices Bakery and a haberdashery, dispersing through a warren of *gänge*.

"David, David!" cried Brigitte, as the knots of shouting and frightened Lübeckers began to realize what had happened and started turning toward Sebastian Kringle.

"I know you must run along, young man, so I will say goodbye now" said Kringle to David. The big man scrambled away toward his bakery and left the boy where he stood, clutching his rucksack and looking about for Brigitte whose shouts he had heard above the din.

Brigitte approached at a run and embraced the boy. She was shaken, but did not allow tears or any other sign of her distress to betray her worry. "Young man, may I accompany you to your office?" she asked, winded.

"*Frau* Brigitte! Did you see what happened to *Herr* Kringle? Look at the mud on me! And now on you!" cried David. The boy could smell the earthy scent of the perspiring woman, and this seemed to calm him as he continued to hold himself close to the young woman.

Brigitte gathered the boy to her side and hurried him away from the scene. She stopped after a short distance and brushed the loose mud from the boy's clothes and her own. The stains would have to wait. How easy it would have been to lose him, Brigitte thought as they resumed their excursion. The thought of parting with the boy was upsetting to the point that her face worked, and tears began to fill her eyes. She managed to hide her anguish by looking down and fussing with her hat until she had recovered. Her life with the Rosenbergs had begun at David's birth, when *Frau* Gabriele had employed her as her housekeeper and nanny—two nearly full-time occupations save for *Frau* Rosenberg's interest in being the better part of David's care and upbringing. Brigitte began to chatter about the scene outside the bakery and asked David if he was worried that his mother would not allow him to go out alone after the news reached her. He assumed, of course, that his mother knew instantly, even as *Herr* Kringle was being harassed, and would forbid him from roaming Old Town alone. Brigitte's presence, he felt, had been preordained by his mother, but testing, he asked, "*Frau* Gitte, where were *you* going when you came upon me?"

Brigitte replied, "I was going to visit the greengrocer. Cook wants something special for your grandmother."

"I am to meet *Frau* Deming at the greengrocer! Do you know *Frau* Deming, *Frau* Gitte?"

"Of course, David. How many times has *Frau* Deming brought young Tom to visit you?"

"Oh, yes, that's right!"

The sidewalk was becoming increasingly crowded as they approached *Mengstrasse*, and Brigitte had trouble keeping the boy in sight, as he skipped ahead. She became uncomfortable as she moved through the crowd. She was a country girl used to open spaces. The closeness of the Old Town walkway always made her self-conscious, and she took her steps as carefully as she chose her words in confession. David ran farther ahead and crossed *Mengstrasse* on his own, stopping to wait for Brigitte, whose image waved in and out of the crowd passing him. When she caught up to him, she took his arm and smiled saying, "Young men don't usually run away from *me!*"

David laughed, and looking at her knew that she must be right. She was slim with very dark hair and a pretty face and large green eyes. Perhaps a little hairy, as he remembered the incident when he was stalking an imaginary beast through his family's house and burst in upon her bathing in her room. David yelled as he entered the room with his toy sword held above his head ready to strike. Brigitte was standing sidelong to the doorway, pulling a wet cloth up her belly and into the tight gap between her full breasts when he opened the door. David saw the dark fluff of pubic hair that refined to fine black fringe along her bare arms and legs and thought, is she a man? He ran, leaving the door open and thinking, "*They* have hair, also!"

The pair neared *Fischstrasse* to the sound of a ship's bell and the chuffing of a small tug taking strain on lines from a large barque. David stopped to watch a harbor pilot standing in his large boat shouting commands through a megaphone and waving an arm down, then up, then out from his chest, as if conducting a chorus. The ship's company was busy tightening and slackening lines from the quay and from the ship to the tug as the vessel moved away leaving almost no wake. Following the progress of the ship down the harbor, David ignored the noise and imagined the exercise conducted in silence. He was excited by the mystery of the ship's destination as he watched its Danish flag being run up to hang limp in the still air. He wondered if he would see the barque tied up at the quay again.

"David, shall we go?" asked Brigitte after a few minutes.

David turned to leave just as a cloud of coal smoke from the tug enveloped the street. They waited a moment before continuing, and as the air cleared, the woman and boy were startled by a group of workmen walking single file in the gutter below them. The men smelled of their labors and coughed as they emerged from the tug's exhaust, their heaving chests swinging the implements resting against their shoulders.

The men's gait was marked by the sound of their lunch pails bobbing against their waists and their heavy work boots slapping the shiny pavement. The queue regained fresh air and as their coughing ceased, they began humming a chorale tune David recognized. As the last man passed, the boy felt immense delight in the beauty of the melody issuing from the dirty and surly looking line of laborers escaping their toil, and he began singing the words as he acknowledged

Brigitte's gesture to continue ahead.

The shop and warehouse fronts were bright in the afternoon sun, their brick courses in their best phase of color, in many shades of red, dun, and brown. The dull suits of office workers became dark chocolate and deep grape, and the strolling ladies, graceful sidewalk eddies of cream, claret and blues as they turned to speak to friends and companions. David imagined the myriad hats as flowers crowning the women and tabs of stone topping the men as the crowd moved about him.

As the pair approached the bend in the river near *Beckergrube*, in the distance he caught sight of a large procession of Lübeck flags at the *Holstentorplatz*. The flags' panels of white atop deep orange moved many abreast in a long line away from the north tower of the old gate toward the river. He could hear a brass performance of Brahms' rendering of *Das Mädchen und der Tod* floating up the river harbor and echoing off the buildings. It brought a smile to Brigitte's lips, and she sang:

A gentle girl, of a morning early,
Went to a flower garden, youthful, happy and lively,
She wanted to pick many flowers
To make a wreath with them, of silver and of gold…

As Brigitte and David approached, three very well dressed young men talking outside a shipping office arrayed themselves in a small arc before them. A smiling blond fellow bowed and began to sing the next lines of the song:

There came edging up to her a very frightening man;
With skin faded and no clothes;
With no flesh, no blood, no hair;
His flesh and muscles were all dried up…

Brigitte smiled at the group, pulled David around to her opposite side, and continued walking. The young men closed back into their talking knot, but the blond called for the pair to stop and sing with him. Brigitte continued on her way, singing:

O Death, allow me to live, take all my house servants!
My father will give them to you if he knows I live,

For I am his only daughter...

Brigitte and David could no longer see the flag demonstration and heard only the musical echo as they walked between the buildings and a series of neat stalls lining the sidewalk. The stalls were shut, but they reminded David of the upcoming spring *Ausländerfest,* when each of the foreign companies granted harbor space would bring performers and foods from their lands to entertain the Lübeckers. The boy remembered the 1892 gala, when his father was the event's *Vorsitzende,* and how he was passed onto the shoulders of merchants from Denmark, Sweden, Holland and Russia, and finally to those of the burly old Englishman, Hugh Twinge, who led the *Nationen* Parade. *Kapitän* Twinge, as he was known, was not a sea captain at all. He was the leader of a vast trading consortium headquartered in Boston, Lincolnshire, and for all who knew him professionally, a man whose presence was a dispensation of class and social order. Everyone felt that he stooped to know them. In a few weeks, the foreigners would be raising their national flags on poles set along the *An Der Untertrave* and *Kapitän* Twinge would open his company's flagship, actually his yacht the Orestes, and offer a tumbler of English pale ale to any of the public stepping aboard.

Hugh Twinge was David's godfather, his father's closest friend and, father-in-law of Margaret Kitchen, his father's secretary. *Frau* Kitchen was the mother of David's best friend, Tom Kitchen. It was never referenced, but Hugh Twinge was also an English peer: the Earl of Boardcroft, Hugh Algernon Geoffrey Twinge.

The pair was past *Braunstrasse* when Vollmer's, the greengrocer's shop, came into view. A three-wheeled Benz-Patent Motorwagen was parked along the curb in front of the shop with *Frau* Deming, Herr Schlarp's assistant, and her daughter, Astrid, sitting on the narrow seat watching them approach. "Hello, David" Astrid called out as her mother stood and beckoned the boy over to the vehicle.

Frau Angela Deming was a petite woman of thirty with dark eyes and rather large, pale hands. She wore a broad white hat that was encased in a white sheer fabric that was pulled down and tied under her chin. Her black dress was made from a shimmering fabric, but was severe with three narrow blood-red stripes gashed across the breast and a collar of black lace wound tightly around her neck. As she stood, her dress roiled out below her waist, crawling over her daughter's knees and nearly enfolding the girl's lower body.

"We shall have to walk, David. Mother will follow in the automobile," said Astrid.

Frau Deming's thin, pallid lips offered a slight smile as she reached over her child and pulled her skirt away while Astrid gathered her own and prepared to step down from the vehicle.

With a nudge from Brigitte, David stepped to the curb and offered Astrid a hand. The girl took David's hand and stepped gingerly toward the tiny footstep extended below the Benz's frame, her skirts covering her groping foot. She was nearly sitting when her foot finally found the step, but as she put her weight on the tiny tab of steel, she slipped and fell onto David, both children collapsing to the sidewalk. Astrid's face brushed David's, and he smelled her hair and felt her breath as his arms closed instinctively around her waist. Her dress rustled and hissed against his clothing and their buttons jammed against each other and popped away as she moved across his frame, trying to raise herself.

Frau Deming was off the little car in a second, her black skirts flying out and her hat falling behind her head, its thin material illuminated against the sun. "Young Rosenberg! Release my child!" yelled Frau Deming. The little woman was shaking and slowly raising her hands and splaying her fingers.

Brigitte had immediately tried to help Astrid, whose pearl-studded gloves had entangled her hands in the lace of her sleeves. The girl rocked from side to side on David, her face flushed and frantically moving about. Brigitte asked her quietly to lie still and gently pulled David's arms away from her waist. She knelt and lifted Astrid's shoulders enough for her to move her elbows under her chest on either side of the boy below. With Brigitte's help, the girl managed to sit and finally stand astride David, who had begun laughing. A small crowd had gathered around the group, their faces appearing over David in a comic procession of noses, bearded chins, toothed and toothless mouths. He felt himself pulled, almost snatched, to his feet and joined in his laughter by a few men.

David noticed a couple of weather-beaten old salts, a nicely dressed businessman, and one of the Vollmer's employees wearing a bloodstained apron. They stood with him for a moment, commenting, "One day you'll have to pay for something like that, young man!" and "Hide your daughters, gentlemen!" and the like.

Frau Deming, helping Astrid, shouted in a shrill voice, "Get along! Get along!"

The men sauntered away, and Brigitte began fussing over the boy, inspecting him for damage and trying desperately to suppress laughter. The housekeeper kept her back to *Frau* Deming, but her shaking frame and the little snorts she emitted gave her away.

"*Frau* Krebs! This is not a laughing matter!" spluttered *Frau* Deming.

"I apologize, *Frau* Deming. May I ask, how is *Fraulein* Deming? Will she be able to walk with young David?"

"Certainly not!"

"But, Mamma, please allow me to walk back to the office!" pleaded Astrid.

"Astrid, look at this boy, so dirty and ill-mannered! You will return with me in *Herr* Schlarp's automobile," replied *Frau* Deming.

"*Frau* Deming, a word, please," said Brigitte.

Frau Deming followed Brigitte out of earshot to be brought up short near the greengrocer's sidewalk window. Brigitte, no longer amused, leaned into the smaller woman's space and said in quiet tones, "*Frau* Deming, you are an employee of that boy's father. Do you value your employment? If so, you will never refer to him in such a manner, again!"

David stood still for a moment and looked up at Astrid while the women had their private talk. She met his gaze and began to smile, just as *Frau* Deming turned back toward the little vehicle. David noticed her moving in his direction and shouted to the women, "Goodbye Brigitte, goodbye *Frau* Deming, goodbye *Fraulein* Astrid!" and looking both directions, skipped across the busy harbor road.

The old salt warehouses loomed ahead across the Trave, south of the bridge leading to the Holsten Gate and eventually he could see past the salt houses. A long structure's dark shadow thrown across the Trave was his father's building. The north end of the T-shaped building rose perpendicular to the *Salzspeicher* along the west bank, its lines of clinker brick were straighter, darker, and much newer than the faded and pocked bricks of the ancient salt houses. The building's gables were simpler than its neighbors' but stately with round, convex extrusions projecting from the middle that housed evaporators installed to heat and dry the interior and to give Sachenzucker Exports the ability to convert from warehousing and shipping to refining sugar. David's Uncle Heinrich had laughed when he saw that the building's design included this feature, but later, when the family's factory went down for extensive maintenance, Heinrich had nothing to say when Jürgen Rosenberg reminded him he could be converting raw product within a relatively short time. The episode had been unpleasant for the family, but Nathan Rosenberg thought the brothers needed this kind of understanding: business was business and blood was blood.

David thought about his friends sitting and lying around the dusty construction site upriver, and felt a little pity for them. He had rarely shared visits with *Herr* Schlarp, feeling crowded each time he did so, like trying to read an entertaining volume of stories with restless bodies pushing against him and heads leaning into his line of sight. "Old Schlarp", as David's mother referred to him, had always welcomed the boys, but tailored his stories to David's ears, keeping his devotion to his employer's son unmixed with the entertainment of the children's antics and guileless observations. As David crossed the busy road, he tripped on the loose cobbles of the sidewalk and fell, twisting onto his back. His white sailor suit was instantly streaked with street dust and brown dirt and his right shoulder began aching. He looked upside down at the mighty *Holstentor* rising before him, the western gate to the city, and imagined the round, pointed towers as dark, giant breasts, burst from a blouse ornamented with crystals and brown stripes. He lay like this until *Frau* Deming and her daughter happened to come upon him as they drove back to the Sachenzucker offices to return *Herr* Schlarp's motorcar. Astrid motioned to her mother to stop and she hopped down from the car and ran over to David, pulling him to his feet.

"Are you all right, *liebling*?" asked *Frau* Deming. The daughter knelt to him and began to brush away the dirt and dust from his clothes as *Frau* Deming came to him and took his face into her hands and looked at him with worried eyes. "I am so sorry to have been unkind to you, earlier."

"Yes, I am alright, thank you, *Frau* Deming" David said. "Thank you, *Fraulein*, for helping me."

The woman and the girl allowed him to continue on his way, and they passed him as they turned the Benz in front of the first *Salzspeicher* and drove along its boarded windows until they reached the Sachenzucker building. When David arrived, he found the place a hive of activity, with the sounds of horses snorting and shuffling in place before many wagons aligned in waiting and several backed into lanes along the loading dock directly behind the wall in front of him. He turned left through a gas-lit passageway and entered the main office through high double doors to his right. He was met by the matronly *Frau* Kitchen, his father's English secretary.

"Young David!" *Frau* Kitchen said in English. David's father had instructed the woman to speak only English to his son, supplementing the private language instructions the boy received from a part-time tutor.

"Good *efternoon*, Mrs. Kitchen," said David.

"*Ahfternoon*, David, *ahfternoon*," *Frau* Kitchen corrected him.

"*Ahft, ahft, ahft*," replied David, flapping his arms, imitating a seabird.

Frau Kitchen pulled the boy into her arms and pinched his cheek saying, "A real entertainer. I have some cool water for you. Have you seen my Tom?"

"Not since school, Mrs. Kitchen. He will be at lift bridge, now."

"At *the* lift bridge."

"Yes," David said as he handed back the empty tumbler.

"You are here to see Mr. Schlarp, I believe," said Mrs. Kitchen.

"Yes."

"Then I release you! Go forth into the dragon's lair!"

David scrambled away from Mrs. Kitchen's embrace and pushed through double glass-paned doors and entered the accounting room. He ran through the narrow passage dividing the sea of clerks' desks, their Duplex Adding Machines working, and the sibilant shifting of paperwork filling the air. David stepped onto a curving staircase at the back of the room, scurrying up the middle of the broad carpeted steps, his suit's jumper flap waving him forward. As he reached the first floor, he heard the lift cage open and met *Herr* Schlarp stepping out of the amazing machine. The elevator seemed an otherworldly device to the boy; that a human could ascend without effort was nearly flying.

Herr Director Schlarp stepped out to the landing and smiled at David. He was lean, not quite gaunt, with straight, gray-blond hair swept back from his lined forehead. He said, "Well, *Junge,* it seems that you are on time, as usual."

The man led David along the long landing to his office, perched above the rooms occupied by *Frau* Deming and Mrs. Kitchen and their staff of secretaries. David looked out an enormous multi-paned window that leaned out slightly above the clerks working below and watched the pageant of papers lifting, dropping into wooden trays, and being collected by hurrying young men darting between the many desks. *Herr* Schlarp's office walls were paneled with brightly polished dark wood and the air was pungent with strong pipe tobacco. Light from a bank of windows on the opposite side of the wide room that looked out upon the delivery and shipping yard was at its brightest of the day as the sun was leveling with the building on its journey toward the horizon. An elaborate model ship was displayed within a large glass case on a table to the right of the Managing Director's desk, and an upright case filled with an ostentatious military uniform, swords and a large dagger, an *Yemini Jambiya,* stood standing free to the left.

Herr Schlarp walked with a slight limp, and favoring his right side, seemed to be pushed along in his gait. He walked behind his desk and sat down, motioning David to sit in one of the chairs placed opposite. The boy settled into the heavy wooden chair and felt the smooth wood of the sculpted seat with his hands as he pushed himself to the back's ribs that fanned up to a narrow curved top.

"*Junge,* tell this old soldier: how is your dear grandfather, Matthäus?"

"He is well, *Herr* Schlarp."

"And your dear grandmother?"

"Well, also, *Herr.*"

David knew that Dietrich Schlarp had been a high-ranking soldier in the Russian army and that his grandfather had known him for many years, but most of the Managing Director's history was a mystery unknown to the boy, as well as the Sachenzucker employees. How he came to the firm was never explained to David, and Schlarp's presence provided a perpetual stream of questions through the boy's mind. In the end, David felt a warm kinship with this man who welcomed and delighted him with stories of fantastic creatures and heroes.

"Well, young Rosenberg, shall I tell you the story of the *Earth Tree?* Before waiting for an answer, Schlarp began: "Before humans lived upon the ground, they lived in a tree as large as the earth." *Herr* Schlarp raised his arms and opened them widely, his fingers fluttering. "They made their homes in the burls and stubs of low limbs and upon the tops of roots which crooked high into the air and shrilled with a fierce wind that blew over and below the roots, tangled and splayed across the world. The humans were restless and ceaselessly climbed away from the roots where light was shaded and dimmed until it became dark where the roots touched the earth. The humans sought gaps in the mighty tree's bark and climbed upward, as if climbing through dells as wide as the valleys of the Alps, so huge was the tree. They climbed toward the light that shot through the tree's canopy-crown and settled for a time near pools of sweet, nourishing sap that the tree allowed to come forth from its core to drip and run until it was caught by wedges sunk deeply in its bark.

"The humans wanted for clothing and had no time to develop language, obsessed by the light high above as they were, and sought only to climb higher and higher toward the branches looming over them. Near the top of the trunk, the humans would gather on ledges of the massive bark, far above the area of the sap pools that had sustained them with nourishment and stand in the brilliant sunlight. They began to jabber and raise their voices in hoots and screams, becoming mad with joy and the desire to climb still farther into the branches and amongst the shiny, emerald leaves that were so huge, each resembling a ship wider than the Trave. But in their madness, the humans ignored how glossy and smooth the boughs above them were, and when they pushed up and away from the bark, they found that they could not grasp the tree further and each fell, almost forever, back into the darkness below.

"One day, a young fellow standing atop the bark watched humans falling away from the branches above him. Through the din of voices, he leaped upon the back of his neighbor and pulled himself up to the fellow's shoulders where he reached down to another fellow and pulled him up to his shoulders and motioned for another fellow to crawl up the human ladder he had devised. The ladder became ever higher, lengthened by thousands of humans until it reached into the lowest leaves of the Earth Tree.

"The men and women finally began to tumble into the shiny green leaves shot out of the lower limbs and found themselves splashing in streams of dew and eating nectar that appeared along the veins of the leaves. The people began to rest and call to each other in grunts and new voice sounds and soon, they began to understand each other. But as the people gave a sound to everything and began to find that they could understand each other, the Sky, looking down, became lonely, finding that the humans were no longer attracted to its light and became jealous of the tree that supported the humans.

"The Sky became angrier and angrier and its face became dark with clouds until the Sky released its rain and wind upon the tree and washed nearly all of the humans away from the Earth Tree's leaves.

When the Sky saw that the humans had disappeared, he pulled his clouds back into his body and all became calm again. But the Sky did not realize that a few humans had clung tightly to the leaves and hidden themselves. These few humans remembered how they had completed their journey to the top of the Earth Tree and reappeared, each one reaching their arms up toward the light until the Sky saw them and was pleased. The Sky gloried in the reverence of the humans and allowed them to multiply and heard their voices praising him as their father. Finally, the Sky's pride swelled his body so much that its light began to reach out beyond the Earth Tree and cover half the world, bringing the humans living on the tree's gnarly roots down to walk for the first time upon the earth. The Sky's daughter, the Moon, was pleased also, and being just a baby of the Universe, began to play with the Earth, turning it over and over so that the Sky's light would reach all of its surface and the Earth would begin to bring forth plants and animals for the humans to watch over and use to live."

Schlarp had brought his arms down, and as he told his story, worked them around in motions to interpret his words. He crooked his arms to imitate roots, cupped his hands to simulate leaves, and shook his limbs to illustrate the fury of the Sky's jealous rage of violent wind and rain.

David sat transfixed upon the images cast before his imagination and started in his chair as Old Schlarp gave motion to his words.

Finally, Schlarp put his hands together and said, "Thus ends today's story, my dear boy."

As David rose to leave, he noticed a new, framed etching set against the wall space between the large windows that looked out upon the legion of *Herr* Schlarp's clerks. It depicted a house set on wheels with a half-raised drawbridge and men flourishing what seemed to be feathers from turrets set at the top of the house around a dome. In the background, a mountain rose, supporting an ancient ship. A banner stretching above the cupola on the house read, "16 COLLEGIUM FRATERNITATUS 18." David asked, "*Herr* Schlarp, what does this picture mean?"

"Mean, my son?" said Schlarp. "I think we'll save that story for another time; it is getting late." Schlarp walked around his desk and held his hands out to David, who took them and gave them a hardy shake.

He looked at the tall, thin man with loving eyes and said in English, "Until we meet, again, me mate!" Words he'd heard Captain Twinge's crew say to each other.

David took the lift down and, as he entered the first floor atrium, he met his friend, Tom Kitchen. Tom excitedly described the afternoon adventure with their friends at the bridge site, especially the attempted theft by one of the boys of a mason's tool bag. The boy, Casper Kirchherr, was grabbed by another mason, swung around and around, tossed to the owner of the bag, and bound hand and foot. Then poor Casper was hung from a small, swinging crane and held out over the Trave, where he was raised and lowered, raised and lowered, until the construction foreman demanded that he be set free. The workmen where all laughing! Tom's frantic description, a mix of English and German, was not easy for David to follow, but he understood.

Mrs. Kitchen had taken all of this in and admonished the boys. "Masons are strong and spiteful. Do not go near them, again! Now, let us get Master Rosenberg home, Tom. Please ask *Frau* Deming to bring *Herr* Schlarp's motorcar around."

"Yes, mother," said Tom. He hurried away, and David went outside to await his transportation. The sun was now sheltered behind the neighboring building, and a chill had begun to creep into the shadows around David. The Benz, with *Frau* Deming at the helm, appeared, and David stepped up to take his place beside her. She looked over at him and nodding, accelerated forward, bumping out of the company's yard. David looked over at his chauffeur, noticed the outlines of a once gentle face and imagined *Frau* Deming without her hat and severe dress, wearing something loose, perhaps gathered gently around her waist, with her hair flowing about. He wondered at the conventions that held everyone so bound, and it appeared to him, uncomfortable.

They duly arrived at David's home, and he hopped down to bow to *Frau* Deming and thank her for taking the trouble to drive. He walked up the three steps and entered the house, where Brigitte met him and marched him towards the kitchen and his final meal of the day.

"Any word from Papa, Gitte?" David asked.

"No, my love; we must be patient."

Elisabeth walked into the house, giving Brigitte a warm embrace. David had gone to his room to play until bedtime, and the two women sat in the library next to the conservatory so filled with Gabi's blooming plants. The grandmother took the young maiden's hands into hers and said, "I fear the worst in our dear Jürgen's dealings with that horrible brother of his, my dear."

"I must confess, *Frau* Elisabeth, my heart aches for this man. I know it improper, but I realize how he has loved his father's legacy for years." She began to cry fiercely. "I am just a country girl and know my place, here, but *Herr* Jürgen has captured my heart! I am so worried about his stake in his family's business! How *Frau* Gabi must be suffering for *Herr* Jürgen, also!" said Brigitte.

"We all know that you adore our Jürgen, Brigitte; it is natural that this should happen. Do you not believe that Lotte has never harbored strong feelings for my Bernd? A beautiful young girl like you has not gone unnoticed by Jürgen, I can assure you! Well, I shall take my leave now and prepare for Bernd's return from his office and his books. Pray for our Jürgen's success, *liebes Mädchen*."

After Elisabeth departed, Brigitte thought, if she only knew. She remembered the day when Gabi had approached her with tears in her eyes, saying, "Brigitte, I am afraid that I cannot satisfy *Herr* Jürgen. I think about everything but the marriage bed. For years, only my son, my plants, my family, the church, and social functions have occupied my days and thoughts, and my poor Jürgen has been neglected. He is the most patient of men, but sexual relations are so important to them as to enslave their consciousness. I know that much. It does not matter if they are scholars or farmers, a woman's body is their preoccupation. My sister can attest to that. I want you to approach

Jürgen, allow him to know you and share yourself with him if you so desire. But you must not take him from me; that is all I ask of you. The maid was speechless and could only nod to her mistress, beginning to weep herself. She knows that I love him, she repeated over and over to herself. Finally, Gabi had said, "Thank you, Brigitte," and left her standing in the lovely room surrounded by walls of books.

Gabi had continued to go about her duties and interests, treasuring the quotidian rhythms of her daily life as the wife of a prosperous and important man, never mentioning her confession to Brigitte, but giving her gentle looks and placing her hands upon her, it seemed, each time they passed each other. Gabi's typical evenings with her husband were very formal and regimented: dinner, a hand of cards, and retirement to a separate bedroom. Brigitte was expected to entertain David for the most part, but Jürgen usually joined in the games she played with the boy and help her ready him for bed.

A Saturday came when Brigitte returned from her shopping excursion for the household, having taken in the admiring glances of men everywhere she ventured and turned away one persistent young naval officer's attentions. She found the house empty, and after finishing replenishing the larder and putting away the small things she had bought for herself, she climbed the steps to the top floor where she knew that the sun would be shining brightly through the huge skylight Jürgen had designed into the house. She entered the spacious, square room, and ignoring the writing desk that had been placed directly under the light, pulled a comfortable armchair alongside it, and leaned back, extending her legs to the desktop. She pulled her dress up to the tops of her thighs and allowed the sunlight to bear directly upon them and her face, as she laid her head back into the chair's plump back and gave herself over to dozing.

At length, she awoke and found Jürgen standing before her. She didn't move, except to part her legs a bit and stare up at her master, who seemed fixed in place. She held her arms out to him, and he fell to his knees and kissed her passionately. She was not shy, given her earlier family life growing up with brothers in a small farmhouse, and rose from Jürgen's embrace and removed all of her clothes. She stood within the intense sunlight, lifting her arms and allowing her full breasts to extend before her. Jürgen took her into his arms and ran his hands all over her body, his fingers finding the gap between her buttocks and rubbing her up and down there, he kissed her again. Brigitte pulled his stays down and began running her hands up his chest, but be brought his hands up to hers and held them saying, "I could love you." They stood still, breathing the scent of her left upon his fingers, until finally, Jürgen pulled his stays back up and said, "I must leave."

6

As the morning dew descended outside his favorite windows, three windows unlike any found in the rest of the house, their glass panes bowed out like a modest compass window, Bernd Matthäus, fully dressed for the day in a light gray wool suit, took down a very care-worn copy of *Fama Fraternitatis* printed by Wilhelm Wessel from a high shelf. His wife entered the library. Her sideway entry, breezily performed as she adjusted to the latest style of material that swelled out beyond the width of her shoulders, caught Bernd by surprise as he handled the old document that had held so very little interest, for so long, for most men.

"Bernd," said Elisabeth, "We have news of Jürgen. He will be moved into Gabi's rooms tomorrow." *Frau* Matthäus-Kahn was also ready for her day, save for a morning shawl. Her eyes shone an absolute trust in Bernd, her companion of so many years.

"Where is David, my dear?"

"He is breakfasting with Brigitte, who came over earlier this morning."

"Elisabeth, you must go to Hildesheim, today, if possible. I have heard from *Herr* Schlarp that he believes that David should, per-haps, accompany Captain Twinge back to England in August. We must know that Gabi concurs that David needs the separation, at least for a time," said Bernd. "If she doesn't, it is very important that you persuade her that the boy's mind must be occupied with something other than *her* misery. From my own observations, I fear for Jürgen and cannot trust that this move will help him, but I know Gabi …"

"I will ask Gottfried to arrange transportation, if you can spare him. God knows, his office duties and house responsibilities keep him very busy. I'll consider taking Brigitte; she's a strong girl and could be tremendous help."

"I'll leave it to you, dearest, but don't allow Gottfried to grouse any sympathy from you. I know exactly what he does, and there will be no acceptable excuses from him. Please have Brigitte send a telegram informing Rabbi Graetz that you are coming. He will appreciate the help with moving Jürgen."

Elisabeth kissed her husband and made her way out of the room, leaving a faint scent of *Quelques Fleurs L'Original*.

Bernd looked out of his window through the somewhat wavy panes and recalled a passage from the book laid open on the corner of his almost barren desk: "*... in every kernel is contained a whole good tree or fruit, so likewise is included in the little body of man the whole great world and works. ...*" His grandson's future was on his mind.

He hadn't looked at *Fama Fraternitatis* in the years since David's birth, and wondered if a new binding was in order for the volume. The book was hundreds of years old and had been offered by a destitute old Don at Cambridge when he, Dieter, and Hugh were students together. Coming out of a stern Lutheran and Pietism tradition, Bernd purchased the book with the encouragement of his friends and an accrual against the allowance his parents had been sending him. The tradition preserved through the centuries offered by the book brought the young men, in the beginning, a mysterious and secretive friendship, but eventually, the ideas and flowing Latin gradually melted the shell holding the profound core of each young man's thought and experience together.

The old lawyer replaced the book, hurriedly walked through the house, and found David, busy at his breakfast, in the kitchen. "Good morning, dear boy; sleep well?" asked Bernd.

"Good morning, *Opa*. I am just wondering how long Papa and Mama are planning to stay in Hildesheim. Brigitte said that she didn't know, that something important must be keeping them."

Bernd patted the boy on the head and said, "Your father had important business there, and your mother wanted to join him. Let's hope they return soon. I hear that Captain Twinge is due to visit us!"

Bernd was pained to not reveal the unfortunate news concerning Jürgen, but shielding the boy from possibilities could certainly be justified. The lawyer continued on his way out toward his office two doors away, but he could not forget the boy's sad eyes, the small, unhappy change in the boy's demeanor. He hoped, but feared, that the changes being considered would not help anyone concerned. As he entered his office's front door, Dieter Schlarp stood waiting.

"Good morning, Bernd. I received your note last night and hoped that we might have promising news this morning," said Schlarp, holding a cup of coffee. "And how are you maintaining yourself, old friend?"

"I am tired, but feel fine otherwise. I was looking through the old *Fama*, remembering the days at Cambridge. I never tire of the illustrations. At any rate, my reason for asking you here, Dieter, was to further discuss David's visit to England, but I do have other news. Jürgen is being moved from Rabbi Graetz's home to rooms rented by Gabi. I am most worried, as you can imagine."

"I assume a nurse has been engaged, Bernd. I know that Jürgen's presence has strained the Graetz's household, but as you have related from your visit to the Graetz residence, I have detected nothing but concern and enthusiasm for his care. With respect, is this wise? I ask only because of my regard for Gabi and *Herr* Rosenberg."

"I have asked my wife to journey down to Hildesheim with a servant to see what can be done to help, but I suspect that she will demand that I go, also, or even perhaps, instead. I do not really know Gabi's circumstances and regret that her sister has returned to Baden, so I must rely on you to attend to our concerns, again. I will communicate with you after we have solid answers on Jürgen's condition and, perhaps, David's immediate future."

"I will not hear from Hugh, Bernd, for several days, at least. I am sure that the boy will be welcome and would advise preparing for his departure. All depends, of course, on *Herr* Rosenberg's condition and *Frau* Rosenberg's assent."

"I looked through our old book, this morning, Dieter, and feel stronger than ever that my grandson should embody its teachings.

I feel silly, frankly, indulging in our youthful obsession with building a *truth* for ourselves, I suppose, we, who so mistrusted the institutions all around us that we had to sacrifice our youth to tearing apart the world of ideas ourselves. But still, we will be gone soon, and the old book's essential teachings will be left to him. He seems to have an intrinsically good, and even settled, mind. But he is young. Do you remember the phrase about "the little body of man and his whole great world and works?"

"Like Aristotle's acorn, yes."

"Our lives—that's yours, Hugh's and mine—have carried some part of that book since we were young. Let us keep the wisdom preserved in David. Hopefully, Hugh will not teach him many 'new' English words."

Dieter Schlarp nodded and fixed his gaze on his long, weathered hands. He had aged in the last year and felt, at this moment, that life was slipping away from him. He looked at Bernd with rheumy eyes and placed his hand on his old friend's shoulder, saying somewhat wearily, "Bernd, please make time to visit me to discuss the company."

"I will, Dieter; give me a few days."

"Goodbye, my friend." Schlarp took his leave and after exiting the office door, grabbed for a new walking stick leaning against the building to help him make the distance to his office. He insisted on walking most everywhere and knew that he required the help of the smooth, hooked cane, as he walked down to the harbor and across the cobbled bridge. But he did not want Bernd to know of his weakness. He muttered: "In weakness, youth and age are one. Old men must walk three-footed, weak as babes, and stray like dreams lost in the light of day."

After Schlarp had left the office, Bernd's secretary, brought in his morning coffee and the day's copy of the *Lübecker General-Anzeiger*. She said nothing and tried to deliver these items with the utmost discretion.

"Fraulein Loew, please go to my home and deliver this itinerary to my wife before she leaves for her appointments."

"Yes, *Herr* Matthäus," responded Annaliese Loew, standing very erect, her full bosom projecting forth and over Bernd's desk.

"And if you please, wear a shawl. Thank you very much."

The young woman left the room and closed the door behind her. Bernd was quickly on his feet and turned to remove the bucolic August Becker painting behind his desk to expose his safe. He opened the safe and took out a very old bronze cylinder, inscribed *Rožmberk 1620.* The vessel had been entrusted to him by Nathan Rosenberg during his visit to Lübeck, eight years ago with a fixed retainer—insisted upon despite's Bernd's protests—to keep it in his possession until Nathan's sons had terminated their professional relationship, which Nathan felt was inevitable after his death. Nathan explained to Bernd that his family, including *Frau* Rosenberg, had no knowledge of the contents of the tube, and that the documents contained therein had been passed from father to son, one generation to another, for hundreds of years. In this case, without explanation, Nathan told Bernd that the documents would go to Jürgen, not his oldest son, Heinrich. Nathan told Bernd that he had been advised to get his business organized. Nathan's Doktor could not promise him another year of life.

Bernd did not open the cylinder, but wanted to reassure himself that the container was not missing. He wondered what mystery the documents held, especially given the knowledge shared between him and his friends, Dieter and Hugh, concerning the *Fama Fraternitatis* and the milieu that had brought the book forth, also dated the vessel. The name *Rožmberk* was familiar to him in this context, but he had no idea how, and if, the tube related. He was afraid, with Jürgen's present condition, he might not be able to fulfill Nathan's wishes. He realized that his son-in-law might not live to see the documents. Who could be entrusted with the cylinder until David became old enough to understand the Rosenberg family mystery? Bernd must have a succession in place before he left this world, should he be unable to fulfill his promise to Nathan Rosenberg. The lawyer replaced the cylinder in his safe, and repositioning the painting, regarded it with some reverence since his father had used it for the same purposes. The picture was probably worth something, given Becker's international recognition, if not fame, but for Bernd the painting was just another pedestrian example of a solitary man standing in a dull landscape.

Bernd sat down to his desk and stared at the fine old paneling before him. An ancient leather settee, left from his father's days, faced a new Persian rug, a gift from Hugh Twinge, and the play of the rug's red and blue hues and its fine geometric patterns made the old divan something of a relic. The settee had been refitted time and again over the years, but the style would never be compatible with the rug.

Bernd's thoughts returned to surveying the problem at hand, and it occurred to him that perhaps Kathe, not Gabi, might be the only person who could be entrusted with keeping the cylinder safe until David would be ready to know its contents. Commensurately, his doubts about Jürgen's recovery seemed to increase as the minutes behind the desk increased. He decided to write Kathe a letter, careful to make a copy for himself.

1 June 1899
Doktor Bernhard Gerfried Matthäus, S.J.D.
5 Hundesstrasse
Lübeck
Gräfin Claramond Kathe von Petersruhe-Matthäus
Vogelgesangstein
Baden

My Dearest Kathe:

I hope this finds you well and rested after your journey home to us and trust that my dear Graf von Petersruhe is happy to have his life blessed again, by your dear presence. I write to inform you of dearest Jürgen who, as you are aware, has been confined to medical attention in Hildesheim, and to request your participation in an unusual venture regarding his family, especially as it relates to young David. At present, our hearts break at the fact Jürgen is showing no promise of recovery. Your sister, even in the face of very attentive care, insists on moving my dear son-in-law to rooms she has taken nearby. This, of course, is entirely her affair and even as her father, I will not chance to interfere with her decisions, but have arranged for your mother and Gottfried to travel to Hildesheim, to assist her. Knowing your mother, however, it is I who will likely make the journey!

David, however, is another matter, and I must act with my best judgment as to his welfare. As I mentioned, I have asked your dear mother to go to Hildesheim today, not only to assist her in moving Jürgen, but to speak to Gabriele about allowing David to accompany Captain Twinge back to England after the Captain's visit late next month. The boy grows more morose every day, with no attention from his mother and his preoccupation with his father's absence. An exciting venture, it seems to me, is called for, and I know of no one outside of our family more fond of the boy who might be willing to undertake to keep the young man entertained and busy.

The other matter that I alluded to must be discussed with you in person, but suffice to say for now, legal documents will be drawn up to ensure that my intentions are carried out should circumstances prevent our ability to speak of them. A certain document will pass directly to David when he reaches his majority, from either you or me, should his dear father depart this life before he is capable of receiving it. It is only to you, my dear, that I reveal this possibility, and should I be unable to carry it out myself as it was entrusted to me by Jürgen's father, Nathan Rosenberg, I ask you to execute the presentation of the document. The documents giving you authority to act in my stead and the document meant for David are in my office safe, the combination of which rests with your mother. This must not, under any circumstances, be disclosed to anyone, except, of course, your own Sigi.

And now, my dear girl, I will say goodbye.
Your loving father,

BGM

Bernd folded the letter, addressed the envelope, and called for *Fraulein* Loew. At once, the young woman entered the office and lifting her head, asked, "Yes, *Herr* Matthäus?"

"*Fraulein* Loew, please have this posted immediately. Did you give my itinerary to *Frau* Matthäus-Kahn?" And, reaching for a proffered document from *Fraulein* Loew, asked, "Is this the itinerary? She sent it back to me?"

"Yes, *Herr* Matthäus, after writing something into it."

Bernd unfolded the itinerary and noticed that Elisabeth had written his name, and crossed out hers. He would make the journey to Hildesheim. "So I go," mumbled Bernd. He had work to address, but as his wife decreed, he must put everything aside and prepare to leave.

"Thank you, *Fraulein*. You may leave early; this will be a half day due to family business."

The girl curtseyed and left the room, thanking Bernd on her way out. Bernd could not help but wonder why Elisabeth allowed him to take on this girl. She was a most attractive woman, in his heart, as lovely as his own daughters. She had been a pleasure to behold, as he stepped into his office, in the mornings of the work week. At twenty-two, *Fraulein* Loew was still unmarried and conducted herself with absolute, but at times, abrupt independence, a trait he'd been long used to in the women of his own family.

Annaliese left Bernd's office and walked to his home, to confer with *Frau* Matthäus-Kahn. Brigitte answered the door and stepped aside to allow the secretary into the ante room and showed her into the parlor, where Elisabeth was directing the packing. Annaliese curtseyed and said, "*Herr* Matthäus received the itinerary, *Frau*; I assume that he is planning to go, since he gave me the rest of the day off, due to family matters. I will report to you tomorrow morning, before opening the office."

"Very good, Annaliese, thank you and enjoy your afternoon, my dear," said Elisabeth, handing her a coin. The girls left, and soon Bernd appeared as the last bags were loaded into his automobile. He gave Elisabeth the Graetz's address, in case he needed to be contacted and, with Elisabeth, stepped into the car.

As they drove up to the station, Elisabeth kissed her husband goodbye and wished him a safe journey. She watched him amble into the small brick building with a porter carrying his bags. She had sensed that she might be needed at home and had ignored her impulse to join Gabi and Jürgen in Hildesheim. She knew that Bernd was capable of comforting their daughter and helping her make decisions concerning Jürgen's arrangements, and most sadly, also knew, that should Jürgen's health continue to decline, or that he should die, David would need her attentions. She tapped the driver and asked to be taken home.

7

Kathe woke with a start. She'd been dreaming of standing on a sandy beach, angry and cold with an unrelenting wind flowing around her bare limbs. She could never remember much of her dreams, but she knew that she had dreamed of her long-ago lover. Kathe said his name aloud. "Isaac Becouche-Albukerk" sounded like a spell pronounced by some unfamiliar voice. She looked at the bracelet Isaac had given her years ago that she wore tightly around her left forearm and thought of the deeply tanned skin of his face and hands as they walked the ancient streets of the Levant—from old churches to municipal buildings, from ruins to private homes—in search of manuscripts. She lifted her head from the side of the bed and sat upright in the small upholstered parlor chair she'd pulled from the room's corner to be near David as he slept and drew her thoughts away from her reverie to the reason she found herself in David's room. She had worried that her nephew would awaken to the servants' chatter concerning the late night news and their resulting pre-dawn bustle after her parents received the ominous telegram from someone named Leo Graetz. The boy had not been awakened when Bernd Matthäus telephoned to inform his daughter Gabi of the news of Jürgen's accident. Gabi had asked that Kathe come to stay with David while she and Bernd journeyed together to Hildesheim.

Kathe looked at the sleeping boy through the dim light given by the small oil lamp she had brought to the room and marveled at how neatly his hair fell away from his head, forming its own pattern of gold, white-blond, and something a little darker. She lifted her own blond curls away from her forehead and tried to set them into her wavy mane, but without the pins that had restrained them, the locks fell back, finding their natural place above and around her eyes. What happened to the hairpins? She looked across the broad bed and smoothed the coverlet away but found nothing but the patterned silk shining in the faint light that fell through the bedroom's window frame where the oil lamp burned. She was not surprised or disappointed. *Gräfin* Claramond Kathe von Petersruhe-Matthäus was used to waking to only a flat, shimmering plane of silk when she looked across in her own bed.

Kathe imagined her husband, *Graf* Siegfried von Petersruhe, well into his lamp-led morning routine, already marching across their small estate's paddock at the care required to take a step safe from fresh horse droppings, swearing in French through teeth clenched around his long, tasseled pipe. *Vogelgesangstein*, Birdsong Stone as Kathe called it in English, had survived Napoleon nearly intact and became Petersruhe's in 1880. He was a restless man, somewhat older than Kathe's own father but completely devoted to her and her travel and intellectual pursuits. They had met in Italy, some years after she had parted from her colleague and lover Isaac, and many years after Sigi's family had given up hope of seeing him married. She had been welcomed by Sigi's surviving siblings, despite her lack of noble standing and even though she was the daughter of a free, liberal city. The marriage had never been consummated, and Sigi had governed his attentions according to Kathe's brutal insistence that only one man would possess her sexually, allowing her husband only an occasional intimacy.

Her mind moved back to the scene at hand, and she wondered what kind of outrageous tales old Schlarp had filled David's imagination with the day before. She recalled the evenings when, as a girl, she would listen to *Herr* Schlarp's stories of Russia when he visited her family's home. She had asked Bernd about the nature of the soldier's visits in later years, but her father had only looked at her, twisted his mouth to one side for a few moments, and told her that *Herr* Schlarp relied on him to oversee certain business matters on behalf of his family. She had never met a single member of Schlarp's family.

A small knock on the bedroom door warned Kathe of the pending entrance of Brigitte, whom she had dismissed after the maid's third round of solicitations through the late night. The young woman was obviously slaving to contain her reaction to the worrying news of Jürgen's accident, and with a small halting voice said, "*Gräfin*, please allow me to sit with the *Junge* so you might rest properly."

"No, Brigitte, I shall stay with David until he stirs and then see you at breakfast at seven. You must rest while you can."

Brigitte nodded, curtsied, and quietly left the room.

The *Junge* had turned in his bed toward Kathe, and gripping the sheets, had wedged his fists under his chin. She noticed a slight drool shining away from the side of his upturned lips and settling on the linen and thought with dismay of the tears that would surely soon find a path down the boy's face. She dreaded telling David of his father's condition and planned to heed her own father's advice to say only that Jürgen's return had been delayed by a touch of fever. She knew that David would fear the worst when he discovered that his mother and grandfather had gone to Hildesheim to be with his father.

Tears came to Kathe's eyes as she recounted the conversation she had with the boy the previous day. Notwithstanding David's confidence, her misgivings concerning his enthusiasm for the military had been shared with Bernd and Elisabeth, and though the grandparents had dismissed the boy's interest as "every boy's heroic fantasy," the aunt's adoration and wishes for her family's heritor brought fret and alarm to the young woman. Kathe had sat in the Matthäus conservatory amidst the fragrance of lemon and oranges brought in from Spain and asked her parents if they were aware that the child's intelligence and sensitivity would broaden his obvious willfulness as he grows into adolescence and beyond.

Bernd had replied, "My dear, David can be a little *Faxenmacher*, but a boy's dreams are the better part of his life, and if we can survive *your* formative years, we can survive our dear grandson's."

Kathe wiped the tears that had begun to swell away from her eyes and drew breath into her shuddering breast, now resting against David's bed, as she recalled her response to her parents' resignation. She had reminded them that there is now, truly, a

Germany, and that tiny, free Lübeck was sitting atop a restless behemoth, whose slapping arms included not just Prussia, but now Baden, Bavaria, Wurttemberg, and Hesse, all led by a bellicose tyrant spoiling for a fight.

Bernd had replied, "Captain Twinge assures me that Britain will match the *Kaiser's* ambitions at sea. David will never forget his freedoms, no matter what path he chooses. He will always remember and seek the kind of freedom he enjoys here."

Kathe told her parents, "The *Faxenmacher* running Germany will find a way to make war!" and retired to her room.

Kathe laid her head against David's bed and once again gave herself to sleep, laying the side of her head against the cover, her eyelids scratching against the silk as they blinked and finally yielded shut. She immediately began to dream of Sigi, smelling his pipe smoke and hearing his gentle voice calling to her from the small *Schloss*, as she sat in the shade of a linden tree growing through the long abandoned ruins that had once formed the greater part of the castle.

"Claramond, Claramond!" he called. "Claramond!" His voice grew louder as she sensed his approach. She looked up and beheld him standing with his arms outstretched, then reaching toward her as if blind, his body nearly nude, his head covered with an enormous, elongated, golden miter twitching and glistening in the sunlight as if it had a life of its own. His arms brought his hands up to cover his face, then opening his palms, a doorway was revealed through which she found herself walking. A brightly illuminated rough stone wall surrounded a passage she followed, and descending into a large, open room, with a swirling wind blowing and lifting clouds of documents of torn parchment, velum, papyrus, and fine linen paper. "Claramond! Claramond!" she heard again. She laid down in the wind upon a cool, smooth floor of dry, hard clay and found herself covered into darkness with the settling forms of documents. She swung her hands through the paper, trying to lift herself into light but could not catch purchase and moved as if swimming through sea foam, her breath becoming frantic and stifled until she felt herself float clear, buoyed only by air, with the swirling wind blowing her skirts over her head. Again she heard, "Claramond!" "But, I am Michal! Pitied by the slave girls," she called out.

"*Tante*, are you awake?" asked David as he awoke, his eyes grainy and heavy. "*Tante?*" David slowly pushed himself up against the headboard of his bed and gazing at his aunt's blond wavy hair splaying out against the side of the cover, wondered why she was there.

Kathe's mind rushed into consciousness, leaving her dream as if torn from some strange, intractable problem. "Good morning, David, did you sleep well? I am here to greet you, to make sure that you haven't become one of old Schlarp's monsters!" she said, stifling a yawn.

"*Herr* Schlarp's monsters are not real. You know that, *Tante*."

"Your mother asked me to come to you to tell you that she had to travel last night to your father. Your Papa is a little ill and will be delayed for a few days."

David was now fully awake and instantly asked Kathe, "Where is Papa? Is he still in Hildesheim?"

"Yes, my *Schatzi*, he's resting there. Your Mama and Grandfather are with him."

David sank back into his pillows and stared at the elaborate print of Captain Twinge's ship framed against the opposite wall. He opened his mouth to speak, but immediately closed it, threw off the bed covers and hopped down to the small Persian rug spread at the side of his bed. Kathe stood and helped him into his morning robe and said, "I'll see you at breakfast," remembering to restrain an endearment that had come to her lips. She must act as carefree as she could this morning.

"Will you telephone *Herr* Schlarp, *Tante*? Please ask him to visit today?"

"Of course, David; I'll ask him to lunch with us."

As promised, Schlarp appeared for lunch, greeting everyone in his formal way until he came upon David and Kathe in the dining room. "How is the little menace, this day? Has *Tante* kept you entertained? I can see that she is tired, completely exhausted by chasing you around."

"She is rather old, you know, *Herr* Schlarp," said David.

Kathe pinched his side and Schlarp laughed heartily.

As they sat down, Schlarp said, "And so here we are, midway through the last year of the century."

"Is it different from the end of the last century, *Herr* Schlarp?" said Lotte, who had just entered the room to serve the guests.

"Ah, the amusing Lotte, never at a loss for torturing this old soul," said Schlarp. "As a matter of fact, my dear, life might have been more civilized back then, but I, of course, was not present to bear witness. But we know this much: all you have to do these days to summon old Schlarp to lunch, is to warn him by telephone, and then he comes to his hosts by driving his motor car."

After lunch, David asked, "Have you a story for us, *Herr* Schlarp?"

Herr Schlarp replied, "Perhaps we shall recount an adventure experienced by the world's greatest traveler, Ibn Battutah."

"But, I've never heard of this man. I believe that you have just invented him!" said David.

"Oh, this man was a living soul who wandered over much of the world and returned home to recount his adventures."

"Tell us, please, of one of this man's adventures, *Herr* Schlarp," begged David.

"Ibn Battutah experienced many great and unusual places and people. He was regarded as an important man and found himself in the company of kings and lesser rulers. In one of his adventures, he made a journey to Constantinople, where he met the king. He began this particular journey in the exotic city of Astrakhan, which was part of the land ruled by the great Sultan, Uzbak.

"One of the Sultan's wives, called Bayalun, was the daughter of the Greek King of Constantinople, known as Andronicus III, and was near to giving birth. She obtained permission from the Sultan to have her child in Constantinople and to have Ibn Battutah accompany her, since he was a great adventurer and friend. And so they set out, accompanied first by the Sultan and his Queen, and when the Sultan had to return to his lands, another of his wives and an important Amir, or lesser ruler, were designated by the

Sultan to act in his place and continue with her. Sultans usually had several wives, as you know, but only *one* queen.

"After many days, they reached the territory of the Greeks and the other wife, the Amir, and the soldiers assigned to guard Bayalun turned back and allowed the Greeks to accompany her the rest of the way to Constantinople. Here, Bayalun left all the customs of her husband's religion behind and embraced the Greek customs once again. Ibn Battutah, of course, was of the Sultan's faith and would not practice devotions as the Greeks did, but being a friend of Bayalun, he was granted an exemption from the Greek observances.

"As Ibn Battutah became known in Constantinople, he was much sought after for his wisdom and knowledge of the world, to the extent that King Andronicus III gave him an audience. The King was most curious about his travels and through an interpreter of yet another faith, asked him questions about Arabia, Jerusalem, Egypt and other places holy to him and his brethren. At length, Ibn Battutah was awarded a horse and saddle and a guide to lead him about the great city.

"But King Andronicus III was not the most important person Ibn Battutah met in Constantinople. It was the King's father. The King's father was known as Jirjis, in Ibn Battutah's tongue, but to the Greeks, Georgios. Now this man had given up all of his worldly power and possessions to become a servant of the divine spirit of his religion and allowed his son to take his place as ruler of the Greeks of Constantinople. The old King wore only a haircloth garment, which is very uncomfortable, and a felt bonnet. He had a long, white beard and carried a staff and a string of beads to remind him to pray. When Ibn Battutah saw him, he dismounted from his horse and bowed to the old King, who asked him, through Ibn Battutah's guide, who he was. Finding that Ibn Battutah had traveled to Jerusalem and Bethlehem, the King said, "I clasp the hand that has entered Jerusalem and the foot that has walked within the Dome of the Rock and the Great Church of the Holy Sepulcher," whereupon Georgios, the monk-king, put his hand upon the foot of Ibn Battutah and passed that hand over his own eyes.

"And so, what does this tell us, David? It tells us of the ability of people of different faiths and customs to honor one another, my son," said *Herr* Schlarp. "And it tells us to find a good interpreter!"

8

Bernd Matthäus stepped away from the bed and reached to lift the shoulders of his daughter, Gabrielle. The woman only sank lower into the bedside as Bernd looked at *Doktor* Stein with a resigned and helpless look. Stein motioned for Bernd to step out of the bedroom with him.

"*Herr* Matthäus, I know that *Frau* Rosenberg wishes to move her husband to her own apartments, but I must tell you that *Herr* Rosenberg is in his final phase of life." Stein looked down, his red side curls framing the man's black eyes. He sighed. "I am truly mystified by this outcome. When I first examined *Herr* Rosenberg, he showed strong signs. His condition struck me as a severe concussion, and given that the condition did not show signs of affecting his general health, I was optimistic. His breathing is now very shallow and his heart is much less strong than only a day ago. I advise allowing the man to die peacefully here, in the comfort of this house. He has had the most attentive care by the Graetz family. You have provided an excellent nurse, and you could expect no improvement by removing *Herr* Rosenberg."

"Herr *Doktor* Stein, how long do you expect my son-in-law to live?"

"I do not believe that he will last through the day, *Herr* Matthäus." Stein folded his hands and asked, "Should I speak with *Frau* Rosenberg, or would you prefer to talk with your daughter alone?"

"Come with me, *Doktor*, if you please," said Bernd. "Gabriele is in no state to be persuaded by a single voice."

As the two men, one with a slightly slouching gait and a precipitously fixed pince-nez and the other tall, erect, and formal with tightly intertwined fingers, moved down the narrow hallway, the nurse taken on to help with Jürgen's care grabbed the doorframe to the patient's room and pulled herself around to face the father and the *Doktor*. She was startled by the men's proximity and with eyes somewhat wider than normal and an opened mouth, shook her head, indicating that her patient had died. She said, "*Herr Doktor, please.*" Bernd entered the room with Stein and his nurse and knelt to embrace his daughter, whose shaking frame and soft moans indicated that she had guessed the worst. The doctor bent over Jürgen and whispered to the nurse to inform the Graetz family that the patient had died; the rabbi should know as soon as possible, given that *Shabbat* would start later in the day.

Bernd led Gabi to a chair and helped her sit down. He held his daughter's face against his own as he knelt beside her and looked away to wipe his tears before they began to fall unremittingly.

Gabi rose and standing fully, looked about with wide eyes and recited to no one, to everyone:

> *This Hell I nail myself*
> *This body I twice cover;*
> *This man, this form, I revere;*
> *I dance with all, loath all;*
> *Who are you, my father?*
> *Who are you, tall man?*
> *I shall...*

Gabi walked between her father and the nurse, and as she reached the hall, began to run, knocking over Rabbi Graetz, as she fled the house to the cobbled street and into the path of a heavily-laden wagon pulled by four steeds. The woman was trampled bloody, her face twisted and smashed by innocent and stamping hooves. Gabi's eyes remained opened, one almost out of its socket, and her hair, sprung loose by the impact and trample, flowed over her upper body like a river of light, revealing here and there bloody skin and clothes. Her mouth was closed at one end, though twisted with a slight hint of beautiful, white teeth.

The Graetz's ran out of the house and stopped short of the horror before them. Bernd followed, his mind still dumbfounded by Gabi's words and fell back onto the stone steps before the front door. He looked up, and horror began to wrap him with every movement of people settling the horses, screaming their horror, and calling for the *Doktor*. Rabbi Graetz came to him and turned him away from the scene, holding Bernd against his unconscious desire to face the tragedy a few steps away. *Doktor* Stein, having seen the accident from the parlor window, came to Bernd with a syringe of morphine, which he plunged into the father's arm, an arm offered with such carelessness that Stein was unnerved, surprised. The grieving father gripped his left wrist, and held by Rabbi and *Frau* Graetz, lost consciousness. Stein suggested that the man be allowed to lie back and that all of them carry him into the parlor.

After Bernd was settled and Gabi's body had been removed and wrapped in a white sheet, Rabbi Graetz telephoned Strumond's office and asked that his receptionist locate the lawyer as soon as possible. The woman demanded to know the nature of the Rabbi's call, but Graetz only allowed that Strumond's presence was required immediately to assist Bernd Matthäus. The police were summoned and asked to wait until Strumond could be found.

Graetz asked his wife to oversee the dreadful scene as he retired to his study. He began to shake and tears came to his eyes. What is this punishment these decent people deserve? He rocked back and forth as the ancient Jews had in defiance of infidels who demanded that they walk, not sit at their level on saddled beasts, and began to silently recite the *Kaddish*, and when the prayer addressed his primary thoughts, the awful human suffering he had just witnessed, he sighed at the phrases, *Holy is the Divine, above and beyond any consecrations and hymns, praises and consolations which are pronounced in the world.* He would have to utter these words before his congregation that evening. The portion he would choose to read, he knew, would relate to nothing but *Frau* Rosenberg's accident and *Herr* Rosenberg's death today. His mind would be consumed until, he feared, punishment from God would bring him back to life. He began to fear nothing.

At length, Strumond and a young assistant appeared at the door, and upon being allowed in, made it clear to all that he had been informed of the day's tragic events. He addressed Rabbi and *Frau* Graetz and asked if there was anything their family needed and if the bodies had been removed. He made clear that he was the voice of the Rosenberg and Matthäus families, and that all concerns should be addressed to him. He told the assistant to notify the *Beerdigungsunternehmen* and to telegraph *Frau* Elisabeth Matthäus-Kahn in Lübeck. He then instructed, as the assistant caught up in his notes, that *Gräfin* Claramond Kathe von Petersruhe be contacted via *Schloss Vogelgesangstein*, in Baden. He made it clear to the assistant that he would not be able to assist in locating *Vogelgesangstein*.

Rabbi Graetz presented the death notices that *Doktor* Stein had prepared before leaving with the nurse. The signatures were somewhat uneven and Strumond observed two or three small, oblong flaws in the heavy paper. Dried tears? The lawyer took the documents and gave them to his assistant, moving beyond him toward the doorway. Strumond looked at the prone figure of his friend Bernd Matthäus and remained silent for a short time. He then turned and said, "My dear Rabbi and *Frau* Graetz, the family you have attended will never be able to repay you for your kindness. Only God has the power to reward you for what you have done on behalf of *Herr* Rosenberg and his family. I hope that you will remember that I will always represent their gratitude here in Hildesheim, and I will offer my services gratis should you require secular, legal attention. May I offer my hands to both of you?" Thereupon the three shook hands and nodded formally.

Strumond asked, "If you are amenable, I will have the *Beerdigungsunternehmen* remove the bodies this afternoon and have the ambulance, which has arrived, take Herr Matthäus with me. I will be communicating with you during the next several days and would be most grateful if you would allow another of my assistants a few minutes of your time, as needed, to supervise the *Beerdigungsunternehmen*."

The ambulance attendants rapped at the door and were admitted by *Frau* Graetz. They were speaking loudly as they entered and immediately met the stony gaze of Strumond. The men quietly moved where directed and lifted Bernd onto their framed canvas and carried him to the ambulance. Strumond stepped into the wagon's compartment and watched as his friend mumbled incoherently as they rode to Strumond's home. "Sleep my friend, sleep. We will deal with this nightmare together."

Once the ambulance arrived, a startled *Frau* von Strumond ran out of her residence. "Albert! What has happened?" the dignified woman asked as her husband stepped down onto the gravel drive.

"I have brought Bernd home. What has happened is almost too horrible to relate, my dear." Strumond recounted the day's events to his wife and explained that the next few days will be quite demanding of her time. The ambulance men brought Bernd into the house, and led by *Frau* von Strumond, had them place their charge onto a bed. Bernd lay very still in the guestroom's half light and showed no signs of awakening. Strumond left the room and at the hallway's elevated desk, telephoned his own physician. He knew that Stein would soon be observing the sabbath and wanted someone available throughout the evening.

It was nearly 5:00 in the evening, and the Strumonds decided to have coffee and pastries to ward off the hunger that would surely come as the night's duties began to unfold. *Doktor* Franz von Gernsdorff arrived somewhat later and joined in the modest repast, making it known that he had suffered through an afternoon of hunger at the local hospital. Strumond recounted the day's events to the horror of his wife and physician, and told Gernsdorff that he would be required during the evening. He wanted a physician with Bernd when the effects of the morphine began to subside.

Gernsdorff said, "*Herr* Strumond, your friend is not going to feel very well and knowing what has happened to his family will be very difficult. How old is he?"

"*Herr Doktor* Matthäus is in his middle fifties."

"Then we must take care that his own heart has not suffered."

"*Frau* von Strumond will see to your needs; I must contact *Herr* Rosenberg's brother."

Strumond knew that Heinrich would be preparing for *Shabbat*, and drove his Daimler to the Conservative *Schul* to ask how Heinrich might be contacted. As it happened, Heinrich was walking along the street with his family between two sets of string that stretched back to Heinrich's home's front door, a little distance down the street. The family was walking toward the *Schul* as Strumond approached the modest building in his automobile. These Conservative Jews are so strict, but they do almost nothing to maintain their place of worship, thought the lawyer.

"*Herr* Rosenberg," Strumond called from his automobile.

Heinrich stopped and then began to walk on.

"*Herr* Rosenberg, your brother Jürgen has died," said Strumond. The lawyer was more aware than most of the brothers' disagreements, but he felt that Heinrich should know that Jürgen and Gabrielle had died, as a matter of human kindness and the events involving their business association that would certainly follow, whatever reaction the older brother displayed.

Heinrich stopped, and motioning for his family to stay behind as he walked farther up the sidewalk, still between the strings, to where the street approached the synagogue, placing him near Strumond's car. "This happened when?" asked Heinrich.

"Today."

"I will have my attorney contact you. Good evening, *Doktor*." Heinrich walked away from the Daimler and proceeded, wordlessly, toward the *Schul*.

Strumond sat for a moment dumbfounded, and then drove away, toward his home. He recalled a passage from *The Choephori* as his contempt for Heinrich deepened:

No man may hope to spend
His life untouched by pain
And favored to the end.
Some griefs are with us now; other again
Time and the gods will send.

He'll pay, and pay again, the swine, von Strumond thought.

9

After receiving the telegram from her father announcing Jürgen's and Gabi's deaths, Kathe thought immediately of David. Her concerns for her mother, Elisabeth, at losing her daughter and son-in-law were certainly enormous, but her primary sympathies were with the poor boy, her David. Kathe knew that her role would be great, imposed by the absence of his mother's comfort, and her grief began to weigh heavily upon her thoughts. Sadness followed her around the house and estate, and she wandered through the elaborate gardens her husband so assiduously tended with his gardener, grieving for her sister and dear Jürgen and considering the fate of the boy and her father's wishes to send him to England. She eventually found Sigi, puffing vigorously on his long pipe, and told him of the telegram. Tears welled up in her eyes and Sigi held her in his arms and told her that he would be in soon to help arrange travel plans to Lübeck.

She negotiated the huge, elaborate garden and returned to her rooms in the old *Schloss* and sat down to write to the only person outside of her family who could fully know her pain.

11 June 1899
Gräfin Claramond Kathe von Petersruhe-Matthäus
Vogelgesangstein
Baden
Isaac Becouche-Albukerk
22 Cicek Pasaji
Constantinople

My Dearest Isaac:

My love, my life, I have had little of earthly passion in this awful world, and I have relied upon recalling you, these last few years, when I must allow my mind and body to find solace. Our parting at Orta remains as a dream to me, and I find in my reveries of that time, your presence, your touch and smell. Remember our love? I haven't returned to Italy since our last parting.

I hope that your Eligia is well and that your beautiful Olivia is growing into a fine young girl. I apologize for not thanking you for the photograph of her you so kindly sent last year, but I've tried to observe my promise to Eligia not to interfere in your lives. It seems, however, that I must now break my promise and write to you. I do not wish to intrude romantically, notwithstanding the confession above, which gave me great comfort to write and read back to myself, but my purpose is to write to you concerning another matter, also most dear to my heart.

My young nephew, David Rosenberg, has lost his father and mother, my dear sister Gabrielle, a very good and kind soul. My father has made it abundantly clear that the boy, as he phrases it, "must be protected and guided into manhood" by everyone in his family and anyone associated with his family. It has therefor, been decided by my father that David will be given over to the charge of his dear friend, Captain Hugh Twinge, Lord Boardcroft of Lincolnshire, England. Captain Twinge, as I've known him, has been a constant figure in my father's and dear old Schlarp's life since their university days together in England, and father feels it necessary that the boy experience the adventure of a new setting.

David is very sensitive and growing into a very handsome and circumspect young man. My dear husband Graf Siegfried von Petersruhe and I have no children, and I intend to discuss the adoption of David into my Sigi's noble family as we travel to Lübeck for the funeral of my dear relations. Sigi's sisters fret constantly about an heir and, in truth, worry about their own status on the estate. They should have been presented to young men more aggressively! Their spinsterhood defies understanding: handsome, energetic, independent and well educated as they are!

I ask, my dearest, that when the time arrives that my nephew, likely by that time my son, be received into your world in Turkey that you will guide and protect him and if all things align, you will introduce him to your family. He insists that his ambition is to serve in the army, a notion extremely uncomfortable for me, but I am certain that I can persuade Sigi, given his connections, to have him assigned to the Federation's mission in Constantinople. I can only guess what the future holds for David, but in time I will write again advising you of the boy's status.

I close, as I've always done, with my fondest memories of our time together.

Yours,

Kathe

As Kathe sealed the letter and took it to her maid for posting, Sigi walked into the hall and asked how she was feeling. She admitted that David seemed to be her primary concern, but she wanted desperately to go to her mother. She told him that she would be leaving for Lübeck that day. Sigi frowned, but he called for one of the servants and instructed her to assist Kathe in packing. He then told Wok, his *Kammerdiener*, that he must prepare to take Kathe to the rail station in Stuttgart within the hour. The Count walked out of his small castle and assisted Wok in hitching the carriage, and with Wok at the reins, led the horses out to the graveled circle in front of the great house. The luggage arrived and was placed on to the coach, and soon Kathe walked up and allowed him to open the door and help her into the coach. They kissed and said their goodbyes and Sigi gave Wok the signal to shake the reins and get underway.

Sigi wondered at the cruelty of it all: two vital young people dead as a result of accident. He shook his head and returned to his walled garden of black soil, manure, and flowered rose vines running along arched iron trellises around the perimeter of the moldy wall. The huge area was crisscrossed with finely manicured lawn

paths dotted with flat walking stones and divided into two sections
by a mile-long gravel path in the middle of green lawn, several
yards in width and bordered with tall willows. The garden culmi-
nated into a circle of black poplars, in the middle of which rose a
simple stone gazebo Sigi called *Wissembourg*, the name engraved
on the entrance lintel surrounding a huge cross of like stone. A
solitary bench stood in a corner.

He walked down the center path, greeting two men pushing cylinder mowers along the length of the dividing lawn and entering
the gazebo, sat down on his cool stone bench and re-lit his pipe. He
remembered the 1870 battle in which he witnessed the slaughter of
parts of his army by the new French rifles and the horror of close
fighting within the city called Wissembourg, but watching the two
fellows approaching behind their mowers, he began to feel at peace.
Both were once his soldiers like Wok, and he employed them to remind himself of the honor of leading men into war and to help him
put to rights the horror of that responsibility. After he had accompanied his Duke through the duties at Versailles, and the war with
France was settled, he even brought back a very young Lieutenant to
his home, and with the old *Graf* and *Gräfin* and their staff, nursed
the brave boy back to health. He would never forget the pleasure
of watching the recovered young soldier climb into the family carriage waiting to take him home to his own relations. Sigi had put
away in his safe a letter of gratitude left for him that day. My dear
Wittgenstein, where are you these days? Sigi thought.

As he puffed away, he thought of his wife Kathe and the joy she'd
brought into his life. After he had inherited the estate in 1880, he
spent his days bickering with his sisters, who held a solid front on
the matter of his bachelorhood. They wanted an heir before Sigi
abandoned them in death and made their remonstrations separately
and together. He couldn't imagine marrying. His life had belonged
to the army and his Duke, but a young woman came to visit his
learned younger sister, a remarkable scholar of Latin whose library
comprised the books lining the shelves in the *Schloss*, and his sister's
young friend, with her beauty and intelligence, captured his heart.

He felt younger and joyful during her stay, and he asked his sister to inquire of her situation.

His sister Bertha said, at once, "She is unattached, and like you, you selfish tyrant, will probably never marry."

Nevertheless, Sigi approached Kathe one morning, joining her, uninvited, in a stroll through the garden.

Kathe said, "General, you have a lovely garden. It is truly a work of art and dedication."

"Thank you *Fraulein*, these grounds I have dedicated to the men who followed me into battle. I have a humble memorial at the end of this walk to the men who fell under my command. I visit it every day. Would you allow me to show it to you? I must warn you: the walk is nearly a mile."

Kathe replied, "I would like to see the memorial, General; thank you for inviting me. Bertha has business in town, so I *shall* take advantage of the opportunity to enjoy the pleasure of your company."

They walked to the round, stone frame and Sigi explained the significance of the name *Wissembourg*. The town represented his first real test of arms, and many of his men fell on the day his army attacked. The Germans won, killing the French general, and Sigi carried on though the Franco-Prussian War, never suffering a scratch.

As they sat on the stone bench, Sigi asked Kathe if she would honor him by accompanying him on a visit to his friend, a retired Colonel, that afternoon. Kathe accepted, and after they had returned to the castle for an early lunch, they were met at the head of the drive by Wok, sitting atop the coach. After a drive of several miles, they turned toward a solitary farmstead resting at the head of a tall hill. The ride was bumpy, and Sigi and Kathe found themselves tossed into each other several times. At last, the coach stopped, and Wok opened the door to allow them to step out. Sigi excused himself and walked ahead to the house and rapped on the door. A tall man named Helmut Mertz, somewhat younger than Sigi, answered the door and at first saluted, then embraced him. Kathe walked up and introductions were made. Mertz invited them inside and bade them sit at his long table made of a single plank of finely finished pine. The table was set with a variety of cheeses, a large loaf of pumpernickel bread, and two unlabeled bottles of wine. The room was neat and clean, the plain white walls bare, save for a solitary photograph of Mertz's late wife, Claudine.

"Well, General, I must say, I am surprised to find you in the company of such a beautiful young woman! An old bachelor like you giving court to the most handsome woman who has visited my hill since my dear Claudine! You old rascal! I shall tell your sisters!" He laughed heartily, slapping Sigi on his shoulder.

As the conversation continued, largely dominated by Sigi telling Mertz that he should mind his own business, Wok unloaded a number of crates filled with food and wine onto Mertz's front porch.

"*Herr* Mertz, you have a wonderful home; the aspect from the road is beautiful. Are you one of the General's old comrades?" asked Kathe.

"Why, the General gave me the honor of serving on his staff for many years, *Fraulein*. He and I saw the best and the worst, hey, General?" replied Mertz.

"I don't know why I kept him, but I suppose I needed someone who could draw a straight line on a map," said Sigi.

"And the beautiful woman in the photograph? Your wife, *Herr* Mertz?" asked Kathe.

"Yes, my dear Claudine, the love of my life, now gone to God. And this old fellow was responsible for our meeting!" Mertz said, pointing to Sigi. "As we fought our way through the Rhineland, the General sent me back to a town called Wissembourg to confirm casualty numbers and to see what could be spared by the population to help feed us poor soldiers. I went into our hospital, and there she stood, wearing a bloody apron and ordering our men, our *German* soldiers and *Doktors*, about in firm command of the place. She saw me and said, 'And, now, what do you want, soldier?' After the war, I went back to find her, and I worked my charms on her!"

"Ha! Charms! You're a brute, Mertz; you probably abducted her!" said Sigi.

"Well, that depends on your *definition* of abduction, General.

Nevertheless, we had ten wonderful years together, thanks to old General Sigi."

They continued talking, with Mertz distributing cheese and bread and pouring wine for everyone, until Sigi announced that he must be getting back to those harpies, called Bertha and Emma. They rose, and Mertz came around the table and embraced Sigi with tears in his eyes, and said, "God bless and keep you, General."

Kathe came forward to say goodbye and thank you, and whispered, "Maybe I can get the old bird to marry me, eh, Colonel?"

Mertz immediately laughed and put his massive arms around Kathe and whispered back, "You could do worse, but not much!"

Lastly, Wok shook hands with Mertz and said, "May we live forever, Colonel!"

On the drive back to *Vogelgesangstein*, Kathe found Sigi's rough hand and held it for miles. She told him of her desire to be chaste, that her love of independence and freedom, now, took precedence over her desire to commit passionately to one man.

Sigi told her of his loneliness, that his desire was for companionship, and if she were so inclined, he would be honored to offer himself to her on her terms.

10

Dieter Schlarp found Elisabeth overwhelmed with grief, leaning on Kathe, her face hidden in a handkerchief. A messenger sent from Kathe had informed him of Gabi's and Jürgen's deaths. He said, "This news is so unkind; come, let us sit in the conservatory." Surrounded by Elisabeth's plants and flowers, Schlarp did not try to initiate conversation, only to hold the hands of the two grieving women, ask the servants to bring them coffee, and alert the family's physician of the news and ask him to come at once.

David sat next to Kathe, who held him firmly as he slumped into the couch and wept.

Elisabeth finally said, "My poor Bernd has taken ill! I pray that I not lose *him*, also!"

The coffee arrived, and Lotte served Schlarp and the women, and then retired to await the arrival of the *Doktor*.

Schlarp said, "I will inquire about Bernd, but you must also rely upon me for anything you might need for now. I will stay and help here, my dear girls."

Soon, *Doktor* Casper Zuber arrived, a young man who had recently inherited his father's practice. He expressed his regrets, offered his sympathies, and administered mild doses of soothing sleeping draughts, which helped David and the women calm themselves and finally, seek the comfort of their beds. He advised Schlarp and the servants to keep the house quiet and when David, Elisabeth and Kathe awakened, to offer them chicken soup. He gave Schlarp his private telephone number and told him to call if he was needed again.

Brigitte approached Schlarp and asked if there was anything *he* needed.

"Yes, please bring me the telegram from Strumond."

The maid obtained the telegram from Lotte, who had been given possession of it by Elisabeth, and handed it to Schlarp. He read the message and found it to be most tactfully composed, but further inquiries were certainly in order. He wrote out a message for Strumond asking about Bernd's condition and authorizing him to act on the family's behalf in supervising arrangements as well as provide payment for having the bodies transported to Lübeck. Next, he composed a telegram to the *Beerdigungsunternehmen,* explaining that Strumond had been asked to act on the family's behalf and to communicate to him any problems and details of the arrangements as soon as they could be disclosed. After sending Brigitte on her way, he sat back into a comfortable chair and addressed Lotte, who had just entered the room, concerning the *Doktor's* instructions. He then waited through the day, for any more news and the reappearance of the women and David.

At about 5:00 p.m., Kathe entered the conservatory, waking Schlarp who had fallen into a light sleep an hour before. "I hope you are feeling better, my dear" he said to Kathe. "I have dispatched telegrams to Strumond and the funeral home and await news from them. You and your dear mother must not worry about anything until all is settled here in Lübeck. I have the situation in hand and will inform you both of the arrangements. Now how are our David and your mother?"

"He still sleeps, *Herr* Schlarp; Mother is moving around."

"Well, my dear, I must return to the office to give the employees news and conclude any business that might need my attention. Your mother should be receiving replies from Strumond and the *Beerdigungsunternehmen* soon. If they do not arrive this evening, please do not worry; I will take care of any matters in the morning."

Kathe embraced Schlarp, and he held her as his own daughter. He looked into her eyes and said, "Be brave and do your best for Elisabeth and David. I will see you in the morning, child." He then left.

After Schlarp had addressed the firm's staff and closed Sachenzucker's business for he day, he walked up the short flight of stairs from his office to his room. Elongated barrel straps at both ends of the room bound the bare boards, and a pervasive odor of heather filled the air. He looked at the lacquered bedside table and the fading photograph of himself and his wife standing and smiling in front of a small cart and remembered her laughing insistence that he allow her to hold a small whip over him as the picture was exposed. He missed his companion and thought how like Kathe Matthäus she had been: eager for learning, adventurous, but sadly, childless. He decided to begin a letter to his friend, Hugh Twinge:

Freiherr Dietrich von Schlarpheim
Managing Director, Sachenzucker
Lübeck
10 June 1899
Sir Hugh Twinge, Lord Boardcroft
Boardcroft House
Ruskwick
Lincolnshire, England

My Dearest Brother Hugh:

Please accept my deepest sympathy for the worries that have beset your family. I am especially aggrieved by the effect that these circumstances have had on your daughter, my dear Mrs. Kitchen. I have had no further news of Captain Kitchen beyond the telegraph we have from you, but we have chartered a vessel that will depart on tomorrow's tide to return your daughter and young Tom to you. Please expect them in Boston 1 June.

I must also send tragic news of Herr Rosenberg and his dear wife. As I telegraphed some time ago, Herr Rosenberg was unfortunately incapacitated by an accident while returning from business in Hildesheim. I am sad to report that, alas, he made no improvement, and unfortunately, he and his wife have passed on under very tragic circumstances. Bernd has granted me powers to act on the company's behalf until our dear friend has completed business with Heinrich Rosenberg, Herr Jürgen Rosenberg's elder brother and erstwhile business partner.

Bernd, our dear friend and brother, has suffered much with the loss of his daughter. Indeed, he himself had what his Doktor has deemed, "a mild heart condition." Bernd has asked me to become de facto guardian to young David, a privilege, and as my first act, I must ask you to entertain the notion of accepting our young friend as your guest and, perhaps, a useful companion to your own Tom. I propose that he sail back with you after our annual meeting, assuming circumstances allow you to honor the date set. I believe that David would benefit in absenting himself from the stress surrounding his family and bring solace to your grandson should the worst regarding Captain Kitchen be confirmed. He is obviously too young to attend university there—I often recall our own happy days together at Cambridge—but your society would certainly help improve his English and broaden his understanding. He needn't be feted by the Bishop of Lincoln like our "brother" Comenius, but our old tradition of honoring Comenius's peaceful and fruitful world would certainly be nurtured in the boy there. As I recall our studies of that horrific period that followed in the German lands, I can only be comforted that the Hapsburgs are contained, at least for the present, but with the old Junker gone, a German Catholic marriage could upset life again! How long has this fear plagued Europe? I know this must seem naïve, but together, perhaps, we can offer dear David a worthy portion of civilized life before something upsets the continent again.

Please let me know if you are agreeable, and if so, be kind as to propose a date for young Rosenberg's arrival there.

Your Brother in Remembrance of Our Cherished World,

Dieter

Our Cherished World, thought Schlarp—a world when men's minds were again curious and expanding beyond the medieval traditions into which they had become locked. Nothing, however, could restrain his grief. The presence of Jürgen and Gabi were most cherished, and he pondered their premature deaths. How very cruel. He began to force himself to consider other things, something useful he'd learned on the battlefield in the face of unspeakable horrors. Recalling his letter to Twinge, his mind wandered to what he had learned of those distant few years of peace in his land, when his ancestors, quiet *Junkers* tending their domains south of the Baltic Sea, heard nothing from their Dukes and never wondered that they had descended from so-called pious men, the Teutonic Knights who had appeared in these lands and slaughtered every native they could find. The thought of this "religious order," depressed Schlarp. These violent ancestors, after helping defend the last vestiges of German presence in the Holy Land, were hired to clear northern European lands of its native inhabitants. He disavowed his heritage and chose to honor those few years of peace that he, Bernd, and Hugh spoke of incessantly at Cambridge and had bonded them to a pledge to assist others and to read regularly the sacred books presented during that brief era before Germany was torn apart by religious factions and the ambitions of the rulers who wrought the horrors of the Thirty-Years War. Schlarp had always questioned what the moment was like after whole states had crumbled, when the warring nobles were overcome with exhaustion, when they could not believe that fighting any longer would bring about their desires.

The apparent irony, Schlarp thought, that he became a soldier and served a foreign ruler, would never be understood by most who knew him. Would the army capture David's ambitions, or would he be able to hold himself apart, just enough to retain his identity as a Lübecker, a descendant of a great house, and continue in the tradition of the Matthäus and Kahn families? He considered the opportunities available to him as a young man and vowed to do what he could for the boy. Schlarp had reclined against the cushions in his chair and considered what was to happen to David now that life had struck a blow. He knew the boy was restless, and now grief, a great inhibitor, was enshrouding his heart. Bernd's decision to send him to England would probably benefit not only David but also Tom and certainly Hugh, who craved attention and good company. But beyond the prospect of David's life in England, Schlarp could not imagine how the boy would make his way in the world.

The next morning, after reviewing the day's upcoming business and offering his best regards to the departing Kitchens, he drove to the Matthäus house to confirm that his telegrams of yesterday had been answered and to help Elisabeth and Kathe with any other trials that might surface during those terrible days. When the door was opened to him, he found Bernd standing before him, somewhat haggard but bright-eyed and most happy to greet him.

"Why Bernd, I thought you were ill. When did you arrive, home?" asked Schlarp.

"I arrived earlier this morning. My dear friend, the lawyer Strumond, drove me the entire distance. He didn't trust me to find my own way. I had been given a very potent injection of morphine."

"I've come to confirm that the telegrams I sent yesterday had received proper responses, and planning was going as expected," said Schlarp.

"Yes, yes, everyone has played their roles well, and we expect our dear children to arrive tomorrow. The funerals are planned four days hence. Do let us sit down; I am a little tired," said Bernd.

Kathe entered the parlor where Bernd and Schlarp sat and announced that she would be returning to her home that day. She had telegraphed Sigi and asked him to prepare for a journey to Lübeck the day after tomorrow. She was composed and seemed well rested to Schlarp, and he marveled at her energy.

"Why don't you just stay, my dear, and allow Sigi to travel up alone?" asked Bernd.

"I want to see my husband, father. I have my coach and driver and feel most anxious to get back to the estate, if only for a day, to help Sigi before he has to make the journey."

Elisabeth walked into the room with Lotte who carried a tray with coffee service and pastries. "My dear Dieter, what would we have done without your help yesterday. Bernd, Dieter was indispensable." She embraced the tall, thin man. "I am, however, most disappointed that my Kathe wishes to leave today, but one accepts and tries to move along with life, doesn't one?" she said, lifting her chin.

"Mother, you have Father and dear *Herr* Schlarp. Everything is settled, and I shall return in two day's time. Surely you can spare me that?" said Kathe. With those words and departing embraces, she went around to the rear of the house and joined Wok to begin their journey to *Vogelgesangstein*.

Schlarp said, "I wanted you both to know that I have written to Hugh concerning David. I will inform you of his reply as soon as it comes. I am certain that Hugh will be most pleased to accept a visit from the boy, and his Tom will appreciate his company. Both families are in pain, and perhaps a dramatic change is in order for everyone's benefit."

11

Kathe and Wok had arrived in the early morning hours the day before, exhausted and relieved to be home. Poor Wok had to endure driving rain and muddy roadways and a broken coach wheel after retrieving her from the Stuttgart rail station. Hours were lost, and the journey back had been most trying. Kathe made certain that Sigi rewarded Wok for his indefatigable service to her. She had gotten adequate rest, though the prospect of returning to the city for the funerals was deeply depressing. But she had Sigi now, her rock and the hero of her practical existence.

The early morning of the journey began in a burst of activity. Sigi's sisters Bertha and Emma were up and about helping with breakfast and indulging themselves by instructing Maria, much to her immemorial annoyance, on her duties. Sigi, like an ant crawling on a lump of bread, inspected the luggage carriage, spoke to the driver, Weiss, and then walked to the lead carriage. He stood on the recessed step and reported to his wife, who had just entered with Maria, that the journey to Lübeck could begin.

The weather was somewhat dominated by low clouds hanging over the Count's estates east of Egerten, close by a thick forest. After taking his seat in the carriage he swore, in French of course, at Wok the driver, manservant, and house manager, and impatiently flapped his hat out of the window and banged it against the carriage's sloping frame as the horses began to step forward. Wok knew his employer and former commander well and accepted that life was always a half step behind the Count and Sigi's rage against the usual *natura naturans* of most, even industrious, humans.

Kathe looked at the old Count, and with a cock of her head, asked him not to light his pipe.

He held up the sleek block of wood, and watching the attached tassel swing to and fro, calculated the time and distance before he could light the old instrument. *Graf* Siegfried von Petersruhe, or "Peter's Rest" in some more Eastern tongue, a joke old Peter Wok liked to tell at every opportunity, had held that his pipe would always be a mark of his survival since he started smoking after becoming an officer in his Grand Duke's army. He recalled smoking with his cavalry contingent the night before entering Versailles behind Grand Duke Frederick, and with every puff since, he had felt that, like Wagner's *Siegfried's* magic cloak, he has been protected from the world. If the world would *just keep up*. He looked at his lovely young wife and rejoiced in her beauty. The north German blond, the large blue eyes, and her rarified poise bound him to accede to her every demand, which in reality, were very few and modest. Sigi held his pipe out of the carriage door window and knocked all of the fresh tobacco onto the cobbles leading away from his home.

Today was different. Kathe's sorrow at the deaths of her sister and brother-in-law knew no bounds. Though she had always deeply admired her husband, and after their few years together, had come to love him for his absolute defiance of life's cruel possibilities, his vigor and strength on this day, a day of impossible, unfathomable bereavement, would see her through the long journey to Lübeck. The miserable and the happy were bound up in each other and for Sigi could never be separated. He took the loss in his wife's family as he had taken the horrors of the battlefield, as part of a narrative thrown upon humankind by some disinterested, unknowable force. He hadn't substituted some self-apparition of what he realized or imagined in his character, nor had he surrendered to the grasp of religion. He simply lived in courage and ignored what many of Kathe's friends found as frenetic, unending, false comfort: convention or the social or intellectual masks. He had aged gracefully, and his sixty-seven years were unaccounted in his appearance. His slightly ruddy, scarcely lined face, strong and vigorous movements, and when covered by a hat, his thinning gray hair would not suggest his age. Though she had made a sacrifice in leaving Isaac, a man in whom she dwelt, she knew that

Sigi had fulfilled all she'd asked for, except as a lover.

Kathe put down her book, *Memoirs of an Idealist,* and said, "Mother has told me that even before Jürgen's death, Gabi had been overtaken by melancholy. My poor sister had apparently lost all control, asking before she and Jürgen died that the boy not be brought to Hildesheim, that Papa act as his guardian. Father intends to send David to England, I hear."

"Why England, my dear? I would enjoy having the boy with us, if, of course, your family believes we could help," said Sigi.

"I really don't know, Sigi. Father was educated in England, and Jürgen had strong business ties there. You've heard us discuss Hugh Twinge, Lord Boardcroft, I'm sure, and of course you've met Dieter Schlarp. Those men are my father's oldest friends and all spent their Cambridge years together. Papa means to send David back with Captain Twinge after Twinge visits Lübeck in late July. Apparently Father hasn't revealed how long the boy's visit should be, but I trust that it will depend upon many conditions."

With Wok turning around to indicate a coming turn to Weiss and offer an obscene gesture to the baggage coach driver, the two carriages rumbled on, the coaches passing through Bietigheim and Rheinstten as they made their way to the Rhein's Karlsruhe ferry terminal, where they planned to move up the great river toward Mainz. As the carriages were carefully loaded onto the ferry's barges, Sigi had their servants join the couple in a large inn for a late luncheon before leaving the river town. The river had played such a huge part in his formative life. How many times had he crossed it as a young soldier, and how much danger had it represented to him? He suddenly wanted to make this journey more significant than the reason it occasioned. He knew that he needed to pay his respects to a man and woman he little knew but liked immensely, but a nagging thought to consider his own legacy worked at him as well. He looked across the table spread at Kathe and remembered her father, whom he regarded as a circumspect and prudent man, and decided on the spot what his heart had really desired and planned to stay a few days longer in Lübeck and, if appropriate, ask for a private evening with Bernd.

The carriages left the great river at Mainz and began the most challenging part of the journey. After a night's lodging near Frankfurt, and Kathe's occasional weeping, the two carriages began rumbling northeast to their destination again. The route bypassed Hildesheim and continued to the east, turning north at Brunswick onto numerous country roads until finally crossing the Elbe and finding suitable barges at the Am *Kanal*. The waterway made its first long eastern turn to finally become the Elbe-Lübeck *Kanal*, and Kathe smiled at the familiar countryside. She wondered if all had gone well with the transfer of Jürgen's and Gabi's bodies and if her mother Elisabeth had been able to manage. The young wife's thoughts were interrupted as Sigi returned from the water closet in the second carriage, swinging the door wide and bounding into the coach like a man thirty-years his junior.

"Kathe, I wish to stay in Lübeck a few extra days. Perhaps your presence would be especially beneficial to your father and nephew. It would also give me an opportunity to speak with your father about some family matters if he is up to it."

"I would be grateful if we could find the time to stay, Sigi. May I ask, what is the nature of your family business with Papa? Is there anything *we* need to discuss?"

"I have flown through most of this life alone, to the anxiety of my parents and sisters. Finally, there came you, my dearest, and this recent tragedy has brought to light certain factors I've never cared to consider. Frankly, I do not have an heir, and when I leave this life, I would wish to leave knowing that I have not burdened you with the greed of squabbling cousins and the machinations of intriguing sisters. I, therefore, wish to discuss a legal adoption with your father."

"And whom do you wish to adopt, Sigi?"

"We are ages away from concluding if what I have in mind would be possible, Kathe, but my thoughts concern young David. Time will tell. I wish to consider discussing adopting the boy as my heir with your father. And, of course, discussing the matter further with you."

The carriage went quiet as the barges continued their journey, occasionally laying-by to allow other traffic through and at times bumping the shallows, eschewing the two barges and their pulling boat at angles, somewhat out of order. The banks of the *Kanal* were at times lined with livestock chewing hay or at play and a great many children sliding through gaps in the rusting fencing strung along the banks.

Kathe began to consider Sigi's words and wondered how far such a path would lead.

"You know, my dear," said Sigi, "a man's life is the sum of what he brings to it. It is like a vessel that needs filling. The emptiest of us just disappear, and though I am not a philosopher, I believe that life is the reward of one's investment in living."

Kathe recognized these sentiments, glanced at the book resting in her lap, and remembered the others she had read and admired. She could have told Sigi that he thinks beyond philosophy and that he kicks away the guises that define, or hide, most lives. "And you believe an adoption will 'fill the vessel,' Sigi, or will it just satisfy some legal questions?"

"I hadn't a care in the world about my legacy before our marriage. Now, happiness demands! David is a fine boy, and I would be proud to give him my name. That, of course, would probably, *finally*, silence those harpies Bertha and Emma and settle the dreams of other family members."

"I have deep fondness for that boy. What he has lost will not be ameliorated by his father's family, certainly, nor would I acquiesce to his being raised by those people. It is not their religion, Sigi, but their lack of *humanity*," said Kathe.

Sigi responded, "I have no dislike of Jews, my dear, but there is widespread prejudice against them. The name Rosenberg does not necessarily identify a Jewish family, but it is a popular Jewish name. The boy is nothing but a delight to me, and his mixed heritage is of no consideration. Frankly, I know almost nothing of Jürgen's business affairs or his family, so to my advantage, I have no burdens to consider in that respect. I would assume that your father and *Herr* Schlarp will resolve whatever matters surface regarding those considerations, and David will receive a fair inheritance."

The Elbe-Lübeck *Kanal* provided another buffer of sleep against the tediousness of travel, and the couple stretched comfortably in their coach as the smooth, green ribbon of water flowed under them. At a lay-by, a huge contingent of naked children ran along the high bank above, shouting and twirling and moving quickly past the barges. Young women were in quick pursuit, holding their dirty skirts above their knees and laughing at the pack of young energy before them. One of the women stopped and peered down into the couple's carriage. Sigi, awake, stole around the opposite side of the carriage and mounted the driver's seat, where he extracted his little pistol and shot into the air, frightening the curious woman, whose yelping followed her until she caught up with the other women. Sigi and the driver nearly lost their balance and fell into the water, screaming with laughter. Kathe, awakened, was less amused, as was Weiss, who walking around his horses, was nearly trampled by the frightened steeds.

Finally, as night approached, the barges neared the crossing at Lübeck's outskirts. The carriages were pulled carefully up the diagonal ramps and the horses were again fitted to their carriages. They drove through the *Holstentor* and onto the *Altstadt*, amongst the old-style buildings, reaching the Matthäus house at 11:30.

They found Bernd and Elisabeth waiting, comforting each other and dreading the coming memorial. They embraced Kathe and Sigi and spoke for a short time before all sought the comfort of a soft bed.

The next morning, golden sunlight streamed through the town, and the smell of the Baltic was in the air. Sigi was up by 5:00 a.m. as usual and waited for the rest of the family to join him. Lotte and Brigitte were busy with their morning preparations and had made certain the old general was plied with coffee as he sat in the conservatory looking out of the unadorned windows. He was unused to city life, and the confined scene of the Matthäus back garden was of little interest to him but offered, at least, an organized and manicured microcosm of a walled country garden, complete with fountain.

He knew that the day would be consumed with preparations for tomorrow's funerals and pondered how he may be of use. He had brought only a formal suit, leaving his dress uniform behind, knowing that these Lübeckers were little impressed by the military and rendered service there only as required by the Federation. Trade and commerce were their fields. They were more open to the world and accepted foreigners without instinctive suspicion. Their world relied on trust, and their way of life had stood the test of centuries. He knew that Dieter Schlarp had military associations, but as they were rarely mentioned, did not pry. But the desire of David to pursue a military career, expressed at such a young age, intrigued the old soldier, and he wondered: where did that originate?

The other members of the family eventually joined him at breakfast and discussed the plans for the day. Sigi was treated like the guest he was and went about the day entertaining David by talking about his old campaigns and the army life. He explained the order of battle of his last command and the tactics of the German army. They discussed weapons and the proper use and deployment of them and how David would, eventually, should he still desire it, begin his career. Finally, he warned David that, in the hard army life, above all, one must learn to live with one's decisions and their consequences for the lives of comrades and innocents alike. His heart reached out to the beautiful boy, and he pledged himself to safeguarding David's chosen *métier*, whatever it proved to become in the years before them.

12

Marienkirche was filled by most of Lübeck's merchant families and the many relatives, employees, and socially obliged of the Matthäus and Kahns. The day was mild, and summer crept through the great church in the subtle drafts allowed through the massive west door that swept into the nave, flowed indifferently around the altars and memorials, brushed the innumerable epitaphs, and found some moment's rest in the highest places, and then swirled back down and out through the open door of Epistle Chapel. The bodies of Jürgen and Gabrielle Rosenberg were brought through, and as the bearers made the turn toward the old purple and granite altar, the choir began to sing to the accompaniment of the massive organ, ever improved to perfect the strokes of the church's newest heirs to Dietrich Buxtehude's middle fingers. The warm breeze met them as they entered the side of the sacred edifice, cooling the tears of some and helping others forget the stiff collars wrapping their necks.

David stood by his grandparents, Dieter Schlarp, and his aunt and uncle, *Graf* and *Gräfin* von Petersruhe. All were raising and lowering handkerchiefs to their faces, unordered and undirected like the notes of saddened bell ringers, but if sound could have been applied, their shared sorrow would perhaps have reflected a cacophony useful to the new tide of serious European music. Their heads lowered. The coffins were placed side by side and covered with plain white cloths. The assistant pastor began the service and to the relief of all, the *Lutheran Book of Worship* and the *Lutheran Hymnal of Lutheran Worship* required repeating and kneeling was kept minimal, especially to the relief of old Schlarp, Bernd and Sigi.

David watched in silence, and in a disconnected sense, could not believe that he was bidding his parents goodbye forever. He thought of the joy of Lübeck festivals, and the arid, impartial ledgers filed along his father's and grandfather's offices, and he could not fully concentrate on the pitiable scene before him and the people gathered to comfort his family and pay their respects. Wails echoed through the church as Gabi's, Kathe's, and Elisabeth's old friends, many who had been Gabi's youthful playmates, could not and would not be consoled at the sight of her coffin and that of her husband's. They remembered Gabi's rebelliousness and longed to relive the days of their own youth, when romance was possible, but through the veils of convention, unmanageable for most of them.

Against usual Lutheran tradition, but on request by the family, the pastor, his hat tilted forward as he looked at his notes, most reluctantly solicited remembrances of the two dead from the thronged pews. Immediately, a woman clad all in white with a red ribbon swung diagonally across her breasts and hip, stood up and clambered, with the help of another woman in matching attire, to the altar to offer a few words.

"My name is Hedwig Dietelkamp, and Gabrielle Rosenberg was my friend and fellow soldier in the fight to have the Loyal Women's Leagues recognized officially by the government's Colonial Office. Three times my dear friend and fellow sister of Protestant mercy, Gabrielle, accompanied me to Berlin and Potsdam to present petitions to officials, and one time she allowed her sister, Kathe, to visit one of our stations in East Africa to formulate a report of our activities. We have made progress! But I am here to pay homage to my dear friend and to recognize that she was more than the best of Lübecker women, she was the best of Protestant German women! May our collective tears comfort her son, David, her sister, and her parents during this time of loss! May we all heed the ancient saying, 'There is no life without suffering,' but struggle against travail where we find it. This family has suffered in rude proportion to their share of living. Goodbye to Gabi and her dear Jürgen! May they rest."

The last was said as the pastor was moving toward Gabi's distraught comrade. His gown actually came to touch the extended red ribbon of the woman's dress. The two were clearly at odds. Again, the pastor asked if there were more comments to be expressed, and was answered by the rising walking cane of *Herr* Schlarp. Much to the pastor's relief, the man was sitting in the family row and had little distance to cover to gain the altar.

Eventually, old Schlarp brought himself up to his full height and walked behind the long, old altar. He looked out amongst the great crowd, and before he spoke, paused to wipe tears from his bleary eyes and find the correct pocket in which to reinsert his modest handkerchief. He tried to speak, but he could only croak a few, unintelligible sounds as his lower face worked, obscured behind his long, veiny hand. Finally, the words came.

"I am Dietrich Schlarp. I have had the privilege of being the Managing Director of Jürgen Rosenberg's company, Sachenzucker Exports, for the last several years. I owe my long life to the kindness of men like *Herr* Rosenberg and have always had the great good fortune to encounter men like this great man we honor here at times most critical to my life. I know loss, I know risk, and I know bravery. *Herr* Rosenberg was a man whose purpose called him to leave the conventions of his family, to embrace our family here at *Marienkirche*, and to fearlessly confront the risks of founding a great and prosperous company. I must speak to the great loss of my dear friends, Bernhard Matthäus and *Frau* Matthäus-Kahn, the Kahn family, and of course young David Rosenberg, son of the dear couple lying at rest before us here. May God give you strength and may the real spirit that has preserved us as people of this land endure in you, my dear David. We place in you our faith that the future will keep you and bring you joy again."

Old Schlarp found his way from the altar and carefully navigated the steps toward his seat. He stopped and bent down to whisper in David's ear, and then sat at the far end of the family pew. He nodded at Bernd, who returned his gesture knowing that their pact to protect David would never, even in death, be broken. After the deaths of David's parents, Bernd had broken the cylinder's seal and shared the contents of the brass vessel with Schlarp. The two men had worriedly discussed methods to ensure that the contents were transmitted to

David and had finally agreed that, as Bernd had hoped, the cylinder should be given to Kathe and Sigi, that they would all hold a meeting with David after his return from England to discuss its contents.

The service finally ended, and the bearers took the caskets around the north side of the great church to the family plot. The ritual was performed for both deaths, and the bodies were lowered into the graves at the same time. David alternately clung to his grandmother and grandfather and tried desperately to hold back tears.

The pastor led the multitude to the *Briefkapelle*, or Epistle Chapel, a part of the cathedral owned by the city, where an elaborate buffet had been prepared by Bernd's servants and Sachenzucker Exports employees. Tables were set nearly against every wall, allowing only room for servers to stand behind to offer the mourners the feast. In the middle of the room, a place of honor in the form of a round oak table had been prepared for the pastor and the grieving family, but most everyone wandered through the crowd greeting and thanking the attendees for the honor and comfort of their company. The distinct smell of the meeting room pervaded the reception, and for those unfamiliar with the room, the aging wood's odor and the oil preserving it became almost too intrusive to allow them to enjoy their food. David took in the aroma mixed with the copious food and fixed in his mind an image of this day, one he would recall again.

The affair had been conducted with as much dignity as Lübeck could muster, and at length, the hall began to empty, allowing the mourning family to return to the comfort of their home and privacy. The entire family had lined the creaking wooden floor as the mourners began to stream out into the late afternoon sun. There was no urgency, as the light would persist until after 10:00 p.m.

At one point, Schlarp came to David, and looking his most serious, said, "Who is to know, my dear godson, if life has chosen a special path for you with this loss. Grieve properly, but rise in your heart to know that all of your mother's and father's past have made you who you are."

Later in the comfort of his home, old Bernd sat with Elisabeth, Kathe, and Sigi and asked, "Do you think Dieter got home, safely?"

David had been long consigned to Brigitte's care.

Elisabeth replied, "I saw him driving off in the Benz. Lotte had fetched him."

Bernd said, "David is traveling to England with Captain Twinge in late July. You all know this. We have to determine how long to allow him to stay away. Dieter believes that the documents that had been moving between Jürgen and Heinrich will ultimately result in a proposal by Heinrich to take over Sachenzucker. As Jürgen's executor, I am reluctant to allow this, even if it means the end of the company. There is no debt, and all of the facilities are in excellent condition. A lease to a suitable competitor would seem to appeal, but Dieter knows of no suitable company. But mind you, he has not undertaken to find one. My concern is that at terms put forth on other matters by Heinrich, the company will certainly be undervalued. All indications from Dieter and Strumond are that if this path is chosen, Heinrich's changes will fail, all will be lost to the Rosenberg heirs, and if we sell Jürgen's company, we will see the facilities crumble and our Jürgen's life's work come to nothing. Strumond has grave reservations about Heinrich and warns me not to engage him directly. He'll need to be lured out, and Strumond has agreed to review all communication with the man, instructing him to correspond with both of us. As far as the daily operations of the company, Dieter will continue to act in his present capacity, consulting me weekly. As for any minor changes already in effect, we will operate according to Jürgen's wishes."

"Is Dieter fully aware of all this?" asked Kathe.

"He is. And more. Dieter, Hugh Twinge, and I have agreed to look after the welfare of David. We claim no more love for the boy than any of you, but practically, and in a very strict sense, spiritually, we are in a position to add to his welfare. "

Sigi said, "Father, Kathe and I have thought for some time about my own legacy. I know that this is somewhat distracting, but we would like for you and dear *Frau* Elisabeth to consider allowing us to adopt David. I would approach the Archduke about transferring some of my titles to him now and all that remains after my death.

The *Kaiser* would have to approve but given our family's service, it should not be unexpected."

"Sigi, there are things you must know before you pursue an adoption. Please be patient. After David returns from England, we will be able to reveal everything. We must wait for the boy to get a little older, and he must be first to learn of these facts."

"As you wish, Father, we will wait."

Heinrich Rosenberg had spent the day in Hildesheim composing a letter to Strumond.

13

Lord Boardcroft, having recently arrived at his estates from his offices in London, surveyed the grounds within the boundaries of its faraway walls until he caught sight of the very tip of the gate tower marking the western extent of his parkland holdings. He knew that much of what he saw was derived from the wealth generated from his much larger holdings—the unobservable surrounding lands under cultivation lying outside the estate's bright limestone-topped walls. He noticed his grandfather's old folly, the *Temple of Poseidon*, with its three tall pillars of mottled and swirling patterns of Lincolnshire limestone supporting a greened copper dome all gleaming in the sun. The structure was open to the winds but for the huge, bronzed anchor resting in the middle of the roundel floor, salvaged from his first ship.

Boardcroft announced to his barefooted man servant, Ibn Rasheed, a middle-aged Indian of deep complexion which contrasted starkly with the white linen kaftan and ocher whirling skirt that concealed his body, that all seemed satisfactory. He could detect here and there the tops of the various fruit trees planted far and near the perimeter of the sunlit brick walls, beyond and atop the park's undulating terrain and discern new leaves, a green, somewhat darker than Rasheed's gleaming lime-colored turban. The trees' promise of abundant yield was at last beginning to inspire hope in his cossetted, at least in his Lordship's mind, household, whose membership yearned for juicy, fresh produce of the *Rosaceae* variety: pears, apricots, peaches and cherries. He thought of them as a *The Cult*, so bent to ritual and habit to serve his needs and pleasure; Rasheed, of course, was the exception. Behind him, the great southern aspect of the house spread out in various shades of Lincolnshire limestone, and unlike those of most of his wealthy neighbors, was clean of the ever-pervasive soot and grim borne of England's burgeoning industries and filthy heating coal that swirled throughout his beloved *Albion*. This cleanliness was helped by the estate's location—well isolated from cities and towns—but mostly by Lord Boardcroft's employment of a small army of cleaning men, all of whom dreaded his visits home.

"Tell me, Rasheed, has Hughie behaved in my absence? And have you seen his grandmother?"

"No, to both questions, my Lord."

"Hughie's not dabbing it up with the sheep again, I hope."

"I'm afraid so, my Lord."

"Damn and blast! Who caught the little nickey this time?"

"The gamekeeper and Mrs. Marston, my Lord."

"To think that gentle woman, probably out just to enjoy the rounds with her husband, witnessed the boy having it up with an animal. What would you Sufis do with him? Speak plainly, Rasheed."

"We would probably ask him to leave the order, sir."

"Well, I can't very well ask him to leave the family! I'll have him arrested, by God. Where is Tom and Mrs. Twinge-Kitchen, Rasheed?"

"Probably in the library, my Lord, mourning Captain Kitchen."

Lord Boardcroft strode rapidly from the hideous *Phönix* automobile given to him a few years ago by Jürgen Rosenberg, who had still preferred horse-drawn coaches. He stomped through the opened door, ignoring his numerous servants all bowing and curtseying, and swept into his library, where he found his daughter and grandson both sitting in a window seat, weeping.

Boardcroft went to them straightaway and enfolded them in a heavy embrace, whispering, "My dears, my dears." He looked at his daughter and grandson and said, "Margaret, Tom, we have quite possibly suffered a grievous loss, but we must bear up. I won't ask where Hughie is, but you both know that my love for you knows no bounds, and I suffer along with you. We must not give up hope, but we must face the fact that the news from Portugal is not promising." Captain Kitchen, Lord Boardcroft's son-in-law, had been reported lost with his ship in the Atlantic after debris washed up along the Portuguese coast.

"In a few weeks, I will have to return to Lübeck to settle rates with my partners, and I have decided to bring young David Rosenberg back with me. You both know of his own and his family's travails, and I have been asked to bring him here to be a proper companion to you, Tom. We will teach him what we can of our own, beloved country. Perhaps the dear boy will provide some solace for us, should the worst be confirmed." Boardcroft kissed his grandson and daughter and drew them even closer to his dun-colored, sea-scented veneer of long coat and loose, dingy, turtle-necked sweater.

"I am so glad to know that David, poor lamb, will be coming to us, father" said Margaret Twinge-Kitchen.

"I just hope Hughie will leave him alone!" said Tom in mournful tones.

"I will have to keep Hughie in check; I'll give him a swat with a holy water sprinkler, if necessary! Leave him to me, my son. Margaret, you must allow me to deal with Hughie, without protest; I must preserve our good name and try to teach that boy how to *behave!*"

Boardcroft left the grieving mother and son, and encountering his housekeeper Mrs. Ward, instructed her to attend his mourning relations, which to Boardcroft meant make certain they eat. He then walked into his study and sat down to make his reply to his friend Schlarp:

22 June 1899
Hugh Twinge, Earl Boardcroft
Boardcroft House
Ruskwick
Lincolnshire, England
Freiherr Dietrich von Schlarpheim
Managing Director, Sachenzucker
Lübeck

My Dear Dieter:

I received yours of 11 June and thank you for your kind words. No news of Captain Kitchen, except the possible recovery of a body resembling my son-in-law off the rocks of Beira.

Please extend my most sincere sympathies to our Bernd and family, and know that young David is welcome to return with me after our meeting in August. I look forward to seeing you,soon.

Yours,
Hugh

Lord Boardcroft looked about his study and allowed his thoughts to wander. He remembered the days after the death of his own father and the black mourning his mother, no doubt in imitation of her queen, affected for the days until she announced her departure with a young sea captain to Australia. He had adored his mother, but when she left just after his eighteenth birthday, he was determined to forget the vulgar woman and threw himself into the family business, which he ran from his Cambridge rooms. He told his appointed guardian that if he enjoyed life, he would be advised to stay out of his affairs. The guardian, an uncle, made no contest and only asked for a steady supply of a certain exotic brandy regularly imported by Boardcroft's company.

Lord Boardcroft left Cambridge with a somewhat less than stellar degree in engineering and continued building the family business. His friends Bernd Matthäus and Dieter Schlarp had introduced him to the entanglements and mysteries of sixteenth- and seventeenth-century German history. He never became as interested in the small interval of hope and enlightenment before the Thirty Years War as his friends, but he never failed to call James I "a right bastard" when punting amongst buildings associated with him on the Cam to visit a raven-haired farm girl he had seduced amongst the willows that topped the river's banks. Through the years, the friends' conventional bonds were based upon commerce, but the less-known emphasis of their investigations were sometimes remembered amongst them privately and in their correspondence.

"Hughie!" yelled Boardcroft as the young man strode past the study.
"Grandfather?"
"Hughie, young David Rosenberg is due to visit for an indefinite period later this summer. You will behave as a gentleman in his

presence. I trust that you understand."

"Grandfather, I always behave."

"God Almighty. The memorial service for your father will be held at St. Botolph's next week, barring more promising news. You should be comforting your mother and brother. By-the-by, I intend to speak to you about your future soon, young man."

"Yes, Grandfather; I look forward to hearing your views on my future."

"Don't get your hopes up. Now, get out."

With that, young Viscount Hugh Twinge-Kitchen continued on his way, no doubt into more mischief or only God knew what. The old Lord tried not to think about it.

Lord Boardcroft shook his head and decided to relieve the depressing thoughts that had started racing through his consciousness by taking a long walk to visit his estate manager, Roger Tinker. He hadn't seen Tinker for some time and decided his frequent absences of late might have loosened the yoke on the man he depended upon to coax the most from those working the Earl's soil. He rose from his desk and walked from the rear of the house and past the enormous fountain with a detailed and doomed Phaethon elevated with water running through him like Zeus's thunderbolt. The fountain was dedicated to King Charles II with the caption, *In Primis*. Priorities, thought Boardcroft, keep the business out of danger of young fools. From atop the statue, a peacock craned his neck to look down upon the Earl, then snapped it back when Boardcroft said, "Ahoy, Hermione."

Roger Tinker saw his master marching down the narrow cobbled lane with his arms swinging and his boots beating a steady, incessant gait upon the stones. Tinker told his wife, Imelda, to prepare tea and then disappear *quickly*. Tinker was a man of medium height, and like his father from whom he had inherited his present job, had very black hair, a fierce beard adorned with two tangles of gray below his chin, and suspiciously, at least for the tenants, if not Boardcroft himself, Welsh heritage. Universally known on the estate as "Black Rog," he had a reputation for fiercely, usually, drunkenly, *protecting* his young, beautiful Spanish wife from imaginary suitors by occasionally borrowing a shotgun from the gamekeeper. The gamekeeper invariably anticipated this and unloaded real shells, hid *all* of the ammunition, and substituted blank shot for Tinker to punish his suspected "Paris Bastards," as he liked calling the men he perceived as formulating designs upon his wife's virtue. Tinker's right shoulder endured a perpetual soreness, not wholly ascribable to age and labor.

"Good afternoon, Tinker, keeping busy with that Iberian beauty, what? Well, how're my beloved tenants?"

"They're just a lot of silly bastards, my Lord."

"What seems to be the matter, Tinker?"

"To tell the truth, my Lord, they're lazy as God's own sloths and now, they runs off every time that Thugger of yours rolls by in his wagon."

"Well, let's be clear, that's *my* wagon, Tinker; Rasheed just drives it for me. He's not a Thug; how many times do I have to remind you, Tinker?"

"Right you are, sir, right you are. But, the tenants get the running shites when that Thugger rolls up. If he steps out and starts one of them dances of his, and now he's waving that great knife you gave him for some reason, God only knows why, you can't find a fucking crofter until you're the other side of Somersby, my Lord. Why, I found one, sat drunk as a lord, begging your pardon, my Lord, in Cleethorpes last week. I says to him, 'Dickie, old cock, drowning your sorrows, again?' Old Dick says, 'I'm sat here, by God, until that brown devil stays out of me fields, by God.' So I says, 'Dick, the Thugger just finds himself a small hill and does a little jig and then moves along; don't be such a cunt, for God's sake.'

"Then Dick says, 'Me own son, I'm telling you, *me own son*, nearly twenty years of age, has started going about in a skirt like that Thugger. Damned embarrassing, Tinker, to hear one's friends describing the boy twirling around the fields in his mother's clothes, I'll tell you. That's why I'm sat up here in Cleethorpes just trying to avoid folk, for Christ sakes,' he says."

"Ibn Rasheed is a particular kind of Indian man, Tinker. He is a Dervish whose religious practices harm no one. I brought him back with me five years ago. Can't the bastards get used to the man? And he is a man, not a genie, goddamnit!" said Lord Boardcroft. "You tell the tenants that I'm off to India to gather up a load of *Indian* tenant farmers who have never heard of Cleethorpes, and I'll set them up on my fields if they don't like seeing Rasheed. Who, *again*, is not a Thug!"

"Aw, me Lord, they're just a bunch of twats who needs a good shaking! You'd think they were, every one of them, from Grimsby, for Christ's sake. I'll deliver the message, count on it, I will me Lord. It wouldn't hurt if old Rasheed would leave that great knife of his in the wagon, though."

"That's very good tea, Tinker. By-the-by, half of the young men on the estate are showing signs of powder flash. Know anything about that?" Lord Boardcroft looked at Tinker with one eyebrow slightly raised and asked, "Where's that wife of yours?"

"Well, me Lord, she had work in the henhouse; you knows how them Spaniards loves them chickens."

"Well, Tinker, the next time I see powder flash on my workers, we'll have to investigate. You couldn't spare me a drop of something stronger in the tea, could you, Tinker?"

"Course, me Lord, let's have a little dribble." Tinker poured brandy into each cup.

Boardcroft asked, "Strange how gunpowder will stay on a man's face, what Tinker?"

"Aye, my Lord. You just hate to see a young man with the whole of his life ahead with all them little dots ruining the side of his face. Breaks the heart, me Lord."

With that, the two men began to talk earnestly about the coming harvest, and for the ninety-third time, the fact that old Cromwell's men sank a barge full of stolen cathedral bronze off Cleethorpes while Boardcroft's fourth grandfather watched.

Mrs. Tinker walked quietly behind her husband as he and Boardcroft sat in the modest kitchen. Lord Boardcroft couldn't resist giving her a wink and watching as she turned about and ran out of the back door. "Tinker, why haven't you taught that wife of yours the English language? Should I have that strapping young groom I recently employed come over and work with her? I hear that he's literate. Why, they could do lessons together! I can just see the young man reading poetry aloud to that little spitfire of yours!"

"My Lord, you can stop having me on, now. We wouldn't want you to have to go to the trouble of that investigation, now would we?"

"Now, now, Tinker, steady yourself. Listen, old son, I have it on good authority that the Viscount has been dabbing the sheep again. Furthermore, Tom and Mrs. Marston caught him in the hideous act. Know anything about this?"

"Well, me Lord, Jelly, that's Mrs. Marston, came running into the house one evening screaming bloody hell about seeing the young lord bare-arsed behind a sheep. Said he had the poor animal's legs stuck in his wellies and was having it off most brutally. The poor woman was shaking and crying and my Imelda had to get her steady with some of that Spanish wine you brings me on occasion."

"Tinker, I want you to let the tenants and the Marstons know that I intend to put an end to these outrages. That boy, *my own flesh and blood*, God help me, has gone just too far," said Boardcroft. "Poor bloody animals."

"Well, it pains me to tell you, me Lord, but the young lord has also been known to make, shall we say *disquieting*, suggestions to some of the young farm hands also," said Tinker.

"Leave it with me, Tinker." With that pronouncement, Boardcroft took his leave and started walking back to the great house.

Tinker's company hadn't done much for his mood that day and Boardcroft shook his graying blond locks as he considered again what Tinker had to say. He had given Rasheed the run of his property, to do as he will, trusting the intrinsic goodness in the man. He was the ideal manservant—quiet, efficient, wise and without complaint. Boardcroft had taken the Dervish out of his quiet world because Rasheed had asked to know more of the world when Boardcroft and a few of his fellow merchants were in India at the invitation of the government and were being feted at a reception near the Afghan border.

Rasheed's Order had been allowed entrance to the after-dinner polo match, and Rasheed had walked up to Boardcroft and said in very good English, "Sir, may I have the honor of acting as your manservant while you are in India?" After inquiries were made, Boardcroft asked the local governor to contact Rasheed and have him brought to the company offices in Karachi, where in time, Rasheed departed India with Boardcroft.

Then Boardcroft thought about Hughie.

14

David looked up at the new *Levensau* High Bridge as Captain Twinge's yacht, the *Orestes*, motored west through the Nord-Ostsee-Kanal, under fair late July weather. He wished for a camera to take pictures of the great *Kanal,* which his father and grandfather had recently visited in part to witness the Kaiser's dedication of the waterway's improvements to his grandfather, Kaiser Wilhelm I, and in part to assure themselves that the work had been completed and larger merchant ships could traverse it. The water stretched for miles ahead, like a ribbon of shiny blue wound with reflected wisps of roving white clouds.

The sea journey would take only three days, and the boy almost hoped that the massive boat would slow and allow time to curb the grief and sorrow that dominated his waking moments. His grandparents had explained to him that Captain Twinge's world would offer him true solace, that the pain of the loss of his parents could only be assuaged by dramatic action, by challenging himself, as his grandfather expressed it, by seeking a new and unfamiliar life.

Captain Twinge had known him since a very young child, regarded the opportunity to comfort David as a duty to his old friends and business partners, and made every effort to keep the boy busy as a deckhand, instructing his crew to teach the young German the ways of knots and whipping lines. Twinge also thanked David for accompanying him back to England to be a companion to his Tom, who had given up hope of seeing his own father again.

As the yacht moved on, at times tying up to bollards strung alongside the canal to allow other ships to pass, David's curiosity began to grow, and he keenly observed the other watercraft: some small and battered from a challenging North Sea sojourn, some majestic, unblemished and towering over the *Orestes*. A ship called *Electra's Promise* steamed past, throwing up such a wake that old Twinge was on his feet screaming English words, unfamiliar to David, the gist of which he had no doubt. Three of the crew standing on the stern of the great passing ship offered a glimpse of their bare behinds in reply. This caused Captain Twinge to begin loading an old brass cannon used for salutes, creating a general panic amongst members of the crew. In the end, as the cannon lanyard was pulled, two of Twinges' crewmen had managed to haul it off the deck, almost out of Twinge's grasp, and point it skyward before the improvised ordnance—a couple of marlinspikes, a wooden block, and all the bullets dislodged from Twinge's ever present Webley Mark I pistol—shredded the clew of the jib and killed an unlucky passing gull.

"Holy, Jesus, Cap!" yelled the first mate.

"Thought I'd try to teach those buggers some manners," said Twinge.

David began to laugh at this scene and could not stop until several of the crew walked over and stood silently above him. He had to resist saying "buggers" several times to his shipmates as they dispersed to duties, but he eventually forgot the word and mixed it with "Meyersbug," a name he'd seen on one of his aunt's books. He "Meyersbugged" the seaman casting off from the shore as the yacht got back underway and received a look of puzzlement and a smart yell, "Piss off, Kaiser!" which, of course, caused David to begin hooting and holding his sides. Captain Twinge had achieved his purpose: he'd brought the boy out of his sorrow and reintroduced the world to him. Not that he wasn't aiming at *Electra's Promise*.

The accommodations were small, but David had enjoyed the day on the canal and felt relaxed and tired as he finally dropped into his bunk. The *Orestes* began to heave into the North Sea, sail was bent on the schooner rigging, and the ship started its reach for a compass point somewhere southwest to put her on line with Boston harbor. He was asleep within a few minutes and dreaming of the *Holstentorplatz*, with Lotte and Brigitte scrambling up each tower and singing into a dissonance of folk tunes. The dream morphed into a bird's-eye view of his parents, each with garden tools tending the plots of their neighbors, then scattering groats over a sheet of linen covering a well. He would remember nothing when he awoke.

The next morning, the yacht was still well out to sea somewhere off Scotland, Twinge reported. David rubbed his sore but roughening hands together and asked Captain Twinge how long they would be out of sight of land. The old merchant told him that they would see lights to starboard when evening approached. The boy sat on the deck watching the hands moving the sheets to and fro as the wind had them close-hauled and heading straight to their destination. He slept in a hammock Twinge had strung for him, and the sun moved on and off his face with every dip into a trough or rise away from the foaming sea. He felt well and thought fondly of his grandparents and their obvious efforts to comfort him. He did worry about Bernd, however, and hoped that his indomitable grandmother would be a challenge to any danger to the old man's health. He rose and walked the deck until he found Captain Twinge holding to a stay and "offering" instructions to one of his crew.

"*Kapitän* Twinge?" David looked up at the ruddy, blond man, "Will Tom and young Hugh be home when we arrive?"

"Both of the boys will be there, although it's hard to account for Hughie. Remember, David, you must begin to accent your pronunciation in English. Call me CAP-TAN Twinge. By the by, you will notice that most people will refer to me as "Lord Boardcroft" when we are in England. Take no notice and continue referring to me as CAP-TAN."

"I know that you are an English noble, and, as you know, my aunt's husband, *Graf* von Petersruhe, would not stand to be called anything familiar by a boy!"

"You are my friend, David, like Dieter Schlarp and your grandfather, Bernd. You will never be required to refer to me as a member of the nobility."

"Thank you, sir."

At length, the yacht became embraced in darkness, as the evening's veil fell. David continued to look for signs of the British shores and was rewarded with sighting the light, near Whitby. The night grew cooler and suddenly the small ship was encased in fog. The sails were furled, the engine engaged, and speed was adjusted to slow. The foghorn began its deep, mournful sound. The boy became somewhat agitated, bumping the aft mast, and standing near the helmsman, whose eye was usually occupied with the binnacle, and counting the seconds. David's mind began to drift, and he tried to differentiate the German and English nobility, as explained by Kathe after her marriage. There were too many ranks and qualifications, and soon he was ready for his bunk.

As he went below, Old Twinge came out of his cabin and asked David if he'd like to hear a story. He was an expert storyteller.

"Of course!" replied David, proceeding into the comfort of the *Orestes'* saloon. He sat down and, as Twinge prepared himself a tumbler of fine scotch, wondered if Twinge could weave a fantasy as well as *Herr* Schlarp.

"Well, a long, long time ago a strong, young sailor named Odysseus became shipwrecked and the captive of a very beautiful woman named Calypso. She wore nothing, had long golden curls running over her shoulders, and her skin was the color of honey. Some say she was a goddess. The sailor was grateful to be her guest, but he grew to miss his beautiful wife, Penelope, whom he hadn't seen for many years. Every time the sailor began to speak about his wife, his eyes filled with tears, and he would sneak out to a rocky headland and cry out her name, though she lived many, many miles from him. The beautiful goddess wanted him for herself.

"One day, one of the great Gods heard his pleading for his Penelope and took pity on him. The greatest of the Gods, Zeus, sent his messenger, Hermes, to command Calypso to help Odysseus return home. She cried out, 'Oh, you cruel Gods!' forgetting that she had cruelly kept Odysseus to herself for so long. And so, to the great sailor's surprise, Calypso allowed him to leave. And where did he end up? On another shore, in the arms of another woman!"

Twinge laughed and said, "Davy, sometimes only one woman will capture your heart, and you'll do anything to keep her! Now, off to bed!"

Twinge looked in on his charge several times before he sought his own bunk. The thought of the loss of the boy's dear parents filled his heart with sorrow, as did the realization of the sacrifice Bernd and Dieter were making in sending David into his care. How they must grieve! He knew that Bernd had long ago come to peace with the fact that his own name would die with him. His daughters captured his deepest love, and this boy, this golden boy, had become the blessing of his life. What strength his old friend, his brother of their youth, would have had to summon to let the child go!

The next morning as the fog began to lift, the lookout spotted a huge array of warships approaching from the south. Dreadnoughts, cruisers, and lighter ships were spread thickly and deeply before the bow of the *Orestes*, indicating no intention of parting formation to avoid the yacht. "Jesus Christ, Cap! Those bastards are not altering course!" exclaimed the First Mate.

"Well, tell the wireless to send a message out saying that we have a royal onboard, and if they ram *Orestes,* someone's career will follow her down."

"Aye, sir. That ought to wake them up, by God."

After a few minutes, a message was received saying that the home fleet also had a royal onboard, and that it is advised that the master of the little dinghy should make to his starboard smartly. The home fleet shall alter to their starboard, two degrees.

"Tell them that we have the Kaiser onboard," said Twinge.

"We have a reply, sir! "Our royal replies that if you fail to alter, he will see to it that less shy aspects of a certain German princess dallying with a certain southern German prince shall be shared with the press!"

"Bloody cheek, I daresay. All right, put the helm over, goddamnit!" said Twinge. The *Orestes* swung quickly to starboard, catching David by surprise. He had been walking along the starboard rail when the little ship swung over and had to grab a stay quickly to keep from falling overboard. After the yacht settled, David ran to the stern and watched as the mighty fleet passed them. He was amazed and began to appreciate all of the talk amongst the adults about the Kaiser's naval ambitions.

The next morning, the *Orestes* approached the Lincolnshire coast, passing fishermen and churning through what had become darkening muddy water. David could make out the small towns situated along the North Sea coast using Twinge's glass, and he noticed smaller watercraft moving in the distance, across the yacht's bow.

"Those ships are making for Boston, David," said Twinge. "In three or so hours, *Orestes* will begin her turn to starboard, and we'll follow them into port."

After the yacht altered course toward the *Wash*, the channel markers began to appear, some with ringing bells painted red, some without bells and painted green. The crew began furling the sails they'd hoisted at dawn and the engine shook the ship to new life. At length, a pilot from Boston harbor came alongside and was swiftly assisted to the wheelhouse. David watched as the river channel narrowed and Hugh Twinge become more animated with the excitement of approaching home.

The old sailor wondered after his family, his daughter, and grandsons and longed to hear their voices. He knew that Ibn Rasheed, his Indian manservant, would be waiting at the docks with his battered old wagon, and he looked forward to hearing the Sufi dispense his faith's aphorisms and stories.

David thought the coast looked like northern Germany and Denmark, perhaps not as clean, but with broader swathes of coastal grasses dotted here and there with what appeared to be fishing shacks. As the *Orestes* moved farther down the channel, a huge church tower came into view and grew larger and larger, amazing the young Lübecker with its height. The "Stump," as Captain Twinge called it, was reaching up to heaven like a sailor overboard, reaching up for a piece of flotsam to keep from drowning. Suddenly, the great bells began to announce 2:00, and the streets flooded with young children running in every direction, fleeing their school day.

Skiffs came alongside the *Orestes,* and their sailors yelled, "Can I help you onshore, my Lord?" and "Do you need my boys at the wharf, my Lord?"

Finally, the pilot moved the ship into place alongside the company warehouses, and the crew tied up to the bollards anchored well into the turf. Twinge gave orders to various members of the crew to slacken here, tighten there, and finally, to lower the gangplank. David tried to stay out of the way and stationed himself amidships near the mast, until Captain Twinge ordered him to climb down to deck and follow him off.

David's legs felt wobbly, and his body still had the sense that he was shipboard and moving through the waves. He was able to keep up with his great friend as Twinge turned off of the cobbled street and followed a gravel path to a massive brick warehouse. They entered, and Twinge peeked around a corner and said, "Good afternoon, gentlemen. Is anyone doing any work today, or will I need to dismiss two or three to get things moving, eh?"

"Good afternoon, my Lord," said four male voices in unison.

A stout woman appeared and said, "Might as well throw out the whole lot, me Lord; all they do is make bloody great messes for the likes of me to clear up, they do!"

"Well, Mrs. Hatch, I'm happy to see that you've been monitoring office productivity, as usual. Got any fresh jokes?"

"None what I can tell ye in the presence of this fine-looking young man, me Lord."

"Everyone, may I introduce my good friend David Rosenberg, late of Lübeck, son of a proud family."

All of the employees shook David's hand and nodded greetings.

"Well now, Mrs. Hatch, would you be so kind as to announce that there is still work to be done and that if activity doesn't begin rather quickly, I will entertain your suggestion concerning the future employment of your companions," said Twinge in a rather loud voice.

Mrs. Hatch said, "All right, you lot, you heard his Lordship!"

"Goodbye, everyone" said Twinge.

Captain Twinge, or now, Lord Hugh Boardcroft, led David out of the office, and together they walked down the wharf-front road, turning up a side street and finding a public house called *The Whipped Sheet*. They went inside.

"Well met, me Lord!" said the proprietor. "Who's this, then, another wash-up from Grimsby, God help us?"

"No, no, Sheet, this is the son of some of my business associates in Lübeck, David Rosenberg."

"Well, my Lord, he's about big enough to put to a mast. What are ye drinking, my Lord? The usual?"

"Give us a pint there, Sheet, and see if you can find a small one for Davy here."

Mr. Sheet pulled a pint of ale for Lord Boardcroft and poured some watered-down lager for David.

"That's majestic Sheet. Now tell me what's been occupying Boston since I left, please."

"Well, me Lord, the authorities finally caught old Slate stealing line off the wharf, but he didn't go quiet-like, no sir, he said, bugger you boys and jumped right into the Haven after he'd broken free from one of them screws. Haven't seen him since. Then, there was the matter of the new girl, me Lord. A certain official man, let's say, got himself caught bare-arsed with this new girl, down from Retford, I hears. Seems the sheriff's holding things down until he can get someone to vouch for the Right Honorable. Other than that, two knifings, a collision between a buggy and an automobile, and old Merton's eighteen-year-old wife running bollocks-out naked down Skirbeck Road, calling after Merton's brother to return her clothes. That about captures the news of late, me Lord."

"*Bollocks-out*, you say. Sounds like things are under control, Sheet, except for our Mr. Slate, of course. Let's have another, my good man. No sign of Slate, eh, Sheet? Has the magistrate or the constable mentioned how they might deal with him after he shows up?"

"Well, me Lord, they neither of them has any apparent designs on the old boy, except to bring him to trial, but he'd damn near have to walk into the court and ask to be found guilty and sentenced, I fear" said Sheet.

As Boardcroft and David were having their second glass, the tall, turbaned Rasheed entered the establishment and said, "My Lord."

"Indeed. Good evening, Rasheed. By-the-by, how would a thief be dealt with in your land?"

"A hand would be removed, my Lord."

"Just one hand, Rasheed?"

"It could be worse, my Lord."

"Sheet, please trot next door and invite the magistrate and constable in for a dash of brandy."

Sheet came from behind his counter, entered a solid door to the left of his establishment, and soon returned with Herbert Swift, the constable and Sir Herbert Sutton, the magistrate.

Lord Boardcroft greeted them. "Ah, here we are, the H and H Justice Dispensary! Welcome, gentlemen. Sheet, please pour these good fellows brandies."

"Consider it done, me Lord," said Sheet.

"Gentlemen, I have been told that our dear old Slate was recently observed, yet again, stealing line from the docks. May I presume that Mr. Slate can expect something inconvenient to greet him upon his inevitable reappearance in Boston?"

"My Lord, we shall do everything we can to bring the outlaw to trial," said Constable Swift.

"Gentlemen, once Slate has been captured, may I suggest that an encounter with my man Rasheed be arranged? You see, Mr. Rasheed is a Gurkha from the Himalayas and carries a rather menacing knife, which in his land, is used to remove the hands of thieves upon their capture."

"My Lord, I am a Sufi, not a—"

"That will do Rasheed. A declaration of modesty isn't required, here, my good man."

"But, my Lord—"

"Rasheed, please," said Boardcroft.

"My Lord, we can't just allow Slate to be mutilated without a proper trial," said Sutton the magistrate.

"Well, gentlemen, Slate has been known to *resist* arrest from time to time, as long experience amongst the most hardy of our officers of the law can attest, or am I mistaken, Constable?" said Boardcroft.

"Right you are, my Lord, the bugger is rather slippery. Gave me a black eye once, he did," said Swift.

"My Lord, Slate never commits enough of an infraction against society to warrant a severe sentence in the eyes of the law," said Sutton.

"Indeed, the 'eyes of the law.' Well gentlemen, most of the line he steals is used to secure my ships and comes from my stock. I do hope that word might be gotten to Mr. Slate that Rasheed's knife has the most convenient curvature of blade as to make a merely an accidental swing, as Rasheed might be inclined to use as he repositions his knife on his person, rather unfortunate for someone's misplaced hand," said Boardcroft. "Perhaps, old Slate could be persuaded to make another roost for himself in, say, Liverpool, if he knew that the 'eyes of the law' were apt to be momentarily blinded by the bright light of swift justice here in Boston?"

"My Lord, you are expected," said Rasheed.

"Well, aground again, Sheet, time to pull the hook out and kedge to the house," said Boardcroft. "Rasheed, I presume that you are ready to leave."

"Yes, my Lord, if that would be convenient."

"Thank you for your hospitality, Mr. Sheet, and the pleasure of your company Constable Swift and Sir Herbert," said Boardcroft. "By the way, Rasheed, this is Tom's friend from Lübeck, David Rosenberg."

"My Lord, I suspect that Slate will become aware of the speculative consequences entertained this evening, should he wish to return to our humble city," said Constable Swift.

"Well, gentlemen, we can only hope that a domestic redeployment might occur in Mr. Slate's case. Good evening, all!" exclaimed Boardcroft.

Waiting in Rasheed's wagon was Tom Kitchen, who jumped down and hugged David. "It's so good you've come, David!" said Tom. "I trust you had a comfortable journey."

"Yes, yes! And Captain Twinge bought me a glass of beer! My first!" said David.

"All right then, gentlemen, shall we ascend Rasheed's chariot, now?" Boardcroft asked. The boys leaped into the rear of the wagon, sat upon cushions. and covered themselves with a wool blanket Rasheed had provided. It was nearly dusk as the wagon pulled away from the harbor district and began the excursion toward Boardcroft House.

"Rasheed, why don't you learn to drive a motor?" asked Boardcroft.

"My Lord, the beasts are my companions. They are pure of heart and use no petrol."

"They are also slower, Rasheed."

"I do not wish to be a slave to that which I desire, my Lord. The wagon balances and distills the correct balance of utility and necessity."

"Rasheed, please pull the wagon over. Time to drain the *kraken*" said Boardcroft. He jumped down and irrigated a clump of brush just off the road. When he had returned to his seat, he turned around and asked, "Are you two gentlemen hungry?"

"Yes, sir," replied Tom.

"Any idea what cook has on for us tonight, Rasheed?" asked Boardcroft.

"No, sir. As you know, I prepare my own food and never visit the kitchen."

15

The boys crawled along the damp, slimy narthex skirting the west front of Lincoln Cathedral. They occasionally peeked over the low wall to watch the *Corpus Christi* Feast Day procession snaking through the damp Exchequer Gate. David and Hughie could follow the writhing of the devout flowing down the undulating path of Steep Hill almost to the arch of the limestone Guild Hall, with its inverse cones of mildew falling from its window ledges pointing to the pitiably covered heads of the determined throng. The boys whispered to each other of the probability that they were trapped until well into the evening. Their dread of Lord Boardcroft's fury seemed to tighten around their consciousness as each hour of their exploration of the great old church passed. David hated Hughie, but took his dare to jump from Rasheed's farm wagon behind the Chapter House and sneak into the cathedral through a small arched door in the Little Transept.

"Why didn't we just go to Stow St. Mary, Hughie, and see the Viking inscriptions? Old Ibn Rasheed is sitting out there somewhere waiting for us. He's soon to alert someone," David said with his slight German lisp. "I should have listened to Tom." Tom had stayed behind to comfort his mother, who was having a particularly acute morning of grief for her lost husband.

"Tom spent too much time in Germany with you poltroons. He's become pathetic," said Hughie. "Look at our mother now—a grieving witch! What did Lübeck do for her except lose our father?"

"Tom only got into as much mischief as I did, Hughie! And your father went missing at sea. He didn't run away from you, *Dummkopf!* He sailed out of Lübeck at your grandfather's request!"

"Anyway, Stow's too far, as far as I'm concerned. And bugger my daft old grandfather!"

David recalled his first visit to Stow Saint Mary with Lord Boardcroft—the exciting drive down the Lincoln Edge, the long ridge fringing Lindum Hill, the old town center, and the short journey through the village of Sturton-By-Stow, the flat land there reminding him of northern, pastoral Germany. He marveled at the old minster, the mother of Lincoln Cathedral and seat of the bishop. Lord Boardcroft had come to meet the Bishop and contribute money toward the building's ever-begging restoration. David was delighted when one of the priests showed him the visible phases of the church's history: the added height, the three distinct windows representing Saxon, Romanesque and Medieval periods of the church's history, and especially the Viking scrawls set into the side of a stone pew.

"Let's just sneak back into the tower and try to make our way into the nave chapel; there shouldn't be anyone there," said Hugh with false optimism. "The door will creak going back in, so we'll have to be quick and crawl like snakes to make it to the south tower door. Let's hope we don't meet someone coming up!"

The boys slid their way through and down the tower's cool, dark passage, feeling their way along, until David's foot landed on the narrow side of the winding steps. Helplessly, he found himself sliding, twisting and falling backwards down the rest of the steps to the open bell tower, rolling into the corded ropes and pulling down one side of a bell. A faint ring came forth and Hughie froze in his tracks in the dim light, but suddenly, momentarily, incontinent. He hissed a curse at his German friend, who, in spite of his excellent English, had no idea what Hughie had said.

"*Gottverdammich!*" David untangled himself and rubbed the bruising his limbs sustained in his tumble. He felt slightly disoriented and nearly fell again when Hugh grabbed his shoulder and muttered, "Bloody hell, the Chockers will be on us in no time now!"

The boys scrambled down another set of winding steps and peeped out into the nave at the crowd shuffling by the trefoil arches over the long-robbed tombs barren of bronze and jewels taken by the soldiers of Henry VIII, and later, Cromwell. The boys made their way to the dark stone font, hiding under the fearsome animals and grotesques carved into its sides and holding to two of the short columns hidden from the pilgrims as the crowd lumbered by, interminably. Slowly, David and Hugh, dressed fashionably in velvet navy outfits, tried to blend into the crowd and avoid the surveying eyes of church officials. They made their way to the shrine of "Little Saint Hugh" at the corner of the southeast transept and wiggled their way through the throng into the dim light of the Dean's Eye at the back of the Great Transept, just before the crowd turned south before the pulpitum. There they were met by the large presence of Ibn Rasheed, who even in his green turban, seemed welcomed in the cathedral by the Dean.

The Dean said, "Couldn't you two have picked a quieter day to explore God's holy building?"

Ibn Rasheed fastened his monstrous hands on Hugh's right ear and David's left and trotted them out of the north arm of the cathedral's cross, up along the ornamented wall external to the first choir, and out through the Little Transept, to the farm wagon he had parked near the church's Chapter House. They had been spotted by denizens of the cloister, daring vagrants, churchmen, and visitors to stare at the green-turbaned "heathen" push along the two scowling friends making noises of suppressed pain. The three reached the wagon, and the huge Indian grabbed the boys' lapels and threw them onto the weathered wagon boards that a day before had carried hay from the estate fields to lofts. Ibn Rasheed shook the reins and backed the horses out and down to the road below and began their long journey back over the Wolds to Boardcroft House.

The boys tried to find some ease in the corners of the wagon bed as they bumped along the ancient Roman road toward Lincolnshire's southeast plain, but there was little comfort offered by spreading their arms along the wagon's sides to brace themselves against the movement of the stiff wheels. As they passed the dilapidated Roman gate, the Wolds rose and fell before them like the North Sea swells David had sailed through. An occasional clump of housing arose to the left or right. The wheat was coming up, and rape had been recently planted along the hills. A shepherd guiding his flock along before them spread the animals apart to allow the wagon passage, reminding David of the schools of fish that parted as Captain Twinge's ship bore him toward its homeport of Boston and to a new life. Eventually, the boys stared out at Somersby, old Tennyson's croft, but found little to interest them but dull, white bed sheets drying on a line, blowing like loose sails as the ride continued through the late afternoon.

With nothing better to do than provoke his companion, Hugh said, "Your old grandmother has completely lost her senses, I hear."

"My grandmother is ill and still grieves for my mother. Now shut it, you Chat."

"And your grandfather never wants to see you again, you berk! If anyone's a louse, it's you, German!"

"You have no idea what you're talking about, *Scheisskopf*."

"You're due for a throttling, German boy, and when we get off this wagon, I'm going to give you a thorough one!" said Hugh.

"Your brother should teach you better manners now that *your* mother is mad, and your *father* is dead, *Scheisskopf!*"

Finally, the northern wall surrounding Boardcroft came into view, and the boys grew quiet. The outer bricks were a deliberate mix of color, topped with the familiar slabs of shiny limestone. Occasionally, obelisks milled from the light Lincoln stone jutted out to support incongruent, flat-bottomed stones, mementos of Lord Boardcroft's voyages. David had asked Lord Boardcroft why the stones were not set atop broad columns, and the old man replied, "Those stones aren't meant to remain for all time, my boy, only a little while, perhaps the length of a man's life, and then they fall to earth as new visitors to this English turf, to be pulled into God's great Earth forever." The boy had been reminded of a story, but the details eluded him, and he began to think of his own life in England like the stones—an exile from all he'd loved.

In future years, the Boardcroft parkland wall would be surrounded by clumps of volcanic rocks, once living sea-bound reef rocks, granite from North America and large pieces of marble, regularly increased and inspected by the present Earl and his descendants.

Finally, the wagon bumped through the arched gateway, and the boys jumped down to be met by Tom Twinge-Kitchen. "Where have you been? Grandfather is thundering that you are two hours overdue!"

"Just a moment, while I deal with this fucking berk!" said Hughie.

In the next second, Hughie leaped toward David and Tom's fist found Hughie's left cheekbone. The brothers began to fight. Hughie swung; Tom ducked and gave Hughie another crack in the same spot. Hughie fell to the ground, and in the next instant, Ibn Rasheed had them by the scruff of their necks and was moving the belligerents toward the great hall.

David was startled by the grinding gravel and quick, violent movements of the brothers throwing it up before him. And he was shaken by the sight of Hugh falling back, his brown hair tossed away from his forehead as by a great wind, and his swelling cheek and eye, already drawing closed. David found himself alone as the Earl's man-servant hustled the brothers toward the great hall, and the young Lübecker looked to the other servants for ease and some kind of guidance, but most had stepped away from their duties and ignored the boy.

Within a few moments, a pretty maid came over to him and led him to a broad, stone bench set into the outside wall of the south wing of the great house. In silence, she flashed her eyes at him and walked away toward the back of the great house. He looked after her swinging rear and thought she may as well have been a duck. He was out of the forecourt, away from the sight of all but the gardeners working around the long, sloping lawn that led to the present Lord Boardcroft's private folly, his *Temple of Eidothea,* as he named it, with its statues of seals set between Corinthian columns open to the sky. David wondered what his dear friend wanted to recall when the folly was constructed.

Rasheed stepped out of a window next to the bench. "Are you alright, Master? Those brothers, when put together, cannot control their passions. I must apologize on my Master's behalf for the behavior of the young Viscount Hugh that led you into the cathedral. And for Lord Twinge-Kitchen, who forgot all restraint. Will you be so kind as to come with me to visit Earl Boardcroft?"

David stood up and followed the Indian through the window and into the labyrinth of the house, moving through the silken, multi-colored walls of bedrooms and parlors until he reached the paneled library. He was guided through a great door and into a room filled with oddly matched leather-bound volumes, three variously sized tables scattered around the large space, and Mrs. Twinge-Kitchen's huge arrangements of flowers on pedestals in all four corners. David's great hero, Captain Twinge, rose out of a large, well-worn armchair of fading brown leather, surrounded by several slobbering and rather large dogs.

"Well, my boy, I suppose you've have a full day! Please sit and let us enjoy each other's company for a few minutes." At that, the master of the house yelled, "Rasheed!"

The Indian appeared from an unobtrusive door set into the long wall of books and asked, "Tea, my Lord?" Several of the dogs had moved behind the chair to take up familiar positions behind Boardcroft's sudden shouts.

"Just the thing at teatime, wouldn't you agree, David?"

"Of course, my Captain."

Rasheed's dark face directed a haunting, disappointed glance toward the young Lübecker.

"Old Ibn Rasheed, he'll never understand why you call me 'my Captain.' He could ask, but even knowing, he'd disapprove."

"Captain Twinge, how long will Tom and Hugh be staying with you? When you go back to sea, may I go with you?" asked David.

"Both questions, my young friend, are problematic. As you know, Captain Kitchen, the boys' father, is missing at sea. His mother, my daughter, is suffering from a nervous condition brought on by her husband's absence, and, of course, concerning you, we have your own family's travails. Hugh will go off to school soon, thank God, and Thomas will stay here another year before entering public school. As for you, my boy, you will stay with me until I hear from your grandfather that life has settled down in Lübeck and I make my annual passage there."

"Captain, I can't seem to get along with Hugh, and I'm afraid that—I think you put it this way—I won't be able to keep from my temper."

"You are a guest in this house, the son of my dear friends, your father and grandfather. You will be treated as such by everyone here. I assure you."

"Will you have time to allow me to accompany you to your offices, Captain? I am going to miss going to Papa's office and talking with Herr Schlarp."

"Perhaps."

After tea was served and David was dismissed to his tidy room on the house's second floor, he indulged in a small nap before dinner. As he slept, he dreamed of his aunt Kathe, who became the young maid he'd encountered earlier in the day. The girl's eyes flashed luminous gray, and she said to him, "You must find your father, and I will help you. Let nothing guide you but my eyes." Suddenly, he was awakened. He had been pulled off the chair in which he'd fallen asleep and found Hugh's contorted face inches from his own.

In a hissing whisper, Hugh said, "I'll see you castrated before I leave, you homeless shite! Here's something you'll like!" He pulled his erect penis from his trousers rubbed it across David's face as he held him with fists of his blond hair.

David kicked the boy, who was only slightly larger than he was, and yelled, "Get away from me, you savage!" David shoved Hugh away, and ran out of the room and downstairs to the hall where he met the same young maid busily dusting the railing.

"What is the matter, young sir?" At once she knew it was a sentence she was forbidden to utter. "May I help you?"

David could only think of his rage in mixed German and English and ran down to the servants' washroom to scrub his face. He knew that he might encounter Ibn Rasheed, but instead he ran headlong into Lord Boardcroft. "What is the matter, David?'

"Hughie, *Gottverdammich*. I'm sorry, Captain Twinge, but please keep that boy away from me!" cried David.

"Hughie!" yelled Boardcroft, "Hughie!"

Hughie approached, trying to conceal a smirk, and was ordered to the library.

When the two were alone, Lord Boardcroft said, "Hughie, you will leave this house tonight. Ibn Rasheed will take you to an inn in Grantham, and from there you will be locked away, or you will be taken to a session of the Lincoln Assizes where you will be dealt with in the utmost severity, I can promise you. If you cause trouble in Grantham, I will ask my friend the sheriff to incarcerate you for any crimes you commit there, plus homosexuality and bestiality! If you behave, you will become a member of Her Majesty's military in a short time. I will send your mother to visit you before your training begins at Sandhurst, if they will take you, God help them. Have I made myself clear?"

Before Hughie could respond, Rasheed had his bent Kukri knife to the boy's neck and led him, somewhat gingerly, out to the old wagon. There, Hughie was tied to one side of the back of the buckboard, the vehicle's lanterns were lit, and the two of them vanished into the still night air.

When Boardcroft left the library, he found David and Tom trying to comfort Mrs. Twinge-Kitchen in the front parlor. The woman was shattered, shaking with emotion, and flooding her hands with tears. "What have you done to my poor boy?" she wailed to Boardcroft.

"Only what would have been done earlier if he'd been out of Rugby. I am sorry, my girl, but your Hugh is rotten fruit! I am giving him an opportunity to mend his ways amongst people who will provide proper discipline. He must rise to his station in life instead of trying to shatter every norm of Christian society."

The party eventually went to bed, and while David and Tom smiled into their dreams, Mrs. Kitchen cried. At first light, David rose and began a letter to his grandparents.

2 August 1899

Dearest Oma and Opa:

I hope you will forgive me for not writing sooner, but I'm afraid that I relied on Captain Twinge to telegraph our arrival. All is well, but Tom and Frau Twinge-Kitchen are truly heartbroken at the loss of Captain Kitchen. I cannot think of my own dear parents without becoming upset, but Captain Twinge, or Lord Boardcroft, as he is referred to by everyone here except me, has made my time away interesting and entertaining. Tom has been anxious to show me his country, and of his friends I have met several. These English are mad for Fussball, but usually ignore the offside rule. Tom's brother, Hughie, has been sent away to join the army! We are very happy.

Love and thoughts your,

David

I hope this English is good. I would rather write in German!

David sealed the letter and changed out of his nightshirt to wander downstairs. The house was already alive, as he had known it would be, and he went into the dining room to help himself at the sideboard. Rasheed poured him a generous cup of coffee, Lord Boardcroft's preferred morning beverage, and David sat at the table waiting for Tom. Presently, Boardcroft came in with his dogs, and after pouring each a saucer of coffee, had Rasheed pour a cup for him as he sat down.

"Rasheed, did all go as planned last night?" asked Boardcroft. "Any trouble?"

"Nothing beyond my capabilities, my Lord. The innkeeper was very cooperative."

"Damn well should have been, paid him two pounds!" said Boardcroft. "How old is that boy? He must be eighteen, what?"

"He is old enough for Sandhurst. Or you could consider the BAI, sir."

"The British Army in India," repeated Boardcroft. "We'll try

Sandhurst first to keep his mother at bay. If he's back-termed, God help us."

"Shall I prepare an itinerary for a visit, sir?"

"Yes, do, Rasheed. Check the rail schedule at Newark, and I'll have you drive me there in the Benz at the appointed time. I thank God you learned to drive a proper motor!"

"David, my son, are you ready for a new day? Goddamned dogs, such a mess, Rasheed, but coffee, that's the stuff to keep the brutes regular what with all the game they catch."

"Yes, sir, I agree. They are astonishingly regular, especially indoors."

"Now, you old Dervish, we have maids to clean. No need complaining, right Davy?"

"Ibn Rasheed only looks to your comfort, Captain."

"Yes, yes, I'm sorry, Rasheed. God almighty! There goes one, now! Get that beast out of here! *O Gesù*, as the Italian's say."

Presently, Tom appeared and sat for breakfast, asking his grandfather if he and David might ride with him down to Boston this morning. Tom wanted desperately to be out of the house today.

"We'll take the Benz," said Lord Boardcroft. "Rasheed, please have the motor ready at 8:30."

"You are driving, sir?"

"Well, of course. There's only room for three. And a dog, if the boys will hold it."

"Very good, sir. The motor is due for service, however. I took the liberty of tightening the brake bar," said Ibn Rasheed.

At 8:30, the party made for Boston, traveling first to Long Sutton to allow Boardcroft to inspect a load of cotton, and most importantly, to call on clients and share a drink with them. The day became somewhat overcast as the car carried the group through the fens of south Lincolnshire. The boys watched mile upon mile of green fall behind them before the little car came into the shadow of the Boston "Stump." They saw the *Orestes* at anchor and shouted at the crew busy at their tasks. When the Benz stopped at Boardcroft's facilities, the boys hurried away from the warehouses and approached the famous old church. They entered and looked up and down the white walls, the windows, and, finally the great tower. A church warden walked to the boys and asked if they wished to see the cells where famous dissenters had been imprisoned.

David was repulsed by the tiny whitewashed cells and could not bear to linger before them. The multitude of people described to the boys, who in earlier times had passed through this church, amazed them. At length, they were anxious to leave, and as soon as they stepped out of the church, the Benz appeared before them and the boys mounted the car. The bustle of the waterfront fascinated them and Boardcroft described for David all of the merchant houses and warehouses they passed. He was reminded of home, wondered again how his grandparents and *Herr* Schlarp were, and began to become somewhat homesick. The death of his parents was never far from his thoughts, and he felt tears welling into his eyes as the little car began developing speed.

As the car began its return journey, Boardcroft asked David to sit with him in the front seat. "My boy, I've heard about Hughie and hope that his behavior has not caused you any harm. He will now undergo training in the army, and I do not expect to hear from him for some time to come. Tom, please get that damn dog out of my face!" Tom pulled the hound away from his master and kept his arms around him for a few miles. The Captain said, "Lady Boardcroft will be returning soon, probably tomorrow, and she will provide a somewhat more formal presence than you have been used to with us. Poor Rasheed, she thinks of him as an infidel, which of course he is, but she twists her impression of that good man into a kind of devil, if you will. You'll have to keep to Tom. He's learned to adapt. Be careful with women, my boy. God only knows if there are exceptions, but for the most part, they're a hell of a bother!"

After the little car reached the estate, the boys and the dog jumped down and ran about, throwing sticks for the dog to retrieve and laughing at Boardcroft's description of his wife.

"Does not your grandfather love your grandmother, Tom?" asked David.

"I have no idea. I can tell you that I didn't see her for a couple of years. Anyway, she tends to annoy Grandfather no end. Best to keep from between them, David, and only reply to Grandmother's questions in single words, if possible. She invariably gets me and Hughie mixed up when she comes up from London."

"How shall I address her?"

"Call her Countess Boardcroft. Grandfather calls her Sally."

"Does not Captain Twinge get lonely, Tom?"

"Hardly. He keeps a German lady in the dowager cottage. You'll probably find her along for the next cruise to Lübeck."

"What is a dowager? She lives in Lübeck?"

"My late great-grandmother. No idea; I only ever see her here."

"Captain Twinge visits her in this cottage?"

"Frequently."

"How old is this woman?"

"Old; probably twenty-five or thirty."

"What do they do? Isn't the Captain too old for romance?"

"I have no idea, but he's always happier after he's visited her for a couple of days."

"And the Countess does not object?"

"God, no. She says, 'Please go off and amuse yourself with that *Fraulein* of yours while I'm here.'"

"Nothing like my grandparents, eh, Tom?"

"Hardly!"

16

Lord Boardcroft was lying in bed when his wife, the Countess, or Sally as the Earl usually referred to her, entered the room. The numerous dogs lying on the bed either snuggled closer to their master or fled through the bedroom's open window upon hearing the Countess's voice. One mastiff remained concerned only to the extent that he opened an eye and stretched along the foot of the great bed, not giving up an inch of that luxurious territory.

"My God, Hugh, I've returned to find you still in bed at the unholy hour of 7:00 and am greeted with the news that our Hughie has been exiled to the army! His mother is inconsolable! Hasn't the loss of his father been enough for the poor boy?"

The mastiff lifted his head and looked out of the window, his nose in play.

"That boy, madam, has done nothing but abuse sheep and little boys for the last several years. You might muster a sentiment for his lost father! I will not hear from my own servants and tenants, mind you, another word of his scandalous behavior! Rasheed!" Boardcroft was incensed that this woman, who had abandoned her husband and daughter for two years, felt entitled to express any opinions concerning the Twinge family. He was beginning to feel his anger when the door opened.

Immediately, the Dervish appeared in traditional skirts, at the Earl's bedside. Today was a special day for his order, and he observed his sacred days with a severity that dimmed any real conviction the Countess may have harbored about anything or anyone. "My Lord?" Rasheed asked.

"Please recount the reason for my present circumstances for the benefit of Her Ladyship, Rasheed."

"My Ladyship, his Lordship, in attempting to return to his estate from the military academy, was attacked with a Major's baton by his own grandson, the Viscount, and rendered unconscious yesterday. His Lordship suffered a wound to the back of his head and upon gaining the estate, asked to be helped into bed." A hound stuck his nose further into the bedclothes.

At the bedroom door, Tom listened with keen interest to the conversation. He absolutely feared his grandmother as much as he adored his grandfather and made certain, by stealing around in stocking feet, that there was no indication of his presence. He was glad that Hughie was gone. His behavior had been shameful, and all of the boys who would normally associate with the brothers had made no attempt, except when forced by their parents, to visit or associate with them in any fashion. Hughie had his "friends," as he liked to call them, but the years of the sheep business had made his acceptance amongst Tom's peers impossible.

Tom had dreaded the return of his grandmother from the London House, knowing that her presence would re-excite an immense expression of grief from his mother. He missed his father as well, but he had been able to contain his mourning while his mother teetered at the edge of tears and *ennui* continuously. His grandfather had telephoned his grandmother as soon as he felt that Captain Kitchen had certainly perished with his ship, but the journey north had taken Her Ladyship through some of London's most alluring and fashionable shops to accumulate the necessary, and latest, mourning garments before finally depositing her at the estate after three days. Tom wanted the whole business behind him. He wanted to be able to remember and grieve for his father in peace and spend time sharing his sadness with David, his dearest friend. Tom chanced a peek around the door and was met with the Countess' penetrating, if somewhat startled, stare.

"And, what do you want, young Hughie?" asked Sally. "Go and find Thomas and that German boy. I can never recall his name."

Tom, miffed at his grandmother's misidentification, especially given her indignation at Hughie's absence, ran downstairs to the servant's dining room and sat down next to David, who had been served a portion of eggs and toast. "We need to get out of here," said Tom as David continued to enjoy his breakfast. A plate of the same was put before Tom, and he consumed it rapidly. "My mother and grandmother will want to begin planning services for my father this morning, and I'm not going to be summoned every two minutes to listen to mother wailing and to every tick of their planning."

Soon Lord Boardcroft's booming voice was heard calling Tom and David. Having finished their meals, they scurried up the stairs to the library, where they knew they would find Boardcroft. His Lordship was speaking to Rasheed. "And she asked me if I wanted to start *sleeping* with her! I had to remind *her* that a gentleman never sleeps with his *wife* … perhaps his *dogs*, but *never* his *wife* … good God." The old man turned and saw the boys. "Young men, I think that the better part of valor would be to vacate the premises and allow the women to do whatever it is women do. We'll take the wagon, after Rasheed finishes his rituals. Now go and get into some proper clothes for the day."

The boys ran to their rooms and changed quickly into their new khaki suits and riding boots. They passed the dining room where they caught sight of Rasheed twirling quietly and ran out of the open front door to the barn. Tom hitched the wagon and led the horses out to crush through the thick gravel in front of the house.

Boardcroft appeared, examined the horses, and looked carefully at the old wagon. "This wagon has been plying the Boardcroft acres for one hundred years, my boys. I can remember driving over the hill and seeing those younger Tennysons running those great dogs of theirs, and me and my own late father wandering all over Lincolnshire with our own dogs. Rasheed!"

Rasheed materialized at the front door almost at once and stepped up onto the wagon where he silently took his seat. The boys climbed into the back of the buckboard and sat on cushions purloined from the sitting room, as usual, and smiled at the opportunity to get away.

Old Boardcroft looked back at the boys and said, "Don't let your grandmother see you with those cushions. Rasheed, burn them when we get back and just smile if the Countess questions you about their whereabouts."

Rasheed nodded, and as his spiritual ablutions continued in a quiet, mysterious rendering, was not inclined to speak at this time.

The wagon moved forward on the great drive from the house to the road and turned left, following Boardcroft's direction. They followed along the aging wall of brick, acknowledged the estate workers carrying their hoes and spades, and remarked to each other how smooth the road was riding and how still was the standing ditch water this day. His Lordship launched into song, Tennyson, of course:

> About a stone-cast from the wall
> A sluice with blackened waters slept,
> And o'er it many, round and small,
> The clustered marish-mosses crept.
> Hard by a poplar shook always,
> All silver-green with gnarled bark:
> For leagues no other tree did mark
> The level waste, the rounding gray.

"That, my boys, is poetry. Too bad the old scribbler is dead and the drive over the hill will be unmet by his visage, if I might wax a little poetic myself. The great son of Lincolnshire, moving away to the Isle of Wight to kiss the sovereign arse, no doubt. I wonder if his son Lionel is still about. Met him in London. Sensitive plant, him."

The wagon bucked on, keeping the boys alert and gripping anything that came to hand, given the sway or bump of the old drays. Eventually, the wagon started up the hill toward Somersby, having avoided Horncastle, and the old Earl's eyes began to fill as he listened for the babbling brook and looked for familiar faces of the last remaining Tennyson relations. The village was as quiet as usual, the old parish church as dun and greenish as ever. The wagon crowned the hill and began a fall into a valley of wolds, and turning right, it made for Louth, waved on by more bed sheets flapping in the breeze.

"Luncheon, my boys? We'll stop in Louth." The wagon passed a gentleman working at a culvert at the edge of the Boardcroft estate.

"What are you doing, Mosley, my good man?" asked Boardcroft.

"Now, then, look who passes the humble tillerman! Ah, fuck-all, me Lord. Where you be heading?"

"Just taking these two young fellows out for a drive, old duck."

"Her Ladyship a little mardy, there, me Lord? I heard that she has landed hereabouts. We all have to escape on occasion. This mess of weeds should do me until me own bride calms down! I was just looking for a little morning kiss, if you takes my meaning, sire."

"Indeed, Mosely, indeed. The occasional romp is healthy for a man, but remember, *sleeping* with them only encourages contempt. Women just fail to consider the entire scope of circumstances, what?"

"Truly, they be mystifying, to be sure, me Lord" said Mosely.

"Moseley, you haven't seen Tinker about, today, have you?"

"Indeed, me Lord, he passed me not twenty minutes ago."

"Did you notice any weapons on him, Moseley?"

"No, me Lord, thank the Almighty! After that barmy bastard got a sniff of that Spanish girl, he completely lost his wits and thinks every three-legger on the estate is giving her the happy man! Goes about blasting poor chaps, every week; at least Marston takes the shot out of the ammunition and Blackie's suspects only have to fear the powder."

"Well, Mosely, she is a beauty, you know."

"Ah, indeed she is, me Lord, indeed she is, but don't tell Black Rog I said so!"

"Mosely, perhaps you could surprise us all by executing some real work today, what?" said the Earl. "We shall look in later."

The wagon continued until the tall steeple of St. Catherine's Louth appeared, and the road became more crowded. Rasheed eased the wagon through the congestion as market day was beginning to attract its usual early afternoon crowd.

David asked, "Captain, are we near the sea? There seems to be a moist wind blowing."

"We're near enough, young man; Mablethorpe is close by to the east." Boardcroft pointed down a narrow road.

"Rasheed, let's stop at the *Meridian* for luncheon."

Rasheed moved the wagon to a side street and stopped near a small stand of trees. He secured the horses and was instructed by Boardcroft to accompany the group into the old pub, which happened to be located on the prime meridian.

The proprietor immediately approached the group and said, "Good afternoon, my Lord. Mr. Rasheed, you are looking well. Follow me." The man, whose features betrayed Mediterranean heritage, led the small party into a private room, seating them near a large rear window.

"My Lord, we have sausages, leek soup, and plum pud. Would you care for your usual ale? Mr. Rasheed, tea? And these fine young men, sir?"

"Give them some weak beer, Stavros."

The meal was served quickly by two of the pub's matrons, one of whom was somewhat obvious in her interest in Tom. She was probably twenty-three or twenty-four years old, with a large, swaying chest that invited the close observation of most of the young men on the premises.

David was used to sausages and only wished that the British versions were less sweet and were offered with a little *kraut*. The women breathed hard throughout the smoke-filled establishment and the crowd generated a common sheen of sweat. "Captain, the church's steeple is very high. As high as Lincoln Cathedral's center tower?" asked David.

"I have no idea, David. I make a point not to visit churches unless necessary. I can tell you that when Lincoln Cathedral *had* its central spire, it was the tallest building in Europe for a time." He recited more Tennyson:

> *Although I be the basest of mankind,*
> *From scalp to sole one slough and crust of sin,*
> *Unfit for earth, unfit for heaven, scarce meet*
> *For troops of devils, mad with blasphemy,*
> *I will not cease to grasp the hope I hold*
> *Of saintdom, and to clamour, mourn and sob,*

Battering the gates of heaven with storms of prayer,
Have mercy, Lord, and take away my sin.

After the meal, the party boarded the wagon and Boardcroft asked, "Let's go to the coast, Rasheed and swing down to Skeggie and thence, back home."

As the wagon was about to pull away, a well-dressed man about Boardcroft's age walked up to the wheel and said, "Upon my word, if isn't Boardcroft the merchant. The Earl who'll never learn to behave as a proper gentleman and allow other people to conduct his *business* affairs. When's the last time you attended Parliament, Boardcroft?" asked the man.

"My boys, please allow me to present for your inspection a rare sighting of an example of the lesser of our poor species: an aristocrat of the genus, Skeeding. Behold, a Lord Charles Skeeding. A Lord Skeeding occasionally sniffs around the countryside applying its colossal nose to the affairs of the higher beings, men of action such as represented by your faithful servant. We, who are so favored to sit atop the great chain, are awake to the world and pity the Skeedings who usually lie about their estates in idleness, rarely spotted except in Westminster Palace and other halls of government where they regularly turn up to apply great bellows to the arses of each other, to inflate, as it were, their puny and pitiable minds with greed. Piss off, Skeeding."

Boardcroft nodded to Rasheed and the wagon moved away from the bustle of Louth with the boys doubled over with hilarity. Soon, they were traveling along the coast where they made a quick tour of Mablethorpe and Cleethorpes before entering Skegness. The town was seen as developing a resort atmosphere, prompting Boardcroft to comment, "That damn Scarbrough, bringing all this rabble to the area. Isn't Cleethorpes enough?"

But the little community with the unlovely name excited David as he remembered his North Sea excursions with his parents—the hard, cool wind, the great tides, and the little inns dotting the area north and east of Lübeck. His father, always quiet, and his mother chattering away about the wonderful seaside and her own experiences of holidays spent with her family. The boy grew silent as he recalled the earnest and joyful aspects of his parents' life together and the protection and happiness afforded his early youth. Now his parents were gone, and yet, he felt protected and loved by other people who had figured so prominently throughout his life. Hugh Twinge was certainly one of them.

The wagon finally began bucking up the estate drive, and David, lying back, watched behind the wagon a procession of singular, thick clouds, floating perpendicular to the Earth, many thousands of feet in length and moving slowly south, a like a procession of reluctant soldiers to battle. The cloud's hues changed with the late afternoon's setting sun like soldiers change uniforms from white, to gray, to red.

Just before dusk, Tinker was to be seen lighting the gas lamps that marked the top of the walls that enclosed the gravel drive up to the great house, and David and Tom fell into a light sleep, leaning against each other as the party neared the end of their journey. Within a few minutes, Rasheed stopped at the front door and the boys alighted quickly and waited for Lord Boardcroft to step gingerly away from the wagon.

He placed his arms over the boys and led them into the open door of the house. "Quiet, boys, *she* lurks!" They went into the library, where Boardcroft pulled off his boots and invited his brood of dogs to jump onto the rather massive leather divan he'd brought back from Turkey. The furniture was crisscrossed with the marks of sweeping dog nails, and a small indentation had formed, indicating the swale of pressure exerted by weight of Boardcroft's daily naps. The boys sat on the floor below, on either side of Boardcroft's legs on the carpet, another souvenir from Turkey. Each pulled their boots off, each leaving unfortunate muddy marks for a maid to scrub out later.

"My boys," said the old Earl, yawning, "I will be putting to sea again soon. David, you must be prepared to honor us with your presence for, perhaps, another year. Your grandfather has requested that you be allowed to attend school with Tom in the interim."

Lord Boardcroft left the house early the next morning after

Captain Kitchen's memorial and spent a week in Boston preparing
for his annual round of visits to merchant houses along the North
Sea and down to ports around the Mediterranean. After departing,
he passed the Thames estuary twice, and twice ignored the expectations of his class and sailed on, avoiding the great business conducted in London's halls of government, and most importantly, the
Countess, who had beat a hasty retreat to the London House after all
that was needed to be said and done about her lost son-in-law had
been said and done.

As fall approached, David and Tom were introduced to boarding at Boardcroft's old school, Roxburgh, near Spalding, where
they were to receive instruction in Homer, Virgil, Thucydides, and
hygiene. Hygiene, which really meant guidance on how to conduct
oneself within one's social class, was emphasized. Rasheed transported them the twenty or so miles from the estate and left them on
the worn, stone steps of the school's main hall. They let themselves
in and were met by the Headmaster, Dr. Clough, a former private
tutor to a family in York. He pronounced his name as "Claw." He
greeted the boys at once, with great enthusiasm, and had the house
porter show them to their rooms in an adjacent brick building.
It was wrapped in a belt of Lincolnshire limestone with matching
lintels and curved arches divided by overlarge keystones, matching
the first building they had entered.

They were instructed to be at table at 8:05 that evening, with the
rest of the boys who lived on campus. David and Tom settled into
their first floor room and from their window watched the movement of other students approaching the main hall. All were dressed
like themselves: gray felt hats, red coats over gray trousers, and high
boots. The requirement for older students to wear a long white scarf,
which applied to David and Tom, was the only difference distin-
guishing their kits from that of the younger scholars. Soon, their
building became boisterous and echoed with the clopping sounds of
boots on the stone floor outside of their room and above, the bumping knocks on wooden flooring mixed with yelling and occasional
screams for the rest of the afternoon. By 5:00, quiet mysteriously

prevailed except for the sound of a solitary pair of boots and the knock of what was discerned to be a heavy walking stick. At precisely 6:00, the building erupted with the rush of students scrambling out of the building. This lasted for a very short period of time, perhaps, three minutes.

Finally, at 8:00, David and Tom stepped out of their room and began walking through the passage that adjoined the great hall. They were caught up quickly by a herd of boys running past them, pushing and shoving and shouting, and then found themselves alone, watching the backs of the fellows as they ran ahead. The two friends began running after the herd, having no idea where the dining hall was located, and finally ran into a straggling few as they entered a large room divided by a long table punctuated by place settings. A number of servants began serving both sides of the table, now nearly full of boys sitting at what seemed to be prescribed places.

Dr. Clough appeared before the two boys and said, "Twinge-Kitchen and Rosenberg, follow me to your seating."

The boys followed, and as they arrived at their reserved seating, Dr. Clough said, "Twinge-Kitchen, though you have been educated at Boardcroft House and in Germany, I have decided to place you here, at the head of the table. Rosenberg, you will sit opposite, please."

Clough walked up to a low platform with a rather disheveled boy in tow and from behind a dais said, in a booming voice, "May I have your attention, young men? I am happy to see that most of the levels have returned and I can, with some measure of confidence, almost believe that most of you shall last here at Roxburgh through the year. Allow me to remind you:

1. There is no fagging at Roxburgh.
2. All participate in sport.
3. There is no inappropriate interaction between boys and matrons at Roxburgh.
4. Attendance at chapel is compulsory each morning at 9:15.
5. Rowing, cricket, and football teams will be appointed tomorrow by the Sub Headmaster, Dr. Baker, and Head

Boy, who you will notice standing behind me now.

6. With respect to sports, you must apply using the forms supplied under your plates and give them into the hands of Dr. Baker upon your leaving this room tonight.

7. Finally, I am again offering Algebra and Euclid on Tuesdays and Thursdays at 2:00 in course room 4-A. Perhaps a few of you will surprise me by taking up this opportunity."

The Headmaster nodded to the Sub Headmaster and a short prayer was offered. The Head Boy stepped up to the right corner of the platform and yelled, "Commence." The Head Boy was wearing a Grenadier Guard Bearskin hat that seemed to be nearly as tall as he was. Clough then walked behind the long rows of opposing boys who were busy passing huge, depleted platters of mutton up and down the table, the remains of the earlier, 6:00 dinner.

One boy, a lanky, ginger-haired lad sitting next to David said in a Home County accent, "I rather believe that one fares better at 10:00, when the servings must be replenished. This 8:00 arrangement is most meager."

Clough left the boys picking through the bones, though most had given up and were eating mashed potatoes and carrots, which seemed to be in abundance.

David said to the ginger-haired boy, "How does one manage to join the 6:00 or 10:00 dinners?"

"Well, one doesn't know, does one, except to say that the upper forms go first and the lower forms go last? The Claw has ordained the arrangements, and if one wishes to dine, one appears at the assigned time. By the way, my name is Douglass, but I'm called Red for obvious reasons." Red offered his hand, and David shook it and introduced Tom. "Ah, a Boardcroft; good to know, although the older boys will not care who you are when the sporting begins."

Tom frowned and said, "What sport do you play, Red?"

"Football, to my father's shame. He believes that cricket is the only civilized activity devised by the human race."

David said, "Shall we enroll in football then, Tom?"

"Why not? A Boardcroft could never idle away days at a time with cricket, and rowing is for ponces, anyway."

"Then football it is. How can we join your team, Red?" asked David.

"Write, 'Herrings' on the line that says 'Team.' Baker and Head Boy, whoever that is now, will probably be grateful for saving them the work."

A small gong was struck and the boys rose from the table and stepped back, over the oak benches upon which they had been sitting. This process did not conclude until several boys had seen their plates removed from under their noses and Dr. Baker had tapped the laggards on the shoulders with a great cane. The cane was an alarmingly thick piece of ash, tapered slightly toward the lower end that terminated in a three-pronged brass foot, with which he continually tapped the floor.

Baker shouted, "Dismissed!" and the boys filed out of the doors located at the opposite end of the room as kitchen maids came through the entrance to clear up the table. Once the boys were out of the dining hall, they began to run, turning right into another passage and on to their digs in the adjacent building. David and Tom found themselves at the opposite end of the hall of residence and had to push their way through the boys crowding the hall. As they approached their room, bells were rung overhead, and the crowd dispersed into their rooms for the night. A lantern had been lit on the desk in the middle of the room, and David and Tom sat down, each weary from the day.

David asked Tom, "Did Hughie attend this school?"

"He was thrown out."

"Why was he thrown out?"

"For violating rules one through four. Though he did attend the maths that Dr. Clough offered, which I suspect, purchased him some grace before the situation became completely intolerable. He was caught under a matron's skirts in a larder."

The boys rose, turned the lamp's light out, dropped into their beds, and were asleep right away. At 10:00, a rumble descending from the third floor manifested on the first and second floors as a repetition of the 6:00 and 8:00 scramble to the dining hall. David awoke with a start at the noise and looked around, unsure of his surroundings. The din outside his door was at its peak when he realized where he was and what was happening. Fortunately, he was still sufficiently fatigued to fall back and resume his slumber. Just before 11:00, the uproar began as the herd returned, this time waking both boys, who looked at each other through the dim light falling through their window.

Tom said, "No use retiring before 11:00, David. We'd better get used to it."

David and Tom stayed awake until after midnight and seemed to have just fallen asleep when their door was opened, and the porter shouted for them to get up. David pulled back his blond hair as he was hit with a towel and told to "get on with it." The boys looked outside of their room and saw a train of other boys queuing in front of open double doors in the middle of the hall. Most just had towels wrapped around their waists, but a few were still wearing their nightclothes.

David and Tom kept their nightclothes on and joined the line of boys, making their way into the modern washroom. After relieving themselves, they removed their clothes and joined a forest of morning erections under the warm showers, trying not to stare at the sea of nakedness. They showered quickly and retrieved their towels, which they had secreted above a locked cabinet. Their nightclothes, however, were missing and they wrapped their towels around their waists and ambled back to their room. There, their nightclothes lay on their already made up beds, and they found their uniforms pressed and ready to wear.

They dressed and asked each other where the dining hall was, finally just joining the army of boys walking past them. When they reached the dining hall, they filed around the perimeter of the room, grabbing cups of tea, hot bread, and porridge that they had to consume standing with many other boys who were denied seating by the students who had arrived earlier. The bells rang, and they walked out of the opposite end of room, repeating the movements of the previous evening, but instead of turning back toward the housing building, they followed the instructions of the porters stationed at the corner directing the boys through doors leading outside. They stumbled out of the main hall, down high steps, and over fallen boys. Once outside, they heard, "Rowing, here … cricket, here … football, here!" shouted by rather large men holding signs above their heads. They ran to the football section and into a crowd of bored-looking lads making sarcastic and demeaning comments about their fellow athletes joining the other groups, which they referred to as "The Cunts" and "The Pricks." "The Cunts" seemed to have the largest following, all well-behaved and quiet standing behind their instructor, who wore his full kit, including a small straw hat, his sign mounted on the blade of a paddle. The "Pricks" waved their bats about, some attempting to fence with them. They were snarling, and obviously, supercilious churls who spat toward the footballers, who they referred to as, unsurprisingly, "The Bollocks." "The Bollocks" just looked at the rest with obvious contempt and continued their banter while they crossed their arms, slouched, and rolled their eyes.

"The Bollocks" were led by a man named Roland Pouchbath, who, standing well-under six feet, nevertheless presented an air of vigor and intelligence. He had a chipped set of bottom teeth, which earned him the nickname, "The Gnasher" and the boys who had played for him, imitated his wit and often, vulgar language.

"All right, you lot," said The Gnasher to the assembled boys before him. "It seems that our beloved Dr. Baker and Head Boy have been kind enough to leave team selections to the coaches yet again. We have enough of you to make two teams, divided by Form and talent. Now, this thing in my hands is a football. Are there any questions?"

No one raised their hand.

"Very good, gentlemen. Now, I am going to kick several of these footballs amongst you to see how you respond to them."

The Gnasher punted seven balls high in the air and watched as most of the boys ran to positions to head the balls toward each other. David and Tom, being fortunate enough to determine the trajectory of two of the balls were able to head them back and forth twice.

"Alright, Upper Sixth and Lower Sixth, over here. Fifth Forms and Fourth Forms, here" yelled The Gnasher. "Right. Now, the names of the teams. The higher levels will be called the Herrings and the lower levels will be known as the Trouts. I will be referred to, at least to my face, as, the Boss."

Two boys, their heads stuck into the hold of a sweep rowing boat, approached the groups unsteadily. The swinging bow knocked over two straggling boys looking for their sports.

Head Boy, standing directly before the oncoming menace, watched as the boat was finally stopped at the cricket group. "Don't you Cunts know where to be?" He bounded over, his bearskin hat bobbing, and grabbed the port rail of the boat, bringing the craft and its bearers down to the dusty ground. "Can't you two berks tell a Cunt from a Prick?" he yelled.

All the sporting groups collapsed in mirth, some rolling into each other, initiating a hail of cursing. Amongst the rowers, a round of fisticuffs broke out, and the cricketers flailed their bats about.

David and Tom were Fifth Forms at fifteen years of age, but educationally, could have easily acquitted themselves well as Lower Sixth students. After the boys were back on their feet, The Gnasher put them in the higher group based on his instinct for talent, "You two look useful. You're Herrings," he said. "Now, I'll need ball boys, which we will refer to as 'Bollocks.' You, what is your name?"

"Rosenberg, Boss."

"Henceforth, you shall be known as Rosy Bollocks. And you, ginger?"

"Douglass, Boss."

"Henceforth, you shall be known as Red Bollocks."

All of the new footballers collapsed again, laughing so heartily that one wet himself. He was known thereafter as Pisser Prangham.

A porter appeared before the massed athletes and rang a ship's bell mounted above a brick column that happened to have been donated by Lord Boardcroft.

"All right you lot, back inside! We meet back here at 3:00, sharp," yelled The Gnasher. "Rosy Bollocks, collect the balls, please, and Red, put them in this bag."

After wrangling the footballs, the boys filed behind their classmates and went into the building, where porters were stationed to direct them to their classes.

"And just where do you think you're going, my Lord?" asked a porter.

David had walked past him, still amused by his new nickname. "Well, I don't know, sir," he said.

"What form?"

"Fifth."

"You, my Lord, will proceed to room 1C, thence to 2C, after which you will proceed to the dining hall for luncheon, thence to 3C. Here is your schedule. Don't let me catch you wandering again."

"Yes, sir, thank you, sir," replied David.

The same schedule applied to Tom. He met David in 1C, Homer, and the pair accompanied each other throughout the rest of the day. Finally, at 3:00, they were back on the playing field—this time unbothered by the Cunts and the Pricks.

"Tom, why are the rowers called Cunts?" asked David.

"Because 'cunt' rhymes with 'punt.' And, you may as well know, should you wonder, the cricketers are called 'pricks' because it rhymes with 'sticks.'"

"It's all rather obscene, do you not think? Anyway, they are rowers, not punters," said David.

"Of course it's obscene, Rosy Balls," Tom laughed.

"All right, you lot. Herrings over here; Trouts over there. We'll need to knock some balls around. Rosy and Red, balls, if you please!" yelled The Gnasher.

"Aye, Boss," said David.

The boys played what The Gnasher called 'Monkey in the Middle' for an hour. The game placed a boy in the middle of a circle of players and required him to try to intercept the ball as it was being kicked around the circle. The Gnasher blew his whistle and had each boy, by turns, tending the goal and kicking toward the goal. At last, The

Gnasher settled on goal keepers and strikers for the teams.

The days settled into a routine of classes that were largely translation exercises followed by football practice. The Gnasher assigned David to mid-field with a boy named Plink-Codington, and they began a schedule of matches with nearby schools and estate teams. When the squad played the Boardcroft team, the tenants' and household servants' sons, along with boys from the shipping company, came up to Roxburgh and thrashed the Herrings 6-0. Roger Tinker was the manager of the team and kept taunting The Gnasher throughout the match to the extent that the contest finally dissolved into a bloody brawl, resulting in two Herrings, one of whom was Pisser Prangham, left unconscious on the field while the fight moved like a knot of flailing insects toward the school buildings. After the porters came out in force to assist the referees, the fight ended, but the two unconscious boys were left on the field overnight until The Gnasher found them while straightening the goals back into shape.

Boardcroft House was called, and a doctor and nurse were dispatched from Long Sutton to attend the unfortunate boys. Later, after the teams appeared at 3:00, The Gnasher took David aside and said, "Listen, Rosy, Tinker purloined our balls. You need to get down to Boardcroft and get them back. That bastard does it every time! Now have those balls back here tomorrow!"

"Right, Boss" said David. He caught up with Tom. "Tom, you need to get word to Rasheed that we have to get our balls back. Tinker stole them and The Gnasher wants them back by tomorrow!"

The boys found The Claw, explained the problem, and asked for a night's leave to retrieve the balls.

"They always steal the balls. Pouchbath knows that! But he never does anything to prevent it." Dr. Clough said. "Jesus Christ, go on, call Boardcroft House, and see if the balls can be gathered up for you, and I'll have Porter Jenkins drive you down."

Tom used the Headmaster's telephone and called home. Rasheed answered, "Ahoy, Boardcroft House."

"Ahoy, Rasheed, Tom here," he said in an elevated voice. "I will be traveling down to retrieve our footballs. Could you please gather them from Mr. Tinker for me?"

"I have already secured the balls, Master Twinge-Kitchen. I anticipate this every year."

"Thank you, Rasheed; I shall see you, soon," Tom almost yelled.

After arriving at Boardcroft House, the boys and the porter were brought into the dining hall and feted by Tom's mother. The food, roast beef, herring, a variety of vegetables, and a pudding was most welcome. Mrs. Twinge-Kitchen said, "I'm so pleased to announce that our Hughie will be returning for Christmas break!"

Tom groaned.

Rasheed appeared, and anticipating the coming winter, gave the boys foul weather kits. He handed them small folios of translations of Rumi done in his own hand. "May the great poet bring light to your souls," said Rasheed. He handed the balls, gathered into a canvas sail bag, to David, along with a sealed note from Tinker to Pouchbath. "Mr. Tinker sends his best regards and looks forward to bringing his squad back to Roxburgh to remind you of the rules of the game."

"Please tell Mr. Tinker that we will have a surprise for him," said Tom.

After Mrs. Kitchen executed a tearful farewell to the boys, the group left. Tinker himself came up to the drive and saluted them off with two extended fingers that he turned out to execute an obscene gesture.

It was late October, and the cold night air followed the motorcar back to the school. After Porter Jenkins put the boys out in front of the main hall, they went inside each wearing foul weather coats and pants over their uniforms. The waxed material was heavy, but with the wool clothes they wore under the kits, the boys were comfortable.

"What the devil?" The Claw asked upon seeing the boys. He pulled their hoods away from their heads. "At any rate, did you get the balls, young men?"

"Indeed we did, sir," said Tom. "You'll pardon the foul weather kit we were instructed to wear against the cold air, sir. Boardcrofts try to be prepared, sir."

"Take the balls to your room, and don't forget to have them back to Mr. Pouchbath tomorrow."

"Yes, sir," the boys said in unison.

It was 7:30 in the evening, and the boys knew that the 8:00 dinner rabble was preparing to hurl itself into the hall, so they hurried back to their room, shed their foul weather kits, and prepared to join their dining fellows. As the bell rang, they charged out a step ahead of the rest of the hungry boys and made the dining hall in time to be the first to take their seats.

Red Douglass sat down next to David and said, "The Gnasher will be in a mood tomorrow, I'll tell you. We'll run the field for over an hour, I dare say. Did you retrieve the balls?"

"Yes," David smiled.

"Oh, thank Jesus!" Red said. "By the by, Jones and the Pisser will be missing for the rest of the season. According to Gnasher, being knocked unconscious and left in the cold overnight induces pneumonia. He blamed the team for not taking care of our mates when he stopped me and Morley in the hall. He also said, 'Never leave a man behind, you lot!' Unfortunately, Plink-Codington was standing nearby and replied, 'Morley always says, I hate to leave my friends behind!' which caused Morley to smash Plink-Codington in the nose and The Gnasher to yell that all will run the field until he says stop, since none of us lot can behave. Poor Plinky had to run to the nurse with blood pouring from his nose, and he collapsed as he was rounding the east corner. The Gnasher pulled him off the floor, and we had to help carry him to the nurse. There he is now, with rather an extensive wrap across the face."

"My word, Jones and the Pisser were fullbacks! Who's going to stopper the back?" asked Tom.

"No idea; Gnasher said we'll have a change-up and reform tomorrow, God willing and the balls arrive."

The next day, with "balls and the Grace of God," as The Gnasher put it, the formation was changed. David was to play defensive middle, which meant that he was now required to cover the field back to the Herring goal. The rest of the season, he ran more than he'd ever run, and by the Christmas break, his fitness was at a peak. The Herrings amassed a barely winning record, and the Gnasher announced that he "had to admit, some of you lot have proved useful. Happy Christmas."

Tom and David arrived back at Boardcroft House to the bustle of Mrs. Twinge-Kitchen directing servants as she flung herself into the art of holiday decoration in anticipation of Hughie's homecoming.

Lord Boardcroft was delighted to see the boys and greeted each with a small glass of beer. "My boys, Hughie will be fetching up here soon, so if he gives you trouble, get word to me," he said.

As the December days drifted by, Hughie decided to leave Sandhurst a few days before dismissal, and he and a new friend made their way to King's Cross station to board a train scheduled to stop in Newark-on-Trent, a few dozen miles from the Boardcroft estate. Viscount Boardcroft-Kitchen and his companion alighted from the late London train and after assigning their baggage and telling the driver of a coach-for-hire their destination, they boarded. The air in Newark was freezing and the young men found their uniforms and greatcoats no match for the gusting, northeast wind. There was a threat of snow and most of the recent fall was pushed along the street curbs, but an ominous swirl of flakes intruded into the cab behind the cadets as they reached to close the door. Hughie and his companion, whom he referred as KoKo, but whose real name was The Right Honorable Nigel Nance-Minnis, had decided to surprise the Boardcroft household, especially Hughie's grandfather. The two young men snuggled and held hands as the carriage jerked forward and turned sharply to follow the community's concert of lights, bright here, dull there, and nearly absent as they began to exit the town.

KoKo was a slight young man, somewhat lost in the faint light as he leaned against Hughie who had pulled him close, almost onto his lap. KoKo's face was long, but in proportion to his height, and somewhat exotic in the way light played off of his reddened cheekbones and light eyes. He was lean, with an almost translucent complexion that Hughie found pleasing. It reminded him of the characters in a performance of the *Mikado* his mother had exposed him to in London some years ago. Hence the nickname, KoKo.

The two young men had met during their first year. KoKo's lean and graceful movements, especially the up-tilt of his face when he spoke, had attracted Hughie. He had had companions whom he had known in different stages of intimacy throughout his youth awaiting his entry to the academy. But KoKo, or to most others, The Sprite, had won the Viscount's heart, and he served upon the delicate boy all manner of homosexual sport, which KoKo absorbed as acts of love. Indeed, now that the light was dimming as the coach clattered down the country lanes, KoKo prayed for a warm kiss from his lover.

KoKo had been a quiet boy, but a troubling presence in his family. While his sisters rode incessantly and played badminton amongst themselves and with friends, the slight, solitary boy busied himself with the keeping down of small animals that were unfortunate enough to wander onto his family's estate. He was an excellent shot, but in the event of merely wounding an animal, especially a rabbit, he relished the chance to finish it with an enormous hunting knife he had stolen from the gamekeeper. Indeed, the gamekeeper had complained to the boy's father many times about the imbalance of small to large animals. All were disappearing. There were scarcely any birds to shoot, so when KoKo's father, Lord Minnis, realized that hunting parties were no longer practicable, he managed to enroll his son in Sandhurst, where he knew Nigel would prove himself a fine man with a rifle.

Hughie had growled his way through his first year with KoKo, but so cut, swollen, and occasionally stitched up were his lips from fighting, he could barely articulate at times. Hughie pushed, spat upon, and struck most of his peers until even his oldest friends began to distance themselves, so brutish did his behavior become. The young men who challenged him learned to take him on in threes and fours, until an uneasy understanding evolved into a disquieting norm. It seemed that all cadet eyes except KoKo's avoided Hughie's gaze by the end of his initial year.

Hughie's marks were very good. Indeed, he neared the top of his class. One of his instructors did remark that he appeared "bloody clumsy" and that the cadet was always damaging his face. This dissipated, as Hughie was given a wider and wider berth by his fellow cadets. Now that he was in his final year, most of the cadets just wanted to leave the troublemaker alone and allow him to "carry on," as it was termed, with his Sprite.

The carriage finally reached the estate after the incessant cresting and falling away of the wolds and entered the two-mile long gravel drive within the property. The driver swore as he had to slow to carefully round a tall memorial to the Viscount's great-great-grandfather, who had done something in the Crimean War. Lord Boardcroft had tall gas street lamps alight around the memorial during the Christmas season, and this helped lead the carriage up to the great house. KoKo had by then fallen asleep against Hughie, and Hughie watched the approach up the driveway as keenly as might an ancient helmsman maneuvering his boat through miles of treacherous rocks. He shook his lover and said, "We are here."

Out of the house came Rasheed, holding his Gurkha knife and demanding to know who was approaching his master's home.

Hughie stepped out of the carriage holding Nigel's hand, "It is I, you WOG. Now, pay the driver." Rasheed's head snapped back, and he glared at the couple as they passed by him and went into the house. Rasheed paid the driver nearly all of the household money he carried. He stood for a few moments in the cold air and allowed Hughie enough time inside for Earl Boardcroft to notice his grandson. It did not take long.

"What the Hell are you doing here, you brute?" asked Boardcroft. "And who the hell is this little bugger?"

Rasheed decided to go inside just as Hughie's mother swept into the hall to greet her oldest son and his companion. "Oh, my word, my boy, come here and give your mother a kiss. And, who is this handsome young man?" Mrs. Twinge-Kitchen pulled back her hands into an attitude of prayer.

"My name is Nigel Nance-Minnis, ma'am," replied the tiny young man.

Hughie had let go of Nigel's hand upon the approach of his grandfather, but Boardcroft was still eyeing them suspiciously.

Also observing the scene were Tom and David, who stood somewhat back, within the recesses of the library. Both boys dreaded the coming days. David had grown remarkably since Hughie had been sent away to the academy. Now just over six feet, he was roughly equal in height to Hughie and felt confident that should Hughie attempt to treat him rudely, he would at least be able to put up a respectable defense. Tom and David approached the cadets and offered their hands.

"Well, look at these two! Gentlemen, please allow me to introduce The Right Honorable Nigel Nance-Minnis," said Hughie. Tom and David looked at each other and shook hands with Nigel and Hughie.

Rasheed stepped in and offered to take the young men's greatcoats and caps and discreetly nudged David back from the cluster of people.

Suddenly, old Boardcroft grabbed Hughie and flung him against the solid oak door. He put his mouth to Hughie's ear and whispered, "Any misbehavior will be met with a soak in the Haven, my son! I expect to enjoy a fine Christmas!"

"I see you still have that Jew around, Grandfather."

Boardcroft gave Hughie a punch in the stomach and turned and smiled at the Sprite. "We have some unusual ways of greeting family members here at Boardcroft. Boys, tell me what happened today." He put his arms over Tom's and David's shoulders and led them back into the library.

Mrs. Twinge-Kitchen took Hughie's and Nigel's hands, led them into the dining room, and called for a footman. "You young men must be famished!" She told the footman to tell cook to prepare for two more at dinner. "Hughie, I've received such outstanding reports from the school. Oh my, how ever did you acquire these scars on your face?"

Hughie was a tall, somewhat lean young man with very thick

dark brown hair and a hint of whisker around his chin. He had the bounding Boardcroft gait and stood very erect. His brown eyes moved constantly, and he had a habit of squinting and blinking in any light or setting. His uniform was correct. He had always taken great trouble with his appearance, but he was no dandy. His facial demeanor would always betray a dismissive and impatient attitude, and the few friends he'd managed to acquire during his lifetime had learned not to be taken in by his fashionable tastes.

The Sprite spoke up as Hughie was opening his mouth, "Hughie was hurt during a cavalry exercise, ma'am." Nigel looked up at Hughie and smiled as Mrs. Kitchen put her hand to her mouth to suppress her horror.

While the servants began filling the room, the family found their seats at the great table. Hughie was seated next to his mother, and Nigel was placed between Tom and David.

As the courses were being served, Nigel looked at David and said, "I have no conflicts. I could kill you anytime. Hughie's brother is delicious, and I might tell Hughie. What do you think Hughie would do?"

"Do what you wish, you little girl," said David. He looked up and met Hughie's gaze from across the table. Hughie mouthed the words, "You are dead."

Dinner concluded and Earl Boardcroft repaired to the library. He asked David to accompany him and left the others on their own. Boardcroft lit a cigar and told David that a letter had arrived from *Herr* Schlarp and that arrangements were being made for his return to Lübeck. David would be leaving the next day on a packet out of Boston to Hamburg, where he would be met by *Herr* Schlarp. "My boy, in these uncertain times, if you need my help, please tell me. Here is a letter of introduction that you may use at any of my offices in England or overseas. It is sealed in a waxed envelope. Do not lose it."

17

Sam Yoffey sat on his front porch reading the Saturday edition of the *Mobile Daily Register*, when his wife, Anna Jane, opened the black screen door, stepped out of the house, and walked over to stand in front of the doctor. Her hands came to rest upon her hips. The two ceiling fans whirred above and shouts of a couple of mullet fishermen standing a few yards off the beach could be heard as they cast their nets simultaneously into the bayou waters shimmering behind her. Her thick, light brown hair was pulled up tightly, and her light gray eyes began to narrow as she spoke, "Sam, what's this business about Palestine I hear from your daughter? What have you been putting into that child's head, mister?"

Sam looked up and observed the lovely figure standing before him and immediately took on a look of astonishment. The fishermen began making triumphant noises as they pulled their nets back from the shining waters. Sam could see flapping fish winking in the nets. Anna Jane stomped her feet impatiently, and Sam responded by crinkling his paper toward his lap. "Are you practicing for next year's Purim, darling? I'd recommend putting a little more heel into it," said Sam.

"Samuel Yoffey, don't you get smart with me. If you don't give me a proper answer, you'll find yourself in a world of trouble."

"Well, my dear, your daughter has been reading that massive Bible you keep in the parlor, and her cousins in Charleston have been talking about how it's the duty of every Jewish person to support a new Israel in that ancient desert we were supposed to have claimed as Hebrew land before the Romans threw us out. Not to mention the talk coming from my little brother, the real *Zionist* in the family," Sam said, his head moving back and forth and his eyes wide with his best don't blame me look.

"Samuel, Hulda is talking about *going* to Palestine! Now you just hush that make believe witlessness. Do you know where Palestine is, mister?" Anna Jane stood slim, and her lustrous eyes had not lost any of their beauty in the thirteen years she had been married to Sam. She held out a magnificent bosom, lifted her arms upon her breasts, and flashed her eyes, now opened widely to exaggerate her complaint.

This was, in Sam's judgment, another example of his wife's feigned outrage that their only child might have *Zionist* "ambitions." The word, *Zionism* itself was new around the household. To hear the thirteen year-old spouting it amused her father, and Anna Jane wanted it clearly understood that it concerned her mother.

"I know I joined the 'Tribe,' Dr. Yoffey, after you wouldn't leave me alone and finally insisted that I marry you, ignoring my contentment with the Esther Sisters, but this business of you telling that child she can go and join the Zionists is outrageous! My poor old Catholic mother and father thinking, it's not enough to have our youngest daughter seduced by an Israelite who forced her to convert to his ways! Now, they're going to hear, 'Mammow and Pap, I'm going to Palestine to become a *Zionist*!' I declare, those are two of the gentlest souls. They're blessed to be rare, rational, white Catholics! Now the poor old things are surrounded by *dagos* escaped from New Orleans thinking nothing but Mardi Gras, Mardi Gras! Why, they can't even go to church without being hustled around by packs of *dagos*! Lord, I wish Admiral Farragut had stayed in Mobile. He would have kept the coloreds, but being a civilized American, would have run those *dagos* back to Louisiana. God only knows why Mr. Jefferson was compelled to buy that place from Napoleon. I declare, he should have made that little Napoleon take all the *dagos* back to France.

"Darling, I always thought *dagos* were Italian or Spanish." said Sam.

"Same difference! We started Mardi Gras, anyhow. My poor mother and father, those dear old souls, here they lose not only their loving girl to a black-headed Israelite like you, sir, but they have to endure the worry and anxiety of believing that their only grand-daughter is planning to leave them thousands of miles behind and join a black-haired rabble in a dusty old desert! Lord above, they deserve better!"

Sam had brought his paper up to his face as his wife held forth, and before she had finished her tirade, he said, "I thought *dagos* were white." He resumed reading, and enjoying the sea breeze that had built through the Sunday afternoon, began humming a piece from Brahms he'd remembered from his youthful piano lessons. After Anna Jane had gone quiet, the doctor finally pulled the pages down and said, "Sister James, how about a glass of that wonderful sweet tea Miss Gomey fixed this morning? You know standing there, you look like one of those beautiful Mobile Camellia Maidens. All you need is the hoop skirt, and I swear, the entire male population of Mobile would swoon, *dagos* included."

"Well, Dr. Yoffey, for your information, I *was* a Mobile Camellia Maiden, but that kind of talk won't get you anywhere, sir. Sometimes I think that I should have waited for Ephraim to come of age if I had to marry Jewish. Sam, if you keep trifling with me, I'm going to tell the old Mother to stop using you at the Esther! Anyway, I wish I could summon Mr. Charles Darwin here right now. I bet he could trace *dagos* back to *your* kind! God forgive me, what my folks must have been thinking about *you* all these years."

"Now, having Mother throw me out of the Esther sounds like something our Yankee Rabbi would welcome. You know he's in love with you, don't you, Sister? Anyhow, he'd rather I tend to the rich houses, especially the rich *Jewish* houses across the Bayou and let Bettoli care for the poor folks on the Hill. By the by, darling, I think that if you look into it, you'd find that Mr. Darwin is no longer amongst the living and breathing."

"Oh, you just hush up, Samuel."

Presently, Gomey stuck her head out of the screen door and asked, "Miss, it's nearly 1:00. Do you wants to wait on Mr. Ephraim before we serve?"

Anna Jane replied, "Gomey, we eat at 1:00, period. If that boy can't get himself here on time, that's his loss."

Anna Jane marched toward the screen door after Gomey had

allowed it to shut, and putting her hand on the worn metal handle, stopped for a moment, looked back over her shoulder at Sam, and flashed her beautiful eyes, as if to say, "Pay attention to me, *mister*." She stepped inside the house and met Linny, Gomey's young niece, who said, "Do I needs to take them ham bones out the beans and greens, Miss?"

Anna Jane replied, "No, Linny, it's just us, today. If any Jews happen by, why, I guess we're just caught and condemned."

"Yes, ma'am. Temple been asking for a piece of chicken, as usual."

"Well, give him one, Linny, as usual."

Sam put his newspaper down and gazed at the iridescent blue water spreading out in front of his home. He considered all the good he'd done the Hill and all the wealth he could have accumulated across the Bayou, had he set up practice there. Would he have met the beautiful nun Sister James at the Esther, if he'd chosen the other path? How many people would have died without a full-time doctor attending the Hill? He began to think about Hulda, about her interest in the Zionist Movement, and feared that he would lose her to it someday. He knew, however, that she would have to choose a path, and if offering to help found a Jewish homeland was part of it, well, he thought, there were worse things she could find to do. With the girl finishing high school in two years, he felt that he and Anna Jane could persuade her to study nursing. He would be able to use her soon, and he looked forward to teaching her all he could about medicine. The two fishermen had moved farther south behind the tall reeds that bordered Sam's patch of beach, but he could still see the nets flying up and hear the men speaking in the familiar waterfront phrases.

Temple climbed the steps up to the porch, gnawing a fried chicken leg. "Afternoon, Doc. What you studying so hard about?"

"Hello, Temple, looks like you're having a fine day. I was just thinking that you're getting too big to put in Willard's boat. Is that my chicken you're eating on, young man?"

Following this Sunday ritual, Temple said, "The Lord has blessed, Doc, the Lord has blessed."

"Well, he didn't check with me. I'm going to bless you out, Temple, if you're not careful."

Temple chuckled and twisted his head from side-to-side. "Doc, I don't ask for a penny from you to guard them women folks what comes over here to work for you. I takes them down to the Bayou to catch Willard's boat in the morning and takes them back down in the evening, rain or shine, summer or winter, night or day. Now, that's practical slavery, boss. Where else you gonna find it? All I gets is a chicken bone on Sunday." Temple licked his fingers with comical affectation. His pants legs were rolled up to mid-calf and his open shirt betrayed a noble, sturdy torso. "Yes, sir, that's all I'm worth to white folks 'round here—a chicken bone."

This, of course, was fiction. Sam had started giving Willard a two-bit bonus every week, knowing that Willard would pass it on to Temple, who, additionally, consumed dinner leftovers like a hound. It was often the case that Willard took Temple out in the Bay, where they caught a mess of snapper or sheepshead or grouper or mackerel, depending on the season and sold the catch to old Jones, who would also part with a little ice for them. If the doctor wanted some fried fish, he'd tell Temple to bring him a mess for Gomey to fry up and Temple would always say, "Doc, now where is I gonna get you some fish? I don't own no boat! I sees what I can do, I just don't know," and magically, Sam would be eating fresh fish that evening.

Temple moved toward the steps, sucking loudly on his chicken bone, and stepped down to the front walk leading to the Bayou. As he was nearly to the end of the limestone and brick walk, he took time to remove his chicken bone and yelled, "Don't forget to tell Linny to save them chicken backs for me! I be talking at you, Doc!" The young black man swayed when he stepped as if following the rhythm of an immemorial tune that rose up from the narrow beach in front of him. As Sam followed the boy's progress, the shimmering water seemed to absorb him to albescence, and only when Temple turned toward the dock that stretched out to his left did his form partially return to the doctor's vision, his ears resembling handles of an ampulla pulled up from the sunlight's silver brilliance spread across the water. How old is that boy? wondered Sam.

"Okay, then, Doc." Gomey's voice came through the screen door, signaling that dinner was ready to be served.

Sam rose, folded his paper, and tucking it under his arm, strode through the screen door, its black spring bringing it nearly shut behind him, causing him to stop, reach back to pull the handle, and bring the door within its frame. He made his way to the dining room and when seated, pulled out his newspaper and resumed his reading.

Hulda had already taken her place at the table. "Papa, I heard you and Mama talking about Zionism, again. She won't let me talk to Rabbi Fischer about it. I know Uncle Ephraim talks to him about it."

"Listen, child, you'll have plenty of time to worry about where Jews are going to try to keep from being bothered. *I* think they should *all* just come right here on the Hill. I need the business," said Sam.

"Papa, you're just like Mama says, *impossible!*" The raven-haired girl stomped her feet and added a pouty twist to her mouth.

She was growing fast, Sam thought. In another year, he'd have her in a nurse's uniform.

"Why, Uncle Ephraim was telling me about all the Jews trying to escape the Pale. I bet you don't even know where the Pale is, Papa."

"Oh, yes, ma'am, I know where the Pale is. Your uncle reminds me quite often of the unfortunate events visited upon our Eastern European brethren. In fact, I'm ready to buy him a ticket to somewhere where folks will listen to him spout off *all* about it."

Presently, Anna Jane came in and took her seat at the end of the dining table opposite Sam. "Sam! Put the newspaper up! I don't know why you read that snobby old rag. It's only good for wrapping fish. Those Mobile, Alabama 'aristocrats' have nothing but Confederate memorials, fancy balls, and Yankee money on their minds!" said the girl from Mobile. "Why, if this town had a decent newspaper, I'd insist on you subscribing, but it's worthless, too." Anna Jane frowned, but she winked at Hulda while Sam was placing the paper on the edge of the credenza.

"Miss, is you ready?" asked Gomey.

"The Yoffey family is ready for dinner, Gomey."

Linny, tall and graceful, came into the room with a platter of fried chicken, followed shortly by Gomey with bowls of pole beans and mashed potatoes. Linny's next trip brought gravy, turnip greens, and a side plate of chicken gizzards, favored by the doctor.

Anna Jane sniffed. "Samuel, Rabbi says we aren't supposed to consume the internal organs of animals."

"Well, my dear, you tell Rabbi, who if, I haven't mentioned it lately, is still in love with you after all these years, that he made me a *Reform* Jew, so I get to pick and choose my own personal rules. And yes, I know they're called mitzvoth, Miss Torah of 1903. What he needs to do is try one of Miss Gomey's fried gizzards. It would change his life. Hell, I'll have Temple take him a mess of them!"

"No you don't, you vulgar philistine!" said Anna Jane, falling into her most refined Mobile accent.

"At least I'm not a red-headed Yankee rabbi who wears a skullcap to hide a bald spot. I'll send him *mullet* gizzards instead. My South Carolina daddy loved mullet gizzards."

"I declare, Samuel, you are *impossible!*" said Anna Jane. "I suppose you're still trying to impress me with your shillyshally *South Carolina* ways. And, it's not a skullcap, it's a *kippah*, you apostate, you. I declare, here I am again, a lapsed Catholic having to teach *you* Jewish ways. Do I have to give you Torah lessons too, doctor?"

"No ma'am, I'm just trying to get you a little less corseted by rules and traditions. Come to think of it, I might just have to loosen that corset by hand, if you don't watch it, Missy."

"Samuel! There's an innocent child present!" said Anna Jane, prompting Linny to guffaw loudly as she stood by the door ready to serve. By the time Anna Jane looked over, Linny had disappeared into the kitchen, from where there was heard another laugh, this time from Gomey. "You're embarrassing me, Dr. Yoffey."

"Well, Sister James didn't mind a little foolishness once in a while, may I remind you Mrs. Yoffey?"

"Eat your dinner and hush, Sam. Anyway, Sister James was just an *innocent* Mobile girl when you started your carrying-on!" said Anna Jane.

Thus went Sunday dinner at the Yoffey residence. After a dessert of dewberry pie was served, Hulda spoke up with some news. "I've decided to start going to church with Mammow. I'll be spending the next month in Mobile."

"And I suppose you want me to inform Rabbi of this?" asked Anna Jane. "And just what do you think Rabbi is going to think of his best Hebrew student going to attend Catholic services, young Miss? I declare, the poor man will just despair."

"Hell, darling, she doesn't even go to temple on Friday nights unless you drag her with you to visit that lovelorn Jew while he entertains the rest of his women admirers. Let her get a taste of those papist wafers. It won't hurt her. I know it'll make your Mama and Daddy proud to have her. She's about got that Mobile accent down pat, thanks to you. Might as well use it. By the way child, when you see Uncle Hubbard, tell him I'm running low on that chewing tobacco he makes. What does he call it? 'Silts from the Fountain of Youth.' I'll give you a plug to try darling, and if you don't like it, you can give the rest to Miss Gomey. She'll be your best friend for life after that."

"Lord have mercy, a Jew with a mouthful of chewing tobacco! Mother Simon tried to warn me, but I sort felt sorry for you, Dr. Yoffey, and out of the kindness of my heart, I traded my habit for a housewife's clothes. At least I gained this precious child," said Anna Jane. "I broke that poor old nun's heart when I told her I was leaving the order, but at least it didn't last long, since after telling her about you, sir, she just got plain angry. You, Doctor Yoffey, can leave my dear, sweet Hubbard, out of your nonsense. I do wish he'd quit that tobacco chewing, though. He goes down to Papa's mill in the morning wearing a fresh white shirt and by lunchtime, the front of that white shirt has turned brown from tobacco juice. He never could spit like my Daddy, poor soul."

"Yes, ma'am, looks just like a *dago*, I declare, poor boy!" said Sam. "Now, getting back to your religious curiosities, Hulda. If you want to attend Catholic services, which will be fine with me, you go and attend Catholic services. You can convert, if you wish, and you won't hear a peep out of me," said Sam. "Just stay away from those Baptist lunatics, like the ones who go to hear Rabbi Fischer every Saturday morning to get the Old Testament rubbed real good in their faces. Rabbi does know how to wring the money out those poor chumps. I do have to give him that, though. You know, I went downtown one Saturday morning to get some chewing, I mean, some iodine, and I'll be doggone if every shop was closed. I asked a colored boy toting a cane pole down to the waterfront by himself if a hurricane was coming. He said, 'Not that I know of, mister sir.' So I asked why the shops were closed, and darned if he didn't tell me, 'It's because Mr. Rabbi was preaching at the white First Baptist, and all the shopkeepers had agreed to close, because there wouldn't be any trade with everybody going to listen at Rabbi!' *God have mercy on those folks!* I could have sworn that the only noise down there was the spilling coins into the offering bowl or whatever they call it."

Anna Jane rolled her lovely eyes and said, "Now child, you listen to your Mama real good. Religion is serious business. Your father is nothing but a heathen with a devoted Jewish little brother, born to a loving Jewish family. He's got about as much business instructing you on holy matters as Temple Luke. Do you understand me, young lady? And to your comment, Samuel, why, I believe it's wonderful that Rabbi can appeal to our brother and sister Christians."

"Yes, ma'am, but I love my Papa, even if he has some heathen ways about him."

"If that isn't the purest Mobile accent I've ever heard, darling, I'll be hanged!" said Sam. "Thank you, child, I love you, too. Why don't you take Sister James' Rabbi admirer with you to Mobile and see if old Mammow can wring some of that Yankee-ness out of him? You know, I walked into my own office one day last week and there he was, *feet on my desk,* sipping on half a glass of my best bourbon. I said, 'Mike, next time I see you and that thing on your head, you better have me a bottle of good whiskey.' And *now listen to me,* he said, 'I'm just a *poor* Jewish Rabbi, living for the Torah. How do you think I could justify buying a bottle of this expensive bourbon, Sam?' I said, 'Hell, Mike, with what those poor deluded Baptists pay you on Saturdays, that should *not* be a problem!' And he said, 'Sam, those folks are poor like

me and just want to hear the Word.' To which I replied, 'If they want
to hear the *Word*, you carpetbagger, they need to go out to Gomey
and Temple's neighborhood when *their folks* push up a revival tent
and then they'll hear *The Word*, Rabbi, let me assure you!'"

Hulda said, "Now Papa, you know if you aren't more kind to
Rabbi and you and Uncle Hub get into trouble again, Mama's going
to pronounce another inquisition on you both and have you signed
up for Red Cross Relief, like the last time, when she had you and
Uncle Hub sent to Galveston after the hurricane."

Sam went quiet and Sunday dinner finally concluded. Anna Jane,
and then Hulda, stood up and waited for the husband and father who,
as usual, was still nibbling a gizzard. Startled, he stood up as soon
as he noticed his lovely wife and daughter with their arms crossed,
striking impatient poses, and looking down at him. He nearly tipped
his chair over, but caught it with one hand behind him, a reflex he'd
refined elegantly over the years. Sam sneaked a last sip of iced tea
and grabbed the last gizzard from the side plate as he slipped out of
the room. Anna Jane and Hulda sat back down, and Gomey brought
out the pie again.

"Miss Gomey, Papa says I better watch my eating, or I'm going
to get as plump as those Yankee girls moving in across the Bayou. I
better not have another piece of pie."

"Now child, everybody knows that at your age, nourishment only
goes to the bones! You better get them bones strong. Now, come on
here." Gomey placed a slice of pie in front of the girl.

Hulda looked at her mother, and Anna Jane said, "Child, your
father knows about as much about the young female physiology as
your Uncle Hubbard. Now eat your pie, and don't pay any attention
to Papa."

"Yes 'sum."

When Gomey returned to the kitchen, she looked at Linny and
said, "Mercy me. That's white folks."

18

Graf Siegfried von Petersruhe, walking with his much-used ash cane his father-in-law Bernd had given him some years ago, approached his nephew with swollen pride and affection. The boy rose from his cold iron chair to meet his *Onkel* at one of Berlin's leafy, outdoor cafes and celebrate the top school marks he had earned at the Prussian Staff College. Old *Onkel* Sigi looked down the way at *74 Unter den Linden* and recalled his time there and the other provincial staff courses in his home state of Baden and hoped that David would have as much success as he had enjoyed himself as a cadet and officer. Though he had participated in numerous battles behind his Grand Duke, Sigi had never suffered serious injury, and this day, he felt, seemed the fulfillment of his long-ago chosen path. That much had changed politically, including the incorporation of his beloved Baden into a greater Germany, made the former General more comfortable with David's desire to enter the Prussian school rather than academies closer to Sigi's home.

Sigi's hands grasped the top of his ever-present cane, and with his head leaned slightly down and his eyes focused, he seemed to be contemplating the physics of the cracked and crumbled sidewalk's coating of ice. David stepped carefully along the frosted walk, and he wondered why his *Tante* Kathe had not accompanied his dear *Onkel,* but, in reality, he was not surprised by her absence. *Tante* Kathe, she appears like a sudden breeze but rests always in his heart, the young man thought.

Sigi knew that David would have been expecting his aunt, and as he shook gloved hands with his nephew said, "*Tante* Kathe sends her warmest greetings and apologizes for not being able to see you today. Frankly, my boy, since our short visit after your return from

England, she has been too upset to see her dearest David growing up—and now entering the Staff College. The Prussian military has had no place in her heart, and while she prays for your success, she wants to calm herself before seeing you in Lübeck."

"I believe that I know how she feels, *Onkel*, and while I certainly miss her, I can understand that it is best to visit when the Christmas season raises her sentiments and she is with *Oma* and *Opa*. I hope she will have become more accepting of the idea of my army career—an ambition of mine she has dreaded, I am afraid, since I was twelve years old and before my visit to England. I find that I am comfortable with this life, *Onkle*, as perhaps you were yourself. It is so wonderful to see you, sir."

Even before your visit to England; those words meant *before your parents died*, Sigi thought. "David," he said, "I have come to congratulate you, of course, to accompany you to Lübeck, and also, unfortunately, to advise you of your grandfather's ill health. Your *Opa* has been losing some strength over these last few months. But you must carry on, and leave his care to the rest of the family. Captain Twinge has made a visit, and *Herr* Schlarp, who isn't so old considering my age, helps with *Opa's* practice, now that all is settled between Sachenzucker and your *Onkle* Heinrich. Your *Opa* is enormously proud of you and has placed your inheritance in a legal trust so that you may begin deriving income from it at age twenty-one."

"Thank you, *Onkle*, I have worried that my time in England and the loss of my parents most profoundly upset *Opa* and *Oma*. *Opa* repeatedly assured me that he felt that I should see the broader world, especially with Captain Twinge guiding me, and that our family would benefit in the future. I had quite a visit, I must admit!"

"David, the time has come for certain facts to be shared with you. During this Christmas break, you, your grandfather, and I must have an extended conversation regarding your inheritance—and not just matters financial, my boy. There are things you must know and things about which you must make decisions." A taxi pulled alongside the curb and the old man asked the young man, "Shall we go?"

The two took the train to Hamburg and changed to Lübeck, arriving in time to join the family for dinner. David was quickly surrounded by his grandmother, *Tante* Kathe, and female servants, while his grandfather Bernd, *Herr* Schlarp, and *Onkle* Sigi stood at the entrance of the smoking room. They had lit their pipes, and after a few moments the women began greeting Sigi and Schlarp with great affection also.

David went to his room, discarded his greatcoat, and changed into more comfortable shoes while keeping on his cadet uniform. As he returned to the observatory where everyone had gathered, he was struck at the toll time had taken on his beloved family members. He ached for his parents, who would certainly have been present, and imagined them standing amongst the group, pulling him into their embrace, and passing him from relative to relative.

Elisabeth announced that dinner was to be served in one hour and herded everyone into the parlor. As he passed the kitchen's serving room, David noticed *Opa* had kept his word and a magnificent roast of venison was laid among the various other choices of beef and fowl. David told stories of his academy days incessantly, and after dinner, Bernd asked him to join him, his *Onkle,* and *Herr* Schlarp in the smoking room.

As the men sat down and began to relax, commenting on the recent snow, the behavior of Britain's government, the *Kaiser,* and other topics, David felt that the meeting Sigi had mentioned to him was about to begin. Bernd, ashen-faced, had sat down, looked at his pocket watch to ensure that enough time could be allowed, then nodded to *Herr* Schlarp to begin.

"David, we have brought you here to advise you of several important facts concerning your family and your heritage, things that have never been revealed to you. I will try to simplify where possible. First, I want you to know *my* story. I am *Freiherr* Dietrich Matthäus von Schlarpheim, your grandfather's older, half-brother. I was born into a noble family, but since the revolutionary actions of 1848, our family had been out of favor with the former Prussian crown. Matthäus is my family name, the name of my father, and your grandfather's father, and I have been proud to share it with your grandfather, although throughout most of his life, I had been at times exiled, working in the service of the Russian Imperial family. The Matthäus family has thrived in Lübeck for centuries, but at the time of the French occupation, my father, your great-grandfather, led resistance to Napoleon and was ennobled by Frederick William III of Prussia. Your great-grandfather, afterwards, settled in an estate granted him in East Prussia where I was born in 1847. I never really knew my mother; she died before I was two years old. In time, my father remarried.

"The Matthäus house had been retained here, and shortly before your *Opa's* birth, our father moved back to Lübeck. After 1848, he quietly gave up the East Prussian lands to appease the *Kaiser,* who had been displeased with our father's liberal political views. It is true that your grandfather and I attended Cambridge University together along with Lord Boardcroft, but I was unable to attend—due to military service—until they were old enough to attend. We were allowed to keep our title, but my father pushed me into the Russian service until Wilhelm I died. I felt enormous respect for our father's views, ceased using the title, and adopted the simple name Schlarp after settling back here in Lübeck.

"After your father, may he rest in peace, established his business here, it was decided that I would act as managing director of his company. I am simplifying, but the relationship between your grandfather Matthäus and your father was more involved than just legal and familial, as I will explain. Your grandfather Rosenberg warned your grandfather Matthäus that certain matters of your inheritance were expected to cause deep and sustained trouble within his family, if unmanaged. Your grandfather Rosenberg was a very wise man, as you will see. Did you know that your grandmother Rosenberg was not born Jewish? Nor your great-grandmother, nor your great-great-grandmother, and beyond?"

"I had no idea *Herr* Schlarp. Why? My grandmother seemed resentful that my father had married a gentile."

"These claims were made by your grandfather, and we can only trust that they are truthful. We have no way of knowing, of course, and simply feel that proceeding with this in mind, at least, preserves the chronicle of your family as he wished it to be known. David, here is a very interesting, if fantastical, history that again we take on faith that your grandfather Rosenberg was completely sincere when he related it to me and your *Opa.*

"During the time preceding the Thirty Years War, the Elector Palatine, Frederick V, was Protestant and married to the daughter of England's King James I. After Frederick V was crowned King of Bohemia, conflict began, and to simplify the story, many families were slaughtered because they were either Catholic or Protestant. At the time, your family was Protestant and—*Opa* Rosenberg claimed—lived as Rožmberks, whose center was an estate and *Schloss* of the same name. The name translates in German as Rosenberg, and faced with the horrors of a religious war, the family patriarch, being a practical and clever man, gave his son to a Jewish family to be raised as a Jew, to avoid the bloody conflict between Catholics and Protestants.

"Jews would likely continue to be persecuted through the years, he knew, but at least, for his time, he believed that his actions might preserve future generations of his bloodline. The Jewish family was given a large amount of money and contracted to retain it for the care of the adopted child. The child grew up with the surname "Rosenberg," was made aware of his origins after he became of age, and the original contract and other papers were given to him to pass down to the next generation. The documents were kept sealed in a brass tube, the one I now show you, to be presented to the worthiest son of the next generation. Unfortunately, the documents do not reveal *which* Rožmberk initiated them, and we have no way of tracing your true ancestors. Your grandfather here, gave this cylinder to me for safe keeping until the conflict between your uncle Heinrich and your father could be resolved, after your grandfather Rosenberg's death.

"*Your* father, the younger brother, had been selected as most worthy to receive the documents. His marriage to your dear mother, a gentile, was very convenient and avoided your grandfather

Rosenberg having to reveal the contents of the vessel to the brothers to persuade them to marry a Protestant and have her convert and live as a Jew. During his visit to Lübeck, your grandfather Rosenberg came to me and your grandfather Matthäus and explained that he must entrust us to carry out his family's wishes, as he had recently learned that he had contracted a terminal disease and wanted to settle matters as best he could before his impending death. He asked us to give and explain the documents to your father, our dear lost Jürgen, may his soul rest. Since Jürgen had converted, unknowingly, *back* to the Protestant faith, we felt that we could wait until you became of age and present the documents to you both. Then we could bring a complete resolution to this matter for all time, saving your father the trouble of telling you, his only son, this convoluted and fanciful story. But your father, sadly for us all, died unexpectedly. We therefore kept the documents for you, until we felt you were old enough to understand and appreciate their significance."

David had gotten to his feet and moved around while listening to Schlarp. He felt Sigi grab his arm, implying support, and looked at his grandfather for confirmation. Bernd nodded his head and put forth both hands toward Schlarp, who continued with the narrative. "So I have no Jewish blood? And my real name is Rožmberk?"

"The days of the Thirty Years War are gone forever, and we have no way of tracing your real ancestors, even if all of this is true, my son. It seems that you may choose whatever name you wish, and that being the case, your uncle Sigi has something to ask you," replied Bernd.

Sigi said, "David, as you know, I have no children. Your aunt and I, for many reasons including our love for you, ask you to allow us to adopt and give you our name. I have spoken to the Grand Duke, who has the blessing of the *Kaiser* to give you my name and the right to inherit my titles, if you will have them."

At this point, David sat, looking from one man to the other, trying to formulate questions. His life, he realized, was probably made possible by the actions of the Rožmberk patriarch. That his father, Jürgen Rosenberg, would have been given this information made the minutes listening to *Herr* Schlarp almost sacred, and the family's almost complete disregard of religion in his daily life, his mother's family's love and acceptance of his father as a presumed Jew, reconciled much for the young cadet.

David looked at his elders and asked if he might be allowed to take a walk. After they nodded their assent, the young man went out into the lighted street and began walking toward the old *Katharineum*, where he had spent that happy afternoon with *Tante* Kathe. It was beginning to snow, and he realized that he had forgotten his greatcoat as the wind brought the cold air to his skin. This would be a short walk. The area darkened, and his rosebushes were now barren entanglements of thorns, he noticed. He asked himself how he could begin life with a new name. He would still be called David, but could he be certain that what he'd heard was not just some fantasy dreamed up by an old Jew who had created this wild story to, perhaps, save himself from an act of prejudice? He looked ahead at the *Marienkirche* and decided that he would trust the men who had spoken to him and go forth, somewhat conflicted, and accept a new identity. Would he ever discover the history of his father's family? Or should he ignore it, and *get on with it*, as the English like to say?

When he returned, he found the elders waiting patiently, smoking, lighting, or digging in leather pouches for pipe tobacco. The room was moderately clouded, even with a window slightly ajar pulling out most of the smoke. Each man had, by this time, consumed varying amounts of Captain Twinge's annual gift of scotch whiskey and seemed a little happier. "*Onkle* Sigi, if my dear *Opa* and great-uncle Dieter agree, I would be honored to share your name and become your son."

"Have you considered a name, David?" asked Sigi.

"David Samuel von Petersruhe-Rožmberk."

At that, old Sigi rose and embraced David, turned, and said, "*Herren,* please join me in a toast to my son, your grandson and nephew. To David Samuel von Petersruhe-Rožmberk, may he follow his conscience and honor both of our families as one!"

"So, *Herr* Schlarp, you are my great uncle!" said David with delight.

"Now that, my new young nobleman, is almost as complicated a story as your heritage!" said Schlarp. "Shall I go into the Huguenot blood, Bernd?"

"Oh, spare us, *bitte*, brother! *Der Junge*, would run away!"

The women approached and were informed that all had been settled. *Tante* Kathe looked up at her new son and said, "You will spend part of your leave from the *Kriegsschule* with me and *Onkle* Sigi in Baden, I trust?" asked Kathe.

David looked at his dearest aunt and said, "Of course, *Tante* Kathe; I am most anxious to spend time in my new home!"

The holiday feast was considerably enlivened by the evening's events and plans were made for David to examine the documents with Bernd the next day. Schlarp and Sigi offered several more toasts and, soon both men were livelier than David had ever seen them. After dinner, the men returned to the smoking room, where the elders promptly fell asleep in their chairs.

David wandered back into the dining room and visited Lotte and Brigitte in the kitchen. *Fraulein* Loew had been a new guest—a gesture insisted upon by Elisabeth—and helped the servants, though she had no obligation to do so. David had scarcely known her and found himself gazing at the pretty face and magnificent figure she presented. She was two years older than David, but still unmarried, much to the surprise of everyone who knew her. At length, she walked out of the kitchen with David and they were called over to the parlor by Kathe and Elisabeth.

"My dear *Fraulein* Loew, I hope that you have enjoyed our gathering this evening," said Elisabeth. "You have been a wonderful secretary and our appreciation knows no bounds, *Liebes Madchen*. I am glad that you were here to share in our joy that David is back amongst us, at least for a few days, and hear the news of his adoption."

"Thank you, *Frau* Matthäus-Kahn, I am most flattered that you chose to invite me to share this wonderful evening with your family. *Herr* Matthäus has been most kind to me over the last year, and I am delighted to finally meet your dear grandson properly. I wonder if I may be so bold? May I ask *Herr* Petersruhe-Rožmberk to escort me home tonight?"

"Of course, *Fraulein*, but you cannot keep him!" Elisabeth laughed.

"Thank you, *Frau* Matthäus-Kahn. Now I must ask *Herr* Petersruhe-Rožmberk if he would be so kind as to escort me?"

"Of course, *Fraulein*, I should be honored. When you are ready, I will accompany you. Do you live nearby?"

"Yes, just a short walk off *Fleischauerstrasse*. Shall we go?"

Fraulein Loew rose and thanked the ladies again, and David retrieved their coats. They stepped into the cold air, thankfully into only a slight wind, and walked the *gange* just beyond the Matthäus house, crossed *Fleischauerstrasse* and down another short alley to a small brick cottage. *Fraulein* Loew's beautiful profile held David's attention as she unlocked her door and stepped into the small front room.

"Come in, please, *Herr* Petersruhe-Rožmberk, while I light the fire," she said.

David followed the girl into the cottage, and as she lit several candles, David bent to the wood stacked next to the fireplace and sorted through the kindling and logs. He prepared a fire for the young woman and stepped away, rubbing his gloved hands together.

"Please call me Annaliese, *Mein Herr*."

"Then you must call me, David, *Fraulein*."

"Will you join me in a glass of scotch?"

"Where did you get scotch, Annaliese?" asked David.

"Captain Twinge gave me a bottle on his last visit. He insisted that I give him a thank you kiss, however."

David laughed. "I can imagine that!"

The two removed their coats and sat down on a small divan and Annaliese poured their scotch into small glasses. She held hers up and said, "To my new friend, David."

They drank and laughed as their eyes met. Annaliese stood and removed her coat, revealing the figure so captivating to David. "Now,

David, you must give me a kiss for giving you a glass of scotch."

David put his subtly trembling hands on Annaliese's shoulders and presented her with a light peck on the cheek.

Annaliese looked at him, and feigning disappointment, put her hands up through his hair, knocking his cap to the floor. She pulled him into an embrace, pausing to look into his eyes for a long moment, then closed her own eyes and put her mouth onto his and kissed him long and passionately. She pulled his hands onto her full breasts and could feel his hands trembling as well as his erection pushing against her as she forced her body against his. Finally, she said, "Thank you for escorting me home, David." She moved away to stoke the fire.

David had never experienced such sensuality. He knelt next to her and said, "I shall dream of you."

Annaliese rose and held David's his coat, lifting it onto him, and handed him his hat. David said, "I must kiss you for helping me with my coat."

"You, young sir, must be on your way!" She guided the blushing young man through the door and watched him walk away. She met his gaze as he looked back but pushed the door closed.

When David returned, the men were moving about looking for dessert, and the ladies were preparing coffee and setting the table. Elisabeth had allowed Lotte and Brigitte to retire early and sang softly to herself as she went about her work. Everyone soon settled back into their places and resumed their earlier conversations except Kathe, who asked David if *Fraulein* Loew had been seen safely home.

"Of course, *Tante*." David looked somewhat sheepish.

"I don't think she will be safe for much longer," said Elisabeth with a hearty laugh. She looked at David and shook her finger at him. "You'll be getting dangerous soon, my dear boy!"

Everyone laughed, and his *Tante* Kathe said, "I finally have a son. I do not believe that I need a daughter-in-law for some time to come!"

David responded, "I don't have time for a wife, my dear *Tante!*"

19

Kathe and Sigi left for *Vogelgesangstein* two days later. The absence of Sigi's blend of tobacco and Kathe's cheerful banter left David quite deserted in a house so familiar to him. He spent time with his grandparents discussing the last few years of his life, especially his time in England and the new information and legal arrangement of his very identity.

After David's return to Lübeck with Captain Twinge, whom he had, in spite of Twinge's wishes, begun to refer to as "My Lord," the boy felt somewhat abandoned by the joy he had experienced in England with his dear friend Tom. Back at home, he began to feel the absence of his parents deepening his sense of isolation and inciting a deep and profound melancholia as the days wore on. He often walked by his old residence, putting a hand to the outer wall or sitting on the doorstep, and daydreamed his way through a life filled with his father's affection, his mother's laughter, and all that attracted him to what he had believed to be his heritage. Though his grandmother seemed as vital as ever and the visit of his *Tante* Kathe and *Onkle* Sigi had instilled interesting and stirring memories to be relished in the years to come, David's thoughts began to move away from his life in Lübeck and settle onto an inert shore of indifference.

His experience in England had been most fulfilling and confusing. The incredible audacity of Captain Twinge's behavior and words had been a different experience for a North German, and Hughie's almost flagrant disregard for public morals, surely unacceptable in any culture David could think of, had left the boy puzzled about the relative nature of human behavior. Roxburgh was baffling in much the same way. Is morality *evolving* or *dissolving*?

His *Tante* Kathe had spoken to him about the constraints of morality and custom, like the circumstances of his own heritage, is human-formed and institutionalized and varies from individual to individual and culture to culture. She encouraged David to look at the periphery of his experience, consider his reactions to human behavior, and perhaps permit the conventions he had grown up with to allow his mind to formulate *thoughts*. Why, for instance, did his Rožmberk patriarch ignore the great conflict of his time and seek to preserve his own bloodline? She asked him, "Is something one understands to be *good* really valuable to mankind, or is it just a concept accepted as such by a majority of a particular culture? Does everything have to be *good* in a religious or cultural sense to be an acceptable part of human behavior or thinking?"

There was no escaping his sadness, however. It settled into his being quietly, and it seemed to him it was not all together due to his reaction to events in his life. He began to look for ways to ameliorate his melancholy and found that trifling with the girls he met at church or during his wanderings along the seafront shops and among the poorer families living within the *ganges* entertained him. He began to spend time with Annaliese in his grandfather's office, and delighted in her teasing, flirtatious treatment of him. In the late afternoon, after studies insisted upon by Bernd, he sought out the sight and company of girls and felt an incomparable fascination with their manner of dress, their shapes, and their *difference*. He never spoke about these things with his household, so dominated by women, and he felt that speaking to his grandfather would betray something ignoble or even shameful in the old man's mind. He delighted in girls, but did not share his fascination in their bodies with his family.

The old books Kathe had given him, *insisting* that he read them, no longer embarrassed him in their plunge into the most elemental aspects of human behavior, as the colorful and heroic, the vain and jealous, exercised their destinies, and in the end, seemed to wander about, pushed along by nothing human. Such was his awakening that remembering the lot of *Odysseus* with *Calypso*, read from the battered copy of the *Odyssey* Kathe had foisted upon him, combined with his recollection of Twinge's rendition of their story, provoked a stirring in his loins, usually resulting in an awkward, but thrilling, tumescence.

David was due to resume his training at the Staff College soon and remembering his success there delighted him. But this kind of pursuit had made little impression on his friends, who like most Lübeckers, hated the Prussians.

After reviewing his progress there, his grandfather said, "I always knew that you wanted to be a soldier. You must look to your *Onkle* Sigi for guidance, my son."

David was pleased when Bernd referred to him as "my son." but that it came from Bernd, and not his own father, delivered a very familiar and sharp sense of loss to the boy. David left for Berlin soon after the New Year and settled back into life as a *Kadett*.

As the winter wore on, David received word from Brigitte that Bernd had begun to experience trouble breathing. Further, Bernd was tired at bedtime, in the morning, and throughout the day. He could barely walk to his office only a half-block away. Although David was not made aware of this, *Fraulein* Loew often found him sitting on the step in front of his office, his head flung back and coat bundled tightly around him. She would help him inside, where he would seek the nearest chair and sit for, perhaps, ten minutes. His coat still on, he would find his way to his office chair, where he would lie his head down upon his crossed hands and rest on the hard desk for half an hour or so, seeming to recover.

Work was grueling for him and *Fraulein* Loew would have to read his correspondence aloud and transcribe them and all his dictated, labored, responses, which had not been Bernd's method. To the eternal frustration of *Fraulein* Loew, a steady stream of friends began to arrive each day, interrupting, the flow of work she had managed to establish for the aging lawyer. Though Bernd was only fifty-six, his life had slowed to nearly stasis, and his friends and colleagues had recognized that his vitality seemed to be slipping away. It was not unusual, however, for a visitor to enliven his attention by mentioning a sighting of David in Berlin. Bernd knew that his grandson was slipping into the throes of late adolescence and that the boy would now be scarce, perhaps even during holidays. To know that his grandson was actually building a career was cheering, but his exuberance, sadly, would not last, and Bernd would sink back into what had become, it appeared to all who knew him, an inexorable decline. When at home, he was often found seemingly winded and asleep, sitting on a plain armchair in his parlor, his chin lowered onto his chest.

One particularly cold and snowy day, *Fraulein* Loew found her employer sitting on the gray stone walkway before he had reached his office and struggling for breath. She managed to help Bernd reach the inside of the building and ran to his house to summon Elisabeth. Elisabeth immediately sent Brigitte to fetch *Doktor* Kaufmann, the family's physician. With *Fraulein* Loew, she was able to get Bernd onto the old divan and bring another chair to stretch his body out. As Bernd lay down, he immediately began to cough and had to be helped into a sitting position, a posture he had been assuming as he went to bed for nearly a year. The coughing was unremitting, terrifying for the women to watch.

When the *Doktor* arrived, he sent the ladies out of the room and administered a small dosage of cocaine, which after a few minutes had a favorable effect on his cough. The *Doktor* had known for some time that Bernd was suffering, and he had asked Bernd if he would allow him to attend him. Bernd's reply was simply, "It may come to that." Kaufmann administered digitalis, inserted Southey Tubes for drainage and within an hour, Bernd was feeling well enough to allow the ladies to help him walk the short distance home. When Elisabeth looked at the physician, he shook his head, and pulling her aside, told her that Bernd had a very short time to live.

After arriving home, Bernd went straight to his bed, where pillows where arranged for him to sit up. He began to cough again but soon settled down. He told Elisabeth that he was sorry that he had to bother her after managing this way for nearly a year. His wife began to cry, knowing that she had heard his coughing in the adjoining bedroom during the night and dismissed it as nothing unusual. She had known that his tailor had been visiting his office, but ignored the dramatic weight loss that was apparent to everyone but, it seemed, herself. She had known that her husband had been slowing down and had ignored his torpor as a symptom of his work habits. She hadn't realized that her companion had been sick until his life seemingly *stopped*. She knew that she had no choice but to begin to try to cope with losing him.

David was sent for and arrived the next evening. As he walked up from the train station, his uniform invited much attention on the short foray along the waterfront. When he arrived, he was shocked to see so much activity around his grandparents' house. Elisabeth told him that his *Opa* was ill and that he would need to stay home, perhaps for a few days. David was terrified that his grandfather could be *that* sick. He went to his room and allowed his emotions to erupt into tears.

Bernd asked Elisabeth to summon Schlarp and to send a telegram to Kathe and Sigi at once. Elisabeth held back her tears and had Lotte go to Schlarp's new home to summon him. Schlarp had moved from his old firm's offices to a room situated behind and above Bernd's office. This visit would not come as a shock to Schlarp, knowing as he had that Bernd had been sick for some time. Bernd struggled to get his body higher in the bed and cursed the effects of the cocaine that had been administered to suppress his cough. He could hear the slightest echo of his breathing at the end of each breath and realized that he had ignored it for so long, he had become used to it. The slight gurgle had become unnoticeable. He closed his eyes, but there was no resting, only the now familiar tussle to adjust and readjust his body to gain a few moments of clear breathing. He thought: How can I go on like this? There will never be another new client! He realized that he must focus on David, as his time was clearly growing short.

At length, Schlarp appeared and looked at his dear brother with knowing eyes. He said, "I've seen this same condition with soldiers enduring three-day chest wounds." He had brought the *Fama* and the sealed tube.

Bernd nodded and said, "It seems that my time may be limited, brother. I've asked Elisabeth to telegram Kathe and Sigi. You must inform Hugh."

"I have already telegrammed Hugh, and if Elisabeth will permit me, I will make accommodation arrangements for the *Graf* and *Gräfin* in the morning before they arrive."

Bernd struggled to speak in the long, expository sentences he was known for as a lawyer. "Give the copy of the *Fama* to the boy and explain that we three, at least, have used it as a way of observing Christianity, of trying to recall and preserve the few years of peace here." Bernd went quiet and tried to regain his breath. "All of those hundreds of years ago, and at least in our lives in our meager way, we did what we could to keep a hope for true social equilibrium in Europe. We have, my friend, only tried to keep the possibility of a new age alive in our own lives and actions, but knowing that we three have kept faith with our ideals has been enough for me." He paused again to cough and rest for a moment. "Now, we must impart it to the boy. He will find value in it or ignore it. With his entering the army, God knows, the Prussians will probably knock it out of him. We must rely on Sigi to remind him of the manipulation the military will impose upon his soul and pray that personal dignity will prevail when crisis comes to him."

Bernd stayed in his bed, becoming progressively weaker as days passed, the difference between mornings and evenings unnoticed by him. Kathe and Sigi appeared and spent time with Bernd discussing David, his heritage, and the contents of the brass tube. Solemn promises were made. David would be looked after. Kathe was inconsolable, often openly crying and found with her hands gripping the tops of chairs or leaning against open door jambs emitting tiny, faltering, moans of grief. But even in her misery, she tried desperately to bear up to the challenge of watching her father fade into death by helping her mother and spending time assisting David's preparation for the military.

Hugh sent the following letter to Bernd:

28 January 1903
Hugh Twinge, Earl Boardcroft
Boardcroft House
Ruskwick
Lincolnshire, England
Herr Doktor Bernhard Gerfried Matthäus
3 Hundesstrasse
Lübeck, Schleswig-Holstein

My Dearest Bernd:

I received Dieter's telegram of 14 January and his following letter of 23 January with profound dismay. I cannot express to you how deeply my old heart aches for your suffering. Dieter asked that I stand ready to honor our agreement regarding our grandsons (with the EXCEPTION OF HUGHIE!) and help guide them through this period of danger instigated by that one-armed, prancing bastard, William (no, I won't refer to him as Wilhelm) and our own lunatics who have given the Navy too much of a freehand to keep building ships. That blackguard, Winston Churchill, Lord Randolph's boy, of whom you may have heard, is edging his way into politics; I do so wish the Boers had managed to keep the little scribbler locked up.

I plan to travel to Lübeck during the first week of February to buck you up and deliver myself of my senseless wife and the trouble Hughie continually causes in the army. Please convey my warmest regards to your family, especially, Elisabeth.

I will see you soon, your friend

Hugh

Bernd was grateful to receive Hugh's letter, but he was barely able to read it, so exhausting was every attempt to move or concentrate his mind. He held the letter to his chest and would not allow anyone to take it from him. After a night of very persistent, vicious coughing, Bernd was completely exhausted and began slipping into a state of semi-consciousness. He seemed awake, but could only, with effort, be revived to take nourishment. His breathing became noticeably even more labored, and the little gurgle dominated his efforts to take breath. He was given morphine by *Doktor* Kaufmann and slept in peace with Hugh's letter resting on his chest under his hands. He found death before dawn.

The funeral of *Herr Doktor* Bernhard Gerfried Matthäus was held a week later in the largest of the chapels of *Marienkirche,* and the swarm of mourners flowed through slowly, most stopping to speak to one or more of the family. The casket was set upon a raised platform, with a plain white cotton sheet neatly placed over the top. *Herr* Schlarp acted as Elisabeth's escort and Kathe and Sigi sat behind them to save space, rising to greet and accept condolences when needed. Hugh Twinge stood with David and Tom by his sides and wept quietly throughout the ritual. At graveside, Schlarp said a few words of gratitude, recited a German prayer. and read from *Fama Fraternitatis Rosae Crucis,* which he referred to only as an ancient spiritual guide.

Wisdom (saith Solomon) is to a man an infinite Treasure,
for she is the
Breath of the Power of God,
and a pure Influence that floweth from the
Glory of the Almighty; she is the Brightness of Eternal Light,
and an undefiled
Mirror of the Majesty of God, and an Image of his Goodness;
she teacheth
us Soberness and Prudence,
Righteousness and Strength; she
understands the Subtlety of words,
and Solution of dark sentences; she foreknoweth
Signs and Wonders, and what shall happen in time to come;
with this Treasure was our first Father Adam fully endued...

Twinge offered a final reading from, of course, his dear Tennyson:

> *I held it truth, with him who sings*
> *To one clear harp in divers tones,*
> *That men may rise on stepping-stones*
> *Of the dead selves to higher things.*
> *But who shall forecast the years*
> *And find in a loss a gain to match?*
> *Or reach a hand through time to catch*
> *The far-off interest of tears?*

Hugh Twinge remained with the grieving family for another day before he took his leave quietly with Tom. Tom embraced his friend David, and both fought back tears as the crew of the *Orestes* made ready to sail. Hugh told David that the future was his to make, but that he should be mindful that the care taken to see him this far would be now mostly extended through his adopted parents. All felt that they would never see each other again.

20

"Rosenberg!" yelled *Kadett* Frederick Mueller, as the two rowed aimlessly during the late morning along the black surface of the *Kleiner Wannsee*, the narrow little lake south of Berlin. Fritz was a large, barrel-chested young man of extremely keen mind and festive demeanor. The two cadets had rented a small boat at the little lakeside concession and spent their day away from the *Kriegsschule*, oaring along the dark water and talking about all things and nothing.

"Ah, you've forgotten already, Fritz. The name is von Petersruhe-Rožmberk, my dear room elder." David smiled and spoke in *Hochdeutsch*, the accent he always used around the academy, one he'd always been required to use amongst his family. He dipped the oars deeply, groping for the muddy bottom, swinging them back and forth, turning the little boat round and round, and knocking their bottles of wine cooling in the lake water against the hull, which annoyed Fritz. As usual, he was in a hurry to get somewhere known only to himself.

Fritz asked, "Why didn't you join the *Kriegsmarine?*"

"I am, as it happens, a good waterman, Mueller, but I wish to study *Auftragstaktik*, as practiced by you, my great leader."

Fritz was unaffected by David's sarcasm, distracted as he was by observing a knot of attractive, and at least to Fritz's imagination, unmarried *Frauen* strolling along the paved path above the shore of the lake. David ignored his room elder, lifted the oars, and began to row with conviction across the lake.

Fritz roared, "*Rosenberg!* What the devil are you doing? Can't you see that I am following those parasols along the bank? Didn't you notice the *Mädchen?*"

The sirens kept Fritz's attention while David stopped rowing and settled back against a basket of food and a wooden crate half filled with beer, various breads, and cheeses. Forgetting his friend, he took a letter from Kathe he'd brought out of his pocket. It gave him news of Sigi and the estate and advised him to find Helene von Druskowitz's work, *Aspasia*. Kathe told him of the recent death of Malwida von Meysenbug, and though David had heard the *Freiherr's* name and associated others mentioned by his mother, grandmother and Kathe throughout his life, he had never formed the kind of interest in them that Kathe had hoped. His adopted mother, however, was determined to keep these and other women she valued mentioned in her correspondence and conversations with him. David occasionally read them with little real interest, but the inevitable associations with Friedrich Nietzsche had fascinated him, given his own interest in the philosopher's work, especially as some of his writings had reminded him of the ancients he enjoyed, where he saw little difference in their import. But he was first a soldier, and achieved success in the defense district examination, which launched him into the *Kriegsakademie*, the hardest challenge for an ambitious Prussian soldier.

"Rosenberg, shall we move a little closer to shore? Perhaps, set out our luncheon?" asked Fritz.

Just in the path of those girls, thought David. He pulled around and headed straight to a bit of shore in the route of the girls, and directed by Fritz, landed perfectly in the middle of the small beach. "All right, Fritz, lay your trap, but don't expect me to keep you from making a fool of yourself."

Fritz jumped out, pulled the boat well onto the beach, and set about smoothing a spot level to place his nest. The beach abutted a beautifully trimmed lip of grass extending from the edge of the paved walk which led to a two-story, stone, French-style house. The house had a thatch of vegetation stretched across beams held up by six fluted stone columns. A wooden gazebo, painted the color of the stone and wrapped in flowering vines, stood in the middle of the lawn. Atop the gray wooden shingles rose a pole supporting a streaming banner, its white and yellow colors twisting in the breeze.

The girls approached just as David was pulling out two tall bottles of beer and turning to sit upon the rough army blanket Fritz had unfolded onto the beach. He looked up to see Fritz positioned in such a manner on the walkway above that the ladies would be challenged to either speak to him, or follow a footpath that looped down to the shore where David had set up lunch. As he predicted, the girls came his way.

Fritz jumped down from the walk above, and in front of the women, introduced himself, bowing and clicking his heels on the sand.

The ladies drew up as one and assumed positions of offense and indignation. A rather petite young lady said, "Sir, I will have my father, an important man, speak to the academy commandant about this rudeness!" The two other girls were clearly suppressing smiles.

David was on his feet, instantly, saying, "I must beg your pardons ladies. My friend has perhaps overstated his admiration of you by his clearly unwelcome antics. Please forgive him, and allow me to assist you back to the path, above."

Another girl spoke in excruciating *Hochdeutsch* that they would consider his proposal and turned around, her shoulders quivering. The third young lady, smiling, walked up to Fritz, and nearly touching him, turned around to David and said, "I will forgive your friend if you would be willing to share some refreshment with us, *Kadett*."

David replied, "That is most generous of you, *Fraulein*. I hope that your friends will join you in this decision. Here is what I can offer you," He opened the crate again and stood back. The three girls looked into the crate and selected a champagne, touching it with the ends of their folded parasols.

David said, "I'm afraid that we only have two glasses, ladies, so I must ask you to share." As David looked to each girl for a reply, Fritz, who had slipped away unnoticed, came down the path carrying three outdoor chairs and smiling. Forgetting the presence of the girls, who had to turn away to vent their laughter, David said, "Good God, Fritz, where did you get those chairs?" He blushed and resigned himself to suffer whatever consequences to which his companion had now exposed them. He merely said, "Ladies, your sitting arrangements have arrived" and helped Fritz arrange the chairs in a somewhat broad semi-circle, allowing the *Kadett Lothario* more freedom of movement amongst the girls.

The young women sat, and David placed the two glasses in the hands of the first, and least friendly, of them. She gave the inelegant, army-issued tumblers to her companions, offering David a fearful stare. The champagne was dispensed between the glasses, and David stood back, holding the bottle at the ready should the ladies approve.

The third girl held out her glass and said, "Excellent, *Kadett.*" He poured her more.

The second girl gave the first girl her glass and David poured for her. The thought of being in the company of unchaperoned girls was absolutely frightful for David and as the minutes passed, he grew more and more uncomfortable. Fritz, however, began to chatter like an ape, without a care or a thought for decorum.

Then, two of the most terrifying words David had ever heard came from the third girl: "Hello, Papa."

David and Fritz froze—David in the process of offering more champagne and Fritz with his mouth open, about to say, "This beer is good!"

David's eyes slowly looked up, and as he pulled back the champagne bottle, he beheld a rather tall man standing on the path above him. The man had a dark bushy beard and wore business attire with a very bright gold chain across his vest, his coat held open by his hands at rest on his hips. The moment seemed to last for hours. Finally, the man pointed at David, and with a jerk of his head, commanded that the *Kadett* walk up the path from the little beach to him.

As the young man arrived, the man looked at David carefully and pulled on his beard for a few moments. He took his watch out and consulted the time. The man took the champagne from David, who had forgotten that he had it in hand, and read the label. Finally, crossing his arms, he said, "This is most irregular, young man."

"Yes, sir."

"I should consult your commandant on this matter," said the man, "but instead, I will require you to present yourself for dinner at my home tomorrow evening at 7:00 to explain yourself to me and my daughter's mother. Do not bring your friend. Here is my card." At that, the man looked down at the girls and motioned for them to join him on the path.

David said, "Yes, sir; I will be there."

The ladies walked up the path.

David bowed and clicked his heels, and as he started down the path, he saw that Fritz had already loaded the boat and was shoving off. Just as the boat began to move off the shore, David swung his body around and jumped backwards, disappearing into the bow and landing with legs flying up and elbows girding himself against the front seat. Fritz was rowing like a madman. "Thank you, room elder!" David yelled at Fritz. As he looked back to shore, the young ladies and the man were standing atop the small hill, all watching and laughing.

The next evening, he was, to his mild surprise, above the beach where he had found himself so embarrassed. The large house, somewhat of the school of *Railway Station Gothic*, was of a prevalent style dismissed by aristocrats. After the housekeeper, Angela, let him in, he found *Professor Extraordinarius* Johannes Meckler waiting just inside the door. His extended his hand welcomed David with surprising warmth. He pulled upon his flowing beard and his face was still youthful, his eyes, clear and blue. He said, "Welcome *Kadett*."

David bowed his head and clicked his heels. "My name is David von Petersruhe-Rožmberk, *Herr Professor Doktor*. Thank you for inviting me into your beautiful home. May I present to you and your family these roses and this bottle of Pinot Noir as a token of my gratitude?"

Meckler accepted the wine and asked his daughter, Ingrid, to step into the room to accept the roses. Again David bowed and clicked his heels, acknowledging the girl by saying, "*Fraulein*, it is good to see you, again."

Ingrid was finely-featured, of medium height with blond hair and a very thin waist. Her face was somewhat round, but beautifully proportioned, and her hair moved away from her forehead with a part along the left side and a massive swirl of locks pulled from left to right that concealed parts of each ear, which were hung with pearl earrings.

Next, *Frau* Meckler approached, an attractive woman of about forty, perhaps more ostentatious in dress and manner but still a diminished presence when standing next to her daughter. "Nothing for me?" she asked.

David bowed and clicked his heels again. "Only my humble hope that my presence will please, *Frau* Meckler."

Johannes Meckler led everyone into the sitting room, handing the wine off to his housekeeper and inviting David to sit. "Petersruhe-Rožmberk, a most unusual name, young man. May I ask of your origins?"

"My family lives in Baden; my father is *General der Kavallerie Graf* Sigismund von Petersruhe."

"You betray nothing of a native *Swabian*. This *Hochdeutsch* was not derived from your countrymen, I dare say," said Meckler. "Tell us, *Kadett*, how you've come to impart such sophistication in your speech."

"I am humbled by your comments, sir; I speak as my family speaks."

The housekeeper appeared and announced that dinner was served. She was a pleasant-looking woman of very dark hair and complexion, impeccably uniformed and smiling as though she knew something interesting was afoot. The professor led everyone into the dining room and assigned seating, putting David next to Ingrid and across from the parents.

As the service began, David decided to broach the subject of their first meeting. "Sir, I wish to repeat my apologies for not observing proper decorum regarding *Fraulein* Meckler and her friends yesterday. I trust that my friend, *Kadett* Mueller, returned the chairs to their proper place on your property."

"All is well, young man. I knew by observing you and the young ladies that your intentions were honorable and that, perhaps, you had been forced into an awkward position. Am I correct in this?"

"Yes, most assuredly, *Herr Professor Doktor*, but in hindsight, perhaps I should have been more aggressive in my objections to the situation as it was developing. I do hope that *Fraulein* Ingrid can be as understanding as you have been."

Ingrid, who had yet to utter a word, finally said, "You were most courteous, sir. I cannot say the same for your friend, unfortunately."

"May I ask what your area of study is, Professor Meckler?" asked David.

"I am a philosopher; I hold two classes at Berlin. My interest is in what is called *Positivism*. That all knowledge is derived from facts, which lead us to a reconciliation of our personalities to the environment in which we find ourselves. That facility which allows us to recognize facts is scientific in nature, and when a fact is observed, it is modified to meet our limitations of understanding, and perhaps experience, to preserve us as functioning beings."

"And from that, sir, you derive concepts? Are facts truth? Do facts dictate, for instance, morality or affirm or deny free will? To quote: 'What in us really wants truth?'" asked David.

"If we are not careful, young man, we shall be speaking past one another," said Meckler. "And why are you in military school?"

"I enjoy the academy life. The problems we are required to confront challenge us to seek solutions that distinguish us as individuals and allow us to serve the Fatherland."

"Glory-seeking?"

"Perhaps, sir. I just wish to pursue self-knowledge—finding one's limitations in a particular field of action while enjoying the camaraderie it offers."

Ingrid began to twist in her chair and *Frau* Meckler gave the professor a glance that suggested that the subject be changed. Silence ensued, and the four diners began to concentrate on their plates as the courses kept coming. The parents were the first to finish, and Ingrid and David felt themselves being observed and losing appetite. Finally, as the last plates were being taken away, the professor suggested that everyone repair to the library for coffee and dessert. The ladies stepped away from the table, followed by the men who clearly were beginning to like each other. As they settled into the room, Angela walked over to *Frau* Meckler and whispered in her ear.

Frau Meckler announced, "Please excuse me, but I must attend to something downstairs. Perhaps father could accompany me?"

David rose as the Meckler's stood, excused themselves again, and left the room.

Ingrid sat on a small settee with David and looked at her hands until her parents had disappeared. She then looked up into David's eyes and said, "My father is trying to marry me off; I am certain this is obvious to you, David."

David was taken aback by the girl's frankness and looked at her, not knowing what to say. He fidgeted and rubbed his hands together, looking up and trying to consider a response. "I am flattered, but do you believe your parents are *that* fond of me?" he asked.

"They are. At first my mother was livid that Papa had invited a total stranger to, as she put it, court me, but when she heard you speak, and of course your *name*, she was delighted. Father is probably a little put off by your ability to parry philosophically with him, but I believe he genuinely likes you. There is something truly mysterious about you, however, and I'm certain that mother will do everything to pull more information from you. I enjoyed our first meeting. Perhaps I was somewhat too forward, but I want to enjoy life, and since we were below my home, I knew that Angela was keeping an eye on me, duly reporting to Papa. I must say, your friend Fritz was insufferably presumptuous, but at least he did not try to take liberties."

"Truly, Ingrid, I do have a complicated life. I don't believe that my history would satisfy your parents, and I am not one to be dishonest with you," said David.

"At any rate, you must tell me! I'm not one to let convention interfere with knowing interesting people. Perhaps we could plan a luncheon without *Mutti* and Papa? Will you plan to come Saturday?"

"Why not? You will have nothing further to do with me after I tell you my tale, however!" replied David.

Frau and *Professor Doktor* Meckler soon returned, giving a short explanation for their absence. The parents smiled, and taking their

coffee and dessert, engaged the young people in conversation concerning the current affairs of their world: the university activities,
their social circle, and the latest of their travels. In short, they held
David as long as they could, gauging his every response against
their own frame of reference. Ingrid announced that she had invited
David for luncheon on Saturday and added that it was a pity that
her parents were planning an outing on the lakes. Could Angela stay
home to chaperone them?

David soon made his excuses and left the party, catching a scheduled cab on the street outside the house. He was glad to finally be
away from the challenges of *Professor Doktor* Meckler. The thought
of his engaging a professional philosopher seemed absurd, and he
chuckled to himself that he would have to describe to Kathe the
trouble her intellectual encouragement had almost gotten him into.
I know just enough to make a point, but not enough to defend it, he
thought. The night was pleasant, though, and he enjoyed the carriage
ride through the Berlin streets, settling into the comfortable leather
upholstery and falling asleep. He fell into a light dream.

His was drilling on the Meckler lawn and Annaliese was conducting the drill. She was dressed like a *Kadett*. A huge ship landed on the
beach below, and Tom stepped ashore, bringing Fritz by the scruff of
the collar to the exercise.

At last, the carriage arrived and jolted David fully awake. A fellow *Kadett* joined him in entering the vast dormitory but passed him
quickly, obviously hurried. As David stepped into his darkened room,
he saw Fritz standing naked and leaning against the windowsill. The
streetlight shined along the sides of the young man's bare, trembling
frame, and the sound of heavy breathing ending in a staccato of
moans caused David to take his hand away from the light switch and
crawl quickly into his bed. He would rise and undress later.

In the following days, Fritz was relentless in exercising his pru-
rient imagination, asking David if he had kissed the girl or caught
a glimpse of her legs. David just ignored his friend, whose curiosity could be encouraged by the slightest hint of "lovemaking" so
David teased him by describing Ingrid in detail, telling Fritz that

he wondered if her hair below matched her hair above. This drove Fritz wild with lust and David said, "I suppose you'll be wanking, tonight?"

Fritz replied, "What is this *wanking*, Rosenberg?"

"A word I heard a lot in England."

Saturday arrived, and David appeared at the appointed time for luncheon with Ingrid. He bowed and clicked his heels, and to Angela's despair, Ingrid only bowed her head without offering her hand. They walked through the house, appointed with African artifacts and a few modern paintings, and emerged under the columns. Ingrid's very blond hair was arranged differently—in an intricate loop of braids that flattered her long, slim neck and seemed to exaggerate her height. She led the way to a table and two chairs arranged in the gazebo and brought her hands under her to control the flowing dress that billowed out as she sat.

Angela hovered nearby and presently served them tumblers of lemonade, saying quietly, "Thank you for the champagne, young man," and giggling, left a full pitcher on the table.

Presently, the young people found themselves alone. The girl looked at the handsome young man and allowed her cornflower eyes to rest upon his face for a moment and then looked him up and down without moving her head or smiling.

"*What* in us really wants truth?" asked Ingrid. "You may begin, man of secrets, with this wild tale I was promised," said Ingrid.

David laughed and nodding, sipped his lemonade. He looked at this attractive girl and against his will, thought of everything Fritz had asked. What are women about? Why do they fascinate me so? Then, what does her bare body look like? Is it like Brigitte's, a little hairy, or milk-white, smooth, and unblemished? Should he tell his story, or try to capture this girl's secrets? He felt rough, sweaty, and dominated by these thoughts. At last, he did as promised and told Ingrid his much-simplified life history.

"Who would believe it?" asked Ingrid. "My parents would have questions to say the least, David. They certainly would not allow me to consort with a Jew or even a young man with a hint of Jewish blood. I don't think my father would believe your story, frankly."

"Yes, perhaps not, but it is mine and I honored my promise to tell you. *That* is the most important consideration." David smiled, looked at this guileless girl, and became silent, waiting for her next thoughts. He drank several glasses of lemonade and looked about the property, pretending indifference but looking for Angela.

Unbothered by his silence, Ingrid observed the blond, broad-shouldered soldier. She finally said, "David, would you escort me down to the beach? It is such a lovely day, we really should stroll, a bit, don't you agree?"

"Of course, Ingrid." David offered his arm and walked with her to the path he remembered all too well. He allowed her to walk ahead, his hand releasing her arm as they climbed down the sandy trail to the beach. The lake was covered in cat's paws, as wind from the north swept over its surface and rustled the trees and shrubs above them. The wind had been blocked from the lawn above by the high stone wall that isolated the Meckler house from its neighbor's and the tall poplars rising uniformly along its length.

Ingrid skipped away over the sand and looking back at David said, "Follow me." She led them into a small hollow among the brambles and wild flowers on the far side of the beach, just large enough to make a small turn into concealment. There, Ingrid pulled down a swirl of vines to close them into privacy and sat down on a large section of driftwood. Pulling up her dress, she slipped off her shoes. "Do you like my feet, David?" she said.

David, sitting opposite her on a smaller shaft of driftwood, had never had the experience of a girl's unshod feet and said hoarsely, "Yes, very much."

"Then you will like my legs?"

"Ingrid," David said as she pulled her shirt up to her knees. He felt himself nervous and slightly shaking as he looked into Ingrid's eyes.

"You must kiss me, David."

Bending over, she pulled the boy between her legs, met his mouth with hers, and ran her hands through his hair. David felt her mouth open slightly and her tongue run across his lips as his shoes dug into the sand under him. She put her legs around his waist and tightened their hold, immobilizing him. She continued to kiss him and placed his hand softly to her cheek, so she might kiss it also. Finally, she slid her legs down the length of his waist, hips, and thighs and brought herself under him, her eyes looking up at him. She shuddered and gave a slight moan as her body found the swelling in David's pants. David held her shoulders up away from him and raised his body to push Ingrid off and into a sitting position.

"Ingrid, I cannot allow myself to indulge in this." He broke free of her grasping hands. "I am very attracted and grateful, but my status as a soldier does not allow me to have intimate relations with respectable young ladies."

"So if I was a whore, you could?"

"That would be worse."

"But, aren't you curious?" Ingrid asked.

"It would be disrespectful to tell you just how curious I am. Incidentally, Ingrid, I have never visited prostitutes."

Ingrid sat up upon the driftwood, leaned over quickly, and reaching through his short coat, grasped David's tunic at the pits of his arms and pulled him into her again. She sighed as she kissed the boy again. She said, "Put your hand here." Holding him against her with her left hand, she guided his right hand under her dress, and placed it against her undergarments. David felt a dampness, and Ingrid pulled his hand up and down against herself, taking David's fingers and squeezing them into a clutch, she leaned back and released them to work into the space between her split, linen drawers. David's fingers explored the wetness, and Ingrid rose, bracing herself on her elbows, staring into his eyes. As David's fingers worked, Ingrid began to moan, and moving her hips up and down, she fell back onto the sand, panting.

She closed her eyes and said, "David, you must wash your hands in the lake before we go up."

The two emerged from the copse, and David rushed to the lake and washed his hands in the cool water.

Ingrid said, "Now, smell them."

David put his right hand under his nose and could smell the girl's scent slightly. Looking up at her, he said, "I am ready."

The two crept up the hill to locate Angela. As they topped the mound, Angela was turning around through the gazebo, looking for her charges. She was about to call out to Ingrid, but in turning once more, she noticed her walking with David along the walkway above the beach. She approached the young people and announced, "Luncheon is waiting!"

They ate lunch largely in silence, but David met Ingrid's eyes several times and held them, imagining all else that could have been his. Ingrid licked her lips as he looked at her, and David admired this independent girl, who in another time would have enthralled him. After their lunch, Ingrid accompanied David through the house, where he asked her to convey his thanks to Angela for a wonderful luncheon.

As they shook hands, Ingrid pulled David toward her and kissed him on the mouth. "Am I ashamed? Never! You are just a man."

The deeply blushing young man left the Meckler home, never to return, except, for the rest of his life, in private fantasy. Just a man.

After returning to the *Kriegsakademie*, Fritz ran David down and pestered him with all manner of lascivious questions. David finally responded with, "She thinks I am Jewish and will have nothing more to do with me, wanker."

21

The landing had been smooth, the new tender gliding onto the coarse sandy beach with very little nudging from the following sea. The ship from which Ephraim Yoffey had disembarked, a twenty-year old steel barque the *Inga*, stood out two miles or so, gleaming in the afternoon sunshine and occasionally twinkling along the lengths of its four masts as it moved, almost imperceptibly, at anchor.

Ephraim had managed a passage on the grain vessel, curiously encouraged to inquire by a stranger who accosted him on the Marseille waterfront. The ship, lately out of Australia, was moored along the ancient stone docks near the ship that had taken him—its only passenger to accompany its cargo of Mississippi cotton—from New Orleans. A party of six shirtless, tanned men met the *Inga's* workboat, and ignoring the tall, less-tanned and fully clothed passenger, greeted the four oarsmen and pulled the boat well up onto the beach. A slender woman of medium height, wearing a plain weathered hijab approached, and after taking a box wrapped in foil from the helmsman, she asked for Ephraim Yoffey.

"I am Yoffey," replied the slim passenger, a man with regular figures and a muddle of dark hair curling from under a boater he had picked up in New Orleans. He took a pair of glasses off his face and cleaned the accumulated salt off them on his black linen coat. Ephraim swung a long leg over the boat's rail after hauling over his battered suitcase and dropping it to the beach. He alighted off balance, forced to hop away from the dingy on his left foot until he encountered a lone crate the welcoming party had unloaded earlier. The young man spilled over the wooden box, and with arms extended as he fell, hands grabbing for his glasses flying away from his nose, he fetched up against the legs of the woman in the *hijab*.

Twisting his face away from the sand, he looked up and said, "Excuse me, ma'am." He sprung from the sand, and as he was stretching to his full height, he felt his boater fly off his head. A puff of wind auguring the expected sea breeze took it into the sparse reeds topping a low dune rising a few yards from the narrow shore. As he took a step toward the errant hat, he stepped upon his spectacles, having missed their glint in the bright sunshine.

The woman watched him and shook her head as Ephraim reached down to pick the gnarled frames out of the light brown sand. Forgetting his hat all together, he focused on bending the thin metal back into useable shape, placed the tortured glasses back on his face, and looked at her.

The woman stared hard at the young man and said in heavily accented English, "Have you never been in a boat, Yoffey? Are you going to leave your silly hat for the shore party to fight over?"

Ephraim walked to the dune, gathered his hat, and walked back to her.

The woman, still eyeing him intently, said, "You will not need this coat for a while, Yoffey. Take it off. Do you think you are here to attend a Zionist Congress? Are you a *really* a Zionist—or just a tourist with an absurd hat?"

"I beg your pardon, ma'am," said the man from South Carolina. "I didn't know that business suits were offensive to you Holy Land Zionists. I'm only familiar with the fancy Zionists back in the United States of America—the ones who raise the money to keep *you people* going, I might add with respect, ma'am. They never disparage a man's hat, either."

The woman looked at the helmsman helping the beach party push the boat back into the water and said, "You! Why did you bring him to me? Do I lack lunatics? You have brought this one to carry on insanely with me?" After her paraphrase of Samuel I, she turned to Ephraim again, shaking her head. "Follow me, and do not talk much, please, if you can. And watch where you are walking, for God's sake." As they started along the trail leading up from the shore, the woman looked back at Ephraim. "So, I am not *fancy*, whatever that means.

You think I am ugly, Yoffey? Just a little too dark skinned for your tastes, perhaps."

"Oh no, ma'am, you're not ugly, oh no. Now Miss, you know my name. It seems to me only polite that you tell me yours. Otherwise, I'll have to call you something you might find rude." Ephraim's patience was evaporating along with the sweat he had worked up since hopping away from the boat, and as he opened his mouth to offer the young woman a lesson in proper manners, she turned around and held up a hand to his face.

"My name is Ruth, but you can call me the name you chose if you dare, my new Zionist from the United States of America with the nice suit of clothes. So I am merely *not* ugly, Yoffey? I should cover my face like an Arab woman, I suppose. Would *that* please you?"

Ephraim looked at Ruth, pushed his crooked glasses up the bridge of his nose, and said, "Where I come from, it's not polite to tell a beautiful woman that she's beautiful until you've gotten to know her at least a little bit, ma'am. And in point of fact, though having never seen an Arab woman, I'm sure that it would not please me if you covered your face like an Arab woman, Miss Ruth."

The two made their way through the dunes to a mule-drawn wagon. They climbed into its bed, the sides caked with layers of mud and dust from wheels to buckboard. The wagon stood on a sandy beach road with a bowed, perspiring driver sporting a grimy rag clamped to his head and holding the lax reins in his lap, asleep. He had the aspect of a beaten circus animal, thought Ephraim.

"*Shmu'elly!*" the woman yelled.

The driver started and the wagon bucked forward after his spate of Yiddish, Hebrew or German—Ephraim couldn't tell which—passed irritably between the man and Ruth. This was to become the slowest and roughest mode of transport the young American had ever experienced. He adjusted his haunches and caught the sideboards with each hand, unfortunately running a splinter into a middle finger that he immediately snatched back before his face to examine.

"Yoffey, how dare you!" said Ruth as she picked up a short board and rapped it against the left side of Ephraim's head. "What, are you not taught proper behavior in America, you *tipesh*! I will break that finger, you brute!"

"Now damn it, Miss Ruth, I was looking at this splinter. See?" He held his finger near her face. "I received that from this filthy wagon. If you try to hit me again, I'll have to report you to … to … somebody. Anyway, how far are we traveling, today?"

"Today?"

"Yes, today, ma'am."

"*Ta'azor lee!*" said Ruth.

Ephraim, thinking that Ruth had called him Lee, said "No ma'am, my name is not Lee, it's Ephraim Lev Yoffey."

"What?" asked Ruth. "And stop this calling me this ma'am, whatever that means. Cannot you speak more quickly, like a real Jew?" Wanderer, who are you, she thought as she dramatically brought her hands up to her face. "Stop acting like these German Jews I must suffer daily. Yes, I am speaking about you, too, *Shmu'elly!*"

Ephraim decided to remain quiet.

The late morning sun intensified its heat on the land, and after a few minutes, Ephraim had shed his coat and unbuttoned the top two buttons of his shirt. So, this is *Eretz Yisrael,* he thought. His companions were quiet now, presumably, knowing where they were going and how long it would take them to reach their destination. The road sloped right after they left the beach, headed toward a broad hill, almost a mountain, and arced around a settlement below. The track straightened and began to climb diagonally up the hill, which was grown wild with scrubby ancient trees and thorns. An infrequent contingent of men and women wearing khaki caps or various styles of turbans passed them moving down the hill, and all would nod and say "*Shalom*" to each of the occupants of the wagon.

Ephraim looked at Ruth and noticed what fine hands this woman had as well as her wide mouth with large, oddly moist lips and remarkably beautiful, caramel-colored profile. A dipped apple, he thought. He didn't stare, not because of his Southern manners, but out of fear that Ruth might notice. God only knew what this woman's reaction would be if she caught him looking her over. He raised his face to the sky and recalled a translation, a poem, betraying the warmer thoughts of the reverie into which the beating sun was now casting him. He dropped his gaze and stared back at the bright, distant Mediterranean and recalled with puzzling relevance the parts of the Mallarme that surfaced from memory:

> then, between her legs where the victim rests,
> in the mane lifting the black open fell,
> the palate of this uncouth mouth is thrust
> pale and rosy as an ocean shell.

Ephraim allowed his fantasy to slide into memories of the Negress he'd come to desire as an adolescent, at home, against every convention that had shaped his life: race, religion, family, education. His eyes closed, and slumber found him and called forth a dream: the woman he met every morning at home, his brother's help maid; a hand, his hand, hoary and swathed in tattoo, reaching for the girl's moist breasts through reeds as they lay together on the warm bayou-brown sand…

As the wagon rocked from side to side, the fatigue of his long sea journey deepened his sleep, and he suddenly found himself awakening in a headlong fall to the opposite side of the wagon, his face finding Ruth's lap. Ruth caught him and brought him up quickly back toward the boards he'd been leaning against, but the smooth linen of his trousers slid his knees along the worn floor of the wagon bed, and he found himself gripping the woman's clothing between her legs until he could turn himself over and sit, his back settling against Ruth's hijab.

Ruth yelled, "Yoffey!"

The unfortunate young man tried to rise away to clear her legs and push his rump off her feet. "I'm so sorry, ma'am, I must have fallen asleep. Goddamn it to hell!" said Yoffey.

"*Sleeping?*" asked Shmu'elly, his first utterance since starting the journey.

"What? You've learned English now, you *ikar*?" asked Ruth. "Well, allow me to tell you. Run back to the beach, swim out to that ship, and tell them to take you and the rest of the Jewish Guard to the United States of America where you can indulge more of your stupidity and greed!"

Ephraim looked up at the man and woman and wondered if they were married. He did not ask. He could see that Shmu'elly had been severely cowed and felt a twinge of sympathy for him. The heat of the day must be making Ruth even more strident than when he'd first encountered her. After helping himself up to the seat boards, he said, "Miss Ruth, you'll have to forgive me, but I'm not accustomed to women like you, and while I may be in a strange land, I regard courtesy as universal. You comprehend what I just said, ma'am? What is the Jewish Guard, if I may be allowed to ask?"

"There you go with the *ma'am*, again! We are Zionists, not little effete tea-sippers, Yoffey. At any rate, so the *Kaiser* was nice to Herzl? And what did that accomplish, I ask you? Jewish Guards is the name of the organization that supplies Jewish settlements with Jewish guardians. No better than extortionists. The *Arabs* are better guards."

The wagon crept on, jarring and flinging its occupants the entire journey. As the sun began to set, Ruth announced to Shmu'elly an incomprehensible torrent of words and the wagon pulled to the side of the road. Ruth told Ephraim that the town of Druzes and Jews was just ahead, but Jews there, except the guards, would be in bed. "No need trying to reach it tonight. Anyway, if the Jews didn't kill us, the Druzes there certainly would," she said.

The evening was beginning to chill Ephraim, and he asked what there was for bedding.

Ruth replied, "Here's your bedding, Mr. America." She handed him a roll of clean white cotton and a shawl of sheep's skin. "You'll need to lie down next to the wagon with us. We hang bells from the animals and wagon in the night." And then she called, "*Shmu'elly! Pahamohn!*"

Shmu'elly lit two small lamps and handed one to Ruth who disappeared into the bush beside the tiny encampment. After a while she returned and handed the lamp to Ephraim. "There are, what you call them, ditches and crags, so watch yourself when relieving, Yoffey."

Ephraim sidled down the slope descending from the road and found a comfortable rock face to lean into as he urinated. An urge to empty his bowels overcame him, and he decided to try to find a suitably stable place within the brush to squat. After wandering for ten minutes, he finally achieved his goal and upon re-buttoning his trousers, he heard a strained whisper from Ruth.

"Did you get lost, Yoffey?"

He hurried up the hill, at times clawing in the dirt with his hands, to the sight of the wagon and the lamp illuminating Shmu'elly's face.

Ruth said, "Now, scholar of English, Shmu'elly, let's get to *sleep!*"

The next morning, after a long, uncomfortable night, Ephraim awoke to Ruth's boot nudging him in the side. "Come Yoffey, have some bread before we continue."

Ephraim got to his feet, stretched, and made his way down the hillside to privacy. After returning and washing his hands under the quizzical stare of Ruth, he took a lump of hard bread and climbed back into the wagon. Shmu'elly drew the reins and urged the mules forward, shaking the supple leather straps, and giving a clicking noise to get the animals started. Ruth was unusually quiet, although Ephraim hadn't provoked her, as far as he could discern.

"Yoffey, where do you come from?" asked Ruth.

"Originally, the State of South Carolina, but recently, Florida, where I moved to live with my brother. And you, Ruth, are you from *Eretz Yisrael?*"

"No, no, I came here with my family from Italy, then Salonika, then Constantinople. Poor Shmu'elly is from Leopoldstadt, the place the gentiles call matzo ball island, near Vienna. My father is a physician in Jerusalem, and my mother is his nurse."

"And how do you find yourself transporting American strangers around this part of Palestine?"

"We are not in Palestine! What are you, a Roman, now, Yoffey?"

"But the Jewish people in the United States call this place Palestine! Everyone calls this place Palestine, Ruth! And, what about the Anglo-Palestine Bank and the Palestine Office?"

"Pure historical ignorance."

Ephraim ignored the remark. "Ruth, what is your father's name?"

"My father's name is Binyamin Becouche-Albukerk, as if it should matter to you, Mr. America." Ruth looked directly at Yoffey with shining dark eyes. "He is a great man. He was born in Italy."

"My brother Samuel, or I suppose, Shmu'elly, is also a physician—a man of great wisdom and compassion," said Ephraim.

"Does your brother approve of your joining Global Zionism?"

"Not particularly. Actually, I joined the Jewish Overseas Association."

"Yes, I know some of those *sich vormachen*, I mean to say, brainless Jews. Global Zionism is a movement to bring all of the Jews to our ancient land, to build a state that protects us from what all these centuries have given us—sorrow and danger."

"I will join *your* movement, Ruth."

"Thank you, Mr. United States of Carolina."

"My pleasure and honor. Where did you learn English, Ruth?"

"I went to a convent school in Constantinople with my cousin. Her father, my uncle, arranged something with the priest there. I learned English from Irish nuns and Italian from my family and the Roman Church. I learned German and some Hebrew. And enough Yiddish, of course, to argue with the Russian Jews."

The conversation died away and the landscaped dulled to the eye as the morning dew disappeared from the brambles lining the rutted, constricted road. The journey began to seem endless to Ephraim, but as he looked from the track ahead of them to the right side of the wagon, he noticed Ruth lying her head in the crux of her slender arm spread along the wagon's rail. He noticed the fine sweep of her neck; the firm, unnaturally smooth skin of her face in profile; and the softened oriental shape of her closed eyelids as her long lashes fanned away from them above her cheekbones. He imagined Artemis at rest among her oak groves as the wagon passed a thicket of trees behind her. He suddenly wanted to prolong the trip, lest Ruth awaken before he had fully taken her into the vault of his memory, where her image would escape into his thoughts, perhaps forever. But too soon, a small set of rooftops peeked into sight above a last hill. Soon both sides of the dirt lane were combed with vines of various types and oddly spaced fruit trees lined the approach to the small town. A small sign with faded Cyrillic lettering greeted the three travelers as they came closer to the cluster of huts and houses.

Ruth woke up and offered a rare smile. "This is our destination, Archie's Spring. This is where we need your help, Yoffey."

"Archie's Spring? I thought you used Hebrew for place names. Who is Archie? What kind of help do you need?" Ephraim and Ruth had dismounted the wagon by this time and he looked at her. He looked at her intently, her features undiminished in this aspect. Amazing high cheekbones; wide-spaced, almond-shaped eyes; and finely formed nose and ears. Her complexion was clear and the light brown color of her skin centered upon those very red and full lips. Ephraim thought: This really is a beautiful woman!

"We're still trying to identify the Messiah. Can you help? No? Then, we'll just settle for some help with water."

Just after Ruth answered, a shot rang out.

Ruth said, "Druzes."

"The Druzes don't like us?"

"Ach, the Druzes just want to let us know they're around. At least they like us better than the Arabs."

Shmu'elly waved goodbye and guided the wagon past them. He mounted the hill onto a level part of the settlement teeming with more people than Ephraim had seen since his few days in Marseille. There were men and women moving by in filthy clothes, some wearing the familiar turbans, some bare-headed, some wearing worn Russian caps, and a couple in fezzes. There were also women wresting unruly children away from wandering animals and a curious cluster of men sitting apart clad in black with wide-brim hats, rocking back and forth and reading aloud from a massive tome.

Ruth yelled at the black-attired men in rapid Yiddish, which she, with relish, translated for Yoffey, "You, you idle *Hasidim*, get back to your hovels in Safed and Jerusalem, where you belong! You have no place in the settlements! Go mumble to your stupid women who tolerate your lazy Torah excuses!" Then, turning to Yoffey, she said, "They're not graduates of *Alliance Israelite Universelle,* that I can assure you!" Ruth let a torrent of Yiddish pour forth that caused the men to scramble away. They picked up speed after she pulled out a small pistol and waved it in the air. "This is how you treat these cowards waiting on God! Now to the well, Yoffey."

Ruth did not stop to recover from the bumps and heat of the trip. She led Ephraim to a deep chasm near the north end of the settlement. They walked into a gulley that eventually became a cave with a bubbling spring and pool of water.

"Yoffey, alright, you've seen the spring. You are to make it flow to grow food on a new section of the *moshav,* which means in English our settlement *cooperative.* It is a new word for me, *cooperative.*

"I can believe it," Ephraim said.

"Now I will take you to quarters. Follow."

The tired young man did as directed and followed the woman, keeping an eye on the gun still in her hand, which she eventually placed into a holster slung over her hip that was hidden by a loose, wide belt of the same fabric as her hijab. He could smell the dust and her body's odor as he followed and wondered what the bathing facilities, if any, would be like. They came to a wooden building with a low-pitched roof and what resembled concrete gun emplacements surrounding it in the all-pervasive dust.

"Are those gun emplacements, Ruth?"

"Yes, but no guns. We like to lie to ourselves that the Arabs will run in fear of our gun emplacements." Ruth banged on a sheet of white-painted steel, and in a few seconds, it opened into the building. "This is the only wooden building in the *moshav,* Yoffey. We found an old Arab taking apart a Turkish outpost nearby, and he was kind enough to allow us to help him. I don't why the Turks hauled all of this wood inland, but we've made good use of it. We traded some fruit for white paint with a Rothschild settlement, and as you see, we have a yellow building. We had to promise to display a Rothschild coat of arms. There it is, above the doorway."

"What happened to the Arab gentleman?"

"We made him a Romanian, and now he wears a vest and trousers to work with us in the fields."

"Why a Romanian?"

"There has been pressure from the *Palestine Agency* leaders to use only Jewish labor. They ignore practicality and insist that we don't deserve to be here unless we work every square meter of dirt and harvest grape ourselves. It only embitters and provokes the Arabs, like we need that to get worse. Have you heard of Arthur Ruple? No? Well, he represents the opposing extreme to those worthless religious Jews I scared away. Ruple is a little too much with the Zionism, perhaps, Yoffey. And so, after the land was acquired, and that's another long story, we liked the Arab. But to keep him, we had to make him not an Arab. We didn't have any Romanians, so we called him our Romanian."

"What is his real name, Ruth?"

"Don't let it bother you, Yoffey. And don't ask *him*."

The front section of the building was arranged in four compartments with low wooden walls split by hallways. Each of the four sections was illuminated by two equally-spaced, low-hanging, bare light bulbs. The sectors held ten beds, each next to a small table with two drawers. A candle was mounted in a dish on each table. The beds were separated by hanging canvas tarps and clothes of various colors and lengths. The rear of the building contained washing and bathing facilities, each entered by a separate door. There were no male or female facilities distinguished. High windows lined the building, most open.

Ruth led the newcomer into the room on his right and counted. "One, two, and three. Here is your bed, Yoffey. You may bathe twice a week, and your clothes will be laundered once a week. You will have to obtain bathing and washing vouchers every week from the office, there."

Ephraim saw a closet-like space with a half door just beyond the sleeping rooms. An old, withered woman sat patiently, waiting to be of service. "This is the men's section, I presume?" he said.

"No sex separation, Mr. Carolina. You'll sleep next to me, as a matter of fact."

"This is highly irregular, ma'am. Where I come from, even table legs are covered, and I don't sleep in pajamas."

"Here we are with the "ma'am". I don't sleep with any clothes. So what? You one of those *meshuga* rabbinical students, Yoffey? We'll talk in the morning. We will eat at the dining hall, and then go to sleep."

The two left the "Residence," a word written in English, Hebrew, Turkish and German above the outside doorway below a large, uncovered clock face. It was 5:20 p.m., and the pair made their way down a slight hill to an open shed lined with tables of all descriptions. A smoking hearth was near the middle, and Ruth invited Ephraim to take a bowl and follow her to the line of settlers queuing along the swinging pots above a charcoal fire. When he took his turn at the pots, he found a thin meat stew, vegetables he could not identify, and some type of dark beans. He was famished and loaded his bowl to capacity.

When he and Ruth sat down at a slightly askew table, she said, "Hungry, Yoffey? Don't keep me awake with your stomach noises, *yafeh*."

"I don't mean to pry, but you never told me how you came to work here. What is your job?" Ephraim took off his glasses and wiped them on his shirt.

"Listen, Ephraim." This was the first time she'd used his first name. "I joined this *moshav* after moving here to be with my parents. I work in administration. I felt, here was my father giving up a good practice in Constantinople, a practice that had provided me great comfort and a university education in Paris, so I should give my talents to help him and the other Jews sacrificing their livelihoods and comfort to help establish a homeland for *all* Jews. I know, I know, we have no state, and believe me, my father and I have some conflicting opinions about *that*, but one day we shall if we stay determined. My other family members are helping also. And they're becoming concerned about remaining in Turkey and will probably follow us here."

"You still have that box with you, Ruth? Is that 'help' from Turkey?"

"Eat your dinner, Yoffey. Questions, *questions*!" said Ruth, raising her hands above her head.

"Alright, let's talk about water. Has anyone ever dug a well nearby? Have you experienced flooding from the cave?"

"We have a well to irrigate the south vineyard and fields, but no well for the north lands. We have never had flooding from the cave spring. We haul water up from there for the settlement and a greenhouse."

"Manually?"

"Of course, if we have to. The Romanian takes a mule cart down there daily, and he fills a tank and brings it up here."

Ephraim looked up and sighed, partly from a filled stomach, partly from observing the primitive conditions of the *moshav*. "We need to dig a test well and devise a pump to move most of the pool from the cave into irrigation ditches. Doesn't seem that difficult."

Ruth looked at Yoffey with a relaxed expression and said, "Yoffey, *nothing* is easy here." She blinked as she stared at him, and resting her chin on the palm of her left hand, she dangled her tin fork with her thumb and forefinger. She stifled a yawn. "Shall we retire early? We can bathe before the others come in and be settled into bed for a little more rest."

"I will follow your lead, Ruth."

They rose from the table and squeezed their way out of the dining facility to find themselves covered in more dirt and dust, gifts rubbed off of the *moshavim* coming through the serving line or milling about looking for seating. Ephraim felt somewhat startled by the jostling and pushing, something unheard of in the genteel world in which he had been reared, and he felt a small but rising anger manifest in his movements. He was tempted to fling an elbow or raise a knee into the side of the determined mass that moved about him. The incessant din of talk and whistling gave him a headache, and he ran his hands through his hair and worked his scalp with his fingers as he made his way behind Ruth into open space.

Finally, they were clear of the crowd, and as they neared the barracks building, Ruth said, "Yoffey, if you do not have a bathrobe, you will need to stop at the clothing exchange just inside the door and ask for one, from old Leah."

The next morning, after a very restful night, Ephraim lay still at first, thinking of the beautiful woman resting in the next bed. Then he had a breakfast of bread and tea before he walked down to the cave. He noticed that the deeper he walked into the chasm, the damper the sand and stone became. That encouraged his hope he would find a continuous source in the spring. Occasionally he would have to move aside to allow *moshavniks*, as he had learned to call them, pass carrying water. As he entered the cave and stepped before the pool, he was startled by a man wearing a patch over his left eye. The man was not surprised to see Yoffey.

In fact, he said, "Young man, I have been expecting you." He wore a tattered shirt, a woolen vest, and a pair of clean cotton trousers in the British military style. "I'm sorry, but my English is not cunning. I am here to help you."

"May I ask your name, sir?"

"Call me Romanian." He picked up a weathered pine stick and with his left hand outstretched, moved toward the pool. "Here, I played as a child. I was pushed into the water by my brothers and my face struck a rock. They ran away to the sheep we had left in the fields above. When I arrive home, much later than my brothers, my father beat me and placed a bandage over my eye. My seeing eye is growing worse." Romanian pointed the stick at the dark recesses of the cave and said, "The water will move back there, in time."

"Were any wells nearby when you were a boy, sir?"

"They were all destroyed by the Turk."

"We will need to dig more. Come up with me, sir."

"I have never been called sir. What does it mean?"

"Honored man."

"Oh, *effendi*, as the Turk says."

"Let's dig a well, *effendi*," said Yoffey.

The two men walked around the outside perimeter of the chasm and several hundred yards north of the gulley. The Romanian had placed a British pith helmet, its covering torn here and there, over his thick graying hair.

Finally, Ephraim determined where to dig. He ran back to the *moshav* and asked for tools and men. Ruth pointed him to the Farm Administrator, who after leaving Ephraim for a few minutes, returned with a delegation of burly men carrying shovels and picks. Communication was mostly achieved through gestures, but in the end, the men began to pick and dig where Yoffey wanted them to pick and dig. In the meantime, Yoffey sought the settlement's shop. The manager, a German, a former university classics lecturer, helped him put together a wellpoint and find about fifty feet of usable iron pipe.

Upon his return to the site, he found that his volunteers had dug an irregular hole about six feet into the ground. The Romanian motioned for all to climb out of the hole and stand in line, knocking them together with his old pine stick. Ephraim climbed into the hole and showed his troop how the well-point would work. He then climbed out and drew a tripod and rope attached to the well-point on the ground.

The Romanian said, "I know how to dig a well. Leave the rest to me."

After several days of work, Ephraim had his well operating with a primitive pump fashioned from bits and pieces of pipe, buckets, and even the remnants of a bicycle. Water began moving out of the deep spring through pipes strung along the ground's surface and emptying into a long, waist-high wooden trough. His workers decided to take baths after the water began to clear, and they stripped their clothes off, showing varying degrees of complexion next to deeply tanned skin. The Romanian remained the lone exception and began to chase the naked men with his stick, catching a few and leaving red welts on their posteriors.

Ephraim laughed at the scene as he approached, leading the mule cart to the well to fill the tank. "This is a sight meant only for the gods' eyes," he said to his workers. "Now shall we fill the tank, gentlemen?"

The Romanian translated his words, and the men dressed and began filling wooden buckets and handing them up to the tank's opening. After an hour, the Romanian determined that the tank was full enough and bade Ephraim to return to the settlement with this new water.

Upon entering the center of the *moshav*, Ephraim saw Ruth standing near the administrative building and led the mule toward her. "Ruth, I present you with water from your new well," he said.

That night, after the evening meal and his bath, Ephraim, wearing his new bathrobe, crept amongst the few candles still burning in the sleeping hall after lights out. He found his tiny room, and after hanging the robe over the canvas partition, sat on the side of his small bed looking at the shadows at play behind the partitions and listening to the pervasive whispering and grunts and groans of the weary stretching into their rest. He snuffed out his candle and found the bed surprisingly warm as he lifted the blankets. After swinging his legs onto the unforgiving mattress and allowing the cover to fall upon him, he realized that he was touching an equally naked figure. He uttered a surprised, "What the ..." as warm limbs moved over him and a mouth found his ear, giving it a small bite.

Then the mouth whispered, "Good evening, Mr. South Carolina." Their last bout of love-making enlarging the pelvic blots marking their passion, their bodies resting in their mingled sweat, Ruth slipped away from Ephraim during the night.

As dawn began blazing up through the high windows, the eastern valley splitting the *moshav* from another settlement, Archie's Spring came alive with workers. Ephraim lifted away from the darker region of his sheets, activity already dominating the facilities. He dressed, too late to wash, and began the day as every day at the settlement, with a stroll to the outdoor kitchen for breakfast. He could still sense the smell of his lover, and as he sat down with his bread and tea, he felt helplessly in love for the first time in his life.

The Romanian eventually approached and said, "You late."

Ephraim rose, returned his cup and plate to the rough boards of the counter, and followed his fellow hydrologist toward the new well. The Romanian stopped and showed him a new manual water pump that had arrived from some mysterious source that morning. The two men went to the Works Department to speak with the Professor about designing a concrete pedestal to place the new pump upon.

As they walked out of the Professor's stone shed, Ephraim noticed Ruth leading two older people around the *moshav*. They sauntered toward him, and he realized immediately that she was with her parents. Their conversation included much touching, and their obvious affection for each other seemed to infuse their cheerful banter and respectful silences as they moved about and greeted the settlers. Ruth's hands were in constant motion as she spoke to her mother and father. She saw the tall, well-tanned, bespectacled young man wearing a dirty *Charleston Seagulls* baseball cap as he lifted the pump onto the wagon and called, "Yoffey!" Ephraim turned to meet the family.

"Good afternoon, Miss Ruth" Ephraim dipped his hat into the air before him, scattering his sweaty, black locks around his ears and forehead.

"Yoffey, these are my parents, Doctor and Mrs. Binyamin Becouche-Albukerk."

"Please call us Bennie and Sophia, Mr. Yoffey," the doctor said with a heavy Italian accent.

"You must call me Ephraim, sir."

"Yoffey is very polite, Papa, a tradition he holds to like *Orestes'* curse!"

"Young man, we must speak together later," said the older man.

"Please join me for lunch," said Ephraim.

Just then, the Romanian approached the group, his right hand set across his chest, his head bowing, bringing the Star of David with a King's Crown that was pinned into his pith helmet into their line of sight.

"My dear, dear, Farraj, *as-salamu alaykum,*" said Dr. Becouche-Albukerk, greeting the one-eyed Arab. He brought his right hand to his own chest, and likewise, offered a small bow. They embraced and twice kissed each other on the cheeks then locked their arms, holding a sacred space between them.

"*Wa 'alaykum al-salaam,* my dear and learned friend," replied the

Romanian. "And I am further blessed with the presence of *Alsayedah*! God is smiling upon this day!"

"My friend, please join us for lunch" said Bennie. "But first, let us leave together for a moment." Turning, he said to Sophia and Ruth, "We will catch up to you soon, my dears." The doctor and the Arab walked hand-in-hand to a Daimler parked a short distance away.

"Come Mamma, Yoffey. We must hurry before the queue forms. Shall we each serve an additional plate, Mamma? If Papa and the Romanian have to queue, we will be finished before they reach us."

"*Si*, Ruth." Sophia took Ephraim's arm.

Ephraim looked back towards the doctor's automobile and saw Bennie give the Romanian a canvas bag, which apparently, inspired the Arab to place his hand over his heart once again and offer another, more solemn, bow. Ephraim turned his attention to the two women, each holding one of his arms, and considered the differences between them. The mother was dressed in fashionable European clothing and wore a white veil of nearly translucent silk. The daughter covered her head with a plain red kerchief and wore khaki pants with a wide cotton sash tied at the waist and a white cotton shirt with two large empty pockets stretched tightly over her breasts. The older woman was somewhat shorter than her daughter, but in profile they favored each other remarkably, save for skin tone. Sophia was light-skinned, with scarcely a hint of tanning; Ruth's face and arms had taken on the hue of roasting chestnuts in the six weeks that Ephraim had known her. Sophia's face was remarkably youthful, given her fifty years, and her stride was as energetic as her conversation. Her body bumped into the young man frequently as she leaned across him to speak in flurries of Italian with her less voluble daughter.

After finally sitting with their food, Ephraim ventured a statement: "So Bennie knows the Romanian."

"Yes, obviously, Mr. America," said Ruth. "I will explain their relationship later."

"Oh, *figlia mia*, tell Ephraim! What is the *segreto*? Oy!" said Sophia.

"Mamma, it would take a Greek year!"

"You, Ephraim, are to be trusted with this *epopea. Si*, Ruth?" said Sophia.

"I will ask Papa to tell him," replied Ruth.

"Oy, the Vatican has fewer secrets than you and Papa!"

Ephraim opened his mouth, but before he could utter a word, Ruth held up a hand. After a prolonged sucking-in of breath, she smiled and said, "Later, Yoffey!"

In the next moment, Bennie ambled up to the table, and offering a warm smile, sat down with Ephraim and the women. "Farraj sends his regrets, as he must attend some business this afternoon."

"We have a plate for him, but I am confident that Yoffey's appetite will not leave it untouched," said Ruth.

"So, young man, it seems that you have captured the heart of my little *moshavnik*. Now, what do you plan to do with it, may I ask?" Bennie looked over his spectacles at Ephraim.

"Papa!" Ruth shouted, startling everyone within five tables.

"*Do tell*, as we say in my homeland, Doctor Albukerk. I believe it would be fair to say that your little *moshavnik* has captured my heart. I will confess that I desire to pay court to her, and with your blessing, sir, if Ruth requires it," said Ephraim.

"My son, you are as smooth as the Dead Sea in summer."

"Papa, Yoffey is interested in your relationship with the Romanian," said Ruth, attempting to change the subject.

"Ah well, Ephraim, we shall speak about that while we walk to the new well, if it would please you," said Bennie.

"Yes, that would be a wonderful idea, Papa. Now, we must hurry our lunch to make room for others. As you *know*, Papa, we have very *limited* space here," Ruth said.

Bennie looked around the tables, and as luck would have it, they were, indeed, becoming crowded. He nodded and rolling his eyes at Ephraim, concentrated his attention on eating.

The meal had been relaxing for Ephraim, despite the doctor's attempt to discuss Ruth's love life. He felt at ease in Bennie's company, but he fought the compulsion to share the joy of his affection for the man's daughter and focused his thoughts on the questions his new acquaintances had engendered: why were they in this land and how could they so obviously differ in their manner of appearance from their daughter? What was his business with the Romanian? As he rose from the table, he felt Ruth's eyes upon him and followed the cadence of the Italian passing between mother and daughter and the affecting counterpoint offered by the doctor's occasional chuckle, sounds that seemed to bring Bennie more and more to life. Bennie's close-set eyes and the exaggerated laugh wrinkles emanating from their corners dropped neatly into his pervasive, but carefully groomed, black beard. Ephraim felt his attention moving from the women ahead of him to the man following him and matched his steps.

Mother and daughter turned toward the administration building and waved to the men behind, Ruth puckering her lips to indicate a momentary acquiesce to her parents' wishes. Bennie led Ephraim away toward the north and the new well. Along the way, he touched his black bowler to the numerous settlers who greeted him.

Finally, Ephraim said, "The Romanian?"

"The man will never be a Romanian, at least to me, you must know. Farraj is an embodiment of this land we call Palestine, despite my daughter's reliance on ancient history to define this little, how would one say it, *un pochino di* soil? She and her Zionists will never be able to see it differently. "

"Are you not a Zionist, Bennie?" asked Ephraim.

Bennie stopped and lifting his hat away from his head for a moment, touched Ephraim's forearm. "I believe that we Jews must recognize the right of the Arabs to live as our neighbors. This notion of a Jewish state only guarantees eternal strife between us, not to mention the Turks. The Arabs, who hate the Turks in spite of the recent revolution that made possible Arab representation in Constantinople, believe that the Turks conspire with the Jews to take their lands and that the Jews further oppress their economic opportunities by excluding them from employment on the very lands they once possessed. It is not *Jews* the Arabs must fear, it is Zionists. I ask you, Ephraim, have the Jews had peace since Og ruled Bashan during Solomon's time? I do not wish to participate in this *new homeland* business and pray that the day will come when my Ruth becomes more sympathetic to my point of view. There will never be peace with the Arabs if the Jews continue swarming the land."

"And Farraj?"

"Do you know why you were put ashore on an isolated beach, Ephraim?"

"I assumed because of the proximity to the settlement."

"You were left there as a, I do not know the English, an *inganno*, a mask, to allow a package to be smuggled to Ruth. If the package had been off-loaded in Jaffa, the *Inga's* real port of call, we would have risked its confiscation by the Turks, who often inspect everything coming off ships there. You see, the *Inga's* master was bribed to put you ashore where Ruth was waiting, and the package was delivered from the hands of one of the crew who brought you to her. He has been working for me under the captain's nose for the last few years as an employee of the shipping company that offers the *Inga's* owners an annual cargo of farm equipment to Jaffa from Marseille, and then, a cargo of fruit back to Marseille from Jaffa after the ship finishes its grain passage from Australia to Marseille. So, it is Marseille to Australia for grain, back to Marseille, then farm equipment to Jaffa from Marseille, and finally, fruit back to Marseille from Jaffa. The Palestine Agency, specifically, a friend of mine and my neighbor's, Albert Ash, who shares my sympathies regarding Palestine, makes himself available to us for the occasional mission such as I've described to you. He, my friend in the Palestine Agency, would certainly be dismissed by Arthur Ruple, the director, if this arrangement came to be known."

"I have *many* question, now, but how does all this relate to Farraj?"

"I gave the package to Farraj this morning. The package contained German currency, which would allow Farraj to purchase what he wants from the German settlements without the Turks becoming suspicious. They usually leave the Germans in peace. You see, it is a payment to Farraj for the very land you are now standing upon. Farraj owned nearly all of the land this settlement was founded upon, but, as is very common, his land was stolen from him by a corrupt

Turkish magistrate, who had the land re-titled in *his* name and then sold to the Palestine Office who established this settlement."

"And you became aware of this, how?"

"I usually take coffee with friends in the late afternoons in Jerusalem, at a café near my office. My friends include Jews and both Christian and Muslim Arabs, and among our little group there are always one or two members of influential Arab families. They are close to Ali Ekrem, the governor of Jerusalem, and one of them had overheard Ekrem discussing the sale of a particularly large section of land to the Palestine Agency. What made my friend take notice was the extraordinarily low price that had been paid by Ruple's financial staff to the Turk, the magistrate I mentioned. My friend mentioned this to one of his relations whose interests reaches deeply into the country beyond Jerusalem, prompting him to investigate the transaction. When the truth was uncovered, my friend could not contain his anger over the injustice done to Farraj by the Turkish officials, and as far as he was concerned, Ruple's office. One afternoon in the café, he challenged me, as a Jew, to confront Ruple and arrange fair, how would you say it, *risarcimento*, a price, with Farraj. I considered the incident and inquired of the details through my friend in the Palestine Office and found that, indeed, something was *schifoso*, you know, bad smelling."

"May I stop you for a moment, Bennie?"

The older man nodded yes.

"May I ask why you use Italian, not Hebrew, when the English word escapes you?"

"But, of course, my son. My Hebrew is *schifoso*, you know, bad smelling!" Bennie laughed with gusto. "You should hear my friends in the café laugh at me and beg me to rely on English! It is just too *teatro*, you know for them!" He laughed again.

"I see," said Ephraim.

"To continue … I decided to take up my Arab friend's challenge, but I told him that I would do nothing that involved the Turks. I made an appeal to our friend in Ruple's office that Ash would like to allow my Ruth, who had arrived from Paris *full of Zionism, I might add*, to join the group being organized to establish the *moshav* here. This was arranged, and I explained to her what I wanted to do for Farraj, and she agreed to assist me. As planned, when she arrived here, she searched for Farraj and found him destroying the home he had made for himself and his family in an abandoned Turkish outpost. He told her that she and the other Jews should leave, because he was planning to burn his vineyards and crops the next day. Ruth explained our plan and asked him to wait until I could arrive to begin discussing a fair settlement with him. He agreed to wait one week, during which I arrived and we came to an agreement. I gave him the first of ten payments in Turkish money and explained that I would have the rest paid in German money to keep the Turks off of us."

"Farraj seems truly happy. I saw how pleased he was to greet you and Sophia."

"After Farraj and I came to agreement, he embraced me and cried. The payment that came with you was the last, and as long as Farraj remains a Romanian, he will be part of the *moshav* and share in its prosperity."

"And your Arab friend, was he satisfied with your wonderful efforts?"

"My Arab friend did not believe me until he accompanied me here to speak to Farraj himself! Now young man, I have entrusted you with a great secret, one that makes us connected."

"I can keep a secret, sir, I assure you. Now, tell me, how did you get the German currency?"

"My brother, Isaac, In Constantinople arranged it for me. He is a grain merchant, as was our father in Italy, and has a contract with the owners of the *Inga* to purchase all of the ship's grain cargo. His office in Jaffa arranges the *Inga*'s fruit cargo, also, which he sells to the ship's German owners, who pay him in German currency. So, when I needed the money for Farraj, I sold my brother an apartment in Jerusalem and he has been paying me with German money. I suppose you are thinking that I have made a sacrifice in this?"

"I would be inclined to say that you have made a great sacrifice on behalf of Farraj, yes" replied Ephraim.

"It is an investment, my son. One day I will need as much Arab goodwill as I can get; I am convinced of this. But my son, what does one really want? Isn't it enough to live honorably and to die with a settled, quiet soul?"

The men walked farther along the furrowed trail formed from the trooping company of irrigation workers and their leaders. When they reached the well, now topped with a four-foot-high casing of masonry and an overhanging iron reel dangling a wooden bucket, Bennie said, "I have seen the well and offer my thanks to Ephraim, Farraj, and Tethys!"

"And, Bennie" said Ephraim, as they turned to leave, "I wish to share a secret in turn with you: I intend to marry your daughter."

22

Herr Wok greeted the young soldier at the rail station in Stuttgart, and uncharacteristically, wrapped his arms around David. Then he pushed him back and holding his shoulders, said, "Fine, very fine, my boy!"

David had finally finished his *Kadett* training and was allowed the traditional leave before he was scheduled to join the General Staff. At Kathe's invitation, he paid a visit to his adopted parents at *Vogelgesangstein,* where he found the old *Schloss* tidy, standing just beyond the thick and dark forest that was exploding with green life and the cries of birds. The old building had grass greening right up to the stone walls, and the staff was in good form, all waiting to bow and extend their warmest sentiments to the uniformed young man, as if recalling the earlier days of their hero and master, the general. The Count and Kathe, standing in the doorway behind the servants, exuded a rather, at least for David's adopted mother, quiet, quotidian contentment.

As he embraced his parents, they offered effusive praise of his accomplishments, and the old soldier, perhaps unnecessarily, appeared extraordinarily humble concerning his role in developing David's career. "You have achieved all that could be accomplished with the Prussians, David." He admitted to the young man that he knew through his contacts that David had been selected for posting in the Levant, and somewhat cryptically, he added that the young Lieutenant would carry a large responsibility to someone at the highest level of government. He promised surprise. His tasseled pipe emitted clouds of smoke as he puffed his enthusiasm.

Later the two men strolled down the graveled lane before the *Schloss* with two of Sigi's ornate Italian shotguns. They took a long walk within the forested surround of the estate, shooting and speaking of David's past life and people who had figured so prominently in its course. David walked with the erect, if somewhat stiff, manner of a Prussian officer, but his large brown eyes seemed to be in perpetual twinkle. Sigi mentioned that *Herr* Schlarp and Elisabeth would probably be coming to live on the estate and that David was not to worry about them. David stopped and put an arm around the old soldier and thanked him for taking this concern from his heart. Sigi mentioned that he had a letter from Captain Twinge addressed to David, which he would share later.

David guessed that Sigi, who maintained that he was just a simple soldier, did not share in the clique of his grandfather Bernd, Captain Twinge, and *Herr* Schlarp, but he seemed to understand and respect the foundation of their youthful bonds. He had been a soldier, but said, "I would have traded it all for the kind of peace those men chose to honor and remember in their friendship and lives. It will always puzzle me, however, why they showed such acceptance for your professional choice, my boy. I suppose that my place as their friend was to impart what wisdom I was fortunate to derive from my military experience. I also imagine, with people throwing bombs in opera houses and assassinating all manner of nobility and government officials over the last twenty or so years, the discipline of soldiering is, at least, a method of discouraging the madness these anarchists espouse. They want to make their message of chaos heard, but as they resist any organization, they have organized conventions themselves! Misanthropy and the worst kind of hypocrisy! Excuse me, my son, but these times rather rile your old adopted father."

"But, with respect, Father, the whims of kings and princes have caused much havoc through the centuries, also. I believe the ideals formed by my grandfather and the others were to rejoice in the lack of the interference of noble causes in the lives of common men. And women, of course."

"I will give you no argument, my son. Your life is a testament to what nobility can impose upon good people. Bernd, of blessed memory, Twinge and Dieter all knew, even at the beginning of their association, that war has been inevitable because of the steady decline of European culture. Especially, our culture. Where are the Fichtes, the Hegels, the Humboldts, the thinkers? Not that I can agree with all of what these men espoused, but at least they challenged society! After old Fritz went to his grave, the best of all we'd worked for, and fought for vanished with him—probably before that, as he was crowned Emperor, for him, a very sad day. We have only *war* to fill the void our leadership encourages. We are now led by buffoons. Now, I fear David, that you and every *German* will do their bidding. You must remember all of us—your grandfather, *Herr* Schlarp, Captain Twinge, your adopted mother, and your tragically lost birth parents—as you move through the world. Your nobility must transcend your times, my boy, and take our ideals into the next generation, beyond the exogenesis of the politics of these last fifteen or so years. My lovely *Athena*, as you've always called your adopted mother, has tried to place in your path the intellectually rare figures to make you think. It has been her prayer that you've realized human decency and *real nobility*, that we must look beyond all of our mortal constructs for real truth."

"Father, I believe that I have achieved some of this; I owe you and *Tante*, now my mother, so much for making life endurable."

The men tramped through the woods and occasionally stopped to relieve themselves, chat or shoot, with dogs sniffing ahead and giving the odd bark. Dried linden, beech, and larch leaves left from the fall carpeted the area and crackled beneath the footfalls of David and Sigi, but neither gave any concern about their noisy approach, absorbed as they were in their thoughts and conversation. Stands of various pines appeared, often upon a small rise, and the other trees, barren during the winter, were now nearly full with leaves and provided the men with shelter against the bright sunlight. Sigi would stop suddenly, listen to a cuckoo for a few moments, and look at David with joy, as if he'd heard the bird's delightful calls used in his beloved Humperdinck's music, streams of which David had heard the general play upon his ancient piano often since he had first visited the *Schloss*. Indeed, Sigi always seemed to start with a series of note couplets that reflected the cuckoo's calling.

When they returned to the castle, Kathe embraced them both as they entered. She led them into Sigi's library and introduced them to a Colonel Stephan von Klages from Berlin, who had arrived unexpectedly soon, as it was revealed. Sigi and Kathe had known that Klages would be visiting specifically to meet with David, but the date fixed in their minds was the next day. Both parents were disappointed that their visit with David was to be interrupted by the officer's presence and had to mask their feelings with effort, lest they offend the visitor.

Klages clicked his heels as he saluted the men and extended his hand to both, Sigi first. "I must apologize for arriving a day sooner than expected, but the force that sent me here is most impatient to enlist our young Lieutenant in the work prescribed for him. First, it must be understood that this is sensitive—"

Sigi was taken aback by the fact that the Colonel launched into a description of his mission before he was invited to take a seat. He interrupted Klages. "Won't you please sit, Colonel? I believe that we would all be more at ease as you describe your mission."

"Lieutenant Petersruhe-Rožmberk, much consideration by important and influential officials has been given to the nature of your mission. First, congratulations for your appointment to the General Staff, but I must inform you that—and here you have a choice as to whether you undertake this assignment—we wish to separate you and ask you to report the results of your work directly to the office of the Under Secretary of State for Foreign Affairs. While we have no wish to circumvent the *structure* of the army, indeed, the army is *part* of this mission, this diplomatic function of our government would, in fact, control your movements. This comes about as a result of the Count's willingness to provide guidance to you, as we know that the probability of conflicting directives will arise, and you must have an experienced voice outside of the usual chain of command assisting you in making decisions. To be rather direct, you will basically be operating on your own within an army command. You must make your presence known, but keep your mission vague, if not completely unknown, to the army at large."

"Sir, with respect, I have not undergone years of training only to be asked to betray the army. Am I not a soldier?" said David.

"Indeed, Lieutenant, it is because of your training record, as well as your family, that we have selected you for this mission."

"May I ask you, sir, to describe the nature of the mission?"

"You will be asked to involve yourself with our country's work in Turkey. The Under Secretary wishes to have direct information coming from someone with a military background since Turkey is moving toward a leadership made up of military men. If diplomacy must be exerted through military figures, you, and others unknown to you, will be available to act in such a fashion."

Sigi interjected, "This is not new, David."

"When will I be expected to leave for Turkey, sir?"

"Two day's time. The Count has all of the arrangements and will speak to these matters in my absence." The Colonel paused. "I apologize, gentlemen, but I must catch my train." He stood, and clicking his heels saluted the men again and was led from the room by Sigi.

When Sigi returned, he was patently unhappy. He motioned for David to sit and said, "David, Klages was not due until tomorrow, which would have given me the opportunity to speak to you about his proposal. This is a *proposal*, and by agreement between me and Foreign Affairs, you are free to reject it if you so choose. The work will involve much initiative and discretion on your part. I cannot see anything but near madness in dealing with the Turks now. You will be posted to a regular unit, but its commander will ignore your activities, as directed by Foreign Affairs. I will have you driven to Freiburg tomorrow, where you will take a train to Marseille. There, you will be met by one of Captain Twinge's ships, the *Imp*, and taken to Constantinople, where you will disembark while the ship lies at anchor or unloads its cargo. You will then present yourself, with documents I will give you, to the ambassador to the Porte who will have made arrangements for your assignment. To simplify, David, I have asked a dear friend, Colonel Witt, who makes his office in the embassy, to oversee your affairs and exert influence on your behalf. In a short amount of time, Witt will have you completely under his authority."

Kathe entered the room and sat down with the men. She asked

David to forgive the unexpected intrusion of Colonel Klages and to consider carefully what the officer had to say. "I cannot advise you on this matter, David, but will support whatever decision you make."

"I will accept the Colonel's, shall we say, *challenge*? I believe, considering the pattern my life has taken, that undertaking this assignment would be, at least, adventurous, and perhaps with the potential of offering more than is usual in a military career, with all due respect, Father," said David.

The next morning, after a quiet breakfast and a tearful parting, David and Wok started for Freiburg in the Count's black Daimler. The journey wasn't particularly long, but David's nervous excitement kept him innervated, restless, and ignoring a part of Germany so unfamiliar to him. He took the time to read Captain Twinge's letter on the way.

Hugh Twinge, Earl Boardcroft
Boardcroft House
Ruskwick
Lincolnshire, England
7 May 1907
Lieutenant David Samuel von Petersruhe-Rožmberk

My Dearest David:

Count von Petersruhe has asked me to be of assistance to you in arranging passage to Constantinople. I have a ship due in Marseille on 2 May and would be happy to accommodate my favorite sailing companion. I have asked my agent in Marseille to find a cargo there and a buyer in Constantinople, which I trust will be realized. The ship, Imp, is due to leave on 10 May but can be delayed for a day if you can inform me by telegram. I hope you have a safe journey and remember your old friend fondly, as you sail the "broad back of the sea." Tom offers his best wishes and regards.

Yours,

Twinge

David made the rail connections, and finally reaching Marseille the next day, was able to find the *Imp* docked and taking on cargo. He walked up the gangway, offered the document he was instructed to give the captain, and boarded a large, new, turbine-driven freighter. The ship's cranes were busily swinging and dropping nets full of manufactured goods: machine parts, rail components, and even two of Emil Jellinek's new Mercedes automobiles secured in odd fashion on the foredeck. Captain Mansell Front led David to his cabin, where he piled his bags against a locker and immediately followed the captain out of the room again to the bridge. The Captain offered David coffee and told him of his good fortune to be appointed to the *Imp* and his fondness for Lord Boardcroft.

"Doesn't Lord Boardcroft prefer being addressed as Captain Twinge, at sea, Captain Front?" asked David.

"By God, he does, young man. Right you are! You must know himself well. He is a fearless, seafaring man, is Captain Twinge. He's slowed down a bit, especially since his son-in-law Captain Kitchen was lost, but the old bull's still going."

David left the captain to his work and went to his cabin, where he took out the little book Kathe had given him to pass the time. *The Longest Journey*, by an Englishman, a Mr. E. M. Forster, rendered him immediately to Morpheus' breast. David slept through the hooting of the French tugs pulling and pushing *Imp* into the harbor and out into the Bay. The ship was up to speed quickly and followed the familiar lanes out and east. Meanwhile, David dreamt.

The doors opened and he stood there with Grandfather Rosenberg on one side and Hughie on the other, looking into a pit with blood oozing down, through the cracks edging the great earth-hole. In unison they said, "We will not weaken." Kathe appeared, nude, and flew up to David, and into her eyes he plunged, swimming miles and miles with the whole earth passing him with mountains collapsing onto the shore, heaving up steep waves, with furrows and troughs and precipices, with fish men smiling up at him as he moved through the water. He, clawing through ether now, pulled himself into an old wagon's bed and felt his body turned over by unseen, soft hands and looking above at a blue man's face shrouded in pulsing, breathing haze who said, "Who has laid it down that wisdom comes alone through suffering?"

Awakening at last, David turned on the cabin light and sorted through his bags, making certain that nothing was amiss. He'd fallen asleep in his clothes, and his body felt oily and his mind menaced by his dream. He felt cursed with the ability to remember his dreams and would, for the rest of the day, fear sleep and resist the creep of his lids over his eyes as long as possible.

The passage was uneventful, and after nearly five days, the *Imp* made Constantinople. David was rowed into the Pera docks and discharged by the small crew onto a slippery set of ancient steps that led to a city of storehouses along the Golden Horn and a mass of humanity of all nationalities, ethnicities, colors, and states of dress. He finally reached the Pera Hotel, where he was given directions to the German Embassy, and with the kindest of assistance from the concierge, was put into a taxi. He looked back down the great hill and saw the diversity of building styles, and in the distance, the zigzagging streets and backstreets crawling with humanity with structures bowed out over the paving or presenting crooked rooftops at all angles. He could smell the driver, and the scent of garlic and tobacco he gave off made David queasy and induced a headache.

At the German Embassy, David had to run in to exchange some money with which to pay the cab fare and elicited a scornful stare from the pinch-faced official who ruled the front desk. After he returned, he handed the man a letter with an official seal and waited. He found a small corner and relaxed, ready to hurl curses at the little man at the desk at the first sign of recalcitrance. After a few minutes, an army officer collected him and led him to the office of one of the ambassador's assistants, a Herbert Witt.

Witt said, "Welcome, my dear sir. If you will be patient with me, I will have you in quarters soon. I hope you had a pleasant journey and will allow us the pleasure of your presence often. As you know, political life in this region is changing, especially with the encouragement of the Russians and others. I will be your point of contact, and together, we will refine the objectives of your mission here. For now, however, I must get you to what we refer to as the barracks: an old hotel, built and bankrupted about fifteen years ago and bought by a concern who enjoys business with the Fatherland and this region. From time to time, you will encounter unidentified men there, who will disappear as quickly as they appeared. Now sir, please follow me."

With those words, both men stood up and proceeded out of the office and embassy. *Herr* Witt was a short, somewhat rotund Bavarian, who would in time, make every effort to help David acclimate to his new surroundings and challenge. The shorter man led the way down the hill from the embassy and turned along a relatively quiet, unusually neat, street, stopping at a once ornate, but now almost nondescript, yellow building adorned only by dark, mustard-colored French shutters. The curving tops of the shutters rose to nearly the bottom of thick, stone window seals and a slight outline behind the shutters could be detected lining the wall. There were small ports of very thick glass set in the middle of the windows, which while appearing real, were only a façade of glass set over steel plate. A double red door was sealed tightly, and a false bell was mounted above the left corner.

Herr Witt pushed a faintly protruding rod set into the wall near the doorway, and the sound of opening locks emanated from the building. A small, quiet woman opened the door and smiled at the men. *Herr* Witt, smiling back, nodded, and the men were taken through a long hallway to a room on their right, where David was beckoned to enter.

"These are your quarters, Lieutenant," said Witt. "By the way, we will require you to be known only by "Lieutenant Petersruhe-Rožmberk," as subterfuge would be offensive to our diplomats and lead others to identify you with something other than a military mission. The room, as you can see, has a spacious sitting area, is *ensuite*, and has telephone service. The telephone is probably monitored, so be careful of your conversation. There are, due unfortunately to security considerations, no windows. There is a convenient side exit, but you must enter through the front. Now, may I present, *Frau* Schencke, our house manager? If you need something, please see *Frau.*"

"I am honored to meet you, Lieutenant Petersruhe-Rožmberk," *Frau* Schencke said. For convenience sake, please just refer to me as Vickie." She was petite, about thirty-five and wore her blond hair in a low ponytail. Her eyes were somewhat dull, an indistinct shade that could be regarded as blue or green depending on the light. She had developed smile lines around her mouth and wore the simple, gray dress of a housekeeper. "I had the pleasure to serve along with our military as part of the Fatherland's nursing corps for ten years, so if you get in a tussle, I can sew you up!"

David thanked his hosts and agreed to meet with Witt in two day's time at the embassy. He asked Vickie if she would have his uniforms laundered in the meantime, and received instructions on dining and other, mostly pedestrian, matters that all people must master when relocating. Witt and Vickie excused themselves and taking David's uniforms, left him to rest before dinner, which he was informed would take place at 7:00, sharp. David unpacked his toiletries, Mr. Forster's novel, and copies of some of *Frau* Liliencron's writings probably slipped in by Sigi, and did what he could to revive his several army caps and formal hats. He thought of Sigi and Kathe and began to sit still, staring at nothing in particular, feeling the homesickness of knowing that he'd had so much more to receive from them emotionally before leaving. He did soon, however, begin to feel the excitement of the new possibilities available to him: new people to know, a foreign world to explore, and the prospect of interesting work to demand his attention.

Wisdom and suffering, he remembered from his dream. He pushed the recollection aside in his mind, shaking his head and concentrating on removing his boots to free his sweat-conjoined toes and offer the room a whiff of real life.

23

David appeared in the dining room promptly at 7:00, having found the room as he explored the building earlier. He looked about, and seeing no fellow diners, seated himself at the oblong dinner table. The room was full of unfamiliar, geometrically patterned tile and the walls featured yellow-based squares holding blue, eight-sided lines diminishing in size and centered with a yellow, three-edged star. The tops of the walls were trimmed with a crown of solid blue tiles matching the base. The floor was nearly completely covered with a blue-fringed Berber carpet, spotlessly clean. The table was long and adorned with a plain white linen cloth, subtly patterned with lines dropping from the table's edges to brush his knees at the cloth's edges. The serving board appeared to be a long, thin slice of polished white marble, with serving bowls of Brussels sprouts, artichokes, a leek soup and a long platter of roasted lamb, all garnished with yogurt and various peppers and salt.

Frau Vickie appeared, sat opposite David, and was followed by one servant who began filling soup bowls and serving the meal.

"*Frau* Vickie," said David, "Are we the only diners this evening?"

"Please, just Vickie, Lieutenant. We will be the only denizens of *Apfelhaus*, or 'A' house, as you'll hear it identified, for some time, I'm told," said Vickie. "Our servant is Norma Akeseel, a native of Southwest Africa."

David looked closely at the server and noticed her predominantly Caucasian profile, fine skin the color of light tannin, and very delicate manner. "I am happy to meet you, *Fraulein*. You have a most unusual surname," he said.

Norma paused, looked at David briefly, and bowing to acknowledge his statement agreeably, continued with her work. She seemed exceptionally polite and especially deferential to Vickie. Norma looked at her with unmixed affection and smiled with every gesture she issued. When the first course had been presented, Norma left the room.

Vickie said, "Norma is a product of a mixed-race relationship. Her mother was Hottentot and her father, while a physician member of the Society of Racial Health, found that he could not resist one of his servants. He abandoned his poor wife who had followed the German Overseas Society's request for more vigorous, pure German female representation in the colony. The doctor took the resulting child, Norma, back with him to Germany, where he found that his family, especially his brother-in-law, was unrestrained in their condemnation of his actions. His brother-in-law returned with his sister who, sadly, tried to reconnect with her husband. A row ensued and the woman murdered the doctor with an ancient Saxon sword belonging to a noble relative, hacking his body into several pieces and scattering the poor man's body parts in the street below the steps of his parents' home in Berlin. I was just back from *GSWA*, having nursed there for several years, and heard of the unfortunate incident, and with the help of the Society and after five years, I was finally able to adopt Norma, who is now eighteen years-old."

Norma returned and cleared plates to serve the next course. She glided around the table with an unusual grace. Her plain manner of dress, and her exotic appearance seemed angelic to David, who couldn't take his eyes off of her. When she spoke to Vickie, saying, "Are you pleased, *Katzenmutter*?" David found her voice low and strong and pleasing.

"You call Vickie, 'Cat Mother', Norma. Why?" asked David.

"Because she is the noblest and free-spirited; only *her* blood I claim, *Herr* Lieutenant."

David bowed his head and looked at Vickie who was smiling with tears in her eyes. With her dull eyes now beautifully mirrored and her white arms, long and slim, offering food across the table, David saw the woman she really was. She dabbed her eyes and returned to her repast, taking small bites and occasionally, looking up to find

Norma standing near her. She finished her meal and nodded to Norma, who left the dining room to prepare coffee.

The air in the room was light, with electric lamps in every corner casting fine and broad illumination across the table and onto the man and woman. There were no windows, only the single door against the room's isolation. Vickie sat with her back to the open door, framed within the shiny, blue tile casing, her body placed against the hallway's passage with light so low as to discourage entry and navigation. "Shall we move to the sitting room, for coffee, Lieutenant?" asked Vickie.

"Really, you must call me David, Vickie. Even newly arrived, I feel that we are familiar; I seem to know you."

"Perhaps you've dreamed of me! Here in the East, all manner of mystery prevails! Come, let us enjoy the last of our first little feast together, David."

The two were served coffee and sat in comfortable, over-stuffed chairs in the sitting room. David could see into a small alcove off the room that held a panel of several small yellow lights and three telephones. Its black steel door with its wide riveted frame stood open and swung against the pinkish wall. David decided not to mention his curiosity to Vickie and allow her time to divulge the little room's purpose. He looked upon the rows of portraits along the wall, noticing the *Kaiser's* in the middle and its dominating size and grand frame. The others were obviously military men: old Motlke, Sigi's Grand Duke, Schlieffen, and the current ambassador. He looked at Vickie and asked, "May I offer my thanks for a wonderful evening and the joy of your company?"

"You may, David. I hope that you find your room suitable and will allow me to correct any inadequacies you may find. Now if you will excuse me, I have duties, and then I'm off to bed."

David sat alone for a few more minutes and finished his coffee. He felt transported, even joyous, and finally at ease. He eventually left the room and returned to his lodgings to find his bed turned down and a sweet scent lingering in the air. He picked up *The Longest Journey* and read until he could no longer keep his eyes open. He undressed, switched-off the light, and went to bed.

A restrained whimpering woke David later that night. He began to listen intently and could hear the lamentation of a woman. Words like "tried" and "blood" mixed the air with unrestrained moaning and low wailing sounds through the lonely night. He noticed a stroke of light appearing under his door time and again. He rose from his bed, slipped on his trousers, and crept along the wall barefoot and bare-chested save for leather suspenders. He opened his door and walked toward a faint light in the hallway. The woman's moans became louder as he moved along, feeling for both sides of the hallway and conscious of his footfalls. His chest prickled with jets of adrenaline, and his breath became somewhat stifled as he made every effort to quiet his lurking presence.

Suddenly, a door opened, and the form of a woman appeared, her thickly curled mass of hair swinging back and forth, her full breasts silhouetted against the pale, faintly lit wall. As the woman's eyes adjusted, she saw David and straightened and said, "Here, here." The petite figure reached out to him and finding one of his suspenders, pulled him close.

He lowered his face to hers and felt her warm tears spreading across his cheeks and her loose hand now pushing along his bare side, gripping the muscles there. David pushed her toward her door and found himself lowering into a bed, his clothes falling to his feet, his body moving sideways. The woman's body pressed against his own, and as he kissed her and whispered, "I'm here," he felt the movement of the soft skin of another woman pass over them both and settle against his form. He pushed on top of the woman, began feeling for her, and entered her. The other woman rubbed her body against his as he moved into pleasure. Moaning began, and he felt the hot breath of the woman lying under him and receiving his penis. Soon they both sighed, and winded, they rolled away from each other with the second woman stroking them both with her bare body. A voice whispered, "Time to leave."

David lifted himself, and reaching the floor, found his clothing and left, carefully making his way back to his rooms.

The next morning, David rose at 5:00 and washed in his bathroom thoroughly. He left for breakfast at 7:00 and was met by *Herr* Witt, who had come to inquire if a guide would be required for David to explore the city.

"I will show him the town, *Herr* Witt." Vickie entered the room and sat at her customary place. "We will enjoy this wonderful, clear day together, and I will have him back before dinner."

Witt rubbed his hand over his thin, shiny widow's peak, around to the back of his hair, and down onto his fleshy neck. "That would be most convenient, *Frau* Schencke. If you could lead him through Stanbul without seeing him cheated out of his money—which, Lieutenant, you need to exchange at the embassy—I would be grateful. Tomorrow young man, please present yourself to me in my office at 10:00 for a meeting with one of our Turkish friends with whom you will be spending a good deal of time." He paused and looked at the food set on the table. "This is exquisite yogurt, *Frau*! The fruit combination is most appealing. I must watch myself, however. As you can see, I am overly fond of good cuisine!"

Witt was a jolly man, his company a delight to most of his colleagues. He had the habit of rolling his eyes around as he spoke, as if nothing he said should be taken seriously. David would discover, however, that most things uttered by Witt must be given a thoughtful hearing.

Breakfast over and a meeting time agreed with Vickie, David went back to his rooms. He thought about his first sexual experience and wondered if it had really happened. He was almost unable to imagine the dimmed sight of the women, but could still feel their movement against his body, which inspired an erection that would have to be stifled *tout suite*.

He met Vickie at the vestibule of the building at the appointed time, and together they began his tour of Constantinople. They walked down past the *Galata* Tower to a dock near *Yag Iskelesi*, the oil pier, and found a small ferry, the owner of which argued vehemently over the toll with Vickie until they finally set out across the *Golden Horn*. The waters smelled of fish and oil and were crowded with swooping gulls and the hooting of vessels of all descriptions. The ferryman sang a Turkish song for them and then switched to Armenian, which told Vickie that he was proudly Armenian. He rowed them across the busy waters, and defying a strong current, deposited his passengers at a stepped-down pier near the *Goth's Column.*

They walked past shacks that served as taverns as they made their way up to the *Wall of Byzantium* and continued to the *Stoa Basilica,* where they looked over at the top of *Haghia Eirne* and the ancient building and grounds of *Haghia Sophia.* They stopped at the *Palace of Antiochus* and decided to take a taxi through the western part of Stanbul up to the *Theodosian* Walls. The buildings were in turn, spectacular and ramshackle, leaning out then into themselves, swayed to one side and then the other. The place looked shaken as they made their way slowly up and down the narrow, dirty, ancient—or modern over ancient—streets and passageways. David noticed a steady noise of windows being pushed open above them, and the occasional drift of dust and lint as women shook out clothes, sheets, and small rugs over their heads. The variety of costume, headgear, and animals was amazing to David, but Vickie took little notice. The taxi stopped as near the walls as possible, and the pair got out and walked up to the antique walls, with toppled stones and loosened bricks lying all around amongst the vegetation and the hovels built into the sides of the long structure that once and again would protect the city.

Finding a shaded lonely corner carpeted with acorns and running briars, David turned to Vickie and said, "I have no restraint, no will against the joy of your presence. Kiss me, again." He reached for her, and she pulled back, looking at him with her dull eyes.

She seemed to groan in small measures and turned to the wall and then back toward him again. She raised her hands and put them together, pressing them against her breasts as a number of low-hanging birch saplings growing from the wall swayed down and almost touched their heads. Vivki said, "I have given you all you need of women for now, and you are ready for the world. Accept it as it was and ask nothing else of my body or my heart. My daughter and I have stood you up and offered you to the world in which you now find yourself and given you knowledge to confront it. Leave us alone, now, please." The shadows encasing them seemed to increase to gloaming and the two were suddenly concerned about the time. "We must leave, now, David," she said.

David nodded and accepted this without really understanding. But he was grateful, and he knew that he would have to live with his heart aching for her. The night had been a gift of awakening and confusion.

They walked for a little longer, Vickie continually pointing out the unending and various landmarks and monuments of the city. They struck off at *Tekfursarayi*, the old Byzantine palace, and headed straight to the seawall and finding the path below it, went down to a café opposite the *Church of St. Mary of the Mongols*, and had a Greek lunch of broiled lamb and potatoes, offered with a kind of ale served in enormously tall, thin bottles. David asked for another bottle and after quaffing half of it down, felt himself drunk, for the first time in his life. Becoming voluble, he allowed the ale to be his voice and talked about Captain Twinge and their sea adventure and about Sigi and Kathe. Finally, Vickie gave the bottle to the waiter, who, in turn, presented his bill. She helped David find the proper amount. She prompted David to get up and to follow her into the narrow lane called the *Goat That Farts* until they reached the *Cisr-i Cedid*, the "new" bridge and crossed back into Galata, taking a taxi back to *Apfelhaus*, where Norma was readying dinner.

David went into his rooms, and as he had the day before, picked up Mr. Forster's novel and put himself promptly to sleep. He dreamt.

A narrow lane and a woman singing in an unfamiliar tongue. Bright sunlight dappling a small body of salt water and the woman's voice still singing. He was walking, blind, in light, and his feet were wet and his trousers began to float up to his tunic as he approached a floating object. The object was a tree, and he began to hammer nails into the tree, and the tree flew up and away from him. He was on the shore, sailing over the Wolds in *Orestes*.

David awoke with a start. He suddenly remembered a poem he had read repeatedly from a book of Tennyson old Twinge had given him, and he hurried to his top bureau drawer to retrieve the volume his English friend had given him and found the text.

> *Home they brought her warrior dead:*
> *She nor swooned, nor uttered cry:*
> *All her maidens, watching, said,*
> *'She must weep or she will die.'*

> *Then they praised him, soft and low,*
> *Called him worthy to be loved,*
> *Truest friend and noblest foe;*
> *Yet she neither spoke nor moved.*

> *Stole a maiden from her place,*
> *Lightly to the warrior stepped,*
> *Took the face-cloth from the face;*
> *Yet she neither moved nor wept.*

> *Rose a nurse of ninety years,*
> *Set his child upon her knee—*
> *Like summer tempest came her tears—*
> *'Sweet my child, I live for thee.'*

"David," said Vickie, interrupting his thoughts as he tried to work out why he had remembered a poem he hadn't read in years. His suspenders were loose and flopping along his shanks and his shirttail was released from his trousers as he opened the door.

He looked at the woman and asked, "Yes?"

"Dinner will be served in thirty minutes. Tonight, we have *Herr* Witt and his wife, also. Won't you allow me to help you with your toilet? Your uniforms are in this closet, and I suggest that you wear one, given the present state of your clothing."

"Oh, no, I'll be ready in thirty minutes."

Herr and *Frau* Witt were waiting in the sitting room as David came out to greet them. *Herr* Witt was jovial, as usual, as was his wife, and the three engaged in small talk until Vickie came in and asked them to follow her into the dining room. *Frau* Witt walked with the sway of a plump and slightly wide woman, but she exuded great energy. All were seated and Norma began the service after *Herr* Witt said Grace.

Frau Witt asked, "Vickie, have you heard from your brother? Isn't he to be posted here?"

"He is in Berlin and has indicated that he will come out in the next year or so."

"Ah, we shall look forward to meeting him. *Herr* Witt expects to be here for some time yet. The embassy seems to get busier and busier."

"Busier, every day, my dear," said *Herr* Witt.

"*Frau* Witt, may I say that you look lovely, this evening?" said David. "Vickie treated me to a tour of the old city today, and I am delighted to be concluding the day with your company."

"Really, Lieutenant, I was not advised of your charm! Perhaps we should keep him locked up, eh, Vickie?" said *Herr* Witt.

"If that is your wish, Colonel, I am sorry, but I will have to ask the embassy for funds to install more interior locks to keep him at my mercy. Bread and water for him, sir?" Vickie said.

"Nothing more. Bread and water, slipped through a panel in the door!" Witt laughed himself red-faced and coughing.

"I am your servant, sir, and will not undertake to steal your own opportunity to give *Frau* Witt the adulation she certainly deserves!" said David. All laughed and began to look up for the arrival of the second course.

The meal progressed and Vickie asked Witt, "And which important personage do you have our Lieutenant meeting tomorrow, *Herr* Witt?"

"Well, my dear, you may remember Izgot *Pasha?* He has asked to visit. Really, he just wants a sip of my cognac!"

"Well, I must admit my dear friend, we did not regret seeing the back of the man the last time you were forced to hide him here!" said Vickie.

The meal concluded and the Witts bade everyone a goodnight. David went to his rooms, and wide awake, thought about his day. He remembered Vickie's words at the ancient wall and decided not to give them further scrutiny. He decided to write a letter to Sigi and Kathe.

David Samuel Petersruhe-Rožmberk
Embassy of the German Empire
14 May 1908
Graf Sigismund von Petersruhe
Vogelgesangstein, Baden

My Dearest Parents:

I arrived safely in Constantinople and am settled into my new quarters. I have had a tour of the old city, remembering some of the sights Mother described to me. I hope you are well, and as my duties become clear, I will be able to reserve the time to write to you. Please write in care of the embassy for now.

Your loving son,

David

David sealed the letter in an envelope taken from the stationery Kathe had packed into one of his bags. He put the letter out in plain view, so he would not forget to take it to the embassy for posting. He decided to try sleep, and putting on cotton pajamas, he turned off the lamp and lay down, instantly appreciating the comfort of the bed. Soon, he was asleep.

The next morning, after breakfast, he presented himself to *Herr* Witt at the embassy. *Herr* Witt had become Colonel Witt, standing behind his desk as David was presented by one of the receptionists. David immediately saluted and clicked his heels and the gestures were returned in kind by the plump officer.

"Well, young man, I promised you a Turk, I believe. You may as well get used to being kept waiting. Turks are never timely. Izgot *Pasha* should present himself shortly, but while we wait, I'd like to explain his relationship to the mission here. Izgot works as a spy for the Porte, for the restless young Turks in Paris, and for us. He has been asked to accompany you to Salonika to introduce you to the garrison there and to some of the army officers and impatient politicians who are returning to Turkey from Paris and other cities. Many of these people were under self-imposed exile, but some of them have a price on their heads. When I say 'heads,' I mean 'heads.' Izgot will take you through the country and help you familiarize yourself with the peasants and the townspeople you encounter.

"Ah, my dear Izgot *Pasha!*" exclaimed Witt, as the Turk entered the office. "Thank you for agreeing to meet with us this morning. May I present, Lieutenant David von Petersruhe-Rožmberk, late of Berlin?"

The Turk bowed and pressed his hand across his breast. He was dressed in Western clothes and held a bowler in his hands. He said, "Welcome to my humble country, Lieutenant. The *Oberst* honors me by presenting his fellow countrymen to me occasionally. I understand that we are to embark on a small journey."

"Let us speak about that, Izgot *Pasha*. I would like for the young Lieutenant to travel through your land to Salonika and to have the honor of being presented to your country's garrison there, and perhaps, to some of the more active members of your empire's society. If you could make the arrangements, the German Empire and I would appreciate your efforts. May I present these documents for your safekeeping? If you have occasion to present them to the proper authorities, please do so with my compliments."

"*Oberst,* I will make the necessary arrangements. Shall we say, for Monday, next?" said Izgot *Pasha*.

"That would be most convenient, sir," said Colonel Witt. He shook hands with the Turk, who offered his to David and exited, leaving a hint of body odor.

Witt looked at David, and smiling, gestured toward a chair. "Izgot is a dangerous man, my dear Lieutenant. Do not take this man at his word, and be very careful of disclosing any details of your presence here. Should he ask, I would prefer that you tell him that you were provided lodging here at the embassy. By the way, how have you found your arrangements at *Apfelhaus*? Is *Frau* Schencke taking good care of you?"

"Yes, sir, she is. I am curious, however, about Norma. Vickie told me Norma's story, but it seems too sad to believe, sir."

"My dear boy, the German Empire's rulers and enthusiasts like that lunatic, *Frau* Liliencron, would have all of us believe that a perfection of character reins and that the sons of Germany carry no faults into new lands. Have you ever heard of Shark Island? Our military placed nearly two thousand prisoners taken during the conflict in Southwest Africa on a rock in the ocean called Shark Island and allowed nearly all of them to perish. The guards violated the young girls, and the men were beaten regularly. Norma is with us because of the unbridled lust of one of our noble settlers, a *respected* physician, sent out to help his fellow settlers and the native population. This was before much of the unrest. Moving ahead, as *Frau* Schencke has probably told you she adopted Norma. Unfortunately, Norma had to endure a few years in an orphanage in Germany before she could be legally adopted. She was fortunate to have *Frau* Schencke looking after her during this time, and when the officials cleared the way for Norma's adoption, she had the good fortune of joining a waiting parent.

"*Frau* Schencke, herself, has endured some serious unpleasantness in her time as a nurse. My wife befriended her many years ago during her own tour in Southwest Africa with the German Overseas Society. Vickie had been a lively girl, full of enthusiasm for her mission and extraordinarily attractive. Unfortunately, she went missing for several days. The army found her bound and barely clothed in the bush about ten miles away from her station. She had obviously been violated, as a subsequent examination confirmed, and my wife took her into her own private quarters to keep her from reliving the horror of being abducted from the hospital. *Frau* Schencke never spoke about the incident, except to say that she must atone for what had happened to her. My wife brought her back to Germany, and after our marriage, we 'adopted' her, after a fashion. When the necessity for the safe house, the *Apfelhaus*, became apparent to us, here, we could think of no better person to entrust with its management. There will be times when you will be asked to stay here at the embassy, Lieutenant. *Frau* Schencke does receive specialized care occasionally, owing to her old trauma. Now allow me to give you a tour of the embassy."

David wondered what 'specialized care' for Vickie really meant. He could imagine how horrible her experience in Africa had been and wondered what 'adopted' meant to Witt. He looked around the Colonel's office and noticed a photograph of the *Kaiser* mounted on the wall, a wooden spear hung behind Witt's desk above the window, and a map of Europe hung on the wall to his left. *Frau* Witt stared out of a frame resting on his desk. He also noticed the beaming image of a young man next to *Frau* Witt.

"Colonel, may I ask, who is this young man in the photograph, here?" asked David.

"Oh, that is my nephew, Lieutenant Sigmund Gerhard Schneider, or "Gerd," as we call him. He is due here sometime in the coming months. Or years, God knows."

Witt guided David through the embassy, introducing him to the various members of the staff, not including the ambassador, Marschall von Bieberstein, unfortunately, and pointing out various elements of the building. At about 11:00, Witt consulted his pocket watch and told David that they would be lunching at the Hotel Pera.

The two soldiers entered the embassy's official limousine at about 11:30 and motored to the Pera, where the nexus of the Western World seemed to gather. The men were welcomed by the doorman and made their way to the dining room, which was already filling up with elegant men and women representing most European nations. A slim man of somewhat dark complexion and wearing an Italian-tailored suit stopped at their table and nodded to Witt. "*Herr*

Witt" was the extent of his greeting. He looked at David and back at Witt who said, "My dear Isaac," and with a smile, nodded farewell. The waiter took their orders and the pair relaxed while they waited. The broad dining room's atmosphere agreed with David. He studied the various architectural styles that seemed to blend gracefully and thought: how very different from the embassy!

"I knew your dear mother, *Gräfin* Kathe von Petersruhe, you know," Witt said. "She used to pass through the city often, looking for manuscripts and ancient artifacts. I've been here for so long, I suppose, I just come with the furniture, as it were. Other officials come and go, but I've had the good fortune to stay in place and develop many friendships these many years."

The meal was pleasant, and in time, Witt, called for the car, and they returned to the embassy. Witt told David to make the most of his free time and dismissed him at about 2:00 p.m. David walked out of the embassy and wandered around the streets for a few minutes, idly making his way back to *Apfelhaus.*

The next morning, after a somewhat restless night, David was awakened by a woman's scream. He put on a robe, dashed into the hallway, and followed the voices to the front door. There, looking down at a small wooden crate, were Norma and Vickie, shaking and holding each other. Norma was whimpering and Vickie was only slightly more composed. David knelt, opened the crate, and found himself staring into the eyes of Izgot *Pasha.* He picked up the crate, set it into a corner of the vestibule, and said, "Vickie, please telephone Colonel Witt, at once." He brought Norma into his arms and led her to the sitting room, where they sat down together, and he held her shuddering body close.

Soon, Witt appeared and examined the crate. He looked at David and muttered, "*Mörderisch* monsters! I'll never get used to these damn Turks! Izgot played a dangerous game, but to have his head delivered to representatives of Turkey's only real European sponsor is insulting. I'll take this horror with me and ask Clara, *Frau* Witt, to help you with the ladies. Do not mention this to anyone, David."

"Understood, sir. I will stay with the ladies until you instruct me otherwise," David said. He'd noticed that Witt had called him "David," probably betraying his own abreaction to the dreadful sight. Norma was beginning to calm down, and soon he heard *Frau* Witt's solicitous voice in the hallway and the door closing. He saw Vickie and the older woman walk past the sitting room, with Vickie leaning into the side of her friend.

Norma patted David's knee and said, "Thank you, sir. I will resume my duties, now." She rose and left the room, leaving David to himself. He left the room after a few minutes and went to his quarters to prepare for the day.

Very soon, David was called to the embassy, and dressed in a field uniform, he entered Witt's office. "Sir, send me to Salonika. Find me a translator, and I'll sweep up information for you. I am ready."

"I am ready also, Lieutenant; things are about to get out of control." Into his telephone, he told the operator to send in Lieutenant Zimmer and to bring in two sets of captain's insignia. Witt told David that he was appointing him temporary *Hauptmann*, because Zimmer was a lieutenant also. The secretary arrived with Zimmer and later returned with the insignia for David. She placed it on Witt's desk and quickly disappeared.

Witt minced no words. "Zimmer, you are to act as translator to acting *Hauptmann* Petersruhe-Rožmberk. You will do whatever he asks. Get your field kit on, pack a spare, and return here at 7:00 tomorrow morning to be issued a weapon." The Lieutenant saluted, turned on his heel, and left quickly.

"Now, *Hauptmann*, get these shiny objects on your uniforms while I tell you what I want. First, get to Salonika and go directly to the home of Said Ali Said, of the Committee of Solidarity and find someone who might be able to lead you to one of their leaders. Spend time with them, and get back here within a week to report. The Paris branch of this organization has merged with the Salonika group, and soon I expect, you're going to see mutinying soldiers looking for back pay and ambitious political types causing mayhem and making threats. We don't want to be as sleepy as that fool hiding up the Bosporus continues to be!"

"Yes, Colonel, but kindly tell me who else I might look for or whose movements I might wish to learn."

"Enver *Bey* and Niyazi *Bey* or anyone associated with them. There is trouble brewing in Macedonia, so if you need to, make a quick survey of things beyond the city. You're going to have to learn this type of work on your own, unfortunately, but I have every confidence that you will be successful. After you return and report, I will probably send you back to Germany, lest the Turks, any *Verdammt* Turk, gets their hands on you."

The next morning, David met Zimmer at the embassy, and the two men began their journey. They left the massive, angled and ornate building under its hovering eagles perched at each corner-top and walked down the *Galata* Hill from Pera and descended the long steps sloped into each other in the middle. The many dogs lay asleep or prowling about looking for scraps of food from the merchants and families moving in and out of their domains. The men finally made it to the old train station, purchased tickets to Salonika, and boarded with a horde of wool merchants speaking *Ladino* and a number of Turkish soldiers and peasants.

Seated, the two soldiers attracted some attention from two curious women wearing black *niqabs* that hid their faces. David felt the train buck forward, and it was underway, rough and swaying around the track's many slight curves. He soon dozed and jerked awake when he felt a cold, wet nose, nuzzling his folded hands resting on his knees. A young sheep looked up at him, stared for a moment, and then wandered back out into the narrow passage that ran along the side of the carriage. He could still smell the city. The fumes of the coal had soaked into the wooden framing of the train car, and the soot and occasional embers that flew into the compartment were waved off by the women.

Zimmer said, "I understand that we'll be able to smell the flowers of Salonika well ahead of our arrival."

"I've heard that also, Zimmer but don't get your hopes up. We're as likely to smell gun powder, I'm afraid."

The journey was interrupted by arguing Greeks and a persistent

Turkish soldier speaking a mixture of French and his native tongue asking for tobacco. The man asked the women if their men relations were on the train, and when the women tried to ignore him, he snatched one of the ladies up from the seat and clearly threatened her. Zimmer rose and told the soldier in Turkish that the women had been entrusted to his care and to leave the compartment at once. The Turk shuffled away, muttering curses and glaring at the two Germans.

That evening in the glow of gaslights, the men stepped off the train in Salonika and finally separated from the crowd that had consumed them and pushed them forward. The angry Turkish soldier approached them with loud, threatening words. He extracted a long, pitted knife with a filthy cloth wrapped around the handle and swung at Zimmer with incredible force. The Lieutenant fell to his knees at once, holding his belly and doubling over. Like Hector leading his army, thought David, a black figure came from behind, and in long, loping strides, flew up, and with one strike, took the head of the Turkish assassin nearly off. Attached to the body only by a tongue of skin, it separated when the black figure pulled back the small sword he had used to slay the soldier. At once, another black figure approached, and removing her gown, rolled the split man into it and shoved him into a small, fetid, pool of water that had collected under a sitting rail car after the last storm's downpour. The sword-wielding figure took the Turk's weapon and threw it into the open door of the car above. He came over to Zimmer, whose body David was turning over.

"Zimmer should had left that Turk to us," said the taller figure, now recognizable as Norma. She pulled another flowing black gown from an ornate bag she'd been carrying and slipped it over her head quickly. She picked up her small sword and concealed it within her clothing. The other figure identified herself as Vickie and told David to move off, to seek the contact near the Greek consulate and not to be concerned with her or Norma.

At once, David began moving in the direction indicated on the small map Witt had given him, and soon he found himself amidst the roving traffic of the city. He was surrounded by Ottoman reserve troops who shouted in chorus, "*Ankara! Ankara! Ankara!*" They ignored the German soldier until an officer took him aside and stated in very good English, "We will not stay! We demand to be transferred back to our base in Ankara! Go tell your Prime Minister that we defy the Sultan and that the Committee will triumph!" He marched on with his comrades past David.

Finally, David reached the residence of Ali Said Ali, a friend of Turgot Djavid *Bey* of the Committee. He knocked on the door, looking around to see if he was being watched. The swarm of soldiers had been a good shield for him, he thought, as suspicion had consumed him since the attack on poor Zimmer. A man of indeterminate age opened the door and looking carefully at David for only a moment, beckoned him inside.

"I am Ali *Bey* and speak only my Ladino, Greek, or English. May we speak English? You are no doubt from Witt, correct?"

"I am, sir, from Colonel Witt."

"I must say, you speak as an Englishman. Come, sit."

Ali *Bey* led David through a narrow, arched passageway surrounded by beautiful, ornate plaster rendered in complex geometrical designs. Above the back of the arch, a Star of David was molded into the plaster, which surprised David.

"You have come for information. I do not wish to know your name, young man, by the way. First, you must give me your weapon," said Ali *Bey*. David handed the older man his Luger pistol. He looked at it carefully, and handed it back to David. "You are from Witt," Ali *Bey* said, apparently accepting the weapon as Witt's confirmation of David's mission. The man wore light, Western clothes with a red fez and presented a sad, lined face. He stooped somewhat when walking and seemed to drag his left foot, which he took care to place behind his right foot as he sat down. David remained standing.

"You are to tell Witt *Pasha* that there will be a rising originating here within a month. Other disturbances will occur, particularly in Scutari, Monastir, and Resen. The Committee will present the Sultan with demands, and if they are not met, they will order a general march on Constantinople within weeks. It must be understood that all of this nonsense being propagated by the British and others about a Jewish Freemasonry revolution can be completely ignored. Witt *Pasha* must warn his superiors that Germany may play an important role in the military and political changes that are coming. That is all you need to know. Now, tell me, was the Turkish soldier murdered by your guards asking any suspicious questions of you this evening?"

"No sir. He was just an irate Muslim looking for tobacco from me and trying to instruct the women in my rail cabin in conservative rules, I think."

"You must tell Witt *Pasha* that Vickie and Norma should stay at *Apfelhaus* until calm reins. There will be blood for a while. Now you must go. Do not stay in Macedonia. My son will get you back to the station for the late train."

"Thank you, Ali *Bey*. We are very grateful."

Ali offered his hand, while remaining in his seat. "Yousef!" he called.

A young man of eighteen or so came into the room wearing a Turkish army uniform, apparently armed to the teeth with two revolvers at his side, a sword, and the handle of another pistol-type firearm in his tunic. The boy beckoned David to follow him.

As they stepped onto the street, the two women joined them and made themselves to look slavish to Yousef, who marched with David in front of the procession. Yousef raised his arm and a carriage came clattering out of the shadows, stopping before them. The driver never looked back as David and Yousef entered, but the carriage started toward the railway station the instant the door closed behind the party. The street was lit with electrical lights, and the uneven paving stones glistened as David looked out of the window. There seemed to be much more merriment in Salonika than Constantinople. People were about everywhere, spilling out of taverns and gathered to impromptu musical performances, dancing and cheering at every corner.

When the coach reached the railway station, David pulled out the Luger he'd shown Ali *Bey* and offered it to Yousef.

The boy was startled and said, "For me, *effendi?*"

David nodded yes and shook the boy's hand, grateful to have gotten to his destination.

"You stay behind us, David," said Vickie. She led Norma out of the coach and toward the station. When David caught up with them, Vickie handed David a ticket and told him to lead them onto the train. Finding their compartment, Vickie put her finger to her lips, which she momentarily exposed.

The trip back to Constantinople was uneventful. There were no soldiers and only a few drunken peasants pushing small children along before them. David closed his eyes, confident that one of the women was awake. He began to dream.

He butted the walls with his ram and hurled his spear and waited for blood to paint his body. The walls were high and thick, but no one was manning them. A voice said, "Look, ships below us!" And he felt his body hurled through the air and falling into the mainsail of a steel-black schooner, wrapping him up and furling unto itself, crushing and blinding him. A voice, a woman's voice, whispered, "You shall, you shall."

David woke and saw that Vickie and Norma were leaning against each other, holding hands, and whispering with great affection, nuzzling their faces together, and sighing. He thought of Zimmer and wondered what the women did with his body. He was afraid to ask, but he could not shed a sense of responsibility. Witt knew the danger, thought David.

The little group reached Constantinople very late that evening and went directly to *Apfelhaus*. David collapsed on his bed and was asleep within a few minutes. Later, he felt his clothes being removed and he drowsily cooperated, stretching his legs when the cuffs of his trousers where being tugged, and rising a bit when his tunic was opened and pulled back away from his chest. Finally, he felt the softness of the bed, as he lay naked within the sheets, warmed by a thick wool blanket stretched over the top. As he was losing himself again to dreams, Norma slipped into his bed, pushed her breasts into his back, and pulled up her legs into his. And both slept soundly.

When David awoke, Norma was gone, and a fresh uniform was laid out on the chair. He went in to his bathroom, washed, shaved, and made ready for his next meeting with Witt.

24

The *Universität Karlsruhe* had been demanding. After a year's posting in Turkey, David had received a letter from Sigi insisting that David take leave of the army and attend the school to further his career and to be educated as his acquired nobility, at least in the old Count's mind, would mandate. Engineering was always in demand by the army, some ministry, or the growing private concerns.

David enjoyed the school break at *Vogelgesangstein* before the final term was about to begin. When he walked from the breakfast table, he found Colonel Klages standing in the great hall of the *Schloss* talking to Kathe. The Colonel had not changed as far as David reckoned, perhaps he was a little heavier. Without doubt, his presence meant another mission.

"Ah, my dear Lieutenant," said Klages, "your mother has been telling me of your success at university. We need more educated officers! I have news for you. You have been promoted to *Hauptmann,* and you will return to Constantinople. This last *Universität* term, I am sorry to say, must wait. Or perhaps, our dear *Alten Hund* will be able to have you graduating early." Sigi had long been known throughout the army as the "Old Hound" for his ability to detect the enemy.

David clicked his heels and bowed to the Colonel. "This must have something to do with Young Turks, I venture," said David.

"Young Turks and old German Colonels! You are to report by the end of the week. General Count Petersruhe has details of your travel arrangements. And with apologies to everyone, I must now be on my way." At that, Klages bowed to Kathe and saluted David, who returned the salute, and left through the great front doors.

David looked at Kathe and said, "I suppose that duty calls no matter what the circumstances, Mother. I suppose the *Graf* will be along to apprise me of my immediate movements."

"This is most unfortunate, David. I always fear for you, my dearest. What ills I too must learn to bear, as Goethe, says. These Young Turks … were they not overthrown?"

"In and out; it is very difficult to keep account of the roiling Turkish political *tableau*, and with university, frankly, I have not had the time to seriously try."

The old *Graf* stepped into the room through the huge front doors, having passed Klages on his way to his official car. The *Graf* had taken to using a longer, ash walking stick that was wrapped at various points with thin, well-tanned leather. He threw the stick before him with discipline and a kind of ceremony, and walked up to its ground-clutch, hesitating for a short moment, and then beginning his stride again, moved onward. He was as alert as ever, and as usual, smiling. He held his tasseled pipe in his free hand and leaning over to the wall, knocked its spent contents out onto the floor. This part of the great hall had been, after all, part of the original *Schloss'* keep. The housekeeper's assistant had heard the door open and rushed in instantly to sweep the discarded clot of tobacco from the floor and wipe the wall, which had become stained with the several generations of pipes banged along the old pocked stone near the same point. The bedabble covering his high boots had dried during his ride back from his morning shoot with his neighbor, and the unlucky birds he brought back were being plucked at that moment in the kitchen.

The old *Graf* spoke to David. "And so, my son, you are off to the Sultan again. That being the case, as Klages suggested, I will petition *Universität* to award your degree. One term should not prevent a serving soldier from benefitting from all of the time and effort invested there. I am sorry to see you leave, although we haven't had the opportunity to see much of you!"

"Oh really, my dear, we've been in Karlsruhe at least three times a month since our boy returned. But I agree, we will miss you, David," said Kathe. "Now I suggest that you find Wok and organize your packing. How is he traveling, Sigi?"

"Well, let us look at the tickets the mysterious *Oberst* left with me. Appears that we'll have to get him to Stuttgart to depart on the Orient Express, which will drop down to Belgrade and then on to Constantinople. I expect that Witt will be there to meet you. You'll have to ask the Colonel what his *real* name is sometime, *Hauptmann*."

"The man is too kind, sir; I wouldn't wish to offend him."

"It's *Wittgenstein*, son. He is a fine man and proved to be a gallant soldier during the last century in West Africa. An unfortunate scheme, if I may criticize the *Rhenish* efforts to bring the Lord to our darker brothers and sisters. At least Witt was well away during the recent horrible suppression of the tribes *one never hears about!*"

"Father, as far as *Oberst* Witt is concerned, I don't believe that anyone really is who they appear to be in Turkey or Greece, for that matter."

After the usual parting, painful and through many tears, David once again set off with Wok to a train station. The ride was quiet, as always, and David was able to present himself before the ornate, Renascence-styled arches of the train station and find his assigned car relatively early. He boarded the middle blue car of the short train and felt himself lucky to have the opportunity to transit the continent in such comfort. He would have preferred *ensuite* arrangements, but sharing the cabin with only a wash sink with a stranger was most tolerable for a soldier. He settled in, placing his bag under the new folded-down seat, and watched the movement of humanity through the cabin window.

David observed a family of street peasants hectoring a beautiful woman dressed in black who was looking about, starting to move one direction, then another, and finally toward a small shop decorated by paintings of peacocks whose plumage was arrayed with many eyes, attracting many eyes, as, perhaps its artist would have wished. The peasants followed, and then dispersed as a policeman approached, tapping an oak staff loudly. The station became dark, and soon, though he couldn't hear it very well, the terminal roof sounded with drops of heavy rain. The peasants disappeared, as if into the wooden panels from the original construction, and David didn't catch sight of them again until a woman emerged from the shop of the peacocks.

She was dressed in an expensive violet dress, which she lifted, exposing fine millinery as she ran from the peasants, who had appeared again as if from nowhere. Another woman, dressed all in white and carrying a matching parasol came out of the shop with a man who was wearing a top hat and carrying a long, slender package under his arm. As they exited, the sun began to creep through the skylights at either end of the terminal, bringing a gleam to the metal fixtures and the tracks. David noticed the flight of the woman's white skirts as wind from one end of the terminal blew through following the rain. The man raised his free hand to hold his top hat in place, and the couple vanished into the interior of the station to exit into a patch of unexpected sunlight.

The carriage began filling, and soon David's own companion opened the door and stepped into the cabin. He was tiny, perhaps just over five feet, with unruly white hair, an elf-lock, wind-blown, swirling around his face. His facial skin seemed as thin as paper, but his white beard was thick, and the fricative wave of his cheeks as he breathed through his mouth somewhat comically, suggested the indefatigable respiration of gills. He wore a roman collar and a black cloak over a white cassock and carried a black biretta. In one of the three ridges atop the hat, the man had balanced an over-sized triangular package covered in baker's wrapping. He set his small bag on the opposite settee, and looking David in the eye, blinked and said, "I am Father Henry Atreus Youghal, O.P. I am traveling from England to Jerusalem." The man's voice was quiet, high-toned, just audible.

"I am David von Petersruhe-Rožmberk, traveling only to Constantinople."

"Your accent sounds positively Etonian, my son. I'm led to believe that you were born and bred aristocratically in England. Nevertheless, you do have a rather continental surname. But your clothes, your clothes are cut for an English gentleman. My word, you do *tease* one." The priest came closer to David and looked him up and down, giving a slight sniff.

"Father, I have lived in England, but I am a creation of this country. I have fond memories of your country. Forgive me, but what does O.P. signify?" David said, smiling at the tiny being.

"Order of Preachers. We're called Black Friars in England as my cloak reflects, but to the world at large, Dominicans. We were, like other Catholic orders, dissolved by Henry VIII and forced to find new homes in the Netherlands and even now, America. We've managed to introduce missions back into England, but as yet, we've not been in a position to re-establish our priory in Oxford, our original English home. Perhaps, soon." Father Youghal sat down carefully, his veiny hands supporting his weight as he dropped back into his seat.

"I know almost nothing of Catholicism, except as it relates to the Thirty Years War, and of course, our brothers Teutonic, the Hapsburgs. May I ask, where are you from originally?"

Just then, a shout of *en voiture!* was proclaimed and after a short interval, the train jolted to life and slowly the engine began to chuff into its passage. The sunlight steadily peeled through the cars as each exited the terminal, and their deep blue became a charming contrast to the dull grime settled onto most everything the train yard presented the passengers. As the train entered into the patchwork of sown fields just outside of the city and followed the curved track leading through the first covering of forest, the two men sat silently gazing out of the cabin glass, committed to their respective missions and knowing that their journeys could not now be suspended.

"Where am I from? I grew up in a region of north London near Hampstead Heath, quite removed from the great city. Are you familiar with the English poet, John Keats?"

"Somewhat. Isn't that the 'Season of mists and mellow fruitlessness' fellow? I am sorry, Father, but that is nearly all I know of the man's work," said David.

"Well, my son, I lived near his home in Hampstead. I later attended Oxford University, where I became a member of the Catholic Club. The name has been changed, however. From there, I sought and found my vocation in America."

"I've never been to America. I have the impression that we Europeans, with our squabbles and variety, must be a strange group to the inhabitants of that country. May they be spared!" David laughed.

"I can't possibly describe the difference. I can however say with some authority that there is a great deal of sneering from both sides of the Atlantic."

"I wouldn't sneer at any country at peace and not obliged to dance around alliances and disingenuous treaties."

"You go far in criticizing your culture, even your own country, young man." Father Youghal smoothed back his whiskers. His eyes opened wider, and his lips trembled for a short moment. "Where are *you* from?"

"I'm from what we on the *Continent* call a Free City. I grew up primarily in Lübeck, but I have lived with my family in the Baden region for some time now."

Father Youghal went quiet and brought his hands up to his dry gash of a mouth and then around his face, stretching it like waxed paper and pulling his eyes forward. His eyes opened widely, and he said, "Here you are, a fine-looking young man, an *Adonis*, shall we say, a figure that in our ancients' tales would be fated to the whims and desires of Divine beings. But you are real, you have thoughts that *will* your private *raison d'etre*, if any, which in my world, you owe to a *higher being*." The old priest stopped speaking and reached over to pat his biretta, and then after turning it about one way, turned it another. The ancient creature ran his hands through his unruly, white hair, and dropping his head against the fashionable seat's cushion said, almost whispering through his pallid, thin lips, "As Augustine said, the proof presented to us is simply, 'For we brought nothing into this world and it is certain that we carry nothing out.' Isn't the question resolved as the child first finds his mother's breast and the old draw their last breaths? Nothing brought, nothing taken away?" He looked out of the carriage window and closed his eyes. "I am rambling on like one of *your* country's philosophers, I dare say." Then the old fellow stared at David, blinking occasionally and pinching and then relaxing his lips for a few moments, and finally blowing forth breath that had been swelling his cheeks. He turned his head to the window again, and began to huff the invisible gills that seemed to lift his head in little motions. His whiskered chin moved up, up upon imagined stairs, his profile puffed respiration, and his mien suggested alarm and bewilderment. "Look at the white poplars, the effulgent dew still shining in our morning. Dazzling, isn't it, my son?" He lifted a hand against what he saw. Light, cast through a narrow slit in passing walls of an estate, fell on his bushy white hair as a single bright line and disappeared.

David sat quietly. The priest's clothes began to fill the cabin with a sweet scent, as if they had been laundered in light perfume. The sensation was punctuated with the old being's foul breath each time he spoke, but David became used to the combination and accepted his companion. Something about the little man took him back to *Herr* Schlarp's world, but he was challenged to make sense of what he said. David wondered, finally, if Father Youghal was even speaking to *him*. David thought, *an angel*? He had listened closely to the old man's quiet ramblings, becoming fascinated with the little being's manner of speaking and questioning the *real* essence of his musings.

The priest's hands had moved from his head to wrap his shoulders and fall down to splay out over his knees as he spoke, but he continued to hold his face elevated, looking aloft, through the window again, seemingly unfocused. Father Youghal remained quiet for a few moments more, then shifted the back of his tiny frame against the wall nearest the door and placed his spindly legs and tiny feet on the seat. He situated his *biretta* and wrapped snack, smoothed his frock, and lay back. He recited, as if only to himself:

My aspens dear, whose airy cages quelled,
Quelled or quenched in leaves the leaping sun,
All felled, felled, are all felled;
Of a fresh and following folded rank
Not spared, not one
That dandled a sandaled

Shadow that swam or sank
On meadow and river and wind-wandering weed-winding bank.
O if we but knew what we do
When we delve or hew—
Hack and rack the growing green!
Since country is so tender
To touch, her being so slender,
That, like this sleek and seeing ball
But a prick will make no eye at all,
Where we, even where we mean
To mend her we end her,
When we hew or delve:
After-comers cannot guess the beauty been.
Ten or twelve, only ten or twelve
Strokes of havoc unselve
The sweet especial scene,
Rural scene, a rural scene,
Sweet especial rural scene.

And as quiet as falling snow, the religious man closed his eyes and began to snore softly, his cheeks filling and expiring with a whistling sound. David continued looking out of the window, reminded of Herakles returning from the underworld wearing a crown of poplars and poor Zimmer, who had been felled so cruelly. Who, or what, were the Father's *ten or twelve*. He gazed at the countryside of Austria as the train slowed near Vienna and wondered how different the journey to Constantinople would have been if old Moltke had not had his way with the Austrians and the French. Would there *be* an Orient Express?

As the rolling stock entered Vienna Station, Father Youghal awoke and looking about asked, "Are we in Vienna, David?"

"Yes, Father." David had noticed that the priest had started calling him "David," instead of "my son" and wondered if his agent of divinity had disinherited him. He was not bothered. He'd never had frequent interaction with Catholic priests and knew that it was not something with which he was completely comfortable. He watched the old man sit up huffing like an aquatic native hauled out of water and thumbing his rosary, perhaps seeking his formula of salvation. David decided to nickname him, *Die Forelle,* The Trout, and began to hum the opening bars of Schubert's masterpiece. He had heard the quintet several times in Lübeck and *Vogelgesangstein* with Kathe at the piano, the first rising scale of keys always signifying, it seemed, the consent of the composer to the strings to proceed.

"I believe that I will move these old legs around for a few minutes," said Father Youghal. "The train will resume its task quickly; we won't get a very long hiatus before Budapest, when the dining cars will be attached. Please excuse me." He made his way, with quite unexpected energy, through the compartment door and began strolling to and fro in the car. The man's shoulders scarcely cleared the door glass and his white hair resembled a confection topping a pastry as he passed back and forth several times before *"en voiture!"* could be heard from outside of the train. When he re-entered the compartment, he found David asleep with his arms crossed and his hat pulled down over his eyes.

The Orient Express screeched away from the terminal, the carriages joggled, and David's body rocked against the back of the seat without disturbing him. The train moved into the dusk of Franz Joseph's Empire, and his minions continued about their labors as the long day continued. At length, the train began slowing, and the squeal of wheels and rail and the rapid chuffing of the engine announced the Budapest station. David awoke and felt the humping of the dining cars joining the metal entourage, which stirred insistent hunger in him. Father Youghal had opened his small package and had begun mincing through its contents, chewing rapidly. His mouth half full, he said, "The dining car is open, but I'll not be joining you my son. This will serve me quite well, and I will exercise my evening rituals in your absence."

David nodded and rose, rubbing his sleepy face in his hands. The train was moving again, and he could see the wind-blown smoke passing his window in more and more frequent gusts. The car swayed more than he had been used to, but the sensation was probably due to his awakening limbs and limited ability to balance during the motion, as the train bent the rails down to the ties and out toward the edges of the track bed. He opened the compartment door and could faintly smell the aroma of food wafting over the heads of those he joined moving in its direction before him. He finally entered the first dining car and finding it fully seated, moved to the next, where a woman waved to him to join her. He thought he recognized her. Perhaps, Vickie, but he wasn't fully certain.

"Good evening, *Hauptmann* Petersruhe-Rožmberk," she said as she stood to greet him. She was tall and wore her dark hair in fashionable ringlets above long *Romanesque* brows and large brown eyes. She extended an unusually outsized hand of long, thick fingers.

"Good evening, Madam. Forgive me, but I cannot place you in my memory" David said, with some reluctance.

"You don't know me, *Herr Hauptmann*, but if you recall *Frau* Schencke from *Apfelhaus*, you may now identify me as her replacement."

"Ah, I can't say that I am surprised that Colonel Witt is still having me watched over. I assume that you know my history, so may I ask if you've uncovered anything embarrassing?"

"Oh, plenty, my dear sir. At least enough to make you follow orders," said the smiling woman. "Shall we sit? I am Freya von Plehn; I am twenty-five years old; I come from Saxony; and unless *Frau* Andreas-Salome wishes to marry me, I shall embrace spinsterhood with enthusiasm. I am sorry, do you know of Lou Andreas-Salome, *Herr Hauptmann*?"

"I've known of her for nearly twenty years, Madam. She is admired by my adopted mother. My mother has likely corresponded with her, I believe, since childhood, and throughout her career. Please address me as just David."

"You, sir, may call me Freya. Shall we order?"

The wine was chosen and the meal organized to their satisfaction. There was small talk, mostly about Freya, who as it happened, had heard of the young man sitting across from her.

"My cousin, Ingrid Meckler, told me of a handsome young *Kadett* named David once. I wonder if all she said was true. And the things Vickie had to say, well, I *should* be terrified of your charms, eh, David?"

"Ingrid Meckler!" David spluttered, coughing wine onto the table linen. "You'll have to be very careful with that particular story!" David coughed more, blushing red. "And with the greatest of respect, Vickie told you nothing, of that I am certain, Madam."

"Vickie told me only that I might experience a shift in my preferences when I saw you. I must say, you do make an impression. As for Ingrid, well, it *is* a small world, don't you agree, my dear *Hauptmann*?"

The meal went well. The food was excellent and Freya's company charming. As they enjoyed a last glass of wine, David asked, "Am I to be consigned to *Apfelhaus* again?"

"Yes, and you will participate in dedicating the new bridge over the Horn as your first duty. Your second duty will be given you later, but it could be *adventurous*," said Freya.

"We must, I suppose, say good night. Thank you for a wonderful evening, Freya. Will you continue to be my, ah, *je ne sais quoi*?"

"We will leave that to *Oberst* Witt."

When David returned to his compartment, Father Youghal had transformed the seating into bedding. He was ensconced within the lower bed, humming, "Ask if yon damask rose be fair" from Handel's *Susanna*. His hands extended beyond the sheets covering him, his fingers snatching as if plucking the strings of an invisible viola. Noticing David's entry, he paused and said "God Bless and good night, my son" and resumed his performance with real gusto.

The *musical* Trout, thought David.

David undressed, and though he was not sleepy, crawled up to the top bunk and settled for the night. He called down to the priest. "Father, what was the poem you recited earlier?"

"'Binsey Poplars,' by Father Gerard Manley Hopkins."

Eventually, through a slight headache, David slept and dreamed that the pope had died.

The train finally reached the Pera Station and as David said farewell to Father Henry Atreus Youghal, O.P. as they disembarked, Freya stood by, ready to accompany David to *Apfelhaus*. As soon as he had retrieved his baggage, the pair began their journey in an old, mechanically suspect taxi. The driver strapped their bags onto the boot, and they found themselves sitting on a leather seat, slit and stained, surrounded by upholstery shredded and threadbare. Freya gave the driver directions.

Their destination reached a street corner near the *Apfelhaus*, the driver retrieved their luggage and looked at them as if offended. Freya found that the driver had wanted to take them to a building, rather than leaving them on the street. She paid him and said in French, "This is close enough."

Freya pushed the inconspicuous ringer, and in few moments the door of *Apfelhaus* opened to *Frau* Witt, who had grown thinner and somewhat shrunken. In a hoarse voice, she said, "Come in, come in! My dear David, now a *Hauptmann*, no less! And my Freya, how are you?"

The *Frau* instructed Freya's assistant, whom she introduced as Helen, to prepare a small lunch, and on her own, hastened to serve David and Freya cups of delicious coffee. The assistant appeared with plates of *Rouladen* heavily laden with pickles and an unidentifiable sauce mixed with mustard rolled into the beef. David was enchanted with the dish and watched the young assistant move about, a blonde girl with hair severely pulled into a tight braid behind her head and hung over her left shoulder, nearly resting on her breast. She had an upturned, slightly freckled nose, small bright blue eyes, and a flawless complexion set into a well-proportioned face. Her high cheekbones reminded David of Kathe, and he relaxed, looking into her beauty. He said, "I am David von Petersruhe-Rožmberk. Is it *Frau* or *Fraulein*, Helen?"

"It is *Fraulein*, but if I continue to be harried by all of the Empire's officers, I may have to change my status, *Hauptmann* Petersruhe-Rožmberk." She wasn't smiling.

"Oh, poor Helen, imagining every man she meets is yearning to trace 'I love you' in wine on every table top she visits," said Freya, laughing. "Pay no attention to Helen, David, she is already in love with you!"

Helen sniffed and left the room. Her formal gait and the manner in which she carried her head, upright and focused, suggested careful training. She met the pantryman, a new staff addition, at the kitchen door and accepted a plate of bread to offer the newly arrived, and turned around to face them, this time with a smile.

"You see, David, you'd better watch out! She'll finish what Ingrid couldn't!" said Freya.

"Thank you *Fraulein*; I promise not to presume upon your person in any manner and hope that if I offend in any way, that you will correct me" said David. "And *please* do not ask Freya about Ingrid."

"So noble, as to shame great Hector," said Freya. "After our repast, you'll find your old rooms ready for you."

"And do not forget that you are expected by Colonel Witt at 4:00, my dear *Hauptmann*," said *Frau* Witt. "Just ask for him at the front desk. He has moved offices since he last had the pleasure of your company."

The few hours passed, and David, rising from a nap, felt refreshed and rested. He half expected to see Vickie and Norma, but as he moved through the building, he saw no one. He left the *Apfelhaus* at 3:00 p.m. and walked to the embassy. He wore a long cape Kathe had given him that concealed most of his uniform. He moved through the stepped streets, so familiar, but now more invested with the uniforms of the Turkish army and far fewer dogs running about or laying in the paths of the multiethnic throngs. At 4:00, he presented himself at the white-trimmed, rust-colored embassy and was directed to an expansive set of offices set in a back corner of the second floor. There he was met at the front desk by a burly young Lieutenant, ruddy and gruff, who led David upstairs.

Another Lieutenant stood, clicked his heels, and saluted as David approached. They were standing in an anteroom lined with seating. A sign announced the section's purpose: "Cultural."

The young man introduced himself as Lieutenant Sigmund

Gerhard Schneider, aide to Colonel Witt. The young man was slight, fair, and very correct in uniform with a slightly over-sized nose leading his otherwise attractive, finely boned face.

"My dear *Hauptmann*, I see that you've met my aide, who also happens to be my nephew," said Witt, as he came out of his office to greet David. "As you can see, we have moved offices, and in addition to Gerd, we have grown in staff. Come in please, and let us have a few words together. Gerd, please keep us undisturbed for a few minutes." Witt was as cheerful as David remembered, but somewhat more corpulent. He sat down behind his desk and immediately became the Colonel. "First David, you will accompany a delegation to rededicate the new Pera bridge tomorrow. As you probably know, Germany built this one. I will head the delegation, and you will be presented as one of our engineers. That should please you, especially since Karlsruhe is going to wave the requirements of your last term. Second, we believe that war is nigh, and you will be sent out with the Turks when the Western Provinces begin to make trouble. This could happen as a result of internal politics or the aim of opportunistic Bulgars, Greeks, Macedonians, or what have you. Something is bound to happen, even to the extent that the Ottoman Empire will be changed forever. Same as your last visit, only worse. For now, I have a new map room that I expect you to get familiar with, and Gerd, who has been here two or three years, will assist you. So, any questions?"

"Yes, sir. These women at *Apfelhaus* … do they possess the same talents as Vickie and Norma did?"

"Well, they are well-trained and dangerous. Freya is a lesbian, as you might have gathered, and Helen, well Helen, is not a lesbian. They both have special talents with regard to personal defense, and you'll find them both dedicated to your welfare."

"May I ask who is running the present government?"

"At present, and this could change overnight, we believe Mahmud Shevket and sympathetic Committee members are controlling things."

"May I assume that Lieutenant Schneider can apprise me of the changes that have no doubt come to govern our behavior in the city? The government has seemed to change, dissolve, and reform since I've been away. I don't wish to run afoul of the officials."

"My boy, Lieutenant Sigmund Gerhard Schneider can tell you anything about anybody populating his primary area of interest— so-called polite society. He can tell you which official from what country is entertaining the wives and daughters of which official from which other country, and which of our own embassy's male staff is sleeping with which secretary. He is on very friendly terms with a number of Turks, mainly women, who he enjoys meeting at dinner to gossip. In short, he talks too much. He is *not* allowed to visit *Apfelhaus*, though his aunt's protests to me against this stricture are a constant irritation! Freya and Helen are under orders to keep him out. You may assume that Gerd is not an entertaining subject in this office. Now dismissed, *Hauptmann*."

David left the embassy, amused at Witt's irritation, and walked, this time with an assigned guard, back to the *Apfelhaus*. The guard was wearing plain clothes and said nothing. They parted at the usual corner, near the building.

25

Gräfin Claramond Kathe von Petersruhe-Matthäus
Vogelgesangstein
Baden
10 May 1913
Isaac Becouche-Albukerk
22 Cicek Pasaji
Constantinople

My Dearest Isaac:

I must first thank you again for the little notes you have been so kind to send regarding my David, these last years. I shall never be able to thank you and our dear Herbert enough for your kind attention to my beloved son's welfare during his sojourn in Constantinople. You have so kindly watched over my boy! I also wish to mention, once again, my profound sorrow for the loss of your Eligia. I realize that her passing was visited upon you some years ago, but the aptness of your pairing had so captivated me that I cannot but recall her to you, my dearest, that we may cosset our mutual grief and summon our gratitude to whatever fate brought her into our lives.

I have the pleasure to report of my dear Sigi. He is as hearty as ever, but in his noble aging, he does, more and more often, tend to sit quietly in his memorial, all morning usually, recalling, I am certain, the days of his military service and those who served with him. Those men he so dearly loved, he now, I am convinced, dedicates his very breath to their current welfare, sharing his wealth when asked, and for those long dead, offering sincere prayers for the nurturing of their souls.

Our beloved Vogelgesangstein seems to grow nobler, more sub-stantial in our lives, as we travel much less these days and rely upon the estate to fulfill our daily amusement and comfort. It is true that my Sigi is much older than I, and it is true that you, my Isaac, are far from me, but I confess that my selfishness, my very need for two great men in my life, has lifted my existence beyond thoughts of the mere human. I, just contentedly, am like a cloud wrought by the intercourse of the sun and earth. I dwell in the repose of my heart, a construction of love, of ideas, and of desires built so long ago by you and Sigi. I pray that I have served you both, offering your lives a homophrosýnē as a woman, as a helpmaid, and when time decrees, as your Abishag.

But my David is my deepest heart's defender. Now that he is in your midst again, I do so desire, if I may be so bold as to admit it, that you may permit him into your life. I see the young boy, the golden boy, in my thoughts every day—his sweetness and his beauty, his intelligence and manly strength—as he has grown into courage and mightiness, now ready to be shared like a pro-tecting star, watching innocently our little movements upon the green earth and listening, more intently, to the songs moving our hearts.

How wonderful it would be to know that we might go on, my dearest, that our cherished love would be carried into the days to come beyond our precious time, to light the paths of others. Do you dream likewise, my love? I think of you, I think of you, I think of you. Is there poetry beyond these simple words? These iambs sing to me like the little birds in Sigi's gardens in the spring and that is all you need to know.

Remember me,

Kathe

26

Throughout David's posting in Constantinople, the political situation in Turkey remained in flux. From the beginning of 1912, David had not been allowed to leave the environs of the capitol and obeyed the standing order: "Be quiet and available." His new tenure at *Apfelhaus* had been uneventful, and he enjoyed the banter between Freya and Helen as they went about the administration of the building and other duties: welcoming short-term visitors, entertaining at the embassy, and assisting in the various secretive duties assigned to them by the Colonel. David was now twenty-six and used to the great city, but after continually getting lost in Stanbul, usually while looking through antiquities and their facsimiles, Witt had to forbid him from venturing away from Pera unless in the company of Freya, who if the truth were exposed, Witt was a little afraid to confine to her post.

Gerd had been a good friend to David, and in addition to being a boundless reservoir of information regarding the social scene revolving around the various evening haunts of the foreign and the locally moneyed, he was also an inveterate gossip concerning things diplomatic. His uncle did not approve, however, and the poor young man was occasionally consigned to weeks of drudgery in clerical duties in an attempt to tamp down his enthusiasm for all things social. *Frau* Witt would inevitably rescue him and make the Colonel's life difficult for his interference with Gerd, whom she loved as a son. "I am his commanding officer!" was heard a few times through the months just before poor Witt's next acquaintance with a domestic ice age.

David marveled at the influence of Helen's beauty, though there was never any romantic encouragement. He thought of her standing still and fearless, ready to repel even the lustiest of *gods*. She was quite educated, and in fact, was the niece of the head of the aide-de-camp's staff at the embassy, often disappearing with him on hunting expeditions to Armenia or Anatolia. She would leave the *Apfelhaus* for these adventures wearing heavy boots and riding pants, and she would return padding toward the rear entry carrying her muddy, bloody boots. The sound of knocking and scraping as Helen cleaned her boots could often be heard behind the building and frightened birds and squirrels into neighboring trees or onto the roof of the building. There was never any game. Whatever she had killed remained with her uncle as far as David could discern.

After a few months, Witt summoned David to tell him that he was to accompany a detachment of Turkish infantry to Edirne near the border where the Ottoman neighbors were pressuring to carve farther into the Empire. He received his weapon, another Luger, and was told in the sternest of terms not to give it away this time. He was ordered to observe and meet the commanding officer, a Major Recep Ratib, at the staging area at the Stamboul train station. An interpreter would join him there.

"His name is Lieutenant Lothar Meese. I hope that he is luckier than Zimmer. Now don't forget to get your maps from Gerd. Dismissed," Witt told David.

The next day, David met Meese at the *Gebze* railway station in Stamboul, the old city of the empire. Meese walked up to David, introduced himself, and led him towards Ratib. He said, "This fellow is from Edirne, with family still there." Meese was as tall as David, had thin blond hair, and a wide freckled face. He took determined strides toward the company of Turkish soldiers and stopped abruptly, saluting the Major without clicking his heels. He introduced David, who was received with good cheer, and like Meese, he was offered an Ottoman army cap. David was made to understand that the less attention they drew, the better for everyone. He had worn a spiked helmet with a desire to distinguish himself as an observer, but in an effort to make him inconspicuous, the Turks insisted that he and Meese be as unrecognizable as German army officers as possible.

"Please ask the Major to explain his preference for the Turkish cap, Meese," said David.

"The Major does not wish to appear to be under international influence. The British and French are everywhere."

The German's helmets were placed in an empty rucksack and handed to Meese, who slung it over a shoulder and smiled. The troops boarded the train and began their one hundred and fifty mile passage, taking over two entire cars and moving the civilians into the remaining carriages. As the train left the old city's walls behind, Ratib leaned over to Meese and said, "Those walls will hold, but I fear for this city. The Bulgarians are hungry for Thrace and Edirne is so close to the border, I am certain that we will have to fight them soon."

The *Karaağaç* Station was crowded as the carriages approached Edirne. Porters stood ready with their carts, and clots of *Romany* were ready for the passengers. When the soldiers began stepping off the cars and formed up, the *Gypsies* scattered down the platform, silent and sullen. Ratib led the group out of the station and onto an unnamed *Caddesi* that took them across the *Meriç* River. After marching north, they found a barracks complex in the shadow of the *Selimiye* Mosque.

The two Germans were shown their quarters, merely a room of unpainted wood fragranced with incense. After they had put their packs and the rucksack containing the helmets down, a knock at the door brought them a meal of thin soup, vegetables, and rice. When the soldiers were finished, Meese went to the door to return the *sini* but found it locked from the outside. He set the tray down, and in Turkish, yelled, "*Aç şu kapıyı!*" At once, the door swung open to a squat, red-faced soldier who looked at Meese with startled features.

Meese handed him the tray, but as he was doing so, Ratib walked over to the building and said in English, "You will remain inside room! Orders!" The door closed.

"I had assumed that *Oberst* Witt had a more active participation in mind when he sent us with these damned *pashas!*" said David. "Tell them to open the door again, Lieutenant."

Meese yelled, "*Aç şu kapıyı!*"

The door swung open again, and Ratib stood before them alone. After an exchange in Turkish, Meese turned to David and recounted the conversation. "Ratib has been told that this is for our own safety, that should an attack come, he will free us and lead us to safety. He asks that we trust him."

David nodded understanding, but he told Meese to demand that the door be unlocked. Ratib agreed.

"I fear Turks bearing gifts, *Hauptmann*," said Meese. "Was Ratib locking us in to protect us from Turks or Bulgarians?"

Night fell, and the barracks outside of the city became illuminated by electric lamps strung along the eves of the rectangular complex. More food was brought to David and Meese along with a type of local brandy, which was a surprise to them. The men talked about the noises about the facility—the continual trooping of men and the clang of metal platters and plates. Then the noise died down, and they heard a thousand voices chanting, "*ölüm, ölüm, ölüm, ölüm...*" This continued for an hour.

"What does it mean, Meese?" asked David.

"I believe that the Turks are chanting, 'death,' toward the Bulgarians. The chanting is from high points in the city—probably some ancient custom exercised when war is expected. Perhaps our friends were sent here to strengthen the chorus!"

Just after he said, "chorus," a round of artillery smashed into the barracks complex. Then another. The sound of running, shouts of orders, and finally the appearance of Ratib at the door, convinced the Germans that an attack was underway. The Major motioned for the men to follow him, but as they ran behind Ratib, they encountered a line of riflemen arrayed in an arc and firing at will at the barracks' main gate. The Major went down, and his bloody neck glistened in the electric light. The Germans hit the ground and rolled to their left where a group of Turks were returning fire. Meese asked a Turk what was happening and received the answer, "Bulgarian infiltrators."

David and the Lieutenant pushed forward while a machine gun began raking the Bulgarians, but they were stopped short when a man in a Turkish army uniform turned on them and tried to shoot. Meese grabbed the pistol and pulled the man back onto himself. David drew his knife and cut the man's throat, not wanting to bring attention from the Turks with a pistol shot. Meese and David continued to crawl toward the gate and fire in its direction. Soon nothing could be heard from the infiltrators except screams as the Turks finished them off with bayonets.

David, only now, saw the panning of searchlights inside and outside the camp. Men were rising and orders were passed to form up. The company's Captain found David and Meese and pushed them clear of the wall they had sought protection under, telling Meese that a detachment of men was being assigned to escort them to the railway station. He told them to stay where they were and disappeared into the crowds of men standing at attention or working with medical personnel to remove the dead and assist the wounded.

A few soldiers approached the Germans and pushed them ahead and out of the gate, where they stepped over dead Bulgarians and around Turkish soldiers. They hurried them along until out of the shadows of a long wall, two men engaged them with pistols. They all dropped to the ground except the leader of the detachment. He leaped up onto a pile of rubble and shot the attackers dead with his rifle, and then motioned for everyone to move off behind him.

The city was quiet with doors shut and lighting intermittent. David fell twice and was pulled up each time by soldiers who were not interested in slowing their progress. Finally, the walls of the white railway station came into view, and as they began to cross a short bridge over a slough, three men in the detachment were shot by snipers from behind. David and Meese plunged off the bridge and met under it. The fourth Turk was nowhere to be seen.

"Get the helmets out, Meese!' said David. He grabbed for the dead Turks' rifles.

They exchanged their cloth Turkish hats for their steel helmets and huddled under the nearside of the bridge. David whispered, "Perhaps we should stay here. Maybe they will fade away at first light. If they try to come for us, we'll have to make a stand here, unless we can sidle down the edge of the ditch and get clear." David looked out from under the bridge and spotted the nearest light hanging from a lamppost illuminating the highest part of the ditch. They were still some distance north of the *Karaağaç* Station and moving toward it would have them exposed for another mile or so, but with the ditch partially hidden, David decided they should move east away from the bridge. The men eased their way slowly and quietly and as they passed the street lamp, they found a row of ancient trees that allowed them to stand hidden. They looked back and could see no one along the street they had crossed to reach the bridge. But as they began to relax a bit, three figures carrying rifles crept across the street toward the bridge.

"Let me kill them, *Hauptmann*," hissed Meese. He lifted his rifle.

David put his hand on the rifle and said, "Leave them for the Turks."

The men in the street turned and began running away from David and Meese. David looked at the long row of wooden buildings opposite him and signaled Meese to follow him across the street. They reached a two-story building with a second floor that stood away from the bottom and found that most of the structures were of the same design. There were a few gaps between them, but with rain beginning to pour, they found the upper ledge to be useful for cover. They moved steadily east, eventually coming to an offset of street corners and decided to stay in place until dawn. As they stood in front of the building's front window, a man inside watched the play of their helmet spikes, shafts moving about as if sparring, and wondered what he was witnessing. He was of late middle age and had happened to be preparing for his work as a manager of a nearby *hamman*, where he unlocked the baths and supervised the staff. He crept to the window and saw the two figures shivering and leaning into the window, trying to avoid the rain.

The man could not contain his curiosity. He was educated, not superstitious like many of his countrymen, and knowing that these strange creatures could have broken his window to gain entrance at any time, almost unafraid. He opened his door and peered around the frame at the two men. He asked who they were, speaking in Turkish.

Meese jumped and nearly lost his balance, but landing the rifle butt squarely, held himself up. David had been startled, but merely raised his pistol as he turned toward the householder. The owner of the house fell back a little as Meese answered, "German soldiers. We accompanied a company of Turks from Constantinople but were attacked and had to hide."

"Attacked by Turks?"

"No, *effendi*, by Bulgarians."

"Oh, no. Come in, come in." The man had graying curls about his thinning, black pate and seemed to be very fit and energetic.

"My name is Georgios Sedaris; I am the manager of a bath house nearby. Take off your coats and warm yourselves before the fire. What, may I ask, is that on your heads?"

"Those are steel helmets, *effendi*."

A small woman covered from head to foot in a thick, white woolen blanket entered the room. She had bushy, black hair that escaped the blanket and very dark eyes. She was perhaps, forty, but David could not really tell. Her bulked figure moved in behind Sedaris and whispered something in his ear.

"My wife asks, in English, 'Why are there bloody Germans in our home?'" said Sedaris, thinking that the Germans would not understand. He turned back to her and put his hands out, as if to say, "satisfied?"

But when David said, "We're bloody well trying to survive the Bulgarians," Sedaris turned about and said, "Why didn't you tell me you spoke English?"

"You didn't ask, *effendi*."

"Oh, you can leave off the '*effendi*,' my friend. We're Greeks who have been in Edirne for ten years but have never totally taken on Turkish customs. I had an opportunity to manage a bath house here, but I come from a family of hospitality people on Proasos where there are few Turks, by the way. I learn English from the tourists who visit our island, mostly English sodomites."

"Sodomites?" said David.

"That is where they come from. This is my wife, Dryope."

Dryope said, "How do you do? I also learn English from the visiting sodomites. They had been coming to our island for many year. They paint themselves and often came to our little shop on the beach and buy oak tokens from us. Tokens allowed to enter a special part of the beach."

"And so, may I ask, how did you hear the word, 'sodomite?'"

Dryope replied, "Oh, the Father told us. They like the women to us and painted themselves, so we called them *Ganymede*, you know, men love men. That is what sodomites do also."

Georgios spoke to his wife in Greek, throwing up his hands and becoming more and more excited. The wife started shaking her head back and forth, and then after more frantic movements by Georgios, began shaking her head up and down and crying into her husband's chest.

Georgios looked at David and said, "We all must leave. If the Bulgarians are coming, they will kill everyone, *everyone*! You must to accompany us in my car. We will go back to Proasos but will have to arrange passage when we reach coast."

David replied, "We will take your advice, sir." He told Meese what had been decided.

Dryope disappeared into a small kitchen and began preparing breakfast. The Germans were directed to try on some of Sedaris' hats and overcoats he'd collected over the years at the *hamman* that had been left behind by forgetful clients.

"You leave the steel hats, please" said Sedaris, returning from the back of the house. "Eat, eat, please, and we go. Hurry."

Everyone ate quickly and Georgios and Dryope gathered what they could and packed it in the automobile, a four cylinder *Diatto Clement*. The chassis had been fitted as a two-seater and David and Meese crammed themselves into the back, wearing Georgios' hats and overcoats. They stowed their weapons under their overcoats but maintained vigilance as the car bounced about the roughly paved and unpaved roads. David was amazed at the absence of military movement on the roads, and when Georgios stopped to buy fuel at a pharmacy near Alexandropoulos, local farmers passed them on the road, pulling their hay toward their fields of goats, apparently ignorant of the events unfolding in Edirne.

When Georgios returned to his seat, he looked back at the soldiers and said, "Impressive motor, eh? A *Pasha*, from I do not know where, won it in a dice game at the bath house. He asked me keep it for him, but I never, never see the man. Good thing, eh?" He smiled and looked as if he was on a great adventure rather than a refugee giving up his livelihood, his home, and risking the comfort of his wife. He started moving the *Diatto* and looked over at his Dryope and they snuggled closer than ever.

The sun was well up, and the sheer mountain ledges and spines resembled sleeping creatures, still and brooding, covered with scrubby little trees and an occasional ruin of some type. Lower, there were tangles of black and white goats wandering under barren trees, watched by shepherds sitting above them on mules or milling about them with sticks. The car had to stop several times to allow sheep, cows, and goats cross the road at their leisure. Ruins of various eras and isolated, overgrown houses or barns rose as they rounded corners and negotiated the climbs and steep falls of the roads.

Georgios assured them that he knew where he was going, but David had little concern except that they move south. At one point, as the road turned westward, they encountered a group of peasants walking up a paved hill, waving and extraordinarily attired, wearing flat-topped white caps with flowing, colorful scarfs hiding their hair above shapeless, black dresses. Georgios stopped the car and conversed with the women for a few moments, then proceeded west toward Gümülcine— or to Georgios, Komotini—where they would stop and have a late lunch. Entering Komotini, Georgios drove the party into the ruins of the Byzantine fortress, where all got out of the car, found privacy, and relieved themselves. Dryope poured water for all to wash their hands and handed David and Meese each a cup of wine. She next spread a cloth and motioned for the men to sit and partake of the cheese, bread, olives. and strips of flavored goat shank she had brought with them. Georgios leaned against the sun-warmed ruins and pulled his wife to him, inviting a mock slap from her.

"Georgios, you seem so happy," said David. "You've had to leave everything behind you, quite possibly never to return. I've mourned for you and Dryope. I know what it is like to leave a life and seek a new place in the world. Are you not sad?"

"My friend, we would have had no life if we had stayed," Georgios said. "The Bulgarians are killers, and if my own information is true—ah yes, even a humble man like Georgios heard things in the baths—if all is about to happen, and you, yourself have already experienced something of it, you may rejoice in our deliverance, which quite possibly, you and the Lieutenant made possible for us. I recite you a poem, from my dear poet of Alexandria, sent to me from a cousin living there." He spoke to Dryope in Greek for a few moments, then recited, haltingly and with whispers of assistance from his wife. He recited the "Cavafy," then apologized for having to use Greek. "I hope rhythm at least appealed, my friends."

David nodded his head and said, "Let us be so guided by the gentle sound, Georgios."

"Ah, poet, also."

27

"Must we leave Proasos so soon?" asked Meese.

"The Bulgarians will be here *soon*, Lieutenant, and the Greeks could turn on us *also*," replied David. "If we stay here much longer, I can guarantee that we will not have *a gentle, painless death, far from the sea,* my friend, to quote the poet of these lands."

The journey from Edirne had proved largely a sightseeing tour of southern Thrace. Georgios and Dryope had found relatives on Proasos, and after a huge celebration in their native village, with much wine and food, David and Meese were placed across the island at Stavenaria with a family of hoteliers, the Kastellanoses, struggling through the sodomiteless off season. The smiling proprietors asked for a minimum payment against two-weeks lodging on non-refundable terms. David paid for one room, but after the first night of Meese's exhausted snoring fueled partly by the local spirits, he was able to negotiate good terms for two rooms. The hotel Ritz was facing south in the lee of the persistent northerly winds, but the air was still very cool.

Georgios had given David his new, temporary address, and on the third day of their sojourn, David had Kyrie Kastellanos send a message to him asking for advice on leaving the island. As David and Meese were enjoying a meal of fried fish that evening, sitting in the otherwise empty hotel dining room, the messenger returned with the name, Ionnis, no surname supplied. David looked at the family Kastellanos, who had moved in to hear what the messenger had to say. Spiro, the father, wearing rouge and outrageously bright lipstick, said in good English, "Well, I'll summon Ionnis," accented with a blatant weakness of the right wrist.

As the meal continued, the mother Kastellanos, Penelope, said,

"My cousin Ionnis can be trusted, but do not pay him all he asks before the journey is completed." Along with the numerous other members of her family visiting the table, male and female, she turned and walked away, hands held before them flaccidly, bottoms swaying. David laughed as he followed them through the long, pink room. *Faux* statues of naked Greek gods and heroes lined the walls, and a portrait of an effeminate man wearing an elaborate French-fashioned dress, probably the hotel's founder, dominated the far wall between twin doors.

Ionnis duly appeared in the dining room, pulling out a chair. He summoned Penelope, who had been lurking nearby a statue of Hermes. Knowingly, she brought him a glass. Ionnis poured from the bottle on David's table and looked at the Germans with a silent scowl. David noticed that the man was also wearing bright red lipstick, but he smelled of sweat and the sea, and judging by the condition of the skin covering his hands, the salt and wind were taking their toll this winter. Ionnis spoke to Penelope, and she translated his words to David, "Ionnis, he want know where, how much," she said, cocking her head to one side with a dramatic drop. Five more Kastellanos relatives arrived to listen to the proceedings.

"Tell Ionnis that we want to go to Saros Korfezi, then to Kavak. I will pay 1,000 Turkish lira."

Penelope translated to Ionnis, and with a turn of his head and sweep of his hand Ionnis delivered his answer.

Penelope, crossing her arms and dropping a hand dramatically, said to David, "My dear, Ionnis say no."

"1,200, then."

"Ionnis say, sodomites pay more."

"Please inform Ionnis that we are not sodomites."

"He say 1,500, and he will feed."

"Tell Ionnis if he will buy a bottle of your excellent wine tonight and share it with us, we will agree."

Penelope relayed David's response and turned back, saying, "Agreed. But why you not speak like sodomites?"

"Because we do not wish to imitate women, only to love them."

Penelope placed her hand upon her heart and said, "You, you think you such a Priapus!" She pouted, batted her lashes, and waved a finger. "Naughty, naughty; I tell my Spiro! But if you want love, I send a girl for you?"

At that point, one of the Kastellanos daughters was serving Ionnis wine and Penelope took the bottle from her and hustled the daughter out of the room, looking sternly at David. The men drank the bottle in silence, and as the last drop fell away into Ionnis' glass, he said, "Tomorrow morning, I take. Be ready, and talk no one, sodomites. You want woman for night? I get you one each for 500 lira."

Meese looked baffled and a little drunk. David said, "No women tonight, thank you."

Ionnis stood up and kissed his cousin Penelope perhaps a little more passionately than Spiro would have approved. He then turned and found the rear of one of the daughters to offer a little pinch as he walked away. The girl jumped, and hit Ionnis in the back of the head. A crowd of relatives materialized immediately, wildly gesticulating and screaming at both Ionnis and the girl until Spiro came out of the kitchen, and with one wave of a well-manicured hand, ended the matter with a fan of red-painted fingernails. Ionnis left the building rubbing his head.

The next morning, David roused Meese at 6:00, and after their showers, they sat to Penelope's breakfast of hot bread, a local jam, yogurt, and eggs. Penelope, standing back away from the men with a leg cocked out, wore a particularly low-cut blouse while her daughters waited the table.

Ionnis arrived in a battered, wood-sided lorry that smelled of rotting fish and burnt motor oil. He had David and Meese sit in the cab with him and took them to the east around several points above the sea and finally stopped and parked the lorry into a layby. The road had been a rising and falling, switched-back affair, and when Meese stepped out of the lorry he promptly vomited. "*Scheisse!* I am dying!" Meese complained.

David said, "Shut up, Meese."

A boat was waiting on the beach, and Ionnis, David, and Meese made their way into it and toward the stern. Two other men shoved off, hopped into the boat, and brought it alongside a sizable fishing smack. When all were aboard, Ionnis took the helm and brought the boat into a light, north swell. The boat eased up and through the broad rollers, and after an hour or so it came broadside to the waves. Ionnis followed the troughs as far as he could, skillfully capitulating into the next watery furrow to follow it in the same manner. David sat on the bow rail, watching Helios bring the light over the dark sea, winking here and there on the few misaligned waves that popped up as an east wind began to chill the sailors' faces. Eventually, in the early afternoon, the east wind had become stronger and steady, making a skewed weave of the tops of the waves, and Ionnis' skills began to be tested.

David slid down into the shelter of the boat's freeboard and sat on a wooden crate. As they were roughly forty miles out of Proasos and nearer the mainland, he could hear the thumping of artillery and prayed that as they passed Alexandroupolis, a rush of refugee watercraft, or perhaps warships, would not impede their progress. His calculations had them even with the town and looking up, he could only detect slight haze to the north. Perhaps smoke, he thought. He noticed that Meese had found himself a corner of the wheelhouse to curl into and was sleeping with his face tucked into Georgios' wool cap.

David wondered if he was the only one worried. He tried to remember a few lines from Rumi that Rasheed used to recite when he took David down to the harbor. The words eluded him, and he began to think of Ingrid. *I am just a man.* Then, he slept.

Ionnis slowed the boat and looked behind the broad, open wheelhouse to reckon the sun. His navigation had put them in line with the point south of Enez, entering the Korfezi. He knew that night would be falling in two hours, and when night fell, unknown to his passengers, he would be heading back west. He consulted his timepiece and told a crewman to be prepared to haul up the dingy being towed astern. He would try to put in near Mecidiye, just west of Kavak.

Close enough, he thought, especially after hearing the rumblings of battle earlier. His cousin Penelope would approve, he was sure, and anyway, he was Greek and had no business sneaking onto the mainland of Turkey. But in taking David's money, at least he could ignore the disappointing fall, and now, a bitter winter. All would be relieved when the sodomites return for their annual holiday festivities. *These* sodomites were soon to find a new home!

David awoke and peered over the rail, spotting coastline about three miles in. He got up and went back to the wheelhouse and said, "Kavak soon?"

"Kavak soon. Yes, *effendi.*"

David was shocked to hear "*effendi*" and wondered why the surly fisherman addressed him so. He was instinctively suspicious. The sun was dropping fast into the sea behind them, and David watched Ionnis give an order to a crewman. The man went to the stern of the smack and began hauling in the small boat. Ionnis steered the fishing boat directly toward the shore and slowed the engine. The boat rocked and some spray began to rain past them.

"Get other sodomite to boat. Here, we shore."

David woke Meese, who hadn't moved in four hours, and told him to follow him to the stern. Ionnis approached them as they passed the wheelhouse, and with his two crewmen behind David and Meese, put out his hand. David instantly counted out the remainder of his fee and thanked the Greek by shaking his hand. David reckoned that they were at least twenty miles short of their original destination, but thought the best course was to disembark while life and limb were still intact.

They reached the rocky shore, under the outcrop of a cliff, with a trail wending up the hill just as snow began to fall, the issue of sudden clouds that had struck into the clear air of the journey. Ionnis pointed up, indicating the trail and said, "No beach."

The men accepted a bundle of rations and shook Ionnis' hand again, and then they moved up the narrow trail of small stones and shells placed to maintain access to the rocky ledge below. When the men had reached the top, they stopped to brush clay off of their pants, recently laundered along with the rest of their uniforms by Penelope. They still wore Georgios' overcoats and wool hats and set a course northeast, hoping to find a town with a rail station. After trudging through the night, they finally came to the town of Kesan, where Turkish soldiers were marching toward an old Byzantine fort just outside of the community. Stopped by a Turkish officer, David offered his papers, prepared in Constantinople. They satisfied the soldier, who clearly had Bulgarians on his mind.

David and Meese were directed toward the railway station and lost no time in finding it and a train loaded with refugees about to steam east to the capitol. They hustled aboard in First Class but found themselves sitting in the dirty aisle, leaning against filled seats with their knees up. Unimpeded by the captured rifles they had left with Ionnis, they trusted their pistols to protect them as they embarked on this, they prayed, the last leg of their trip back to their respective headquarters.

Gebze railway station was alive with swarms of soldiers, a swelling number of arriving refugees, and the usual dispossessed that roamed the oldest part of the city, adrift, filthy and constantly seeking shelter. David and Meese struggled through the humanity and its polyglot din of Turkish, Greek and Armenian to make their way out of the station. After an hour's wandering north, they were able to hire a taxi to take them to the embassy.

They entered the grand building and found their way up to Witt's office, where they were met by Gerd, who sniffed and said, "You both smell like goats; wait here and I will bring the *Oberst to* you." Both men had held on to Georgios's coats and hats and deposited them on a chair in a corner of the room next to a clerk's desk. The clerk looked at the coats and hats, wrinkled his nose, and rising from his post, left the room. David and Meese looked at each other.

"We thought you were dead, gentlemen," said Witt as he entered the room. "Judging by your smell, at least, you could be mistaken for the departed. Now, tell me what happened." Witt crossed his arms over his belly and with raised brows, made himself ready to hear David's report. As David recounted the soldiers' adventure, Witt repeatedly uttered, "*Fantastisch!*" and "*Mein Gott!,*" his small eyes protruding and his fleshy cheeks reddening. At the conclusion of David's narrative, Witt said, "Meese, you are dismissed; Rožmberk, get along to 'A' house and tell Freya to prepare dinner to include me and *Frau* Witt. And for God's sake, *bathe!*"

David and Meese picked up their coats and passed the disapproving eyes of the staff members as they exited the embassy. After earnestly shaking hands, the comrades parted ways, David walking to *Apfelhaus* in a slowing gait, growing wearier with every step. At last he reached the door of the mysterious building and was allowed in by Freya, who stepped back holding her nose. "I beg your pardon, *Fraulein*, but there is an explanation. Also, Colonel Witt asks that you prepare dinner to include himself and *Frau* Witt, please."

"Sit here, David, and do not move until Helen has prepared your bath; I do not wish to loose this smell upon the rest of the building!" Taking Georgios' hat and coat from him, Freya held the items well away from her and left the anteroom, closing the door behind her. David sat down, unconcerned that the odor of his clothes might be absorbed into the fabric of the long settee placed along the wall behind him. He was instantly asleep but soon awakened by Helen, who asked him to remove his uniform where he stood.

"Helen, you just want a naughty peek, don't you?" he said.

"No, *Hauptmann*, we just do not wish to contaminate the rest of the building. And please, do not take the trouble to flatter yourself, soldier."

"As you wish, *Fraulein*," he replied and stripped down to his underwear.

"We shall burn these." Helen led David to the large bathroom attached to what had, in the early days of the building, been known as the grand suite. The room was filled with the scent of *Après L'Ondée*, and as he stepped into the deep bath, he realized that the water was the source of the strong fragrance. The scent immediately induced a headache and caused him to bathe vigorously, but thoroughly. He slid under the water and straightaway realized that even the harsh soap he was using might not remove the odor of the perfume from his hair. He would find that he had been correct in the concern.

As he surfaced, he noticed, through filmy eyes, that another set of legs was stepping into the bath. He rubbed his face, rapidly, and beheld, albeit momentarily, Helen's round breasts sinking into the suds. She looked at him and said, "Well, my dear *Hauptmann*, you've had your treat, and now in this hot, perfumed water, I shall have mine."

David could not suppress the stirring of his penis and looked down at himself and at the woman at the opposite end of the bath.

"Oh, do not let it bother you," Helen said. Stay and enjoy the water with me! I have brothers and can say with some authority, there is not very much concerning males I have not witnessed."

Freya knocked, opened the door slightly, and reminded him that the dinner hour was approaching. She looked around the door to give Helen a mock scowl, then left. He finished scrubbing his head with the block of soap Helen had ceremoniously presented to him and rinsed under the chilling faucet water. Then he leaned forward, and with Helen's eyes upon his nakedness notwithstanding her declared indifference, he lifted himself from the bath. David pulled his erection into the towel he had reached lying from a stack within a gold-leaved set of shelves lining the wall opposite the tub. He dried rapidly, putting on a robe left for him. As he walked to his room, he could hear Helen's laughter and felt himself tempted to return and drag her out of the bath, but he decided to just dress for dinner, taking the tease in stride. He thought: Women!

Wearing his dress uniform and boots, and leaving the room with fifteen minutes to spare, he was not surprised to be met near the dining room by the Witts, who always arrived early for any affair.

"My dear boy," said the Colonel, "now you smell like a French, ah, a French perfume shop. At least the ladies will appreciate it, I suppose."

They sat down at the table and awaited Freya and Helen. "David, I was most worried about you and Meese, I must say. The day after you departed for Edirne, we were advised by the Turks that war had broken out, which affirmed the information we had received from our people in those countries the previous evening, probably near the time you were sneaking out of Edirne with your Greek friends. The Greeks, Bulgarians, and Macedonians had opened fronts against the Turks, and we feared that you would be caught up in the fighting. Obviously, you had the presence of mind to make an escape before that came to pass! I must congratulate you; you have demonstrated great resourcefulness. Hopefully, the great powers will put a stop to the fighting soon, and we can get back to just observing the circus of Ottoman politics."

As Freya and the larder man served the food, she leaned over David and asked, "Are you finding it *hard* to adjust to a perfumed body, *Hauptmann*? Maybe I should just have Helen scrub you with soap after your next intimacy with sheep and goats! And Turks, of course."

28

David hadn't noticed her standing behind him, but when he turned to leave Gerd's office, his first sight of the woman was startling. Constantinople, indeed the entire region, had been like this to him. Her tall form was wrapped in a gray *tesettür,* and her face shaped into a black, chiffon *shayla* falling away, wrapping her neck down to an ellipse like the labellum of a sheer, black orchid. She stood framed in the doorway with a gentle light resting upon her face. Still fatigued from his Edirne adventure David thought, she's waiting for me.

In the moment he saw her, his eyes gathered her into that place where everything he knew or imagined about women was retained. She looked at him, holding his eyes, silently asking him to look at her face and forget the old, sad truth of *sic transit gloria mundi,* the glory of the world passes away, he remembered in English, and know that this first meeting would live in his thoughts. Her cheekbones were set high under olive skin. Her eyes were large and green, the shapes of almonds. She parted full wide lips.

David turned around and asked Gerd, "*Wer ist dieses Madchen?*"

Gerd replied in English. "Miss Olivia Iphigenia Becouche-Albukerk, allow me to introduce to you Captain David Samuel von Petersruhe-Rožmberk of the Imperial German Army. David, English is the *lingua franca* here."

Clicking his heels, David said, "How do you do, *Fraulein* Olivia? I didn't expect such a European name." He suddenly realized he was being forward and blushed.

"My heritage is quite diverse, Captain." Olivia stepped forward and offered her hand. "Thank you for using English. It is fortunate that Lieutenant Schneider and I have English in common. I sometimes regret that I haven't studied your language."

"Your English is very good."

"But not always the language I need." She looked at Schneider.

"*Hauptmann,* you'll have to excuse us. We have some gossip to exchange. Will I find you at Pera later?" asked Gerd.

"Very well, Schneider. My day isn't finished, either," replied David. "I'll be there by 7:00. *Fraulein*, may I call you Miss Olivia, until I can remember your surname? That is, if I have the pleasure of meeting you again."

"Of course. Perhaps since we both know Lieutenant Schneider we might have occasion to happen upon each other again."

"Miss Olivia, I am honored to have met you," David said, clicking his heels again. She stepped aside to allow him to pass, but he stood before her another moment, perhaps too long, before he nodded to her and left the office.

"*Liebe* Olivia, my beautiful siren, sit and sing to me!" said Gerd.

"Now, Gerd, you know an old Greek, obviously frightened of women, invented the story of those alluring women. Are you like that old Greek? Or do our little conversations beguile you and entice you to do something dangerous?" Olivia laughed. She knew that he knew she was teasing him. His homosexuality was no secret to her. She tried to give the German her full attention, but her thoughts of the tall, striking soldier she'd just met would not allow her to fully engage her friend.

Sigmund Gerhard Schneider was, perhaps, frightened by her. She was no challenge to his sexual preferences, but her beauty did not discriminate in its power. She captivated everyone who entered her world. Schneider wondered at how little he knew about this woman, and yet, how they seemed to converse with the ease of dear, old friends. He was somewhat unnerved, as a German embassy staff member and army intelligence officer, at how she had moved into his work and social life and had shared observations about her homeland's leadership in whose circles she and several members of her family seemed to thrive. He knew that her conservative attire belied the bloodline she owned, that her clothing bespoke traditional Turkish, or perhaps more precisely, Muslim identity, but she had made no secret to him that she was a Jewess. Her slight Italian accent made her origins clear, indeed, as the daughter of a childhood friend and political associate of influential Turkish Jews, and members of the *Committee*, he assumed that her family also came to Constantinople, like some of the other Jews, from Trieste. These people were mysterious to Schneider, exotic, and seemed, just by their presence in the milieu of 1913 Constantinople, to warrant the, in Schneider's opinion, naïve, views of the British that the Turkish governments, that the Young Turks themselves, were tools of international Jewry.

"Dangerous?" Gerd said. "When you introduce me to beautiful young men like Nahum, yes, I am tempted to do something dangerous! Colonel Witt would execute me personally if he could read my thoughts when I'm around that boy."

"You soldiers, so captured by traditions and morality, I do worry about your future. But you're a successful soldier, first and always! With, I'm told, a coming war to make you famous."

"Yes, yes, with a war on another front, perhaps, thanks to your Young Turks, Dönmeh, certain German admirals, and in the soup somewhere, *British politicians*."

Schneider's embassy office was spare, with a tall ceiling and by some great good fortune, a window. The air was cool, with the wind blowing incessantly from the north and whipping up sea foam and mist along the *Golden Horn* harbor quays—winter's stab into the city. Olivia looked at the small fair man sitting behind the dark polished desk, his uniform extremely correct, his hair combed neatly away from his face in rather shiny broad ribbons and the large, but pleasantly shaped nose. He is like a martial figurine occupying a cut-away room in a dollhouse, she thought. A portrait of the *Kaiser* was hung on the wall behind him and the replica Corinthian *Oinochoe* vessel she had bought for him from an old Greek merchant in Stamboul was placed on a corner of the desk. One filing cabinet stood to the right of the door she had walked through and a table piled with carefully stacked map holders claimed most of the wall to her left.

"Perhaps you tell me too much, Gerd, but with German sailors wearing Turkish uniforms on those two German battleships lying in the Golden Horn, many things seem imaginable."

"So, tell me why I have the pleasure of your company, this afternoon, Olivia. I thought we'd be seeing each other this evening at the hotel," Schneider said.

"I'm sorry to have surprised you, but I was nearby, visiting my father. Are you displeased?"

"No, of course not. You've become a dear friend, one of the few natives I really know, or *wish* to know. You are … what's the English word? An anomaly. The least Turkish of Turks. I'm glad that your family is on good terms with the ambassador and you can come and go as you wish here."

"Speaking of going, I'll leave you to your work, Lieutenant Schneider. I was thinking of dining at the Pera, this evening. May I ask you to be my escort?"

"I'd be honored," Schneider replied. "Will you collect me, or, should I just meet you there?"

"Be good enough to meet me, Gerd. I'll be there by 8:00."

Olivia rose to leave, her clothing giving a gentle sibilance as she slid from the plain wooden chair. She looked at Schneider and thought, "You are one of my only friends. You have no idea how much I might need you."

Olivia's chauffeur, Mentes, a Greek, was waiting outside the embassy and led her to the *Mercedes Phaeton* parked a short distance away on a side street. The elderly man took her to her family's home located southwest of the embassy, off the Rue de Pera, Bayuk Hendek 61. The house was large, with round, fluted Greek columns supporting a portico and tall windows lining the three floors. She went inside the house and was immediately greeted by the Greek housekeeper, Irene, an attractive woman of about thirty-five. Olivia's father came out of the smoking room.

"Good evening, daughter" he said in Italian, their private language established for household secrets by them in her early childhood. The servants spoke Greek. Isaac Becouche-Albukerk was a man of sixty-two, of medium height. He possessed an extraordinarily vigorous and handsome visage, which he kept by walking the two miles down to his office every morning, almost without fail, and in the early evening by visiting the Galatasaray Baths to break his uphill journey home.

He had married late in life, after what seemed a lifetime spent in Trieste working in his family's grain and dairy business. He was offered an opportunity to expand the company in Salonika and later Constantinople, and in moving, found himself welcomed into the thriving Sephardic communities of both cities. His wealth grew rapidly, and he moved amongst the *doyens* of prosperous Jewish families, all of whom, it seemed, were anxious to present their daughters to him. Although Isaac was not religious, he made a practice of attending services at a nearby Sephardic synagogue and came to know the rabbi well enough not to be surprised when the rabbi advised him to marry and have children before he grew too old. Time had passed quickly, he realized. His business exacted most of his time and much of the rest was taken up visiting Greek antiquarians working out of bazaars, searching out ancient papyrus scrolls and palimpsest. His evenings were usually taken up in applying considerable Latin and ancient Greek language skills as he pursued philological studies or translating, or applying the techniques he'd learned as a student in Rome to divine the earliest writing from sheets of palimpsest. But, there was another reason Isaac had not married.

Isaac made periodic travels back to Trieste to visit family members and business associates. When circumstances allowed, he left his business life and traveled to Italy or France to present the results of his philological work to various colleagues, and always with urgency, to renew his relationship with a woman, now the *Gräfin* Claramond Kathe von Petersruhe-Matthäus, but always, his Kathe, also a colleague, but more importantly, the love of his life. But during a sojourn in Orta San Giulio, after a midnight swim in the lake with her, the woman suddenly told him that he should marry as she had done. That her marriage was unconsummated perhaps made this advice easy for her to give. Isaac had not married in part because of his relationship with Kathe and couldn't imagine giving her up for another woman, especially with a commitment of marriage.

Kathe said, "Isaac, perhaps our time has deprived you of something, something that was never possible for me: the blessing of children."

Isaac met the woman who was to become Olivia's mother in Rome, during a short visit during the same year. He was celebrating his forty-first birthday with friends at the Ristorante La Campana when, unexpectedly, Kathe appeared with one of her students. This student was, in fact, the *Gräfin's* choice for Isaac, something she never admitted to him, but he always suspected. The girl's name was Eligia Alfassa Yafey.

Olivia greeted her father the way she had always done, with a kiss and a long embrace. She loved this sanguine, methodical man who had made her know unreserved affection and security, who had in every way he could, tried to fill the empty space her mother's early death had left for them both. She had grown up to be slightly taller than Isaac, and she unconsciously bent to meet his eyes. "Good evening, Papa, you're home early! Old Benetar *Bey* finally succeeded in getting you away from the office before 7:00; amazing." Iacob Benetar, another Sephardi, had been Isaac's employee for over thirty years and for the last fifteen, his general manager. Olivia looked carefully at her father; he seemed subdued, worried. "Papa, what is it?" She took his hand and walked him out to the lush courtyard. They sat on a stone bench fashioned out of a polished slab of marble set upon two upturned *Ionian* capitals that had been salvaged from one of the innumerable ruins strewn about the Levant.

"I have spent a lifetime speculating on harvests, weather, the reliability of transportation and the machinations of other merchants, but now, in the confusion that has become Ottoman politics, I am lost and wish to leave this madness," Her father told her. "I have been planning, successfully, I pray. I have explained to you that things are changing now, in ways I've never encountered. I fear that the pace of these changes increases every day, and that the life we've known, the lives of many merchants like me, will vanish. This country has lost

wars with Italy and others recently. Now the Committee seems obsessed with finding a European protector, according to my government friends. The *Dönmeh* seems to grow! There are German battleships anchored in the harbor flying Turkish flags. Whipping up these
changes are the young men, and as you know, these people concern
me deeply. When they burst out of Salonika, they were shouting liberty! Equality! But these years later, they think these ideas are meant
only for Muslim Turks. Some Jews will probably survive, but after
their lives of politics, they have little to lose, really. Because of their
activities, the British now believe that the government is a Jewish
cabal! Nothing is farther from the truth, and sooner rather than later,
I believe, these Young Turks and all of the lies and half-truths in the
air will destroy us if we don't leave!"

"Papa, I believe you; I see these things also. Your judgment is my
light. Give me my parts of the plan, and now we must proceed. I have
news from Uncle Binyamin. The transfer was successful."

"Your Germans. Concentrate on your Germans, Olivia."

"I will, Papa. Would it be acceptable if I brought one home to
meet you?"

"That would be an enormous act in this neighborhood. The servants will have much to gossip about! I believe that your old father
should know your taste in young men, at least. Bring this German, if
you wish, but have an intermediary invite him, my dear."

"I will Father; it will be no trouble."

Olivia retired to her rooms to prepare for this evening's meeting
with Schneider at the Pera, changing into modern European dress
and adorning her bared hair with an ancient, beautifully polished
diadem. She hoped that this new German would be there. She found
him most attractive and enjoyed speaking English with him. His
English is almost too good, she thought.

As Olivia removed her traditional garments, her young Greek
maid, Christina, muttered, "What is this changing to please these
Europeans? You're a Levant girl and this showing your hair!"
Christina had been brought into the household after Eligia's death
to help Olivia and to give her a companion. She was short and broad

and had an ongoing relationship with a somewhat slim Greek fisher-man, who brought fresh fish to her aunt, Irene, the housekeeper, sev-eral times a week—opportunities acceptable to Irene for Christina to speak to the young man.

"May I remind you, Christina, that I am not married and my hair may be exposed?" Olivia said. She finished and ran down the stairs in a long royal blue tunic tied around a full, patterned dress. She wore somewhat higher heels than Christina approved, but with her hair pulled up and the diadem in place, she was elegantly dressed. Her almond-shaped eyes and olive complexion made her rare and irresistible, much to the sadness of the other unmarried European woman who gathered in the Pera Hotel.

She had Christina summon the driver and walked out under the portico to wait for the motor's appearance. She could hear sounds of unrest carried across the water—the cries of women and occasional gunshots. She thought again of what her father implied: the importance of the Germans. Finally she arrived at the Pera and entered the great establishment with men bowing and women turning their heads away until the *maître d'* approached and led her to her and Gerd's usual table. He was not waiting for her, and when she turned around to look for him, she encountered the new German.

David said, "Olivia, Gerd sends his regrets, as he has been asked to work late. I'm afraid that the Bulgarian aggression preoccupying the entire city demands the attentions of our friend, also. I hope to be an acceptable substitute."

"I must say, Captain, you were not expected."

"I apologize on behalf of Gerd. If you wish to dine alone..."

"No, no of course not Captain, or as you have called me Olivia, shall call you David? I heard the sounds of unrest tonight as I stood in front of my house."

"Do you live near here?" asked David.

"Yes, my family is fairly new to Constantinople. My father lived most of his life in Italy, working in the family firm. His other inter-ests took him to Greece and Turkey often. After my mother's death several years ago, he decided to stay here. His memories of her are mostly here. And where are you from? Where did you grow up and learn this impeccable English, David?"

"I have a somewhat, I suppose, adventurous, history, peopled by interesting and diverse men and women. I was born in Lübeck, off the North Sea, in Germany. I spent two years in England and became a German soldier. My name has changed due to inheritance and adoption, but I have lived a satisfying life."

A waiter appeared and took their orders, vanishing with the expected aplomb. The dining room was beginning to fill with Europeans of many nationalities and David found himself standing to greet, be introduced, or occasionally, snubbed. An old army acquaintance from the German group formed to observe the late Italian-Turkish war took an almost impolite amount of time with David, leaving him somewhat annoyed. He sat down before Olivia and took a moment to compose himself.

"David, may I ask what is wrong?"

"The fellow who was just here informed me of some disturbing developments. Now let us talk about Olivia!"

"I hold Turkish and Italian passports; I speak Turkish, Greek, Italian, English and French. I am descended from ancient families that we trace back to Bagdad. Well, mostly to Spain. I was educated in France and here at a Catholic school. But, I have traveled little."

The food arrived and both ate with enthusiasm, catching each other's eyes as new courses arrived. David looked splendid in his dinner jacket and the pair became conscious of other eyes upon them. The two, shining amongst the mass of the other tabled and standing men and women could not have attracted more admiration for their beauty and the apparently natural fascination they shared. Throughout the evening, a steady coming and going of Turkish police, staging themselves with an unalterable presence around the huge room, seemed to dissuade more of the usual patrons from entering the hotel.

David looked at Olivia and said, "Do not be alarmed, Olivia, but I believe it wise to leave as soon as possible."

Olivia nodded, yes, and David called for the check. Many diners followed the waiter as he presented the bill and David paid, standing to assist Olivia and move toward the exit. Outside were gathered a large force of police and several soldiers on horseback.

Olivia asked, "What is happening, David? Why are all of these police here?"

David had his official papers ready, and in time he was accosted by a plainclothes official asking to examine them. The official looked carefully at David's documents, nodded, and thanked him for his cooperation.

David said, "They are looking for a banker—a money-changer or any of his associates, they say—but really, they are looking for Bulgarian spies. We must locate a taxi."

"No need; there is my driver. Please come home with me. My father would appreciate your presence. He probably knows that this is happening now."

The couple entered the back seat of the automobile and within a few minutes, they arrived at the Becouche-Albukerk home. David followed Olivia into the great house, and immediately, Isaac greeted his daughter and her new friend.

"I have been worried," Isaac said. "There may be another attempt to deflate the lira and anarchists have been encouraged by this Bulgarian and Greek business."

David was introduced by Olivia to her father.

Isaac said, "I have to confess, I've known about your presence in Turkey for some time now. Your aunt, *Gräfin* Claramond Kathe von Petersruhe alerted me that you would be posted to Constantinople. *Gräfin* Claramond introduced me to Olivia's mother."

Olivia stood stunned. She knew that her father's reach for information was extraordinary … but this? "Papa, why didn't you tell me that you knew that David was in Constantinople? And why would his aunt wish you to know?"

"That is a conversation for another time. Please, David, will you share a brandy with us?"

"Thank you, but no sir, I must get back to my billet."

"My car will take you. I would be most pleased if you would agree to have dinner with us soon. We will send an invitation to the embassy."

"Thank you, sir. Olivia, good night, and thank you for this wonderful evening."

"Good night, David." Olivia went to her room puzzled and wondered if her father had been encouraging her to stay close to "her Germans" for *only* political purposes.

As the car pulled away from under the portico, David began to think of Olivia. She seemed like a divine being—so refined in manner and education, so exotically beautiful, such a *presence.* He felt he'd met another shaper of his destiny like Schlarp, Twinge, and his adopted mother and father. However she was placed into his life, he was grateful, excited, and expectant.

He had the driver stop in front of a shuttered falafel shop around the corner of the *Apfelhaus.* He pushed the shaft, and Helen answered the door. Waiting for him in the sitting room was Witt.

"Well, my adventurous young man, it wasn't enough to roam the Thracian countryside, *you* had to meet the most beautiful woman in the Ottoman Empire! Oh, yes, I know. Gerd told me all about it. Is it possible that you could tell me something about her father, the man of mystery, and it is reported, influence?"

"They are worried, like most people here, Herr *Oberst.* I believe that you already know these people, or could I be mistaken that the man we've often seen at the Pera was not Becouche-Albukerk *Bey*?"

"Bulgarians? Greeks? Armenians? Any of the Great Powers?" Witt ignored David's accusation.

"I believe that they are worried mostly about the Turks, sir."

"That's an answer that makes sense, David. By the way, the Bulgarians have the Turks in full flight. Don't fashion any ideas about going to the front," said the portly colonel.

"I have been reasonably good at killing them, sir."

"So I have heard, *Hauptman.* You, however, will stay here, for the time being."

In the weeks following his meeting with Olivia, David remained puzzled by her father's knowledge of his presence in Constantinople.

He saw her often and each time he was more impressed by this exotic, exceptional woman. How could Becouche-Albukerk *Bey* know *Gräfin* Claramond Kathe von Petersruhe? Was it through his *Onkle* Sigi? He thought of Olivia throughout the days, but he told Gerd little, as his friend pried for information and a hint of David's intentions. Olivia, Olivia, he said her name silently to himself throughout the days, dreaming of her twice, and even taking the time to put to paper his memory of one of the dreams.

I rested on sandy ocean bottom breathing, and Olivia's form seemed to be rising above me, trailing an opening, expanding, red rose, swirling into a sheer gown of clear, shimmering jellyfish. The living tissue became suffused with red strands enveloping her shape, then her neck and head, lifting her dark hair into an eddy extending away from her, as if wavering gently in the wind. The gelatinous form protected her nudity, the gown moving the red strands as beckoning limbs. She grew smaller and smaller as I followed her ascent and the ocean suddenly became a small pool and her legs were upon me, enveloping my chest, and I felt pulled into her, held by the red, living streamers.

A day came when he sent her a note asking for a meeting at the Pera, which would, if granted, defy the convention of only the regular, once-weekly dinner arrangement they had established. He became exceptionally concerned, after the note left the embassy that he might have acted too aggressively and spent the time awaiting a reply from her in mounting anxiety. Was there an impulse hidden in the dream he'd recalled that had emboldened him to obvious courtship? Perhaps, he thought, he should *tell* her of his dream, but he feared it might somehow offend a quiet sensibility in her in its imagery, knowing that he had not, and might never, fully step into her world. Finally, the next day, he was rewarded with a positive response. They would not meet as usual, however. She would pick him up at his office, and they would go to the hotel together. His relief brought such a stirring of happiness that he forgot the drudgery his work had become.

He realized that he had acquired, perhaps partly because of Olivia's presence in his thoughts, some difficulty in concentrating on his work. But the endless meetings with Turkish army officers and sitting through hours of useless discussion of their problems, both personal and official, were no longer stimulating. He would walk the distance to Turkish military headquarters and return, invariably shaking his head at the stories of profligate adventures and the woeful condition of the Empire's forces wrought by the Balkan Wars and the turmoil of its leadership. He always seemed to glean something interesting for Witt from these meetings, but when he expressed surprise to his commander that this was the case, Witt said, "Even cavalry charges can get old, my boy."

Olivia's driver stopped in front of the embassy at the appointed hour. David could not reveal the *Apfelhaus*, so he had brought formal clothes to the embassy and changed there, drawing the curious eyes of Gerd and the Colonel. He stepped into the large vehicle and sat down beside Olivia. She wore her traditional headdress of blond silk lined with a stiffened material that wove around her thick, amassed hair. The wrap perched highly on her head and fell away, tying upon her chest and lying flat against her back. It was a traditional Ottoman Jewess fashion, topping a modified dark robe that covered a new high-waisted, low neckline French dress of considerable, but quiet, appeal.

David greeted Olivia, and as the car moved away from the embassy, asked boldly, "Why me? Why does fortune smile so well upon me to grant another evening with you this week? I have been given to understand that you've enjoyed the company of several young men, mainly European, over the last year or so."

The young woman acted startled and looked at David with mock surprise. Her driver remained mute. She shifted somewhat noticeably away from David and said, "I choose as I please, *Hauptmann*."

"Was I too familiar, Olivia? May I ask, also, why you have changed your manner of dress so dramatically? I admire the oriental nature of your ensemble," he said, knowing that the look was obviously Jewish.

"My father objects, but I insist on being myself in a crowd of European women—the wives of diplomats, the "companions" of dignitaries, and wealthy Armenians and Greeks. I'm a *Jewess*, David, and I only adapted my clothing to reflect my origins. Now, who do I know who adapts to German nobility, who started as simply, David Samuel Rosenberg?"

It was David's turn to be startled. "How could you know that? Is my *Tante* so free with information, Miss? I am just a soldier. If you look further, you'll find that I was never Jewish."

"I've known, *Hauptmann.*"

The pair rode in silence until they reached the Pera. David was somewhat nonplussed and hid his discomfort in the formality he hadn't used since he first encountered Olivia. "Miss, may I take your arm?" he asked. He led her into the building, which was awash, as usual, in the very type of people Olivia had described. They were shown their usual table, but Olivia said, "I would prefer sitting near the center tonight."

The *maître d'* placed them as near to the middle as he could, at a large round table cluttered with six place settings. He was obviously unhappy with the arrangement, but had no intention of protesting, except by rather aggressively clearing the redundant silverware and napkins. He barked at a waiter to serve them, adding, in Turkish, "I want this table, soon!"

David sat down near Olivia and smiled. "May I tell you of a dream I had recently? Perhaps we should order first." With that, the hovering waiter bent to them and took their wine order.

"My dear *Hauptmann*, why do you wish to share your dream with me?' asked Olivia.

"Please, let's stop this formality. Call me David, and I'll call you Olivia. I want to tell you of my dream because *some* Europeans believe that they contain useful, scientific, meaning. Certain Jewish Europeans are making much of dreams these days, I hear!"

"You must tell me then. I'll forward it to the *Psychoanalytic Society* and ask them to explore your deepest thoughts. Maybe I'll learn what you're really thinking. What a shame that we don't have a Solomon Molcho to help us, these days."

David ignored the "Solomon Molcho" reference and began to tell Olivia of his dream.

She looked at him intently and occasionally said, "You're trifling with me" and some rather curious Turkish phrases he could not understand.

"There is only one answer. You have fallen in love with me" she said.

"Perhaps that is so." David lifted his head and looked into her shining eyes. "I think of you constantly and crave any opportunity to see you," David replied.

The waiter reappeared, almost rudely soon, and their dinner order was taken. They sat in silence for a few moments. Finally, David said, "I have no idea where the army plans to send me, but I hope that I can stay near you, Olivia."

"You will, I can assure you of that."

29

Isaac leaned over his massive, cluttered desk and reread the note that Yonat Saf, the man once known to him as Emmanuel Levi, passed to Isaac's English friend, Arthur Cohen, a fellow antiquarian and clerk with the British diplomatic service:

> A: You must leave the city as soon as possible. The Germans are forcing an alliance and Talaat, Djemal and others known to you, will likely deprive the rich and influential Jews of everything, including citizenship. I expect the worst, as there is nothing to finance another conflict, especially one contemplated by the Germans. You must leave, my dear friend. Please pass this on to others. ~S

Why didn't Saf just visit or telephone him? Isaac had known the man since both were living in Salonika where Isaac, sympathetic, but in all things a circumspect man, had considered joining the masonic movement under his guidance. They had been in regular touch in Constantinople and had their own shorthand and code, but Isaac had noticed a growing reticence by Saf to be seen in his presence, especially at the Pera. Arthur had come directly from his embassy and left the note with Isaac, who reading it in a growing state of alarm, was ready to put it to flame. But first, he called for Olivia.

Olivia entered his study and asked, "Yes, father?"

"Daughter, I must share this note with you." He showed Olivia the small scrap of cheap, dull paper Cohen had left with him.

"Father, we are ready to leave. Uncle Binyamin has the last of the deposits in the Italian bank. We just need to transfer the rest directly to Italy. I am ready to go to Palestine and will follow you to Corconio in time, but you must alert the *Gräfin* to help us devise a way out. I know the Count holds tremendous sway over Witt, but it seems if war finds us here, we may not have an opportunity to communicate with her. We have looked after David, and the *Gräfin* pledged to look after us, should we need assistance."

"Kathe will do what is required, daughter. I will wire her this evening. Now go have your dinner with David, and I will begin the arrangements." Isaac stood and kissed Olivia, holding her face in his hands for a few moments before sending her away.

"*Seni seviyorum*, Papa," Olivia said at their parting.

Isaac sat back down and jotted a note for Kathe: *O to Uncle. I to lake. Urgent.*

He called in Benetar *Bey*, instructed him to deliver the note to the telegraph exchange, and gave him the address on a separate sheet of paper. "Destroy both after the message has been sent," he told the old, stalwart employee. Benetar nodded and left the room.

Isaac considered what he was admitting to himself: he must leave Constantinople. Perhaps forever. He reviewed all that had been done should this fear become realized: the movements of money, the long established understandings with his family, and the quiet machinations fostered by Kathe through her husband, including the posting of David to Constantinople. Now it seemed all must come to bear to secure his and Olivia's escape. That Sigi could communicate directly with Witt, a man with a long history with the Count General, would undoubtedly expedite matters, now that the ancient city was throwing off its cloak of parastatal influences and coughing up so many who wished for change. Kathe, the consummately guiding hand, moving them all, his imagination told him—a woman the ancients could deify for her beauty and wisdom could, with a few quiet words Isaac believed, offer them safety.

Isaac remembered a day at Villa Elena in Corconio, near Orta. The days, sometimes months, he had shared with Kathe there came flooding back, and his thoughts became infused with the rhythm of speaking only Italian, a triviality and competition they shared. The first of their private days together after returning from a Roman library where they had begun to know each other, were easy to recall:

her mane of blond curls shaken free and her arms full of books as they worked together in his library or passed each other in the vast hall, or the first time they ventured down to his little lake together, finding dense forest enclosing the waters. She was twenty-one and he was nearing forty, a slim, handsome, and vigorous man, but quiet and studious. The path from the villa wound through unusual laurels and flowering dwarf whitebeams, the pink petals of the shrub giving the day an uncanny brightness and compliment to the bare, milk-white arms Kathe had exposed from the plain, sleeveless peasant's shirt she had bought at the roadside country market, whose poor proprietors had spread their homemade clothes and second-hand cooking implements along a few open tables.

They had found the lake surrounded by cypresses and Italian maples in flower. He spread the old blanket offered him by his young housekeeper, Marina, just seventeen, the daughter of his estate manager. They lay down together, wearing the rough cotton and woolen of rustics, the sun fully upon them, and closed their eyes to the bright warmth. Isaac heard Kathe rise and rustle through her clothes, and as he opened his eyes, saw only the bright sun blinding his sight and a beckoning sway of high cypress limbs and high, sparse, streaming ribbons of fraying cloud. He heard her shuffle behind him, turned around, and saw her creamy limbs enfolding her full breasts as she sat upright, nude and cross-legged like a statue of an East Indian goddess. She opened her arms, her breasts fell before her, and she held her hands out from her body, raising them as if holding and balancing Isaac's thoughts. She moved next to him, her haunches unblemished and milk white as she spread herself across the blanket onto her belly. Isaac looked her length: her feet were splayed in towards each other, and a faint pinkness followed her beautifully formed legs, spreading out upon her buttocks. He touched her back and she turned up to him to offer a deep kiss. Then she pulled away, and laughing, ran down to the lakeside where she slowly moved into the cold water. He followed.

Isaac had always shadowed this woman, the *quinta essential,* a being without conflict by virtue of quiet restlessness and action. There seemed to be no dialectic to her life, only a synthetic concord with time, *natura naturata*, as perhaps Spinoza could appreciate. Isaac found his life an unabating toss of a restless mind looking out, wrestling with irreconcilable contrasts of thoughts, an eternal knotting of hopes toward, he hoped, a fabric of belief that might relax his critical tendencies. But would there ever really be peace for this man, always moving in nature, naturing? He was suborned by the whirl of thinking, thinking, dissecting the finite and opposed, but it seemed, never allowed to just slouch into a world like Kathe, as a question answered. Except when he was with Kathe, did he really become self-aware, recognize himself going out to meet his most dreaded suffering, and at the same time his most profound fulfillment. Leaving Constantinople, the worldly seat of his riches and his most trivial thoughts to move toward Kathe seemed epochal and absolute. Perhaps it portended change in himself, a push toward an even path where his eyes could look ahead, uncompelled to fix upon and question all he passed, *Ding an sich*, as perhaps his lover would say.

He remembered more of that afternoon at the lake; his placing the spine of a book, a copy of Lou Andreas-Salome's, *An Aberration*, along the cleft of her buttocks, the pages standing, then slowly falling almost evenly to each side. He remembered cocking his head to read a short passage: "…only you walk like this, as if over the whole world there were nothing but smooth paths, or as if an invisible being were walking ahead of you, smoothing them." He remembered Kathe's walk, the carefree swaying, almost loping gait, her head held up, and her eyes moving easily over the path ahead, ready, but never with disingenuous politeness, to smile. The absence of smile lines upon her mien had never been misleading to Isaac, indeed, they challenged him. But when her face came alive with mirth, she opened her mouth, broadening her lips astonishingly, and her large blue eyes captivated with the lift and rounding of her slanted, narrow, blond brows, to Isaac, like *Romanesque* portals into a contented mind.

Isaac brought his thoughts into the present and took his usual small *kanyak*, the Turkish brandy he preferred, and sipped it thoughtfully, sitting on his bedside. Irene would be in soon to say goodnight, but Isaac knew it was her way to assuage his paternal concerns, to assure him that she would wait up for Olivia. She duly entered and bowed goodnight, still wearing her severe housekeeper's uniform but imparting her contentment in her service with a small smile. Isaac slipped out of his stays and undressed, and after pulling on his night shirt, he lay down, his restless mind unfolding amongst the planning and calculations that were now confronting him and his brave and clever daughter. Finally settling into a light dream of summer heat and a whispering voice, he soon fell asleep.

The next morning, Isaac awoke to a bed in disarray like a sea frozen into heaping waves and tight, wind-blown ripples. Irene entered his room with a tray of tea and the news that a German named Herbert Witt was downstairs to see him. Witt had never ventured to Isaac's home. Indeed, the soldier had been very careful not to acknowledge Isaac unless a message from the Petersruhe's required. He was, to Isaac and a few friends, *Wittgenstein*, a man he met occasionally at the *Ahrida* Synagogue. German, true, but also a fellow Jew. Isaac hurriedly threw on a dressing gown and went down to meet the man who devoted himself to fulfilling the wishes of Sigismund von Petersruhe on behalf of *Hauptmann* Rožmberk.

"Good morning, Witt *Pasha*," said Isaac, addressing Witt in German. "Please, follow me into the library." The men walked hurriedly over the marble floor, Witt's heels glancing loudly on the smooth, polished stone and Isaac walking almost soundlessly in night shoes. Isaac gently closed the doors behind them and turned to his visitor, saying, "My apologies, Witt *Pasha*, but I must ask that we keep our conversation to near whispers unless we may speak in Italian."

"My dear Albukerk *Effendi*, I have no Italian, alas. I wish you to know that I received a telegram at my residence this morning from *Graf* Petersruhe regarding our business. The *Graf* and *Gräfin* received your message of yesterday evening and want you to know that I shall arrange, shall we say, your daughter's *Aliya*. She will be accompanied by *Hauptmann* Rožmberk. I ask that none of this will be spoken of to either of these young people. I will contact you with instructions for your daughter and issue orders to the *Hauptmann*, who will have no knowledge of your daughter's presence until both are *en route* to Palestine."

"Very good, Herbert, please accept my deepest thanks. Would you be so kind as to accompany me to the *Ahrida* for *Shabbat* this week? I will have my affairs concluded next week, and though I am not a religious man, I would very much like to remember my friends in the community, including yourself, in *our* setting. I plan to bring Olivia, and if he can be persuaded, David. Perhaps stepping them closer to the dear *Gräfin's* ultimate wishes for those two, if I may speak candidly."

"I understand, *effendi*. The joining of these two, I've long expected, really formed the basis of the Petersruhe requests to me concerning David. I certainly owe the *Graf* any service that is within my means to provide."

"Herbert, it is time that you called me simply, Isaac, as I am known in my native land."

"I am honored, my friend, and I will be pleased to join you at services as you request. I must be off now, but I ask you to trust me to make the arrangements for Olivia and David. I cannot promise a quick departure but ask that you prepare her for the journey within ten days."

"Thank you, Herbert. I look forward to sitting with you Friday evening."

"Good day, Isaac."

Isaac opened the library door and allowed Witt to pass into the hall. Irene had retrieved his coat and helped him into it. Herbert nodded thanks to her and farewell to Isaac who stood, watching in front of the library doors. I must know this man's story, Isaac mused as the front doors were pulled into each other.

"Good morning, Papa," said Olivia, using their household Italian. "I recognized the man as he left."

"Indeed, my dear?"

"Yes, he is my friend Gerd's uncle; both work in the German embassy. May I ask why he paid you a visit, Papa?"

"May I just say, daughter, that *Herr* Witt wishes to accompany us to *Shabbat* services this week. I would like to invite your *Hauptmann* also. May I rely on you?"

"I must confess, Papa, I have grown fond of David and would miss him after I depart, but I have a *presentimento* that he shall not completely exit my life. I trust you have things in motion?"

"Of course, daughter. Do not worry yourself. Just begin setting aside the things you may wish to take with you. I must begin my day, my love. I will see you this evening." Isaac hurried upstairs to prepare for work.

During the next several days, Isaac began making arrangements for his departure. Benetar *Bey* was asked to look after the business—not an unusual step, as Isaac often came and went to and from Italy. Irene was informed that she must prepare to go to Corconio, as Isaac was expecting visitors there. The conversation was informal and implied no urgency, lest the manager and housekeeper suspect large changes. Isaac knew that nothing stays secret for long in Constantinople and that the movements of prosperous Jews, he reminded himself yet again, were suspect. He continued with his daily routine, the walking and visiting the Galatasaray Baths, and when Friday arrived, he found Olivia and David standing in his home's great hall to meet him.

"And will we have the honor of your presence at services, young man?" Isaac noticed that David was in evening dress.

"Yes, *effendi*, Miss Olivia has kindly invited me to accompany you to the *Ahrida* this evening," replied David in surprisingly good Turkish.

"Good, good, but we must hurry. Daughter, please have Mentes bring the car."

"Yes, Papa."

Soon the party was bumping down the hill toward the Golden Horn and its bridge to Stamboul. The traffic was heavy and the usual throngs of citizens and refugees coursed every direction, brushing against the automobiles and languidly walking before them, clotting the thoroughfares and provoking the police who raced back and forth shoving the cataleptic and drunken crowds out of the roadway. Often a series of pistol shots could be heard ahead and a rush of Gypsies or ragged refugees would run past the car in a blur of colorful clothing, shouting and screaming, and then a uniformed horseman waving a whip would invariably follow. Finally, the car joined the queue in front of the synagogue and soon the passengers were deposited before its door.

Olivia was dressed much as when David had first met her—wrapped in a blue *tesettür,* her face shaped into a white, chiffon *shayla* enclosing her long neck down to a pointed ellipse. Her head was wrapped in gold strands dangling jewels of every color, and her long arms, ringed with golden bracelets, flowed away from her long gray dress. Isaac noticed her unusually kohled eyes and the scent of a new perfume, and his heart worried while he watched David carefully, but with quiet pride, attend his daughter.

They approached the great old temple, resembling, David thought, the Boston stump, rising so dramatically from the ground near the sea. The reddish color of the synagogue made the building a cynosure of the holy sites surrounding it; the aroma of Greek incense floating by, combining with the rot fumes of the waterfront added an even more poignant, exotic aspect to the Stamboul air as the party approached the opened doors. As they stepped inside, Witt emerged from the crowd and offered his hand to Isaac and David, but bowed deeply before Olivia, who nodded and turned to follow the other women to their side of the *mechitza*, a finely made partition of cloth rising from the ancient floor three feet or so, with cloth lattice-work rising another two feet along the top.

When nearly everyone was settled, the rabbi gave an undulating, high-pitched call to prayer in a voice that seemed to refine into a subtle echo and began the service: "O Lord, open my mouth that my lips may utter your praise!" All rose, the men wearing *kippahs,* fezzes, or European hats of the day, and began the *Ma'ariv.*

After the hour's service, finally concluding with an astonishingly loud "amen," Isaac stood for a few moments, looking over the congregation and the men he had known, some with whom he had done business, others merely friendly conversation. The men filed out followed by the women, and Isaac, David, and Witt surrounded Olivia, carrying her *siddur* as she emerged from the great doorway.

As they began walking away, a small, pale man in Western clothes with dark eyes ran up the temple's steps, approached Witt, and in an instant, stabbed him in the left chest. David could see the man's arm raised and the fisted knife, but as it fell towards Witt, his vision was blocked by Isaac, who had caught the man's arm and spun him around. Suddenly, all was chaos, with men and women running frantically away from the scene, but David was able to spot the small man's dark bowler as he ran to a waiting car. The frantic crowd blocked the progress of the car as people fled the startling incident, and David was able to hear the man shout in English, "Run them over, you fool!"

David ran after the fleeing car and caught up to a taxi inching forward that had pulled in between the fleeing car and a tangle of arguing Jews. Entering the taxi, David told the driver in Turkish to follow the car ahead. As the cars moved towards Galata, crossing the bridge, a throng of soldiers was smashing into a crowd of people, blocking all progress. David leaped from the taxi, and the unnoticing man looking ahead impatiently found himself dragged from the car.

David wrestled him easily to the pavement. He pulled the man between the car and the taxi, and with his knee in his back, tied the man's hands behind his back with his belt. He then took the howling little man along with him in a headlock, knocking his bowler over the rail to fall into the waters of the Horn behind them. As they reached the Stamboul-side of the bridge, David led the man down the embankment and slammed his face into the rocks surrounding the butt of the bridge, knocking him unconscious and spurting blood from his face.

David scrambled up the embankment and ran to the opposite side of the road, where he found a small haberdashery, closed of course, but persuaded the owner puttering inside to open the door in defiance of the Sabbath and bought from him four leather belts. The shopkeeper's immaculate red fez bobbed up and down as he closed the door behind David and pulled down the shade. David ran back to his captive and finding him covered in blood and moaning, tied two belts to the belt binding the man's hands and linked them around his throat. He led him up the embankment and along the roadway, pretending to be assisting a drunken partner. Parked taxis lined the street, and as the pair approached the first one, David bent down, shoving the man's face into the pavement again, and reconfigured the belts so that he could tie the man to the bumper of the car with a third belt. David then wiped the blood from his hands, walked up to the taxi's window, and ordered the driver to meet a Mr. Jones, the only name he could readily think of, at the British embassy.

He paid the driver the fare, included a generous tip, and watched as the car pulled into traffic with other drivers honking their horns and waving in an attempt to stop the taxi and save the man being pulled over the pavement behind. The driver just exhibited a fist or the universal two-finger salute and swore at everyone who tried to stop him. The would-be assassin gained consciousness and was shouting, "Goddamn you!" He looked back at his assailant, standing with crossed arms, and began to scream incomprehensively as he was dragged along, bound in his cruel phylactery, the skin scrapeing and burning from his body. David walked behind, picking up the scraps of clothing torn from the unlucky man's body, and eventually collecting his shoes. As the taxi stopped behind the commotion on the bridge, David threw the clothing over the side and ran up to the bloody mess hanging by a thin strand of leather off the bumper, breathing heavily the automobile's thick fumes. In English, he asked the unrecognizable creature, "Why did you stab my friend?"

The man's jaw was still intact and he uttered, "I was ordered to. Let me, let me go, and I will tell you everything. "

"Give me a name, you bastard," David demanded.

"Never, no I can't, I'll be killed!" the man blubbered.

David untied the man, who muttered, "Thank you, thank you." Wrapping the man inside his long coat, he moved him against the following crowd to the side of the bridge. Waiting until he was unnoticed, he threw the nearly naked and tortured attacker off the bridge into the Golden Horn. He watched for a brief moment as the man tried desperately, but in vain, to keep his head above the flowing water. David's last glimpse of him was the sight of his bloody, open mouth receding below the bay.

David walked on to the end of the bridge, feigning calm, chin up, looking ahead, but feeling the night's chill as he carried his bloodied overcoat. He knew that blood had soaked through to his white evening shirt and carried the coat as he had carried the attacker to hide his gory side. He found a taxi and made his way back to the *Ahrida*, where he found the rabbi watching members of the synagogue staff cleaning Witt's blood from the steps.

David approached the rabbi and asked, "Please, rabbi *Beyfendi*, where has my friend Witt *Pasha* been taken?"

The rabbi looked carefully at David and seemed to remember him with Witt during the service. In any event, it would do no harm, the rabbi finally decided to tell him: "He was taken to the German Embassy."

"Was Witt *Pasha* alive, *Beyfendi*?"

"Yes, and speaking."

"Thank you, rabbi *Beyfendi*"

"May your friend recover."

David walked into the immaculate embassy to the stares of the night staff, a few rising from their desks and asking David about his appearance, now somewhat rumpled as well as bloodied. He went straight to the small infirmary and found *Frau* Witt and Freya sitting together, holding hands.

"How is the *Oberst*?" David blurted out and then remembering himself, bowed to *Frau* Witt and offered, "My dear *Frau*, how you must be suffering! Please forgive me for ignoring your travail."

"*Herr Oberst* is fine; sewn up and resting, *Hauptmann*," said Freya. "You look terrible, David! What has happened to you? I am not so certain that we will allow you out of the *Apfelhaus* again. Always, you are in trouble!"

"My dear Freya, perhaps you will finally bathe me?" said David.

"No woman would wish to have anything to do with you, *Tierisch*!"

"May I see *Herr Oberst*?" asked David.

"Come with me," said Freya.

Colonel Witt was awake, but fuming at his condition. "Ah, *Hauptmann*, and where have you been? And what has happened to you? Are you wounded, also?" he asked.

"No, sir, I am well. How are you feeling, sir?"

"I only wish to get my hands on that would-be assassin, David," replied Witt.

"That may be problematic, Colonel."

"Oh, indeed? What did you do with the swine, David?"

"I only asked him why he attacked you, *Herr Oberst*."

"And then?"

"I shouldn't wish to bore you with details, sir, but suffice to say that I threw him into the Horn."

"Alive?"

"Not now, I shouldn't think, sir."

"You are a dangerous man, Rožmberk."

"Yes, sir."

"Now you need to get to *Apfelhaus*, my boy. Albukerk *effendi* and his daughter are safe. I want you to confine yourself to *Apfelhaus* until further notice."

"But…"

"No arguments! Now, out!"

David stepped outside the small room, colliding immediately with a nurse carrying a steel dish filled with instruments. The dish was knocked against the startled woman, and the implements of her trade fell all around her.

"I am so sorry, sister" said David, who knelt down to retrieve the medical tools.

"No, no, no, leave them! They are contaminated now!"

David nodded, moved around the woman, and exited through the infirmary's swinging doors. At once, he saw Gerd, bent, standing with his arms surrounding his aunt's shoulders. Freya looked up, drawing Gerd's attention to David, who went directly to the murmuring little chorus and said, "All seems well; the Colonel is as irascible as ever."

Gerd turned, and assuring his aunt that he would return soon, took David's arm and led him away to a small alcove down the hall. He looked at David and said, "You look a sight! Tell me what happened, David."

David recounted the evening, omitting the more gruesome details of the fate of Witt's would-be assassin. Gerd began to shake, tears welled up into his eyes, and the small, effeminate man burst into uncontrollable sobs. David took Gerd into his arms and allowed his friend to burrow his face into his unbloodied side. The tears of the nephew soaked through to the skin of the man as Freya, listening at the crack of the infirmary's doors, heard David relate the fate of their master's assailant. "There, my dear, friend" David said, lifting the young face away from his shirt, "Our hero lives and shall recover."

"But you are our hero, David. We all hail you who has spared us great suffering; my tears pass and are drying at our feet now. Grief flies away!"

"My dear Gerd, truly, you sound like some overwrought, ancient chorus. Now go; hold your aunt's hand and make her laugh: all is well, my friend."

David led Gerd back into the company of the vigilant women and left, summoning an embassy car to take him to *Apfelhaus*. He felt his head drop upon his chest as he fell into slumber, awakening immediately as the car stopped at the familiar corner. He made his way into the foyer, confronted by the stare of a robed Helen, who nodded, indicating that David must once again shed his clothes, then and there.

"Do you know what time it is, my dear *Hauptmann*? Do you imagine that I keep absurd hours like this? Now, wait here while I draw you a bath. An infant would require less care, God help me!"

As Helen walked to the great bathroom, she suddenly realized that David had dried blood all along his left side and his overcoat was stiff with it, as he dropped it, as ordered, to the floor before her. The coat stood supported by the desiccated gore, the neck forming a peak, eventually slumping over to her feet. Good God, what has he done, now, she thought to herself, shuddering.

The woman returned to find David standing in his undergarments. "Drop them all, now. I don't have time to worry with a robe, you devil!"

David took his remaining clothes off and stood naked before Helen. She took him all in and finally said, "Now move, David!"

David settled into his hot bath, lowering his head under the water and sliding down without his feet touching the far end of the great tub. The lights went low, and as he raised his head above water, he saw Helen enter the tub opposite him, her straight blond hair cascading over her breasts.

"Touch me, and I'll tell my uncle. And remember, *Hauptmann*, I can shoot, also."

"Turn your head this time, Helen, for God's sake," said David, somewhat sternly, "I must stand to wash." David finished his ministrations and sank back into the steaming bath. "Now, your turn." He turned his head and closed his eyes.

"No need, David, I bathed earlier. I only wanted to enjoy the hot water. You know, I'll have to burn your clothes again. I suppose that I'll have to wait for Freya to tell me the story?"

"You are correct. Best to burn the clothes sooner, than later. Now you are getting out first this time, my beauty!"

As dawn approached, Olivia awoke and lay wondering what had happened to David after the attack. She had seen him rush by her and disappear into the crowd and then reappear as he entered a taxi. Eventually, she rose and went downstairs to find Irene, who stood immediately at her appearance.

"*Hanımefendi*, so early? May I serve you tea?" said the housekeeper.

"Yes, Irene, please." The two women sat together and sipped tea quietly, Olivia ignoring the customs of their roles. "Dawn rises on her golden throne, my Irene. Another day to most, but our Sabbath, this day." Eventually, Mentes entered, but, taken aback by his mistress's appearance in the kitchen, turned to leave. "But, Mentes, you must take your tea," said Olivia.

The servant stopped, turned, and bowed as Irene handed him a cup of tea. "Please excuse my intrusion, *hanımefendi*," he said

and disappeared out of the room. But he was back, almost instantly, saying, "There is a German lady who insists upon seeing you,
hanımefendi." Mentes had an uncanny ability to recognize Germans,
owing to long service with another influential, but now dispersed,
Sephardi family.

"I will see her, Mentes, thank you. Please accompany me to the
hall." As Olivia, still in her morning robe approached, she beheld
a shorter blond woman, fully dressed, but somewhat plainly for
the day.

"Please speak German, *Frau,* or is it *Fraulein*? said Olivia. To
Mentes, she said, "You may go, thank you, Mentes."

"I am *Frau* Helen, *Fraulein. Hauptmann* Rožmberk wishes you to
know that Herr Witt is out of danger and that the *Hauptmann* has
been confined to quarters until further notice. He wishes me to assure you that the attacker will bother no one again. He further says,
that he trusts that he will not have to light a fire to purify this house
once he returns."

"Thank you, *Frau* Helen. Please tell the *Hauptmann* that I look
forward to his release and tell him to say a prayer to the bright-eyed
weaver girl and her father who may ask him to brandish his long
spear and save us, his devoted."

"So I will, *Fraulein,* and I promise you that I will protect him until
he sees you again." Helen left the Albukerk house and returned to
Apfelhaus, finding David asleep at the dining table. Freya had not
returned from the embassy, so she prepared a small breakfast, woke
David to share it with her, then told him of her visit to Olivia on his
behalf. "Now, to go to bed!" she commanded.

Isaac rose from deep sleep and greeted his daughter, who awaited him at the dining table. Breakfast was served immediately, and
Olivia recounted Helen's earlier visit. "I think you love this boy, my
child" said Isaac. "Our current situation reminds me of a famous
German's thought: 'We are only in our bliss when we are in our
greatest danger.'" He thought of the golden-haired girl lying asleep
next to him along the lakeside in Corconio so long ago, and he bit
into a ripe plum.

30

Ephraim Yoffey lifted the binoculars from the dock railing and moved a finger over the instrument's bridge wheel. He read the *Fernglas 08* CARL ZEISS JENA markings and absentmindedly ran his thumb over the letters, remembering. The blood is finally gone, he thought. The blood of the *moshav*, when the Romanian held the glasses to his eyes with raw hands, worked to blood by shovel, the stones and the burning, caustic mortar he used to build the cistern under the lip of the ledged hill at the end of the new well's piping. When he and his helpers finished, he looked back at Ephraim, standing half a mile away at the well site and waved a signal to pump the water to him. The Romanian dropped the binoculars against his chest, dirt baking into the blood his fingers and palms had left upon them.

It was nearly noon, and Ephraim felt the warming metal beginning to sting his fingers off the tubes, out of his sweaty grip, and wished the dock were covered like the old boathouse next to it. Ephraim brought the glasses to his eyes and pulled his sight up beyond the narrow spit of land that nearly closed the Bayou and looked into the wide Bay, beyond. He turned the eyepieces and brought the glinting objects he hoped were coming to him into focus. Two men, he thought, just two men. Not Hulda, his niece, the girl still silent, perhaps lost to the desert.

He heard the swish of bare feet behind him and felt the slight shudder as someone brought their weight onto the dock's steps. The wood soon sounded with the *bump-bump* of a heavy man walking out to him. "There is a balm in Gilead to make the wounded whole," the man was singing. "Hey, Mister Ephraim!" Temple called. "That ain't them, too early." The man was tall and well built, his arms straining the cotton sleeves of his clean white shirt. Above his bare black feet, he wore shiny black linen pants. He'd just arrived from church.

"They've been early before, Temple," Ephraim said.

"But not on a Sunday, boss. They mean as hell, them red ferrymen, but they still has to have they church on Sunday." Temple Luke stood three steps behind Ephraim and pulled the brim of his sweat-stained straw hat down against the bright sun. He squinted as he followed the white man's line of sight out to the Bay and noticed the winking object moving over the waves. "You just may as well come on up and let Miss Linny feed you, mister."

That's enough sunbathing, Temple thought. He looked back to the bayou's oyster shell-covered bank, brought his feet up to avoid the parched dock's splinters, turned his upper body, and in a light hop, swung about, and marched away from his employer's brother.

"What has Miss Linny prepared for me, Temple, the usual Sunday fare?" Ephraim asked.

"Ain't nothing fair about Miss Linny. Said she was frying mullet, and if you can't smell it in the air, you got a condition, boss. Better go see Doc *Butt Holie*. I don't know though, he probably wouldn't know what a frying mullet smelled like, eatin' that *wop* food like he do."

"Temple, his name is *Bettoli*, Doctor Tomaso Bettoli. Does he call you anything mean?"

Temple shook his head.

"No? Well then, please don't call him a *wop*, or I'll have to inform Miss Linny."

Ephraim brought his binoculars down, wiped sweat off the diopters, and replaced the one surviving cap over the front lens. He picked a pith helmet up from the decking and pulled its stained, fraying, khaki cover onto his head and adjusted its dented and chipped brim, fingering a small badge set into the front. The badge was a Star of David with a King's Crown at its top. It was hot to the touch, and again Ephraim paused, remembering the fellow who gave it to him. He began to follow Temple Luke toward the shore.

"Linny's *a what* you was thinking too, you know," Temple said.

"*Goddamn it, Temple!*" Ephraim yelled.

"Lord's gonna smite you on this Sunday, boss." He sang very loudly, "There's enough power in heaven, to cure a sin-sick soul. How lost was my condition, 'til Jesus made me whole, and bossman blasphemin' won't be saved by the wop Butt-Hole. Eeee."

Ephraim threw up his hands, knowing Temple Luke would keep it up as long he would listen. At the end of the dock, Temple turned left and followed a path through a stand of cattails to a boathouse next to the dock. He was now just humming the old melody, smiling. Ephraim continued off the dock and up a path and crossed a sandy two-rut trail fronting a shaded, sandy yard littered with leaves and mapped with huge roots, gnarling and jutting away from large oaks and magnolias. He stopped and looked up from the yard at the house before him. He put his hands around the binoculars hanging from his neck, remembering, wishing to hold the recent past to himself, wishing to bring his Ruth to this strange place and his life amongst these strange people of the Hill. He was now lonely, and with the loneliness, the guilt that had become his mind's enfolding companion during the long, dim hours past light began to move through his thoughts. He walked ahead and stepped onto the wide, limestone walkway.

The house standing before him had originally been built by a South Carolinian, a Civil War refugee who guessed, or as he later claimed, knew through his business there, that this part of the South would be little touched by the conflict. His time here along the red bluffs of the northern Gulf Coast were good to him, providing the clay his company needed to produce the bricks his Confederate and U. S. government contracts demanded. Signs of his success were scattered along the coasts as lighthouses, forts, barracks, and occasionally private homes. The mansions faced by his bricks stood tall, immovable, declaring the dividends of a slave-fostered wealth known only to the cupful of souls nuzzled at the top of a barrel of uncounted minions who spent their lives restlessly pushing, swaying, but never climbing.

This house was somewhat less than a mansion, but substantial, also red-bricked with three large, brick columns with brick extrusions flowing around the sides, and a pattern of three rows standing out from the columns winding up the cylinders like Calypso vines. The brick-paved porch under the columns was established several feet above what had been determined the highest watermark left by a hurricane the year of the home's construction on the nearest oak. The house brooded out toward the bayou, its windows framed and capped by dun-colored limestone and broad brick steps fanning away from the porch, the risers fronted by the soldier bricks supporting the corbelled lips above them and finishing onto a broad limestone walk of the same brown-gray.

The original owner had lived there for twenty or so years alone except for a spinster sister and the servants, a Creole woman and her brother, and he rode out the Civil War and Reconstruction until Mr. Chipley brought his railroad to the town across the gentle waters of the Bayou. All four of the original occupants succumbed to a Yellow Fever epidemic that seemed to follow the neighboring town's progress. The home was inherited by the man's niece and later by his great-nephew, who residing in Mobile, Alabama, was completely absent even when the estate was sold to Ephraim's brother Sam, newly arrived from South Carolina himself.

Ephraim entered the house and immediately heard Linny the maid call to him that dinner was almost ready. Sunday dinner in the South, Ephraim had learned as a boy, would be served no later than 1:00 p.m., a custom Anna Jane followed without fail come Yellow Fever, hurricanes, or childbirth. Sundays had been his youth's loneliest days of the week, with most people in church or cooped up at home with a preacher. Only Sunday dinner seemed to cut this day into bearable portions for Ephraim. He took off his helmet—Temple called it a *nubby*—and placed it on the baker's rack in the kitchen and looked at Linny's face, straining back at him across her shoulder and smiling, lovely. She had skin the color of dark rust and a small scar at the bottom of her left temple, reminding him of a sycamore fig nicked to encourage ripening. Again he remembered that other land and the night feeling crawled through him.

"What you studying, Mister Ephraim?" Linny asked. "Temple been working at you, again?" She turned fully around and wiped her hands on her apron. Standing six feet, she was nearly eye-level with Ephraim. "Go on and sit down, and I'll serve you in just a minute." Her long neck and slim limbs reminded him of another dark girl, one that greeted him from the imagination of a long-vanished artist, an image on the side of a tomb he seen in a book, but unlike the painted girl, Linny's eyes were alive and amazing.

"Miss Linny, the Pharaoh's daughter," Ephraim said. He took in her laugh, followed her limbs as she turned back to her work, and imagined Red Indian and Caucasian grandfathers somewhere in her past.

Linny sang, "Go down Moses … tell ol' Pharaoh, let my people go," and then said, "Now go sit down please, sir."

Ephraim moved away to the dining room.

"Good afternoon, young man." Sam Yoffey was sitting at the head of the long table. "I hear you've been out on the dock looking for the afternoon ferry, as usual." Sam was now in his early fifties, still with black hair, but it was thinning at the back. Like his brother, Ephraim, he had a soft South Carolina accent and invariably wore a small *Rod of Asclepius* lapel pin. The pin would appear variously on Sam's collar, on a lapel, or on one of the white cotton shirt pockets Linny ironed and laid out for him every morning. Sam's mind wandered every day to the afternoon ferry also, but he was usually too busy with his practice to walk with Ephraim to the dock to see if, perhaps, his daughter had finally returned.

"Ephi, I'm about ready to run those Jews from Charleston off. They have kept you in their throes for what, nearly twenty years? Shipping you off to Palestine, you, a newly minted engineer from a damn good school. Mama and old Pap so proud, but never to see your success, which by the way, is past due its *fructification*, if you follow me, buster."

"Sam, I keep telling you about the irrigation and community

building projects I participated in Palestine. We're making a new *homeland* for the Jews. Progress is slow. Now with a war on, it's hard to say if it'll get any faster. Or if the Turks don't kill every Jew around."

"Miss Linny, how many Jews do you know, if you don't mind my asking?" said Sam. "Other than these two Israelites eating your delicious cooking here, my daughter, and my dearest wife, though she converted to please that love-struck rabbi, how many of our kind do you know?"

"Well, Dr. Sam, I can't say I knows more than that handful what comes around for a visit here; maybe five, six."

"Ephi, my boy, I kind of like having the tribes scattered around the earth, but as I've often said, I'm always ready to invite the rest to live here in these United States. If we can overcome the sins of slavery, and be forgiven by good folks like Miss Linny, this ought to be a fine enough place to bring the rest of our Hebrew brethren. And don't correct me about Hebrews and Jews, Maimonides. Now, I've just got to get my Hulda back. That would fulfill *my* need for more Jews. That epic you told me about how she got to Palestine is nigh on a year old, brother. I'm going to be jumping up and down amongst your Charleston friends if I don't see her soon!"

"Sam, she sneaked in there on her own! The Society had nothing to do with Hulda joining the goddamned English nursing corps and then making her way to Palestine."

"Hush that language in front of Miss Linny. This is what happens when parents have children twenty years apart. They just don't have the energy to teach good manners. God help us both if Sister James hears language like that!"

Ephraim remembered the letter he'd received in Palestine from Sam about Hulda's leaving.

Hulda was contacted by some long, lost cousin, through the Charleston Society, about joining the damned British Nursing Corp, and ran off to Charleston to catch the first ship out. I swear, that girl is afraid of nothing and looking for adventure. War in Europe: those rich Charleston Jews seem to have something to prove to the old world!

Ephraim looked at his brother and sighed. "Sam, it was a Canadian who reached out to the Society to solicit volunteer nurses; you can't blame everything on them. Hell, the girl's twenty-two years old and ready to get away from the Bay."

"Listen, Goddammit. Sorry, Miss Linny. When I'm not chopping on somebody's body, I miss my child. You should get married and have some children. That'll teach you."

Ephraim began to think of his Ruth still in *Eretz Yisrael*, building the *moshav* where he'd worked with her and loved her. He thought he'd convinced her father to allow her to accompany him here to the Bay—at least until after the war. But every day, looking out from the dock, there had been no sign of her. Her last letter was dated months before the war began:

11 April 1914

My Ephi,

It has been a year since we last saw each other, and I ache for you. My role with the settlement has grown and I sometimes wish that I could just go back to helping you and the Romanian move water around this Israel dirt. My cousin Olivia plans to come to Jerusalem to visit my father and mother, but I have heard nothing from her. Please come back to me, my Ephi. I will go with you to any place you wish.

My love,

Ruth

Ephraim knew from his Society contacts that the war hadn't reached Palestine yet, but he feared that the Turks would make trouble for the Jewish settlements or ignore attacks by the local Arabs. During his last talks with Binyamin and Ruth, he made certain that his contact information recorded his home address, his brother's telephone number, and the addresses of friends associated with the Charleston Society. He wanted Ruth and her family to be assured of their safety with him in the U.S. The possibility that the strip of land, so often named and renamed, so long fought over, was not finished soaking blood was ever present. Now that the Turks and Germans had allied, Britain would make strong efforts to protect the Suez Canal, and knowing their penchant for hegemony, look for opportunities to pare down the Turkish Empire.

Anna Jane joined the men at the table, offering Ephraim and Sam silent greetings. She had grown quieter as her worry for her child had grown since Hulda left the Hill nearly a year ago. Her hair had begun graying and her beautiful, lustrous eyes were often cast down as she went about life with Sam. Her once frequent trips to the Esther had fallen off her routine, and she only sent Sam's nurse around to look in on the old Mother, who was now very feeble. She kept to Sam's office during the weekday mornings, returning home for lunch and to occupy the balance of her afternoon with sewing clothes for the little hospital's less fortunate inmates.

After Linny and Gomey had served the table, Anna Jane looked at Ephraim and said, "Has there been any news from Palestine?"

"No, ma'am, nothing, yet."

"I so wish that we could have left you there, Ephraim, but, and I realize that I've said this many times to you, Sam simply couldn't take the time to make the trips to South Carolina to settle your mother's estate. You can't know how much we appreciate your return, as would Sam's patients, if they only knew. We are all so sad these days missing our love ones. You must begin making arrangements to return to your Ruth where, hopefully, you can find us some information about your niece."

"I fear, darling, that since Hulda's presumably on the British side of the line over there, Ephraim will be completely cut off from her, but maybe the Jews have a way of getting around that little dust up," said Sam. "Ephraim, Anna Jane is right. It's time to get you on a ship."

"I'll pay a visit to the steamship companies in town tomorrow," said Ephraim.

After dinner, Ephraim went up to his room and sat for a few minutes, allowing memories of Palestine to flood his thoughts. He thought of Ruth, sleeping next to his empty bed now.

31

Sergeant Harry Eccles knew someone else had struck the water. The faint cry, the spray rising through the moonlight, and the tug of his own body as the man displaced the water nearby, convinced him, in his muddled state, that he was not alone. But knowing he had a companion in the sea did little to help still the signs of panic that immediately began welling through his body as he watched the burning ship turning sharply to port and increasing speed, leaving him. His mind pushed away the realization that the ship could not be reached, and he kicked up and to his right, bringing his head higher above the chop and coughed saltwater out of his throat. Looking toward the sound of the splash, he put an arm up to swim but allowed it to fall as he saw a young man floating not more than a few feet before him. Eccles realized that he was floating also, and he knew he owed their lives, at least to this point, to the ship's first mate, who swore at anyone not wearing a life vest while on deck.

Another assault of white water slapped Harry, filling his open mouth as the chop and the wind pushed the breaker up from the Mediterranean. There seemed to be only now, a present, the ordeal dissolving his thirty-one years, leaving only the sense of this minute, this second, and the relentless waves crushing any sense of time. At least he could orient himself to the man floating with him on the back of the ancient sea. The man, moaning, began to cough and struggle against his buoyancy and the lack of foundation beneath his feet, perhaps somewhat aware of his own predicament in the rising, falling, but never with opened eyes. Eccles called to him, grabbed the straps of the man's life vest, and pulled him onto his chest to bring them both into his own struggle to find breath between the troughs and the foaming ascent to top the waves.

Eccles knew they were miles out to sea. He recalled the crewmen earlier in the day discussing the heading, apparently a straight course to Alexandria, closing an angle from Malta along North Africa. How far from land were they? In the gloaming, through a light, wispy fog, he recalled a dim light he'd watched from the ship's starboard rail as the vessel moved easily over the waves, the indifferent giants now slapping him and his groaning companion. The long minutes of dusk that began just as the torpedo struck the ship were revealing a faint moon, risen just enough for Harry to notice as he rose to the crests and allowing him a bearing, a thimbleful of knowledge to bring him out of his tightening world, toward the movement of time, safety and relevance. He noticed a light, was it the light he'd seen from the ship? The light was brighter, now; was he moving toward the light? Was the water pushing the men toward the light, directing their drift to a shore?

The man clasped to Eccles screamed and shook his head gently from side to side, causing Eccles to pull his chin away from the man's shoulder. In an instant, as his eyes moved from the struggle and noise, he sighted a large, white object rising toward the crest of a breaking wave to the left and then slapping down the trough it met behind. Harry knew immediately that he'd seen a lifeboat, surely blown away from the ship like the two men, and the object brought a measure of resolve into his mind as the sea's disorder assaulted his wits and senses. Harry looped an arm under one of the shaking man's armpits and began to kick and pull himself with his other arm through the water toward the damaged boat. As he moved toward the white hull rising into and then falling out of his vision, Eccles could hear its slapping and pounding struggle against the waves and the scraping slide of whatever tackle it held moving against the deck. As he got closer, he could see the top half of the transom rising away and then falling against the ravaged hull, striking with force and offering a loud bump to the sea noise and loud babblings of his companion. He knew the slamming wood would be dangerous to approach, so he worked along the hull away from the transom to find a grip, and he prayed for the right dip in the waves to allow them to struggle into the boat.

Harry found himself in a trough as he reached the boat. He grabbed for an oarlock along the rail and found enough purchase to hang on and then pull the boat's rail down toward him and kick his legs to pull himself and the man, now quiet and unmoving, far enough up to straddle the rail to where he could shed the man's body, dropping him into the dark, gaping space and into the curve of the little wreck's gunwale. Harry fell back, and as the boat rose away from him, he caught his chin along the strake of the hull and the lapped boards strummed a quick and painful bruise. Harry brought his legs together again and pushed far enough up to gain the oarlock. He hung alongside the tossing, noisy boat until his strength and a suitable trough of water allowed him to pull into the hull and fall next to his companion. The men rose out of the trough, buoyed on a plane, and cresting a wave. For the first time since he found himself overboard, Harry began to calm himself and allow some hope to stir through him.

As the light dimmed to darkness, Eccles and the injured man bounced, sometimes nearly out of the shattered boat. But he was a strong man with powerful limbs, and he fought the movement and held onto the man. In the crashing and noise, and now the night's cold air, Harry began to long for sleep, but to relax for a moment, he feared, would bring only a return to the water. As the many black hours passed, Harry's eyes began to close, but a sudden scraping, a creaking and pounding as wood met rock, brought him fully awake, startled and instantly afraid. The boat seemed to be hammering through a knot, its shaking sides crashing and banging and causing, finally, the transom to completely separate from the hull. It flew over the men with the wash of the surf, and jamming between rocks above them, settled just at the top of the boat's prow. Eccles reached and found the edge of the transom, and wrapping the man between his legs, used both hands to pull them from under the curving wood above to the top of the wreck, the boat at last unmoving, for a moment wedged between black rocks pulsing with white water and spray.

The ravaged hull rose and fell gently between the rocks, locked into place, tightly hinged, riding the movement of the water pushing into and withdrawing from the gap. Eccles brought his companion up next to him, and as the hull's stern began rising, he grabbed the transom and lifted himself to a squat. He looked through the moonlit spray and made out the line of shore along a headland to his right. He hoped that the tide was high, knowing that his refuge among the rocks would abandon him if the water rose. He looked at the man lying below him and knew he was still alive because, like himself, he was shaking with cold. It had been some time since the man had moved his head or made a sound, but the quivering gave Eccles hope that he would not have to spend yet another night with a corpse in the endless war enslaving him. He sat down and pulled the man's head into his lap and sitting on the detached transom, leaned against the boat's rail and fell helplessly into a deep sleep.

Harry awoke with a start as he began sliding down the hull. The sea had withdrawn enough with the retreating tide to ease the stern down to rest evenly on the rocks. The man against him began to stir and lift his head. Harry grabbed for the rails of the boat, and turning on his side, lifted him up. The man steadied himself against the gunwale. Eccles looked at the his face, lit by a rosy dawn, smiled and said, "Weel, tha's arisen. I hope we're out of this posskit soon. Sorry I had to hopple thee, but tha' might have been tossed out without my grip. I'm Sergeant Eccles, 4th Shropshire Yeomanry, and I can tell you're an officer."

"Lieutenant Thomas Twinge-Kitchen," the man whispered. Harry's companion rubbed his face and tried to speak again, but pain began wracking his body and he slumped down. The officer's right knee was exposed, swollen, and gashed. His left shoulder bled under his khaki tunic, and blood was running down from his hairline and across his face. He gripped the boat's rail with his right hand and closed his eyes. Although soaked through, it was apparent that his uniform fit him particularly well and his boots were of quality.

The night wore off, and the cold began to flee the rising sun. The wind diminished. The two men longed for warmth, each unspeaking and shivering in their places against the hull, and occasionally approaching sleep. As the day spread before them, Eccles looked out to a calming sea blending into a pearl horizon that was slowly becoming lighter and seemed to be separating itself from the water. He turned to shore and saw that during the night it had reached out toward the boat. The water was clear, and beyond the rocks he could discern a sandy bottom.

Harry shook the Lieutenant awake and said, "Sir, we must leave." He crawled down the rocks, holding onto the boat and stepped-off into the water, daring its depth. Tom raised his head and looked down the length of boat and the watched Eccles step-down, out of sight. He managed to pull himself toward the lower end of the boat and was trying to raise a foot over the last brutal rock when Eccles came back and reached to help him.

"Ast thou the strength, sir?" said Eccles.

"Sergeant, you must be South Yorkshire, born and bred," replied Tom.

"Right sir, Penistone."

"Yes, the wonderful viaduct."

Tom gave Eccles his hand and managed to get over the rock and into the clear, shallow water. He could see that they were about one hundred yards away from a beach of light-colored sand set between twenty-foot mounds of broadly striated rocks. "How deep is the water, Sergeant?"

"Just here, about four feet, sir."

"Let's get started, then. What did you say your name was, Sergeant?"

"Eccles, sir, Harry."

"Well then, Eccles, you'll have to be good enough to loan me a shoulder."

"Pleasure sir, thou took quite a braying last evening. We'll osse on, but if thee needs to rest, tell me."

The men moved carefully along the slick rocks, the sergeant guiding the officer to the water's edge. Eccles jumped down, away from the rocks, and held his hands out. Tom gripped one and allowed the other to close upon his tunic and pull him gently forward. He managed to move into the water, and the men began making for the shore.

It was a cold, painful struggle. They tripped once, Eccles falling to his knees and Tom following him, the water covering their chests. Finally, they reached knee-high water about twenty yards out and stopped for a moment. Tom tried not to allow his agony to show and resumed the slog to the beach. He could imagine his old grandfather laughing at his progress and immediately wished to see him rising from the waves before him, offering his huge and mischievous smile.

Tom and Eccles reached the beach and sat down to rest. Tom lay back and tried to sleep, but the cold that had built within him during the night would not abate. Eccles rose and walked several more yards inland and began digging a huge, elongated hole in the sand. Eventually, he came back to Tom, and dragging him by his epaulettes, slid him into the hole. He shoved two feet of sand over Tom's body, placed his life preserver over his face, and said, "This fooking desert will warm thee, sir."

Eccles lifted his face to the rising sun and guessed that it must be about 7:00. He was a hardy man who hated the elements and felt an interminable rage against the weather, cold or hot. He stood and removed all of his clothes, spreading them onto the rocks near the beach like he'd had to do as youth before the hearth after coming home from herding sheep for the family in the rain. He recalled the smell of the lanolin his father collected from the beasts to sell after he'd managed to find a day away from one of Baron Ashton's factories in Lancashire, from which he brought the smell of linseed oil and sweat. The man would toil for his wife and their children, a son, Harry, and a daughter, Eunice. He made linoleum, for weeks away, sleeping in a tiny room he rented above the Blue Rooster Pub in Lancaster. Harry's father had been the most gentle, patient man he'd known, and when he died at thirty-six, an early victim of heart and lung ailments, Harry's heart broke when he was told that the poor man, trying to make his way home, had fallen from the back of a farmer's wagon and lay unnoticed for two days. His mother, a withered and fatigued young woman, told Harry to find his own way in life. At fourteen, Harry was a big lad, somewhat literate, and he managed to bluff his way into the army, and for ten years, he sent his mother and sister nearly every penny of his earnings. Then the war came and a short sojourn the with the French army in France, as the British tried to decide how to conduct themselves against the Germans. Soon, Harry was assigned to the Middle East where, he realized, as he sat naked upon a warming rock, he'd arrived.

"Eccles, I say, Eccles," called Tom after about three hours underground. "Would you be kind enough to help me out of the underworld?"

"Surely, sir, art thee warm enough, then?" The big man pulled on his undergarments.

"I believe so, but I can't seem to rid myself of pain."

Harry leaned down and pulled the sand away. Despite his wish to rise, Tom could scarcely push his upper body away from the sand. With Harry's assistance, he finally managed to lean upon his right elbow, and after a few more minutes, lift a leg.

Harry said, "Hold sir, and we'll hunt us down a stick of driftwood for a crutch."

He ran off down the beach as Tom leaned on one arm, panting. The pain from his right knee was excruciating, and he could not move his left arm without crying out. Wonderful, Tom thought, a troop of Bedouins will be along any time to flay me raw.

Harry returned and presented the Lieutenant with a sturdy piece of faded wood he had found washed up and balanced atop a clump of rocks.

"My dear Eccles, you are a resourceful man," said Tom. "Now, if you please, help me by sitting me up. My left knee seems to be shattered, and I cannot move my right arm."

"Right sir, but if thee will permit, I wish to get back into my uniform."

"By all means, Eccles; I shan't stray," said Tom.

Harry returned, and with the utmost delicacy such a large man could offer, managed to get Tom to his feet and leaning upon his new stick.

"Eccles, perhaps we could just find something to splint my right leg, what?"

"Let us move thee along for now, sir, and I'll surely spot another bit of wood to brace thy leg," replied Harry.

The pair began moving south with the velocity of a chilled snail. After a half-mile or so, Harry spotted another piece of elongated driftwood and carefully sat Tom on a low dune.

"Now sir, we must stretch thy leg out, so I'll help lift it and then … "

"Ah! Goddammit, Eccles! Lift, hell! Is my bloody leg still attached?" shouted Tom after Harry had yanked his leg into place.

"Oh my, yes sir, thy leg is as straight as a yardarm. I'm going to wrap it, now, sir." Harry laid the two life vests he slung behind an arm and began cutting away the straps. He removed the webbing from his uniform and tucked the material under Tom's aching leg, looping it round the driftwood and securing it snugly. Harry lifted Tom, and they began their slog south along the barren beach.

After another mile of progress, Tom asked, "Do we have any water, Eccles?"

"I were just thinking of taking a nip, sir."

The men stopped, and Eccles gave Tom his canteen. "I might have something a bit stronger, sir, if it would help."

"Couldn't hurt, Eccles, surely," replied Tom.

A flask was produced from the recesses of Harry's uniform. Tom took a swig and felt the fiery rum go down his throat. After suppressing a cough, he handed the flask back to Harry, who took a long draw himself.

"Thank you, Eccles. Where did you come by that concoction?"

"Me sister, sir. She works in a distillery. Gave it to me as she saw me out of Liverpool."

Tom's pain was mounting, so he decided to try to distract himself with conversation. "Tell me, Eccles, what does your family do?"

"Well, sir, me father were worked to death by the Williamson's in Lancashire, and me mum, well, she gets by in service to a local squire. My sister married a good old Scouse from Garston what works in the rail service."

"Indeed? Are we speaking about Lord Ashton, Eccles?"

"We be indeed, sir."

"I hear that he's built a grand folly to his wife above Lancaster."

"His second wife, sir, after her death. It should be a memorial to them that made his family rich by their labor, if I may be permitted an observation, sir."

"Certainly, Eccles, certainly. Are you of the socialist persuasion, by any chance?"

"I never think of politics, sir. I just tries to be a good soldier. And where, if you don't mind my asking, sir, is your family from?"

"Lincolnshire. My Christian name is Thomas, and my family name is Twinge-Kitchen. We are a seafaring merchant family of several generations."

"But you are in the army, Lieutenant; what does your father think of that, sir?"

"My father is no longer living, I'm afraid, Eccles; he was lost at sea a few years, ago."

"A great pity, sir; sorry to hear it. Did you have to join the army?"

"Oh no, I just wanted to get away from shipping for a while."

The day was growing much hotter, and as the sun bore straight down, Harry suggested that they rest. The men found a steep dune and Harry eased Tom down against its wall. Tom unbuttoned his tunic fully, and Harry took off his shirt.

"Sir, I'm going to hunt up a bit of wood and try to make us a little shelter." Harry walked to the top of the long dune that seemed to stretch for miles along the beach and eventually spotted a sturdy piece of wood, a parched limb that had fetched up, it seemed by its condition, years before. Harry brought the wood back, and with Tom's walking stick, pushed them well into the wall of the dune above them. He then spread his shirt over the sticks and positioned them for shade as he sat down next to Tom.

"Good show, Eccles; thank you," said Tom.

"I'm not feeling well, sir," said Eccles.

"Probably sunstroke, Eccles. Better drink water."

Harry found his canteen and took a long swallow. He offered it to Tom, who took but a small sip.

"Drink more, Eccles," commanded Tom.

Eccles drank, again, replaced his canteen, and fell back against the dune, his face half in the sun. Tom moved Eccles toward himself to bring him fully into the shade, and both men fell asleep.

Finally, after two hours, Tom heard Eccles say, "Goddamn sun."

He opened his eyes and found himself still in shade owing to the movement of the sun past their dune. "Shall we move on Eccles?" asked Tom.

"We shall, sir." Eccles turned around and promptly vomited.

"Yes, I think we might find a more suitable place to pass the evening, what?" said Tom.

"Sorry, sir."

The men started moving slowly down the long beach. The sun was still high and shore birds began to appear in numbers, squawking and crying to each other. The beach narrowed and the dunes become steeper as they walked, their strength fading with the day. Finally, they were blocked by a long stretch of pocked, pink rock, and found themselves forced to winnow out a point low enough to get over the formation. As they looked about, Harry spotted a lateral depression in the side of the wall and nodded toward it. "We may as well stop there for the night, sir. I'll try to get a fire going, later."

Tom moved silently with Eccles to the small cave and allowed Eccles to help him down into the wonderful shade. "Brilliant, Eccles," he said.

Harry wandered along the beach, finding a passage to the top of the wall. He roamed for an hour, collecting wood for a fire. He returned before the sun had barely moved and stacked the wood before the cave. "Happen to have a lighter on thee, sir?" asked Harry.

"As a matter of fact, I have a Ronson, here. Hopefully, it's dry enough for use." Tom took the lighter out of his pants and set it by Harry.

Harry took the lighter out of the cave and set it in the sunlight, praying that he could get a spark out of it later. He continued his search for wood, and as the sun began to recede, he returned with another armful. He sat down by Tom and awaited nightfall.

"What do you think about this war, Eccles?" asked Tom.

"It's going to be bloody awful, sir. When I was in France, all of my mates were killed in an afternoon. Now I'm sent out hither to fight the Wogs and Gods knows who, no doubt a German somewhere. But I'm paid to do it, and do it, I shall. Where the hell do you think we might be, sir?"

"My guess is that we're on a peninsula, and if we keep in the same direction, we'll find ourselves in the desert, where hopefully, we'll encounter a coastal road and a car loaded with belly dancers waiting for us."

"I wouldn't care if it were a gang of poofters, so long as we could get to a command, somewhere," responded Harry. "May I ask? Are you married, sir?" Harry's loathing of homosexuals had been aroused.

"No, Eccles, but I do have a bit of a courtship going."

"Indeed, and who might the young lady in question be, sir?"

"Lady Evangeline Ismay Rundle-Pop."

"Oh, indeed, a Lady, sir?"

"I'm afraid my mother wouldn't allow just a beautiful, decent girl to contribute to the bloodline, Eccles," said Tom.

"Well then, you must be some kind of lord, sir."

"Some kind, Eccles, but just a lieutenant out here, my friend," said Tom.

"Well, let's see if we can get a spark agoing, sir." Harry rose and retrieved the lighter, gathered his dry kindling, and with the first strike, he achieved a small flame that he fed carefully, as the evening, and finally the dark night arrived.

32

The blood seemed endless, flung and splattered inside and under the buckboard of the wagon and beginning to blacken. The March day had been the first in several weeks without rain—nothing to thin the blood and wash away the dust that settled upon the casualty, upon everything. The sun was full upon his face, shining under the meager shelter offered by the boards strung across the wagon's low sides, as it creaked to a stop before the canvas portico of Camp Wisdom, as its inhabitants liked to refer to it. The soldier was silent and pale after the long and tumbling evacuation. He was dying, and the nurse, Hulda Yoffey, knew it. She looked away from the young man and recalled a scene, only alike in blood and the certain knowledge that life finds an end somewhere, anywhere.

She had been with her father, whose afternoon meal had been interrupted by a quiet knock and the small, dull voice of a shirtless and barefooted ten-year old boy asking him to "see about his mamma."

"You better come with me, Hulda," the doctor had said, "and bring the lady bag." Hulda looked into the parlor where her mother had weighed up the manners of strangers and entertained her many friends, ladies like her, born to the codes of Southern American prosperity. She found the lady bag, a satchel containing the implements her father required when babies demanded birth and mothers begged to get the ordeal over. Hulda rushed out of the room, out of the house, and stepped down to the broad porch, turning around to lock the door behind her. She joined her father and the boy in the buggy, and he the shook the reins to move them toward the boy's home.

"Do we have time to stop by the office to pick up Mama?" asked Hulda.

"Better not risk it, my girl," said Sam.

The buggy stopped in front of a small, narrow shotgun cottage with pale green stucco walls and a small covered wood porch. As he climbed down from the buggy, the doctor said, "I was afraid this was going to happen."

Hulda, like the others, could see a line of bright red running unevenly down the unbalanced chipped concrete steps leading up to the porch. A garnet smear masking the wear of the porch's dull whitewash led over and beyond the home's worn threshold. They could hear someone wailing, a woman, and the crying of a newborn as they approached the house. Hulda told the boy to wait outside as she looked at the scene. The mother's body was lying on the floor, resting on a white sheet in a darkening halo of blood spread broadly away from her still hips. The blood formed an ellipse narrowing up to her mid back and down behind her skinned and bruised knees. A woman, the lifeless woman's mother, held her daughter's head in her lap and tried to speak between her sobs. The woman lifted her daughter's hands to her chest, and Hulda heard her say, "Doc ... Yof." Then unable to continue, she stopped trying and raised her head as the high-pitched cries began again. The doctor found the infant wrapped in a frayed white towel and lying in the trough of a bottomed-out cane table chair. He turned the child to him. The baby appeared to be very healthy, offering bold screams and a ruddy countenance.

"Hulda, please find a pan and warm some water; I want to get this little girl cleaned up," Sam directed.

Behind his daughter, a woman's voice asked, "Dr. Yoffey, can I help?"

"You are a neighbor, ma'am?" asked Yoffey.

The woman nodded, yes.

"Then please go and tell the sisters to come and inform Father Murphy that we have a death here."

There was so much blood. So much blood then, and now, as Hulda came back to the present and another death.

Hulda remembered herself and looked away as two orderlies lifted the Australian "digger" out of the cart and onto the litter stretched near them by two regular soldiers.

A small sunburned corporal came around to her and said, "Another Berber ambush out from Kanayis." He seemed to be nearly in tears and brought his hands up to a dirty head bandage, really just a blue rag, that turned up a mop of blond hair like a ragged sash holding a dusty hank of tow. The corporal turned away and leaned over the side of the stained cart, wishing again that an armored car had been available to get the dying boy to the camp.

Hulda put a hand upon the corporal's shoulder and said, "I'm sure you did your best, Jonny."

"Why don't we have a proper bloody ambulance? A motorized, proper ambulance! I volunteered for the medical corps because I didn't want to kill anyone, but with this miserable, clapped out thing, I can't seem to save anyone! First, do no harm, the doctors are told. No worries, I do it for them!"

Hulda listened to the little Australian, Jonny Pedersson, and as always, was fascinated by his lean, strange accent. She looked at the young man of perhaps twenty and imagined his skin unburned, fair. His bright blue eyes were set perfectly apart above high cheekbones on a face dominated by full, curving lips. He struck Hulda as a statue might, and she imagined his nude, alabaster body unmoving, silent, and posing. She thought him of a different sex, not hermaphrodite, yet both male and female, or something else. What? She was not attracted to the corporal, though he was beautiful and a strange and welcome presence in the desert milieu, a place that had unrelentingly, indifferently, assaulted her senses for more than four months. She put a hand to his shoulder and said, "Come into the tent, and let me look at your head."

The corporal followed Hulda into the first shelter, a low mud brick, tin roof room used for initial examinations. The young man pulled himself upon a clean, narrow table, and Hulda began cutting the bandage away from his forehead. At first, there appeared to be little need for the dressing, but as Hulda continued, she could see that Pedersson had a long, bloody line struck across the right side of his skull. The blood had not seeped to the surface of the wrapping, and the extent of the wound was surprising to the nurse. As she moved the strands of hair away, she could see that a large amount of pus had accumulated behind his ear, stiffening the hair and still running. She stuck a thermometer into his mouth and said, "Lie still for a few minutes." She left the room.

Corporal Jonathan Mats Pedersson, son of Danish immigrants to Australia, had never imagined a life in the army. Again, as he did most days, he thought, what am I doing here? His father was an engineer who brought his wife to Australia in 1897 and now worked in a government office near their home in the new, developing capital. The family had moved to the area that was to become Canberra in 1912 when Jonathan was sixteen, breaking his heart. His life had been music, his teacher, and his mother, and his goal had been admittance to the coming Sydney Conservatorium of Music, a community cause dear to both of his parents' hearts. But his father received the call to assist the group surrounding the new city's designer, architect Walter Burley Griffin, who were to bring the new capital out of the ground. Jonny's mother cried once and alone with the knowledge that they would leave the only house she'd known in their adopted country, his father made a last contribution to the Conservatorium, and the boy found his life adrift and much saddened. The sound of his violin no longer pervaded the upper floors of their Potts Point Victorian. After the move, his music was confined to the small bungalow built on a hill that overlooked the straining machines and legions of laborers building the streets and foundations of the country's new city.

The young violinist found that new friendships were easily formed in the new town. The families of engineers, suppliers, and other prosperous men built their new, mostly temporary, homes near each other, and their children attended the same schools. Jonny found himself spending time with a boy of his age, another engineer's son, whose German family had preceded his own to the area. The boy, Max Weiss, spoke good English, with a noticeable accent, but enjoyed picking up the Australian idioms Jonny constantly threw at him. Max loaned Jonny sheet music belonging to his pianist mother: Schubert, Wolf, and Weber.

When Hulda returned, the corporal's eyes were closed, and he was singing softly, the thermometer jarring about between his teeth.

> In einem Bächlein helle,
> Da schoß in froher Eil
> Die launige Forelle
> Vorüber wie ein Pfeil.
> Ich stand an dem Gestade
> Und sah in süßer Ruh
> Des muntern Fisches Bade
> Im klaren Bächlein zu.

"Jonny! For God's sake, you need to be still! I need to take your temperature before Dr. Villiers comes in."

Pedersson stopped singing and steadied the small glass tube in his mouth. He thought of his friend and wondered how his government could have sent Max and his family away to internment after employing his father to help build its capital. Max's countrymen were now his enemies: it seemed beyond imaging.

Hulda watched the boy closely, and after three minutes by her watch, took the thermometer and noted its reading on a chart she had been preparing. "What were you singing? Was that German?"

The boy replied with a translation:

> Across a clear brook gentle,
> There shot in eager haste
> The trout, so temperamental;
> Quite arrow-like it raced.
> I on the shore was gazing
> And watched the brook disclose
> The merry fish's bathing
> To me in sweet repose."

As Pedersson sang the last line, Dr. Robert Villiers swept into the room, his clean, freshly ironed operating gown rising away from his sides, his presence scented with English lavender oil borrowed from the barrels of the stuff requisitioned for use as a floor disinfectant in the operating room. He was tall and erect, with an excruciating correctness. His clipped, nasal speech betrayed the accent of the Home Counties, and his regular features suggested generations of careful breeding. Hulda stood behind him, regarding the scene with some amusement. The care invested in the trim, handsome creature before her, perfumed and wearing a spotless white gown contrasted by dusty, mud walls and the dirty human lying before him. An urgent rapping sounded as the wind outside found a wayward tin panel above them.

"Right, tell me what we have here, Yoffey," said Dr. Villiers, the words kazooing from him.

"Sir, Corporal Pedersson, J, deep laceration to the right side of the head, infected. Fever. Temperature one hundred and one."

"You are an ambulance attendant, correct, Pedersson? Didn't you bring in those poor souls from Matruh, last week?" asked Villiers.

"Yes, sir."

"Let's have a peep at this head." Dr. Villiers turned the corporal's head to the side and spread the hair roughly away from the wound. "Yoffey, clean this up carefully, and I'll return in a few minutes to stitch up. Pedersson, how did you get this wound?"

"I'd rather not say, sir."

"I'm not interested in your wishes, Corporal; tell me how you received this wound."

"I asked these two poms to help me unload supplies I had taken to the first Matruh station so I could quickly load two wounded digger privates who were sitting in the mud, waiting. The English soldiers told me to piss off. I then invited them to have, ah, carnal relations with each other, as it were, and called them pommy bastards at which point one of them shoved me into the wagon and my head went across the wheel hub."

"Right," said Villiers. He walked out of the exam room.

"You do realize, Jonny, that the Englishman you just spoke to is planning to put a needle into you?" said Hulda.

"He's a bloody freckle, like them all. I'll just have to take my chances, Sister."

Sister. Hearing the word, Hulda remembered her father's words, "go tell the sisters," and she wanted to return to her memories. But she needed to concentrate on the job at hand. She worked quickly, cutting hair away from the wound and cleaning the corruption with Dakin's Solution, removing the scabbing and loose tissue, and stanching the bleeding. She was surprised by the extent of inflammation surrounding the wound. Deep redness covered nearly the entire side of Pedersson's head down to the area behind his ear. This worried her.

After assisting Dr. Villiers with closing the gash, she was relieved to hear him tell Pedersson that he would have a bed assigned to him in the ward. He would need rest and care for several days, at least.

Hulda left the exam room and walked out into the evening's long shadows cast by the station's defense works and tents. The orb was beginning to turn shades of orange and the opposing sky, purple, violet, and darkening blue. The heat of the day was abating and the sea breeze was beginning to settle, nearly forgotten. She walked around the ruined building and looked up the dusty road following the headland. *Ras al-Hekma,* The Cape of Wisdom, reached out to sea. Would she find some truth here, or just a few, mostly unpleasant, memories? She followed the double rows of barbed wire strung adjacent to the camp and down to its termination at the shore. The water was lapping against a stretch of beach set beside low rock shelves, following a long curve behind the camp toward Alexandria. It was crystal clear and reflected a rising, brightening moon.

As she was looking beyond the beach at the dark forms of rocks and seaweed lying under the water, Hulda remembered hearing a report, then another, sounds like muffled gunshots the day, or perhaps two days, before. She had looked out to the horizon and seen a small, intense yellow flash rising up from the sea, nearly aligned with the shore of the headland stretching away from her. There was a rumble, and the tiny flare she was watching became more intense. Then nothing. She thought: a ship, an explosion. Her fear of drowning seized her mind.

The days she'd spent on the ocean during the voyage from the States had filled her with an intense dread. Her nights on the ship were restless, and she spent her days looking out to sea, searching for dark shapes, anticipating things she could not say to herself. Most nights aboard she dreamed of being pulled down and held under water by a formless grip, feeling her hair floating up around her head in a dimming light, unable to move arm or leg. She'd seen drowning victims, bloated and eyeless forms that washed up along the bay at home, deaths that her father had had to certify for the city, bodies that were brought to their house or his little office on the Hill in the back of wagons for him to examine. She had completed the death forms as her father dictated, a task she'd learned from her father's original nurse, her mother, and handed them to the wagon drivers who took the bodies to either the white or colored funeral home morgues. She recalled the faces of some of these victims now, the young and the old.

She continued looking at the horizon and up along the headland; her eyes found only a few patrolling seabirds. Night was falling quickly, so she turned and walked back to the station. The air was filling with the smells of dinner, and she knew, since no wounded had arrived since the night before, that prospects were good for an uninterrupted meal.

After entering the dining tent, she turned to the mail desk and asked if anything had arrived for her. She had not received a single letter since she had joined the British Military Nursing Service after arriving in Alexandria. She had posted a letter to her parents five months before being ordered to the western desert, explaining her situation, but she had no idea if the letter had reached them and little faith that mail from Egypt to the States could survive the enormous chaos wrought by the war. Nevertheless, she began each day with hope that a reply would come. The mail clerk handed her a letter.

Hulda's smile back at the private gave only a hint of her excitement. She took the letter and sat down at the end of one of the two long dining tables and looked at the writing. Her father's hand was instantly recognized, and the postmark indicated November 1914. She carefully opened the envelope and took the letter gently into her hands.

4 November 1914

Dear Hulda,

I am so relieved to know that you are safe in Alexandria. I have not heard from your Uncle Ephraim since he returned to Palestine with instructions from Sister James and me to hunt you up, and have spent every day hoping that a letter from you might get through. I have worried so much these last months.

I know that your vocation has led you to service with the English, but please remember that lives need to be saved here. The sisters ask about you constantly and even young Dr. Kennedy defies his family's bigotry and asks me to send along his regards. Bettoli, the old stinker, is still pining away for you, but I told him to get Father to find him a nice Catholic woman his own age.

Rabbi Fischer, who somehow heard you were away, probably on one of his forays to court your mother, stops by occasionally to check on me, take a nip of my best whiskey, and ask after you (he can never remember your name). He's stopped telling me that I should attend services, at least Pesach or the holy days, so I suppose I'll have to stop telling him to go back to Yankeeville!

I can't pretend to understand why my brother went to Palestine and what he and his friends wish to accomplish there. Damn Charleston Jews and that "Society" of theirs. There's plenty of engineering work in this country! In this little mosquito town, itself! And with you two away, it's just Sister James and me to wave the Yoffey flag (long may it wave).

Please be careful, my dear, dear girl. Our hearts are with you, always.

Your loving Papa

Hulda continued to look at the signature for a few moments and felt her eyes welling with tears. Her mother and father were the bravest people she'd ever known, and she missed their strength of character.

Her shift had changed to early days, so the next morning she rose, ate breakfast, and took a long walk up the peninsula. She had rolled her skirt up, and out of sight of the encampment, bared her feet to walk in the cool water. She was unfamiliar with such coarse sand and so many rocks, but she enjoyed watching the motion of the thick green seaweed that left long strands in and out of the tight clusters of rocks that formed variously sized shrines of debris as the Med, as everyone called it, defended its shoreline. She was a few miles north of the medical station when she noticed two limping figures moving in her direction.

"Yes, sir, they appeared injured," she told Dr. Villiers, who had followed her into the day shift. Hulda had not wasted time getting back to her station. She found her commander filing reports and waiting for the day's casualties to begin arriving. "I recommend that a group be sent up the coast to verify, sir."

"And just what were you doing up there alone, Sister?"

"Sir, I grew up on the sea front (she almost said Bayfront) and having never seen a human out of British uniform along *Ras al-Hekmay*, I felt safe enough to take a stroll."

"A stroll on the beach. Right, well, I'll alert the gentleman, who would *risk his people*, to find out who these men are. Thank you, Sister. Dismissed."

Hulda moved back and turned toward the door. Villiers' eyes followed. The young woman's dark hair pulled under her nurse's cap, the sway under her "kit," and the determined gait held his attention until she was gone behind the thin, shutting door.

33

The sun was blinding the hobbling soldiers, burning the bare skin exposed by their tattered uniforms and their partially clad feet. The rocks were an enormous nuisance, and sea spay overwhelmed the rugged shore, leading the Lieutenant and Sergeant to rest before deciding to climb or detour. The sand was burning, but at least Eccles had most of his shoes. The men were hungry. Each wondered where they were and if they would encounter food before encountering robbers or the enemy. Neither mentioned their state, and both struggled on, occasionally stopping to rest and neither asking nor objecting when one began to slow and disengage his body from the other to slowly sit or stretch down to the sand.

As Harry began to slow, Tom mumbled, "There are people coming toward us, Eccles." Tom saw a wavy and shining presence growing larger and larger, as the two companions stared south along the long curve of the land.

Finally, Eccles said what both had been thinking. "Thee should just wait, sir."

The men rested into the folds of the rocks where they had dropped, relaxing for the first time since leaving the cave and crawling over the stone face that had sheltered them overnight. Now they were facing higher dunes and endless rocks. Tom was asleep within two minutes, and Eccles closed his eyes, but with the sun bearing down against the left side of his cheek, the Yorkshire man brought his shoulder up to attempt to hide the glare from his eyes.

Finally, a cockney voice said: "So, who are you beachcombing bastards, may I ask?" A medium-sized man wearing a British uniform indicating the requisite stripes for a sergeant stood over Tom and Harry, looking singularly displeased to be out in the elements. "I was sent to investigate a bloody nurse's report of two people out strolling on the fucking beach. Now, who are you wankers?"

Tom looked at the man and his party and said, "We are survivors from the *Lillian.* I am Lieutenant Twinge-Kitchen, and this is my assistant, Sergeant Eccles. Sergeant, what is your name?"

"Ford, sir, Sergeant Ford of the 25th Service Battalion, London."

"Well Ford, would you be so kind as to assist us in reaching your headquarters? And a word of advice: don't upset Sergeant Eccles, he is very ill."

"Sir! You men give these gentlemen water and any victuals you may have on you. You two, get back to the station and fetch two stretchers and four more men. Get moving, damn you!"

"Thank you Sergeant," said Tom as he relaxed back into the rocks.

The arrangements progressed, and the soldiers were finally delivered to Camp Wisdom on stretchers and placed directly in hospital beds.

Hulda approached the two men and said, "You both could use baths! Sister Jones!"

And with that, a small conference between the two women produced the disappearance of Hulda and the appearance of pans of clear, warm water to a low table next to Sister Jones, a rather large-boned woman who began cutting the clothes off of Sergeant Eccles.

"I'll not have thee remove my clothes, madam!"

"Oh lie back, shut it, and pretend you're in a Paris bordello, young man. I'll make smart work of you two!"

After both had been stripped and bathed, Hulda returned, received a report from Jones, and began dressing the wounds acquired during the explosion and on the rocks. She asked Tom where his ship had been taking him.

"We were on our way to Aden, Sister," Tom said.

"Please do not refer to me as 'Sister' sir. I prefer 'Nurse Yoffey' or simply, 'Nurse.'

"You are in Military Nursing Service, are you not?"

"That is correct."

"Calling you anything but 'Sister' would be considered disrespectful, Nurse."

"I'll consult the Mishnah and let you know about that, Lieutenant."

"Mishnah?" Tom said as Hulda walked away.

"Eccles, you still awake?"

"Yes, sir. I can't get rid of this stiff one that Sister Jones managed to kick up."

"Go to sleep, Eccles."

"Yes, sir."

Later in the day, Dr. Villiers visited his two new patients, swirling into the room and sweeping to their bedsides like an inspired *danseur*, his robe unfurling and liberating the bouquet of his English lavender oil. "A lot of sunburn, not much to be done there. Must keep infection out of these menacing cuts and scrapes. No broken bones, but the knee will take some time to heal. Nurse!"

"Not Sister Jones, sir!" said Eccles.

"And what is wrong with Sister Jones, young man?" asked Villiers.

Tom reached across the beds and slapped Eccles with the back of his hand.

"Sister Jones is a magnificent nurse, sir," said Tom.

"I plan to evacuate you men with the next packet from Alexandria, by the way," said the doctor.

Hulda began to remember why she joined the Military Nursing Service as she sat on the side of her cot after her shift ended. She had done much good at Camp Wisdom, but Palestine and the Zionist cause were her primary interests. She thought, or had been misled, that she would be able to resign her current posting and go directly to Palestine. The Turks held Palestine and the thought of having the Brits deliver her into the Zionist embrace there, she soon realized, was simply absurd. There must be a way … If she could move closer, to Alex or Cairo, perhaps, more opportunity would arise. Now hundreds of miles away, there seemed to be no hope.

At length, she sought out Dr. Villiers, who by then had retreated to his extraordinarily clean, though somewhat plain, office. Dust seemed to cover every other part of the indoors, but Villiers had a constant servant recruited from a local tribe who dusted and washed the flooring and every wall and object in his room. Hulda knocked and was summoned into the doctor's office.

"Sister Yoffey? How may I help you?" asked Villiers.

Hulda pulled down her nurse's apron, patted her hair, and entered. "Dr. Villiers, may I speak plainly?"

The doctor nodded, yes.

"I am Jewish, and my principal aim in life is to assist the Zionist cause in Palestine. I realize that the length of my commitment to Military Nursing Service is for the duration of the war, but I want to find a way to Palestine."

"But, my dear, the Turks hold Palestine, and I have no idea if we intend to take it from them, anytime soon, at any rate."

"I want to request a transfer to Alex, sir, to be, at least in touch with my counterparts living there."

"Impossible. I'll hear no more of this, Sister. Dismissed."

That evening, Hulda made her way around the camp offices to find out when the next boat from Alexandria would be arriving. She was determined to escape to Alexandria by some means, and the packet back to the city would certainly be the most convenient and quickest. She began to plan and decided to enlist the two strangers who had just entered the hospital. She had dinner in the modest canteen and made her way through the arriving casualties and evening nurses to the bedsides of Tom and Eccles.

"Good evening, gentlemen. Have a restful day?"

"Yes, thank you, Sister, I mean, Nurse Yoffey," said Tom. Sergeant Eccles suffered some inconvenience, but on the whole, we did rather well, thank you."

"You are due to be transferred to Alexandria soon."

"So we understand."

"I am also transferring and have been assigned to accompany you to the hospital there," said Hulda.

"That would be most welcome, Nurse. I would request, however, that Sister Jones be asked to bathe Sergeant Eccles again, before we leave," said Tom, with a wry smile.

"Oh, no, Sister, I'm clean enough for weeks!" said Eccles, while Tom laughed and Hulda smiled.

"Now gentlemen, my transfer is unknown to Dr. Villiers and others, so if you would be discreet enough to keep this hush-hush, I'll be certain to bring enough pain medication to make you very, very comfortable while we sail."

Tom looked at Hulda quizzically and said, "Should anyone ask, I will tell them that you are Lord Twinge-Kitchen's private nurse."

"My Lord," said Hulda as she curtseyed.

"You're a Lord?" asked Eccles.

"When I need to be, my good man."

"What I need from you two, is to allow me to be carried onto the ship under one of your names. I will cover myself with a blanket with a name tag attached and have my colleagues carry me on board first. They will come for you next. All the manifest will show is that you are onboard. I can arrange this."

"That's rather cheeky, Nurse," said Tom.

"I'm an American, and as we like to say, so what?"

A week passed and finally a small, somewhat battered, packet ship arrived with quantities of supplies, two new nurses, and an empty hold for patients being transferred to Alexandria. Corporal Jonathan Mats Pedersson and a bribed local carried a stretcher onboard the ship supporting Hulda hidden under a blanket with the name Twinge-Kitchen attached to it, and situated her so that she would be next to Tom and Eccles. Pedersson made certain the name was added to the manifest.

Hulda had Jonny bandage her face and head to complete her disguise, but the gauze could not keep the stench of the ship's lower deck from fouling her nostrils. What the seriously ill must have to endure, she thought to herself as the hold began to fill with patients. The chorus of moans began to intensify, and Hulda was glad that her ears were wrapped and that she was not attending anyone. Someone reached for her tag near her feet and continued through the ship verifying the passengers before casting off the long pier that had been built to accommodate these visits.

Tom said, "All right, my Lord, we're getting underway now."

There was no reply from Hulda.

The medicine Hulda had promised was handed from under her blanket at intervals of bells, and the men slept most of the time. After nearly a day and a full bladder, Hulda cast off the blanket, unwrapped her bandages, and began to move around the hold in her nurse's uniform. She finally found the head, and after a much relaxing relief, she began attending her wounded shipmates. An unfamiliar nurse holding a bright kerosene lantern accosted her, asked who she was. and why was she on her ship. Hulda explained that she had been assigned to accompany Lord Twinge-Kitchen to Alexandria at the request of his brother, Earl Boardcroft. The nurse, Sister Jagger, pried no further.

The little craft finally came into sight of Alexandria, but as much as Hulda wanted to see the harbor entrance, she remained discreetly below deck. After the small ship maneuvered between a large transport and supply vessel, the many fishing boats and official ferry craft, it finally tied up along the eastern harbor and was met by an army of attendants. She carefully followed one of the stretchers down the gangway and moved into the city, southwest towards Pompey's Pillar. She stopped an army officer strolling back and forth in front of a modern-looking hotel and asked, "Could you direct me to the Jewish quarter?" The officer, a rather freckled Scot, gave her verbal and hand-drawn directions to go east along the sea where she would encounter Jews. He advised following the *Quai Promenade* for two miles or so and then turning right into a street just before a corner being cleared by British soldiers.

She turned around, and in the next street near the harbor, found a public trolley running east. She was about to climb aboard when an army truck stopped, and the driver asked if she needed transportation. She replied that yes, she did, and told the driver where she wanted to go.

"Jews live mainly in the east, Sister, and I have to go near there and will drop you at the corner where we're constructing an installation."

The truck bucked away and after a chaotic and slow ride through the city, Hulda was let off the lorry. She strolled purposely down the busy street, finally spotting a synagogue. There were hundreds of people, people she did not recognize as Jews, moving rapidly along both sides of the narrow road—some in brightly colored clothing and some in business suits with fringes hanging below the coats. She pushed the door of the temple open and found a large dim room with only a handful of people doing odd jobs or speaking to one another.

Presently, a man wearing a fez-like hat and elaborate robes approached Hulda and asked, in Greek, if he could be of assistance. She answered in English, whereupon the man clasped his hands and said, "It is so long that English has been spoken here! A few soldiers, sometimes, but mostly English business Jews give our *Eliyahu Hanavi* temple visits. What is your name, and how can I be of help to you?"

"I am Hulda Yoffey. I have been working in the Military Nursing Service for the last year. I wish to join the Zionists in Palestine."

"Ah, this would be a crime, madam! But *Eretz Yisrael* needs people. You are a sister, a nurse?"

"Yes, a nurse from America."

"From *America?*" exclaimed the old man. "I have rarely seen Americans." He extended his arm toward a set of stairs hidden to the side of the aligned columns, just before the small forest of menorahs standing either side of the altar and the Torah closet. He led the young woman up to a spacious office. "I am Rabbi Avraham ben Yusef, one of the leaders of this temple. I have always lived here in Alexandria, but I have traveled to Jerusalem several times. I am familiar with Zionism, and though a native Egyptian, I fear that the principles of this Zionist movement will prove vital to all Jews in time." The man was perhaps approaching his eighth decade, but he moved with reasonable vigor in his robes. He was clean-shaven with a hint of thick, graying hair under his elaborately ornamented, banded kippah. "Please sit." He indicated a chair to the side of his desk.

"Thank you, Rabbi, for your hospitality. I really had no idea where to go in Alexandria, except to a synagogue," said Hulda, sweeping a sweaty strand of black hair from her forehead She quickly pinned it back and tucked it under her white veil. She removed her scarlet tippet and sat in her white apron, which she had chosen unadorned with a red cross, and smiled at the old rabbi. Her green eyes shone beautifully in the office light, and her unusual height presented pleasingly as she sat in front of the ancient desk. She decided to remove her veil and snood and folded the tubular neck scarf into the head gear, careful to keep the nursing badge exposed and placed it on her lap. She noticed that the office was filled with cabinets with books and boxes of various sizes stored behind geometrically ornamented glass doors. There were no pictures or photographs.

"Young woman, I am not particularly friendly with the British, but I do appreciate their efforts to discourage religious strife. May I ask you a few questions?"

"Of course, Rabbi."

"First, how would you recognize a Nazirite?"

"He would have long hair, Rabbi."

"Second, how many trials were inflicted upon our father Abraham?"

"Ten, Rabbi."

"Third, do you wish to travel to *Eretz Yisrael* within a week's time?"

"I wish to go as soon as possible. I must ask for your guidance in sheltering until I can leave, Rabbi."

"Fourth, why do you wear sleeves with red crosses on them?"

"This is part of the uniform, Rabbi. It was my decision not to alter the sleeves to avoid troublesome questions."

"That is a thing for study, surely. You may reside with my wife and me in our quarters. May I offer you something to drink?"

"Anything would be appreciated, Rabbi, thank you."

"Excuse me for a few moments."

As Rabbi ben Yusef left the room, a woman approached and said, "Miss, please place this shayla over your hair and follow me to the dining hall."

The women went downstairs and into a hallway off the sanctuary and continued down one short flight to a wide room located behind the altar, where a number of tables stood. She wore a long black dress embellished with a wave of several golden rows of intricate needlework wrapping up from the middle to her left side, with a wide golden sash, a muted silver tunic, and white cotton sleeves puffing down her arms. She also wore an elaborate scarf of red and gold brought to a peak over her forehead and held in place with pinned jewels. She said, "Miss, please sit. We offer you orange juice and water."

Hulda relaxed more, feeling the kindness of these Jews beginning to touch her memories of her youthful temple life—a time of inconsistent observance, but a joyful and communal existence at home. She almost wanted to stay with these people, to get to know her brethren in Alexandria. But she knew her mission was demanding, that to betray the nursing corps would demand equal work and sacrifice for an equally worthy cause, a cause certainly closer to her heart than the present war.

The young lady came to sit near her, finally daring to speak: "I am Leah, granddaughter of the Rabbi you were speaking with. I attended the English school here in Alexandria. You are a sister?"

"I am Hulda Yoffey. I have decided to forsake the British nursing corps to offer my services to *Eretz Yisrael,* as a member of the Zionist organization. I have told your grandfather that I wish to go to Palestine. I do not yet know how to accomplish this, but at least I have gotten as far as Alexandria." She drank deeply of the orange juice and took a sip of water. She looked at this young woman of perhaps sixteen or seventeen and wondered how she felt about Zionism.

Presently, Leah's grandfather entered the room and sat in front of the two women. "You should know, Miss Yoffey, not all Jews favor Zionism. Many believe only the Almighty will make way for our return to Israel and no man has the right to re-establish our homeland. There are those in this very congregation who feel this way! Already, I sense the tongues speaking about your presence and fear that we will not be able to keep you safe long. You must stay with us for now. We have an additional room, but we must contrive a way to make a journey possible for you. Please go with Leah, now. When the evening meal is prepared, she will bring you something to eat." The Rabbi smiled and left the room.

"Please follow me, Miss Yoffey. "

"Leah, please feel free to call me Hulda."

"Hulda, would you like to change clothes? I must insist that we find you something more appropriate for the temple." She touched the cross on the material on her right arm.

"Yes please, Leah. Thank you for your kindness." The women went into a sparsely furnished room and Leah said, "I will return with new clothes for you. In the meantime, please rest."

Soon Leah returned with a long dress of several layers, a golden snood, dark leather sandals, and a yellow beret with fringes cascading off the sides. After Hulda put on the clothes, Leah helped adjust the beret to fit well back on Hulda's head, exposing a good deal of her hair. She was given a pair of false eyeglasses and her hair was tied in a peculiar way in the back. A necklace of what appeared to be coins was put around her neck and an unfamiliar perfume applied. "This will be your costume, my Hulda." Leah hugged her new friend in a long embrace. "I will return with food, soon."

Hulda felt extraordinarily grateful as Leah left her on her own. She was surprised she'd gotten this far in her escape and began to wonder what her next move must be. She would rely on the Rabbi to help her work this out. As she began to fall asleep, she heard a knock at her door, and with the utmost caution, cracked the door and looked out.

"Miss Yoffey, I am Lieutenant Ash. I work with Rabbi ben Yusef. I am here to help. May I come in?"

"Of course." Hulda opened the door. They shook hands, and she invited Ash to sit down with her on the bed.

"You look splendid! I understand that you're American, formerly working with the Nursing Service, now seeking to enter Palestine."

"That is correct, Lieutenant Ash. It has always been my plan to work in Palestine. With the war, however, I've found getting there difficult, to say the least! Can you help me?"

"Hulda, I am a committed Zionist, but also a serving officer in

His Majesty's Forces, so you can appreciate the fact that my help may be limited. There is the possibility that I may be able to have you assigned to a unit being formed to support our defensive efforts in Sinai, specifically Kantana. The problem would be getting you from Kantana to Palestine. I will have to make some enquiries."

Lieutenant Ash told Hulda a little about himself. He was from a wealthy trading company that had offices in England, the U.S., India, and China. He had attended the military academy at the insistence of his father, also a *Zionist*, in the event he might be needed to help defend Jews in Palestine. As America was neutral, he told Hulda, there was the possibility that she could be smuggled onto a ship bound for a port in Palestine. In any event, getting her there was going to require some imagination and danger. He wished her well and left the room quietly.

Leah reappeared with food and sat down to speak to Hulda while she ate. "Hulda, what is America like? Are Jews welcome there?"

Hulda replied, "Jews have the same rights as everyone, but they're not always welcomed. We have our organizations to keep Jews as Americanized as possible, but, I can tell you, Sundays are very lonely days for Jewish children. We also have Jewish organizations to help us remember that while we are fortunate to be Americans, we do not wish to forget our own Jewish traditions. My uncle Ephraim has been working in Palestine, recruited by an American organization to support Zionist efforts. He is there, now."

34

Hauptmann Petersruhe-Rožmberk pulled up his wool collar as the wind, whipping down the Pera hilltop and the length of the Golden Horn, brought another hint of fall. He looked down at the narrow gangplank of the *V65,* a somewhat new torpedo-boat-type destroyer. From above, he could see the comings and goings of German seamen and the occasional civilian, moving back and forth between the ship and the dock. The ship was about the size of Captain Twinge's yacht, he thought, but the resemblance stopped there. The *V65* was not a beautiful craft. As he resumed his walk, he took a little caution, as the street became wetter and wetter with sea water, fish blood, and spots of oil. Finally, after pushing away desperate children vying for the chance to carry his canvas bag, he approached the officer standing at the foot of the plank and presented his orders.

"You're lucky. We're heading *directly* for Haifa, sir" said the young Lieutenant.

David proceeded up the gray gangplank and presented his papers to the junior officer standing at the ship's rail. The officer motioned him aside and told a seaman to fetch the Captain, a Commander Martin Holtz.

The Captain was a tidy young man of about twenty-eight, with blond hair peeking out from his hat and a somewhat damp gray tunic. "Having pump trouble," said the Captain. "My name is Holtz." He offered his hand, which had engine black grease rubbed into every crack, line, or wrinkle.

David shook Holtz's hand at once as he clicked his heels and bowed.

Holtz looked up at the taller *Hauptmann* and said, "Captain, it's a pleasure to meet you. You needn't observe ceremony too rigorously onboard the *V65.* We put so much effort into keeping her afloat that military exactitude sometimes falls somewhat by the wayside. Let me show you to your quarters."

"Thank you, sir; I can appreciate your situation" said David. "If I can be of help to your crew, please inform me; I have no problem getting my hands dirty." The men stepped through the nearest door and Holtz led his guest up to the bridge, where he found the Second Officer, Manfred Schmitz, yelling through a megaphone at crewmen near the bow. The wind swirled through the open windows.

"Schmitz, sir," he said, "Welcome aboard."

Holtz turned and passed David and he made his way down two steps, walking several paces, until he stopped at a fairly spacious, open cabin. "Your accommodations, sir. Your hammock is just there, with a small table for your convenience. The head is just down the way."

David went in and sat down on the only chair provided. The steel chair chilled his bones and the hard seat felt oddly comfortable. The room smelled freshly painted and there were signs of vigorous rust removal, the gouges and indentations somewhat smoothed by the shiny gray coating, surprising for a ship that new. They're probably thinking of giving this one to the Turks, also, he thought. He looked through the open porthole and could make out some of the familiar sites of Constantinople, some of which he would miss, along with Olivia, of course, and some he would wouldn't mind forgetting. The waterfront along the Galata section of the city teemed with humanity, as always. The familiar wagons, carts, and automobiles competed for right-of-way, the whole mass curving around the east point where his vision strayed to the blue *Bosporus* and the multicolored specks moving up and down its length. He unpacked a few books and maps and began to consider his orders. He could tell no one of his mission until the time came for action.

The sounds of the ship became louder as the turbines were brought up and officers and men began the final preparations to cast off. The little ship was berthed just inside the *Horn,* and the persistent northwest wind's cold hand gripped the little ship, making every surface

David touched unwelcome. As the Captain ordered the boat to cast free from the dock, the ship floated until the wind had overcome the north side of the city and pushed it well out into the *Bosporus*, turning it about to face south. The craft rumbled from stern to bow and David felt the ship get underway, and he leaned against the propulsion vibrating through his chair. As the boat passed down the strait, he saw all of the great Ottoman features of the Constantinople coast out of the several starboard ports and marveled at the age of the place and the long decline that had overcome the metropolis. He removed his papers from the hammock nearest to the forward bulkhead, and crawled in, away from the memories of the dirty city. Soon he was asleep.

David woke to a sudden jolting, as the ship suddenly dropped speed. He went onto the bridge, half in alarm, half curious, to find out what was happening.

"Oh, *Hauptmann*, you noticed the power down, I presume," said the Captain.

"Yes, sir. May I ask why we are slowing?"

"We have to respect certain precautions, some of which we placed in the waters ahead against our British friends who might be inclined to visit us. We are about twenty miles south of the *Bosporus*, in the Sea of Marmara. We will maintain this speed for some time. I advise you to relax," replied Holtz.

Night began to fall and David enjoyed watching the sunset over the hilly terrain to starboard. The *V65* stayed in the middle of the channel and moved at leisurely speed, vibrating subtly. Darkness soon overcame the evening, and on deck the men became thickened and slowed by the dim. They were all watching, listening, and tense. In the early hours of the next morning, the ship entered the Dardanelles Strait, passing the low lights of Chanakkale and began increasing speed, following a recent charting of mining activities. He had taken a station along the starboard rail and looked out west beyond the water. He remembered the journey he and Meese had undertaken not so far away, and thinking farther back still, the delightful, effeminate Greeks who had sold them food, shelter, and finally a way back.

The Strait broadened, and the hours that David had spent on the bridge and along the rail were barely noticeable in his attention. He stood, cocooned in a heavy navy coat. The only distraction he allowed himself was to finger the toggle buttons that kept him surrounded by the thick, black wool. The chilled, pre-dawn air had kept him alert, just as the crew had remained highly vigilant, looking, looking, looking. As the boat entered the Aegean Sea, a scent approached his body, and he heard, as if dreaming, Olivia's voice.

> *As it was said of old, may the dawn child be born*
> *to be an angel of blessing from the kindly night.*
> *You shall know joy beyond all you ever hoped to hear.*
> *The men of Argos have taken Priam's citadel.*

David turned around at the rail and beheld her. "What are you doing here? I had no idea, you were aboard!" he whispered.

"I came aboard as a member of the *German Overseas Society*. Gerd escorted me. My papers are in order, *Hauptmann*."

"Are you going to Haifa?"

"Yes, first, then I'm going to visit relatives."

Holtz stepped up and offered them cups of coffee. "We have a few turns, but soon we'll be able to make directly for Haifa. The British are chasing our ships all over the Med, but I've received no sightings to interfere with our journey. Captain Petersruhe-Rožmberk, may I present *Fraulein* Olivia Yafey?"

"How do you do, *Fraulein*," said David, clicking his heels. He assumed that Olivia wished to keep her identity concealed.

The *Fraulein* curtseyed and said, "Very well, thank you, sir. I was just thinking that perhaps we are near the site of Troy, Captain."

"Captain Holtz, may I ask where you are from? Is that a Bavarian accent?" asked David in an attempt to refocus the conversation.

"Yes, I started with humble lake sailing and finally joined the naval school. Most of my short career has been spent in East and West Africa working on larger ships. I've had this, my first command, for about ten months now."

The dawn's rose-red fingers cast its veil of ruddy light upon the port side of the little ship and the broad back of the sea. The water was beginning to throw up an unruly northwest swell and the *V65* pitched in and out of the troughs and crested more and more awkwardly over to port. Late in the afternoon, near Rhodes, on the long run to Haifa, the rough sea was following them and David and Olivia settled down into their respective sleeping arrangements. Olivia enjoyed a tiny cabin and bunk, and David slumped back into his hammock. The motion of the boat made the hammock swing front to back and to front, producing a pleasant rocking that had the *Hauptmann* quickly asleep. His last, conscious thought was: she knows Aeschylus.

The ship continued until nightfall, when a sudden reduction in speed and a broach into the wind woke David. He climbed out of his hammock and went on bridge to determine what was happening.

"Had a report of British activity southwest of Cyprus. Waiting for confirmation," said Schmitz.

David decided to remain on the bridge and watched the bow move up and down in the swell, in and out of spray. He listened to the low hum and felt the slight vibration of the engine. At length, clouds moved in, and a light drizzle soon turned to a heavy rain.

Holtz was back on deck as the first big drops began to hit the ship. "Turn her about, Schmitz; this filthy weather will cover us!" With that, the *V65* found the correct heading, shed its static, northwest heading, and resumed good speed. The sea swept over the stern, pooping the little vessel from time to time and some of the crew began stealing out to the rail to allow the effects of seasickness free rein. David wondered how Olivia was faring, but he didn't dare disclose any unusual interest to the crew.

You shall know joy beyond all you ever hoped to hear, he thought. He had known joy with this woman, had written his *Tante* Kathe about his infatuation with her, and had been pleased that she confirmed all that Becouche-Albukerk *effendi* had revealed. Kathe had even sent him a small token figure that matched one he'd seen in Olivia's sitting room. He wondered how deep their association was.

He didn't know details of his aunt's early life, and her secrets stood between them like prizes, yet to be earned and given.

Recently, a letter had arrived from Berlin for Olivia, informing her that she had been made a member of the *Women's Corps of German Overseas Society*, an organization with which she was unfamiliar. The official documents stated that she had completed the requisite training, and she was to precede to Haifa to report to *Jerusalemsverein,* the Association of Jerusalem, as a teacher. She was to leave on 22 October, 1914, on the German warship, *V65.* Clothes would be delivered to her home soon, and she would be expected to wear them during her journey and after she reported to the colony. The cover letter was signed by Clara Yafey, Assistant.

Olivia knew that a Clara Yafey was her aunt, and assumed that this letter originated from her. Clara, carrying a letter from *Gräfin* von Petersruhe, had visited Constantinople just before she met David. The state of affairs between the great powers, the recent harassment of Isaac's business concerns, and the condition of Turkish politics were discussed. It was decided that Isaac's assets were to be transferred out of Constantinople to the care of relatives in Italy and Palestine, with Olivia taking part. Further, that Olivia was to immigrate to a location in Palestine sponsored by a Zionist organization. She had learned that Colonel Witt had arranged for David, the *Gräfin's* nephew, to leave also, and that he would be onboard the same ship. All of this she desperately wanted to discuss with David, who must have been extremely puzzled by her appearance at the deck railing. She was correct that he would not acknowledge their friendship to the ship's crew. The prospect of speaking to him once on land, was urgent, even vital, to her. She wanted to explain, but she would have to wait to deepen her relationship with this man.

The ship finally moved out of the stormy, wine-dark waters, and was able to pick up considerably more speed. The lookout spotted a larger ship running west at high speed across their bow, the froth of the waves hitting and blowing over its starboard side. The prow of the foreign craft, a British light cruiser, dipped and rose, but the ship's crew ignored the *V65,* and Holtz kept speed. Suddenly, the crew of *V65* observed a tiny flash from many, many miles away west—what must have been a large explosion. The small British ship had been racing to the area from which the explosion had originated and continuing on its way, ignored the German. The late afternoon sun kept the cruiser obscured in the spray it threw up, but as the little German ship crossed the tiring wake of the British ship, Holtz preserved a keen eye on the disappearing speck on the western horizon that had become the British ship.

"One does admire the British mastery of the sea," said Holtz, edging up to David, who was standing along the rail. "But I must say, they were a real nuisance for us in Africa." Holtz's light beard retained droplets from the rain and spray, and the man looked as seafaring a being as David had ever seen.

"The British certainly seem to have an instinct for using the sea," said David.

After nightfall, a few lights were observed off the port side of Holtz's little ship, and the Captain ordered quarter-speed. He charted a speed for entering Haifa's harbor in three to four days' time, just after dawn, and against the possibility of enemy activity, ordered Schmitz to have the crew at battle stations after midnight.

Olivia was tired of lying in her bunk and ventured up to the bridge.

"*Fraulein!* Welcome" said Holtz, "we will be in Haifa in a couple of days. May we offer you coffee?"

"Please, coffee would be welcome," said Olivia in German.

"I hope the journey has not been too unpleasant. We hit some rough seas for a time, but thankfully we left them behind some time ago." Holtz was becoming fascinated by this woman, hidden behind the men's gray woolen clothes and wearing a heavy naval cap and a heavy blue scarf. Nothing, however, could obscure the softness of her accent, her exotic eyes, and the fine, high cheekbones of her face. "So, you plan to work in the Haifa community? I hear that the population is nearing 500."

"Thank you, Captain, the voyage has been fine. I will, however, be glad to reach Haifa! If you don't, mind, I would like to take in some fresh air." With that, Olivia stepped down the stairs to the main deck, feeling for the rail. She had to be very careful about Haifa, as she had no intention of working in the German colony. She would only meet her cousin and follow her to her *moshav*. She knew that David would have to report to joint Turkish-German Headquarters within a few days, and she had purposely delayed her Cousin Ruth's arrival for two days.

The dawn finally arrived, and anticipating the early light, Captain Holtz ordered full speed and retired to his cabin. The *V65* followed the land, and then began to close the port angle, bringing features of the northern Lebanon into clearer view. Eventually, the rocky coast became more distinguishable and a few lights from Tripoli glinted, as the dawn began to fade. David spent the bright day turning over the events of his most recent posting in Constantinople. He sensed that Witt had been testing him, asking himself why he had been sent on each mission. What was the real nature of Witt's relationship with *Graf* Petersruhe? How did he now find himself in the company of Olivia? He sat on the foredeck of the little ship, and between naps, he was finally able to brush the questions from his mind, accepting the events of his life as steps forward. Wouldn't life end if he achieved an ultimate goal? He decided that his natural, judicious combativeness was more important than solving the riddle of his destiny. He would just keep the philosopher at bay, and get on with life, as always.

The next morning, Palestine's coastal plain became more and more sandy and narrow until the town of Acre appeared, sometime after the barely distinguishable Tyre. David remembered Captain Twinge telling him that Lord Kitchener stood on a hill near what should be the ship's present position and drew a line on a map that became the border. There was nothing very distinguishable about the coast or the inland features. An occasional plot of green would appear along a hill, leading to some hesitant coloration crawling up sloping mountains. Hooked before them, the Haifa peninsular jutted out, with smoke and activity, buildings and a couple of ships lying off the harbor. Holtz was back on the bridge, giving orders and consulting his binoculars regularly, as he backed speed down and began to bring the destroyer into position to berth alongside a long, sturdy pier lined with German naval personnel. The ship slowly worked its way into the bay and turning around, eased into position, finally tying up around mid-day.

The small ship was only somewhat higher at the bow than the pier. The gangplank was easily slid across and soon Captain Holtz and the Executive Officer, Schmitz, were standing at the rail to consult the harbormaster. David and Olivia appeared and asked if they may leave the ship. With permission granted, Olivia gave a small kiss to her two naval escorts. David shook their hands and followed Olivia, who was carrying what appeared to be a very heavy suitcase, until she was near the stern of the ship, where he caught her up. "This is a surprise, Olivia!" David whispered excitedly.

"Oh, *Hauptmann*, only to one of us," Olivia said. "Follow me to Karmelheim, up the coast, and I'll show you where you'll be staying for the next few days, *Liebhaber*. Shall we share a taxi?"

David was delighted by Olivia's foreknowledge and suspected, naturally, *Tante* Kathe's hand. He walked with her along the wide pier, and like her, grew tired of the heavy clothes. He offered to carry her suitcase, but she politely refused. He noted the substantial chain attached to the case, but he didn't mention it to the young woman.

Arabs were carrying crates on donkey carts, on their heads, and on their backs. Dark Jews with swaying fringes ran up and about the structure and in and out of offices supporting the maritime trade. A few German soldiers marched by with their Turkish counterparts and cleaning personnel were moving up and down the pier.

David and Olivia stepped onto a concrete sidewalk, and David hailed a taxi. A new Daimler pulled alongside them and they found their way into the back of the automobile.

"*Enzhaus, Karmelheim, bitte*," said Olivia, using a slightly Swabian accent.

"Ah, I understand, now. My *Onkle* Sigi has been teaching you what he calls German!" David said. "You will fit right in here, Olivia. From what I hear, these Germans all seem to be from Württemberg and like my *Onkle,* haven't learned to speak proper German. "

"So, who is this Sigi?"

"Please stop toying with me, *Fraulein,* or should I say, *bayan*?"

The car shifted on an uneven part of pavement, and Olivia said, "Oh, my, that hurt!" She had sat the suitcase in front of her legs, and it flew up and back against her, tearing a small, deep cut into her shin. The case handle made the only noticeable noise. There was no rattle or bump to suggest its contents. David at once withdrew his handkerchief and offered it to Olivia. She was stiffened against the back of the seat with pain. David had never seen her face contorted, but he noticed her changeable beauty as she blushed and her long lashes blinked steadily. Her mouth was taut, spread out widely, and bent slightly up at the corners. Her lips maintained their lustrous rose-red.

David asked, "Can I do anything? Could I perhaps move the case for you?"

She looked at him with thoughtful eyes but shook her head "no" and pushed the suitcase away with her feet, which she had lifted, exposing her other shiny, olive leg. She held the handkerchief under her, rolled up her pant leg, and bowed her head until the taxi arrived at the northern end of Haifa, turning right up into the foothills of Mount Carmel. The place seemed to be have been planted meticulously with palms and other native trees, and the road was in quite good shape.

A schoolhouse was evident from the many children playing outside and matronly women, all shouting German, kept the children within the bounds of the property.

Soon, David and Olivia arrived, and a porter ran out to greet the couple. "*Hallo, Willkommen* to the Hotel Prost!" the man said. He was obviously Arab, but he was in uniform and had extremely solicitous eyes and beads of sweat dropping from his forehead against the heat. He motioned for the couple to follow him into the reception hall. David, wishing to maintain as much anonymity as possible, chose to speak only English. He thanked the porter with a small gratuity and addressed the desk clerk by asking after their rooms. He assumed Olivia had made prior arrangements, and when the clerk asked, "What name?" Olivia spoke up and said, "Michael and Olivia Yafey" and presented two German passports.

David was amazed. He failed to understand what was happening, but again, he felt that he knew the origin of the entire subterfuge. The porter strained against the weight of Olivia's case, which was hardly balanced by David's, and he took them upstairs to a large, clean, green room. The room had one bed, two windows on either side of a balcony, and a sign warning in German, English and French that the hotel cannot be responsible for acts of hooliganism regarding behavior on the balcony.

David tipped the porter again and sat down on the edge of the bed. Olivia sat on the bed, somewhat higher, so she could stretch out her injured leg. She asked David to apply a wet wash cloth to the injured area and slowly untied and lifted the blood-soaked handkerchief to inspect the damage. While David was in the small bathroom, a knock came at the door.

David said, "I'll answer it," and he bounded over to open the light green door. Opened, the doorway presented a dark, green-eyed woman with very dark hair. Her olive skin was very tanned, and she smiled a mouthful of beautiful white teeth. She had Olivia's almond eyes and lithe figure, but not her height.

She said, "Welcome, David, I am Ruth Becouche-Albukerk Yoffey. This is my husband, Ephraim Yoffey, an American."

David motioned them into the room and at once, Ruth exclaimed, "What has happened, Olivia? *Oy!*"

Ephriam rushed over to take charge of her care. The leg was elevated, and after a rushing back and forth to the bath, Olivia's leg was wrapped carefully in wash towels. "We must summon a doctor." These were Ephraim's first words.

Completely mystified David asked, "Can someone tell me what has been happening? Are my parents, Kathe and Sigismund von Petersruhe, involved in constructing this meeting?"

Ruth answered at once: "Yes, and so what *Hauptmann* Petersruhe-Rožmberk? This is the woman you have fallen in love with, yes? Well, then, just settle down and all will be explained in time. For now, remember, you are *Yafey!*" David looked at Ephraim, who, in turn, waved his hands in front of his body, as if to say, *Don't worry about it.*

"Do you know why I was sent to Palestine?"

"There's no such place. This is Israel and yes, we know all. Just relax and accept that, David. We have no interest in interfering with your military activities, unless we need you" said Ruth.

David replied, "You are correct: I love this woman! But you will not interfere with my military obligations under any circumstances!" He turned and left the room, anger beginning to ruddy his face. He walked out of the front door and looked down the slope along the long shoreline and the tiny ships resting at piers or at anchor. He was beginning to calm down, and taking Ephraim's gesture to heart, he returned to his room.

He knocked on the door gently, and hearing Olivia respond, "Yes?" he spoke his name and entered the room. There, lying prone with her injured leg lifted by a pillow, she turned to him and smiled. "I'm sorry all of this is confusing you." She lay in a filmy, glistening robe, her hair long and loose, falling all around her. David could see the curves of her figure, the long legs and bare outline of her body. She said, "Come, lie with me, but mind the leg." David removed his bulky tunic and shoes and lay down beside her.

Her hand stroked his hair, and she told him that she was sent to meet Ruth, that all was done to get her out of Constantinople and that her father was to leave also, as soon as he could secure his affairs. Her father had agreed to the plan only because David was to be present on the same ship. He had been correct that his *Onkle* and *Tante* had been intimately involved with both of their lives, especially now as war had broken out. As for Ruth, she lived on a *moshav*, a Zionist settlement she had helped found with her father's financial support. Ephraim had been recruited in the United States to engineer the future development of the settlement, and he and Ruth had married earlier in the year. There is more to that story, also. They have been trying to bring Ephraim's niece, Hulda, out of Egypt since the war began, but have not yet been successful.

As David began to fall asleep, he noticed that Olivia's suitcase was missing, and that a bundle of clothes was resting on a small corner chair. The room was becoming very warm in the deepening afternoon, and David looked into his bag to find his lighter uniform and removed the trousers. Looking back at Olivia, he removed his wool uniform and began to slip into the cooler pants.

Olivia looked up at him and said, "Leave them off, David and come back to me." She shifted onto her side and held her arms out to him, saying, "After all, you are Mr. Yafey. You should be comforting your injured wife." David threw the pants toward his bag and lay into Olivia's embrace. She smelled his body, unwashed for days, but, she allowed his scent to encompass her own odor, and she kissed his mouth long and repeatedly. His hands moved over her and she held his shoulders up and said, "We have two days. Let us sleep for a bit, and then we'll bathe each other." Their weariness overcame them, and their desires subsided. Olivia curled into David's form, as he lay on his side. The sun streaming through the room's window struck his bare arms and face shining with sweat and burnished them as polished metals exposed from Olivia's sheer silken gown laid over his length as one of a pair of glowing wings.

As evening approached, the shadows it threw up chilled David and Olivia awake. He had turned into her, his arm stretched across her hips. He opened his eyes to look into her smiling face. No words were exchanged, but each felt, as they parted their bodies, as if they had peeled away from themselves. They sat, yawning, on opposite sides of the bed. David rose and noticed that an envelope had been slipped under the door. Olivia, her head a mass of flowing, dark, curls, lifted her face to give David a countenance that seemed to say, "Well."

David retrieved the envelope and opened it, reading:

29 October 1914
Tempelgesellschafthaus
Karmelheim Colony

Dear Hauptmann Yafey:

*I hope that you and Frau Yafey have found your accommoda-
tions at Hotel Prost satisfactory. My wife and I wish to offer you
hospitality this evening at our home in the Colony. If you will
kindly respond, post haste, whether or not this would be satisfactory, we shall make due arrangements. Please give a written
reply to the concierge by 5:00 this evening.*

Yours,

Wolfe Yoder

"Well, my wife, shall we accept?" asked David, after reading the
note to Olivia.

"Yes, let us go, my husband," replied Olivia. "But I will need something fitting to wear. These German colonists have a reputation for
simplicity, I understand."

"Indeed, they do, my dearest," replied David. "I shall enquire
downstairs if something can be arranged."

David put his uniform back on and went down to the concierge
desk. The man who greeted him was a German and used an accent
David could not place.

"*Hauptmann* Yafey, I have been instructed by *Herr* Yoder to inform you that our car will waiting for you under the portico at 7:00,
if you accept his invitation."

"We accept, but could you have a seamstress come up to our room
at 5:30?"

Of course, sir."

Olivia was sitting in the bath, scrubbing and humming an old
Italian folk song as David entered the bathroom. "I see that you've
started without me, my wife."

"Get in, *mein Herr*."

David said, "The bath is very small; I will bathe after you."

"But could you wash my back, darling?"

David had dreamed of this woman, now sitting nude before him, her body becoming more and more obscured by the soap residue and the minor bubbles that were beginning to stretch over the surface of the water. Olivia adjusted herself and her surprisingly ample breasts rose above the water as she pushed herself near the back of the tub and leaned over, handing the brush over her shoulder and behind her. David began soaping the brush and then gently moved the stiff bristles up and down her lovely back. He followed her back's shape, punctuated by the subtle rise and fall of her vertebrae, down to her surprisingly small waist.

"All right my darling, you must finish in a hurry. The seamstress will be here at 5:30." David's voice shook slightly, and he had to clear his throat twice as he spoke to her. He felt his entire body shaking as he returned to the bedroom to await Olivia.

Olivia came out of the bathroom wrapped in a thin cotton robe that did nothing to settle the rushing cascade of his body's reaction to hers. He went past her and turned off the faucets she had begun running for him, forgetting to close the door behind him and stripping off his clothes before her gaze. He stepped into the tub and turned, unknowingly revealing his erection to her before he sat down. He reached up to the faucets and ran the water again. Olivia came into the room, took the brush, and began to wash him, scrubbing his back, and as he leaned back, washed his chest and legs.

"My mother sent me a poem, recently, written, no doubt, by one of her friends." David took her hands into his and recited:

> *She stands in deep-blue ocean depths*
> *into which many rivers pour*
> *from distances on high.*
> *A gray fish carries her along,*
> *delighted by her weight's lissomness,*
> *which trickles over his fins.*
> *Out of his gills spews excited*

spraying – bubbling rush of breath.
But into her beauty rises,
coolly, ushered along the waves,
his forever level feeling.

Olivia was surprised by the amount of black hair that covered David's body. It wasn't thick, but it contrasted with his very blond head, and as she lathered him, she remembered Irene's old stories of the Greeks. He stepped from his bath, glistening like a god.

"Come, my husband, you are clean enough. Wash your hair, and I will prepare for the seamstress," Olivia said.

Olivia left the room, shutting the door behind her. She brought herself into the narrow shaft of the sun coming through their window and dropped her robe to feel the final warmth of the day upon her. She rummaged through her bag, found undergarments, and slipped on a blue *pardesü*. The long sequined coat had wrinkled in the journey. She brushed her lovely shining hair back into a ponytail and took out a pair of Western-style shoes she had bought in Italy.

After she had slipped her feet into the shoes, David appeared at the bathroom door with a towel wrapping his waist. He moved sideways to Olivia, reached down to grab his bag, and pulled it with him into the bathroom. As he bent over, his towel slipped, and he comically struggled to regain a tight grip upon the dropping cloth as he made his way back to the safety of the bathroom.

A knock came at the door, and Olivia opened it to a petite German lady holding the handle of a plain wooden box. After some conversation, the seamstress understood what was needed: a proper European dress appropriate to wear in the Colony. She left quickly, and returned by 6:00 with a long, unadorned, cornflower-blue dress. The sleeves would have to be taken up, and the seamstress made short work of the necessary cutting and stitching. By 6:20, she was gone with David's uniform, to render it presentable.

Olivia applied the modicum of makeup and light lipstick to meet the minimum of the standards of beauty she had been taught. She twirled herself before David, who was waiting on his light-weather uniform to be pressed and returned to him. Soon they were downstairs, walking toward the hotel entrance, when their car drove up.

The concierge, himself, stepped out of the driver's seat and hurried around to open the back door for them. The driver pulled away from the hotel silently and started up a steep hill that eventually leveled, splitting a small plane of waving waxflowers and lilies. A lone house of finely hewn stones with a slate mansard roof stood at the end of the road. The driver brought the car to the front of the house, jumped out, and ran to open his passengers' door. As David and Olivia stepped out, a compact sunburned man of about forty-five came out of his house to meet them. "My dear *Hauptmann* and *Frau* Yafey! How do you do? Please come inside!" he said.

They entered the rather plain home, and the furniture and a ticking cuckoo clock immediately reminded David of home. A small, but fit, woman approached them and said, "Welcome to our home!" It was Vickie, who immediately embraced David and shook Olivia's hand.

"My dear Vickie! I wondered what happened to you!" David then told Olivia of their connection, back in Constantinople.

"Shall we dispense with the pretense now that the driver has left us?" asked Yoder.

"Of course we shall," said Norma, who stood at the dining room entrance. "Dinner is served!"

David said, "This is so very surprising!"

Yoder said, "Well, you know our dear Colonel Witt, *Hauptmann* Petersruhe-Rožmberk! Never too much intrigue for him!"

The party sat down and ate heartily a dinner of lamb and fresh vegetables complemented by good German beer. David relaxed and looked at his table partners with great appreciation, remembering home with Sigi and Kathe. He still felt the sea moving him up and down and wondered if Olivia felt the same. As he began to feel himself seduced by the fine beer, his host asked if David would be good enough to repair to the small smoking room for a small bit of conversation.

"First," said his host, "my name is *Hauptmann* Padolsky, and I am here using the Pietist group as cover. I serve in a similar capacity as yourself, Rožmberk, and I must say, Witt seems to be most fond of you. I have asked you here to allow me to reveal your real orders. To begin, Witt has information that the British are moving a naval gun into place near the canal. It will be your job to prevent this from happening. You are to leave here in two-day's time to begin to recruit a squad, Witt wishes to call 'Force China.' I will give you guidance on where to look, especially now that a group of Indians has defected to us, and the British have Indian army units in the Sinai. That's all you need to know for now. I know that you've had a long journey and would like to get back to your lovely wife. You are a lucky man, there, I must say!"

35

Patrols would be along any minute. Before they landed they could see beams of light waving across the low sky, sometimes reflecting off the lake and putting the mainland dunes in relief. Their legs bogged into the loose wet sand, slowly sinking, not knowing if their feet would find a bottom. They slid the boat off the sandbar and into the water using the force of their arms and backs. No one spoke.

The men were excited and relieved, finally off the submarine. The night was colder than they had expected, with a light northern breeze following them off the Mediterranean. Their efforts to get the boat across the broad sandbar and into the lake made them appreciate the crisp air. They were dark-skinned and wore the light khaki of the British Indian Army that blended well in the twilight with the sand. They dipped into the salty water, and with one man at the stern and one on each side, pulled themselves onboard.

Someone's foot rattled a weapon in the bottom of the boat. All stopped, froze in place, and remained quiet for a long moment. Sensing no danger, the leader said, "*Chalna*, go," remembering to stay with English. They started rowing quietly, the water's glassy surface disturbed occasionally by a wading bird rising to flight or a turtle dipping below the surface. They moved the boat through the water toward the north shore of the *Sinai*, to a point in no man's land, a few miles east of Oghratina, well away from the perimeter established by the British near the canal.

The leader checked their heading by a dim torchlight held well down in the boat, tapped the others, and pointed an adjustment to their direction. While the Turks and Germans had recent success in the area, he knew that the reinforced British would become active and requested that his squad be brought in from the sea. The place chosen to land would provide good cover and give the men a chance to hold an adequate meeting with the German contact to carefully assess the situation before moving into the desert. The rendezvous would be tricky, further planning, everything really, depended on the meeting ashore.

The men moved their boat carefully, keeping their paddles away from the freeboard. The leader scanned the western and southern horizons, using the small German binoculars he'd been given in Gaza before setting out in the sub. The remainder of their equipment was stowed in waterproof duffels, but the men were still worried about the explosives. Without the charges, their mission would have to be abandoned.

These were Indians, deserters, or as they would have preferred, infiltrators. They left their infantry regiment of the Aden Brigade nearly a year ago, shedding their uniforms and dressing in native clothes bought and hidden in their quarters over a number of months. They were able to find places on a fishing dhow, which like many other large boats, found mooring in the "Crater," the ancient Yemeni Front Bay, away from the facilities in Tawahi, or "Steamer Point," as the British called it. The dhow crew was comprised of a handful of Arabs from around the Yemen with several black men from Somaliland, though some of the Africans were lighter-skinned than their Indian guests. Although Hindu, the Indians had lived with Muslims all of their lives and gained enough knowledge of the faith's customs to offer respect to the ways of the fishermen and found themselves welcome. The captain spoke good English, making communication straightforward.

The Indians promised three months of *gratis* labor, in return for sanctuary, food, and the promise to be taken to a point north near Jeddah. Captain Hassan ben Ali and his crew accepted the arrangement, and when the Indians completed their obligation and asked to be put ashore, the bargain was kept. The captain put in through a channel bordered with mangrove swamps at Al Lith, a small coastal oasis along the *Hajiz* portion of the *Tihameh* strip north of Yemen on the Red Sea and went ashore with them to meet a cousin from his Arab wife's family. The men found the man, a farmer, among a handful of livestock grazing along a steam feeding the inlet that the captain had used to bring the dhow in to the coast. The captain and the farmer shook hands, kissed and embraced, shook hands again, and began a lively conversation in Arabic. The Indians watched as the men shook their heads, clicked their tongues, and made unfamiliar gestures with their fingers. There was much laughing.

Ben Ali introduced the farmer, Ziad Al-Megrabi, and told the Indians that they were welcome. Al-Megrabi, a North African, was of medium height, dark as a nut, with a narrow face and a lazy eye. He wore a full beard, which he stroked and rolled through his long fingers. He appeared happy to see them, bobbing his head and repeating, "Yes, yes."

The Indians, in turn, said "*As-Salāmu `Alaykum*," to the farmer and introduced themselves: *Havildar* Vinay Prakash, *Naik* Sunil Rai, *and Naik* Ravi Gambhir.

The farmer, Ziad Al-Megrabi, responded with "*Wa `alaykumu s-salām*," and shook their hands. With his right hand touching his chest, Al-Megrabi asked, "Please, may we speak English?"

Prakash replied, "Yes! Honored sir, it would be our privilege to have you speak to us in English, a language we know well." He touched his right hand to his chest and bowed, slightly.

"My family from Tunis, then Muscat and worked. Worked... English trade agent. I am schooled and can write. My father...problems in Muscat...we came here, where peace," said Ziad Al-Megrabi, the farmer.

Al-Megrabi grasped Prakash's hand, walked him over to an area of shade, and said, "My friend, it is good that you have Arab dressing now... when you are travel in this land, do not speak of your country. Are you leader of the men?"

"Sir, thank you for telling me this; I will take your advice. I am their leader, yes," the Indian replied. He touched his right hand to his chest again.

"Come now, honor my family by sharing meal with us," said the Arab farmer, and still holding his hand, he led Prakash back to the others and gestured for all of them to follow him. They moved along the shore of the stream, stepping through soft, dense grass and small puddles until the stream became very shallow. Al-Megrabi stepped from the edge into the moving water, stopping for a moment to look at the Indian beside him, nodding and smiling. Prakash understood that the water was quite hot.

The farmer said, "The heat springs give us comfort in the evening, better for us with many years."

Prakash nodded, wishing desperately to hop back to the shore of spongy grass and pinkish flat rocks. Captain ben Ali looked at him and laughed.

At length, the party approached a few dwellings, rolled after a fashion back toward a series of low hills. The houses were made of stacked bleached and pink stone, with gray weathered wood running through the walls, mortared in amongst the flat, variously sized rocks. Lattice covered all of the window openings, and a dull red awning was stretched faintly asymmetrically across the top of the second-story casements, its wooden supports anchored into the thick, hump-like, stone lintels. The beautifully carved, dark wooden double-doors of the entrance belied the almost haphazard modesty of the house. The fact that the floor above canted out a bit was hardly noticeable under the shade of the awning. To the left of the house, a dusty road meandered away and down a hill below a long series of wooden roofs sheltering town dwellers.

Al-Megrabi pointed toward a small out-building to the right, somewhat behind the main house, and said, "You, my friends, will sleep there."

A young boy came out of the house to greet the farmer who spoke rapidly ordering, the three Indians assumed, the child to announce the presence of guests. The tall wooden doors had remained open a crack, but only when the boy approached were they opened wide enough for the men to notice a woman wearing a shiny black *hijab* and long, dull-black skirt.

Captain ben Ali walked with his kinsman ahead to the out-building, turning to claw down into the air, indicating that the Indians should follow. Once the party was there, the farmer showed them where they might wash and told them that hay would be brought to them for bedding.

The next morning, ben Ali and his dhow were gone, leaving his erstwhile passengers with Al-Megrabi standing over them as they awoke and pointing toward the north. Hospitality, it seemed, had run its course, and as the Indians shared a meager breakfast provided by the Arabs, a Turkish patrol from the south approached the home site and asked to water their animals. The Turks were advised of the Indians' presence and approached them with rifles fixed with bayonets and yelled, "*Oturmak!*"

Al-Megrabi yelled to the Indians, "They want sit, sit down!'

The leader of the Turks, a sergeant, motioned with a German pistol for the Indians to sit and put their hands up. He ordered his men to collect the Indians' weapons.

Prakash said, "Gaza, Gaza, please."

The Turks began to speak amongst themselves. After some conversation, the Turkish sergeant looked at Prakash and said, "Gaza?"

Prakash stood and said, "Germans," offering a marching motion.

The Turks, apparently deciding that the Indians had value as prisoners or traitors, allowed the Indians the use of two of their spare camels. The party moved off toward the north and into the *Hejaz*, skirting the coast as far as Yenbo, where Turks gave over their captives to the local garrison and an officer who was able to interrogate the Indians in English.

"Why you are doing this place?" said the Turkish officer.

"We wish to link with the German army in Gaza or Palestine."

"Why not Turk?"

"Because two of us speak German," he lied. "We were taught at missionary school."

"All infidels, anyway." The Turk shrugged.

Prakash and his men were now finally where they had planned to be: serving the Germans to fight the British. He and the men strung their camouflage and buried their explosives, along the south shore of the lake against dry dunes. As the sun began to rise to the left,

Prakash gathered his squad in a tight group and said, "Now men, we are ready to hit back. It will probably be several days before we make contact with our German commander, so everyone stay hidden and remember the password: "China.""

36

"What do you mean, you have no Hindi, Lieutenant?" Colonel James Minnis-Martin asked Lieutenant Twinge-Kitchen. "Lord Boardcroft, your *own* grandfather, made it clear in his letter to the Postmaster General, no less, that you knew the language, and I quote from the letter, here: "Send our Thomas, he'll go Hindi-Hindi with the brutes and sort them out.""

Tom, who hadn't been invited to take a seat, leaned on his stick and looked down at the Colonel with a pleading look. It was only 10:00 a.m., but the travel through the dusty streets of Cairo had been difficult and confusing. He and Harry inched through shouting hawkers, filthy urchins running in and out of the throngs, and angry porters shouting unintelligible curses as they tripped over squatting fakirs that kept the Lieutenant's eyes in constant motion, taking in the unbelievable scene and trying to catch the Cairo landmarks he'd been given to follow. A sea of crimson and black fezzes bobbed and bowed in and out of his sight and knots of women rushed along, masking the shop fronts with the solid black they wore from head to foot. The occasional engine noise and demanding horns of army vehicles parted the swarms of humanity and forced stray, unhurried animals to the edges and sometimes into the wide open shops, causing the keepers to scream and run at them with long sticks kept for the purpose.

As he stood before the Colonel, Tom still had a hundred smells in his nostrils gathered from the spice and perfume shops, the animal market, and the small fetid streams moving toward the river. He hadn't eaten in hours, but he hadn't felt inclined to look into the modest sack of dates and flat, dusty bread the innkeeper's wife had packed for them before they left for the station.

Minnis-Martin was a man of medium height with a large garnet nose guarded by intense, hazelnut eyes. Even when staring, his eyes seemed to drift up, the effect of his massive dark brows, which moving to the Colonel's mental swings and broad jumps, came together, bounced, and bounded away from each other like hirsute wings. Now, as when the Colonel followed any interlocutors' words, his brows moved up and down in a staccato palsy, punctuating his level of attention and interest. Few enjoyed a conversation with Colonel Minnis-Martin, and most who tried to speak with him developed headaches before leaving his office.

"Sir," Tom replied, "I don't believe my grandfather was referring to the Indian soldiers serving in Egypt. In any event, my grandfather is now deceased."

"What!" the Colonel shouted, his brows rising unevenly, with pauses like separate lifts going up and stopping on different floors. "Then why was the letter forwarded to me and you sent out here? I've spent hours of my time devising a strategy to deal with unrest in Indian ranks. The reports from HQ are relentless! Every week! Finally, I'm told an expert in Indian affairs would arrive from England, and now you tell me that you know nothing about Indians? Bloody hell." The Colonel's desk sounded as he brought a remarkably small fist down to the blotter in front of him. A framed photo of an unsmiling, thin-faced woman jumped in the knock's slight tremor, and the Colonel gave his chair an involuntary push backwards as the picture rocked unsteadily. His brows froze as he regarded the sepia image looking out at him.

"Sir," Tom replied, "I do not speak Hindi, but I am somewhat familiar with Indians, having been at university with a few and grown up under the shadow of my grandfather's man servant. As for the letter, my grandfather wrote his neighbor—an aide to the Postmaster General in Mr. Asquith's government—almost daily. I think perhaps the minister wanted to do something to persuade my grandfather that his grandson could be useful to the government and passed the letter on to someone in the War Ministry who wanted to help you deal with the Indians. Unfortunately, I believe that my grandfather referred to the wrong grandson and meant to mention my brother Hugh, Major Twinge-Kitchen, *Viscount* Twinge-Kitchen now Earl Boardcroft, who serves in the Colonial Office. Somehow, someone then had the army send me along to report to you. Actually, sir, I really believe that my grandfather was referring to a belief that I, or rather the Viscount, could quell the trouble on the subcontinent itself. The former Earl, as it were, tended to think on a large scale."

"Where is your brother, Twinge-Kitchen?"

"Hong Kong, I believe, sir."

The Colonel stood, stomped his feet on the linoleum, and shouted, "Damn and blast!" His brows began to wigwag, and the Colonel's head went back as he looked up. His pursed lips moved in a circle, and his cheeks puffed out as he tried to find expression to the thoughts assaulting his plans for this young lieutenant. Finally, he said, "Never mind Lieutenant, you leave for bloody Sinai tomorrow to join an Indian unit! Here are your orders."

The Colonel handed Tom a set of papers and told him to sit. He then picked up a cricket bat and rapped it against a map behind his desk, pointing to a spot between points marked Kantara and Ismailia. But before he proceeded to explain the mission, he asked, "Who is that large man at attention outside the door, Lieutenant? Is he with you? What kind of uniform is he wearing?"

"Sir, that is Sergeant Eccles. He came here with me. In fact, he rescued me after the *Lillian* sank and managed to get me to shore and to medical help. Like mine, his uniform was so battered during our ordeal, that he joined me in improvising a new kit. He sews elegantly."

"What the hell am I to do with him?"

"Sir, as his entire regiment was lost with the *Lillian*, perhaps he could be reassigned to our mission here, as my clerk."

"Clerk? He doesn't look like a clerk! Oh, very well. Does he speak Hindi?"

"No sir, something less comprehensible, I'm afraid."

"And what is that? Oh, never mind. Are you getting cheeky with me, Lieutenant?"

"I'm sorry sir, it must be the heat."

"Let's get on with it. You are to proceed to Ismailia. You have transportation arrangements in your orders. When you get to Ismailia, go to HQ and find Major Hazard Lawless. Major Lawless will issue you and that man Eccles camels. You do know how to ride a camel, do you not, Lieutenant?"

"We've had some experience, sir," Tom said, lying.

"Right. Major Lawless will brief you on the situation in his sector and direct you to the canal road, to the ferry. After you cross, you will proceed north. A runner has been sent ahead to the Indians, to a *Subedar-Major* Mankad, the chap commanding the unit, alerting him of your trip."

"I'm sorry Colonel, could you repeat the commander's title?"

"*Subedar-Major. Subedar-Major* Mankad, Lieutenant."

"Thank you, sir. Does *Subedar-Major* Mankad know the nature of my mission?"

"God no, Lieutenant! We don't want to give away the show!" said Mennis-Martin, his brows working, seeming to lift him off the floor. He grabbed the sides of his desk and rocked from side to side, as if trying desperately to hang on to the back of a team of wild horses.

"Understood sir, I do beg your pardon. Please forgive the question," said Tom.

The Colonel stopped swaying, lifted his fists, and held his breath. "Russell!" the Colonel shouted to his aide with his first expelled respiration. "Russell, goddamn it!"

Lieutenant Russell, the officer who had greeted Tom as he and Eccles entered the office, almost immediately appeared with a decanter of some kind of spirits, and before he reached the Colonel's desk, he had filled a tumbler with the libation.

With eyebrows moving in a kind of rapid semaphore, the Colonel took the drink carefully and brought it up to his mouth.

Without a word, the Lieutenant turned and left the office.

Tom stared at his current commander with an open mouth.

After a long minute, the Colonel seemed to regain some composure and sat back down. "Eccles, I mean Kitchen, I mean Twinge-Kitchen," he said. "You're pushing me to the edge of my reason! Now pay attention, and be quiet!" The Colonel continued with the briefing. "Lieutenant, you're going to have to devise a method of reporting your findings to me. You are to remain with the Indians for ten days and then get back here to Cairo."

At that moment, Sergeant Eccles appeared in the doorway and looked sheepishly at the Lieutenant and then the Colonel.

"Just what the hell do you want?" the Colonel shouted at Eccles.

"I heard my name called, sir."

"Get out! Damn you, get out!"

Pain coursed in a band around Tom's head, accompanying the constant tenderness in his injured shoulder and knee. Looking at the map of the ancient country behind the Colonel, he felt no relief knowing now why he was sent out to Egypt without regimental orders. He drew in a deep breath, and with dread gripping his thoughts, he knew he had more questions for Mennis-Martin. Desperate to get the meeting behind him, he decided to ask only one.

"Colonel, with the greatest of respect, I do not understand what I'm expected to do with these Indians and what I'm supposed to report to you about," Tom said. He drew his walking stick closer and waited for the storm.

Surprisingly, Colonel Mennis-Martin smiled, and with a small wave, sat back down. He looked at the Lieutenant with his brows winking in a gentle and regular movement, like ocean swells moving along, and gave a patient frown. "Young man," he said with a quiet, almost tender, voice, "You're to find out who the radicals are amongst the Indians, what kind of mischief they are planning to get up to, and deliver this information to HQ, to me in particular, before real damage visits this campaign."

Understanding, Tom saluted, turned about, and left the Colonel's office. No one in the outer office looked up as Tom and Eccles left the building.

Eccles asked, "Sir, if your brother's an Earl, what does that make you?"

"Just a Viscount, Eccles, just a Viscount."

"Viscount woot, if you'll pardon my askin', sir?"

"Just Lieutenant Twinge-Kitchen, for God's sake."

As the two men walked down the steps of HQ and tried to find the motor pool, a set of light gray eyes followed them. Major Nigel Nance-Minnis had stepped to his office window, next to that of his uncle, Colonel James Minnis-Martin, as he heard Tom and Eccles leave. He wondered when Hughie was due to arrive.

But the fact was, Hughie had arrived in Port Said at the tip of the canal. He was, at that moment, watching a huge naval gun being off-loaded from one of the Boardcroft ships. The gun had been in service in Hong Kong guarding the harbor when Hughie had received KoKo's cable concerning his uncle's discussion of placing a naval gun in the Sinai with another, rather more eccentric, Colonel. Hughie appealed to the governor for the use of the gun and received the reply, "If you can get it there, by all means, take it." Hughie had the gun dismantled and placed aboard one of his freighters and instructed KoKo to make the necessary arrangements.

Koko, having no engineering training or experience, consulted his uncle. "Well Nigel, good work, I must say. Just get those blessed Indians to build a position for the bloody thing." KoKo summoned the newly arrived commander, a *Subedar-Major* Mankad, or Mankind, he couldn't remember which, of an Indian Army engineering detachment and gave him his orders.

"But where in the Sinai do you wish to place the position, Lieutenant? asked Mankad.

"Right here." He pointed to a spot on a map laid out over his desk. "I'll arrange for the delivery of materials, which I suppose you'll need to make that … what is it called?"

"Concrete."

"Right. Concrete."

"But Major, the gun will have to be transported to this point. There are no landing facilities here."

"Not your concern, Mankind, just get your men and the materials there, and the gun will be brought to you."

"As you wish, Major."

37

"Bloody *Wog*," Sergeant Harry Eccles muttered to no one in particular. He turned and came face-to-face with Lieutenant Tom Twinge-Kitchen.

Tom said, "Eccles, must you continue to mistake *Subedar-Major* Mankad, an officer in His Majesty's Indian Army for an Egyptian laborer, like the ones who dug that magnificent ditch there below us? And yes, I know that our countrymen refer to the inhabitants of the Indian sub-continent as Wogs also, so save the lecture, why don't you, my dear. In a more *just* world, *Subedar-Major* Mankad out ranks me, you know."

Harry didn't know quite how to respond, except to say, "My dear, sir?"

"Just an expression, Eccles. Don't let's make it important, what?"

Harry replied, "Sir, I'll stop. Thee's right, of course, I'm sure." He picked up his leaking bucket of water and resumed his search for some privacy in which to bathe.

The two compatriots had arrived in the Sinai after Colonel Minnis-Martin finally allowed them to leave Cairo a week ago. They had been billeted in an old hotel built outside of Giza, where Harry had been delighted to take in the view of the Pyramids the ramshackle building offered, but upon noticing that the place seemed to be crawling with vermin of every description, all of which seemed inclined to ignore the intimidating presence of the South Yorkshireman, he took himself outside and away from the shade of the hotel to a spot he'd found under an abandoned work shed.

Tom went about life as if crawling things were not uncommon, but even expected, and usually sat out on the slumping terrace that had, in many years past, accommodated English explorers and tourists. "Eccles, you must have an assignation with one of the modern *Rahab the harlots* we've been encountering. I see that you even have soap with you!"

"Naw, sir. No woman would drop her bloomers out in this miserable place."

"Oh Eccles, I believe you sell your charms short."

"Well fuck it then, sir. *I'd* not bother with them twats in these bloody conditions."

"Indeed? I take it then that you are averse to our current hot, dusty, sandy, fly-cursed landscape." Tom laughed at the banter. By asking Harry to dispense with the formalities of the armed services and using more of his native expressions, his demeanor reflected the humility of his old grandfather.

In truth, Mennis-Martin never gained an ounce of conviction that Harry had really been serving as Tom's clerk, or even, when Tom had been summoned back to the Colonel's office, Tom's clarification that Harry was acting as his surveying assistant. But the two were allowed to remain together with Harry either referring to Mennis-Martin as "the chilly fish" or "the paper porter" to Tom. Tom, unfortunately, couldn't get the "Mennis" name out of his mind, and thought reluctantly about Hughie's KoKo and what connection he must have with the Colonel. He'd spent his days dreading a meeting with the *Sprite.*

Upon their arrival at Mankad's position, having traveled down from Kantara, Tom had dismounted his camel and asked the turbaned sentry to summon his commander. Mankad appeared, offered the Lieutenant tea and asked the sentry to direct Harry to the Q *Havildar* to arrange tents and a suitable location to set up camp.

Now, four days in camp behind them, Tom asked Harry to accompany him to Mankad's tent to discuss, again, the orders Mennis-Martin finally contrived for Tom's cover. As they approached, Mankad, a graduate of Lord Curzon's *Imperial Cadet Corps*, stood behind his work table under the tent's extended awning and saluted the British Lieutenant smartly, and as in previous meetings between the men, asked his *Daffadar* to serve tea.

During the morning preceding this meeting, Tom had mentioned the orders Mennis-Martin had handed down, and each time Mankad had looked at him quizzically. After the men were seated, Mankad, once again with pleading eyes, asked, "Lieutenant, why more trenching? We have a defensive perimeter that would make a French general swoon, if you'll pardon the exuberance. My men have suffered enough, moving sacks of cement General Murray was kind enough to send to us, and as instructed through General Maxwell's staff, are building a concrete wall, perhaps that is too strong a word, if you'll pardon the pun, around the half-mile of our position without the benefit of what is commonly understood to be essential ingredients of the usual concrete recipe: coarse aggregate and fresh water. We simply can't dig any more trenches, your orders notwithstanding, sir. Frankly, our labors here are absurd enough: pumping salty water up to a cistern to pour into discarded bully beef barrels to mix with sand and cement, making a thick slurry to drop into our forms, such as they are, made from the only wood to hand, that being scavenged fruit crates left by the departing Turks!"

Tom knew that the Indian commander was desperate to wave off his persistent twittering and be allowed to go about his business, absurd as it was. He realized that something had to give way before Mankad and his Indians fulfilled Mennis-Martin's worst fears by starting with the slaughter of himself and Harry. "You, sir, are most correct, and I apologize for pestering you with these ludicrous orders. You didn't hear me say that, by the way, Eccles. These orders lying before us only say, 'dig trenches,' and trenches, you have sir, dug. *Subedar-Sahib*, does command know that you have finished your trench works? Have you reported *anything* to General Maxwell's staff? Has *any* staff officer visited your position?"

"No, no, and again, no, Lieutenant Twinge-Kitchen. There are no telegraph lines. There have been no ships or boats since the cement was delivered, and we are too far away from HQ Kantara to risk sending a runner, as if I could spare one. We have no camels of our own. But, for *your* arrival, we should have thought ourselves forgotten," said Mankad.

"Then, inasmuch as trenches have been called for, it appears that my mission is accomplished, *Sahib*. I offer my congratulations! With your permission, I shall write a report to this effect, post-dated to April 20, and with your signature, submit it to HQ as verification of the completion of the orders heretofore outstanding." Tom smiled, Eccles smiled, and Mankad threw his hands into the air.

Mankad said, "Is there any particular rush to get back to HQ, Lieutenant? If not, then I propose that you and Sergeant Eccles be our guests as we celebrate with a day of rest."

"I propose that we make it a couple of weeks, *Sahib*," replied Tom. "We must remain here a reasonable period as if to 'oversee' the construction of the perimeter line, and with no further orders and no desire on my part to disturb the beast resting contentedly behind my tent, I can find no pressing requirement of my presence back at HQ."

"Truly, Lieutenant, if I may be permitted to say, your supervision will be most helpful. More tea?"

Harry looked confused.

"*Sahib*, you strike me as a man of civility and education. You appear to be about my age, perhaps somewhat older. How did you come to the army?" Tom brushed a persistent fly, away.

"Lieutenant, I am a product of centuries of tradition. I belong to a particular group, or tribe if you like, called *Jadejas* and also called *Rajputs*. I was born near Nawanagar, the son of a noble, in what you British call, a 'Princely State.' We enjoy some independence from your *Raj,* and wishing to placate your sovereign, we avail ourselves for military service on his behalf. My father did the same, before me. I now command this small company taken from the India Expeditionary Force F, 10th Indian Division, Imperial Service Brigade, State Force Unit, Army of India, Northern Army, 20th Nawanagar Infantry Brigade. There you have it," said Mankad.

"*Sahib*, I am an engineer by training, and with your permission, I would like to ask you why you've chosen to persist in trying to make concrete without the proper materials under the worst conditions? In 110-degree heat without a proper mixing apparatus and sturdy forms? Your men are nearly collapsing, and many of them are suffering cement burns to their hands and arms, I might point out," said Tom.

"Lieutenant, I will admit to the pointlessness of our activities here, but my troops can't just sit idly by here in this terrible place, waiting for an enemy who probably has the good sense not to come back. Since we've declared a holiday, we will attend to our injuries properly," replied Mankad.

The men sat back and sipped their excellent tea quietly. Mankad eventually summoned his aide and had the word passed for his men to stand down after securing what tools they possessed worth accounting for. As the afternoon wore on, all three men enjoyed a short nap in their hard chairs, the heat pushing into their skins and the ubiquitous flies notwithstanding.

Harry awoke first. "Fooking Hell!"

Tom and Mankad promptly awoke with starts. "What *is* the matter Eccles?" asked Tom.

Harry had a pair of binoculars up to his eyes and said, "I think I see a group of British soldiers heading our way. Fook me to Sheffield, sirs, but it seems that they are pulling some kind of great black object with a *fooking* herd of camels!"

"Give me those glasses please, Sergeant," said Tom. "Fuck, he's right, Mankad! Better get your men roused and into proper line. He's someone important!" He took a much longer observation. "Oh, no, Jesus Christ! It can't be, goddamn it!"

"Lieutenant, what do you see?" asked Mankad

"Something unbelievable, *Sahib*. It is my brother, and he's leading a troop of twenty or thirty camels pulling a bloody huge naval gun!"

"Are you certain that it is your brother, Lieutenant?"

"Oh yes, he's squinting like a maniac, and he has his favorite companion with him—Mennis."

"Like …" Mankad hesitated to say the name. "Like *Minnis-Martin*?"

"Afraid so. The lunatic is the Colonel's nephew or something, I believe. Better pull your men together smartly and as well turned out as possible, *Sahib*. My brother is a slave to regulation as well as being an idiot. Dangerous combination, in my experience. Eccles?"

"Sir?"

"Best hide for a while, if you can."

"Sir!"

The desert air became a gray-brown cloud as it flew into the faces of the scrambling Indians desperately locating and pulling on uniforms. Mankad was shouting and directing his troops into shape when Major Nance-Mennis rode into the camp.

"Who is in charge, here?" Mennis demanded. He knew, of course, that Mankad was commanding.

Mankad, who was far enough away from Mennis to not have noticed or heard him, went on with his work.

Tom, standing some distance from Mennis' camel said, *Subedar-Sahib* Mankad, Major."

"Who the hell? Is that you Twinge-Kitchen?" asked the *Sprite*.

"Yes, Major, it is I. I see that you have my brother in tow. How is the pederast?"

"I'd watch that kind of talk, Lieutenant! What are you doing here, anyway?"

"It's a long story, only your exalted uncle can explain, Major."

"Well, never mind. Couldn't care less, actually," said Nance-Mennis. "Mankad, get your men ready to secure the animals and cover the gun. As you may have noticed, we have many camels and few men, so I expect cooperation."

Mankad had been greeted with these words and began to feel himself a character in a Gilbert and Sullivan operetta, for which during his stay in England for an education, he had once developed a fondness. Alas, he'd never think fondly of them again, he thought.

"Major Nance-Mennis, if I may, do you plan to mount that bloody great gun, here?" Tom asked.

"Well, you, cretin, why the hell do you think Mankad has been out here? He's been seeing to the preparations, you fool," replied Mennis.

Mankad dropped his head and stole a glance at Tom that said, God help and save us.

The newest Earl of Boardcroft, the Major Hugh Twinge-Kitchen rode up to the men. He looked down at his brother and asked, "What the bloody hell are you doing here, Thomas?"

"Long story," Tom replied between gritted teeth.

"Long story, sir," said Hughie. "Are you seconded to these Indians? Or did Ko, I mean, Nance-Mennis' uncle send you out here for a walkabout?"

"Perhaps more of the latter, *sir*." Tom walked up to Hughie and whispered out of earshot, "If you keep trying to humiliate me, brother, I'll break your fucking skull, rank or no. Now, who the hell came up with the idea of pulling a great naval gun across the fucking desert on an out-sized donkey cart?"

"Nance-Mennis, a note, please: Lieutenant Twinge-Kitchen has insulted His Majesty's Royal Engineers by referring to this magnificent caisson as an out-sized goat cart. There's a good man," said Hughie.

"I said, *donkey* cart, damn you."

"Lieutenant Twinge-Kitchen, let us inspect these works of Mankind's to ascertain their suitability to the purpose," said Hughie. "Mankind, you may join us, but do keep quiet."

Mankad felt his blood rising.

And so, the group of senior officers inspected the work of the Indian engineers, and in the end, Major Twinge-Kitchen found them lacking. "The trenches will do, Mankind, but most of the concrete work is weak and often crumbles underfoot."

Mankad recounted his travails with supply and when asked what was to be done, he replied, "Fresh water from Kantara, a proper mixer, sturdier wood and hard, coarse aggregate."

"Why did you choose to waste the materials given you, Mankind?" asked Hughie.

"I had a direct order, sir, from Kantara, to 'make do' with the resources available."

"Indeed. Well, let's not weep over spilled milk, gentlemen. Twinge-Kitchen, you will accompany us about and make for Kantara this evening. Make certain that the men and animals are properly watered and fed. There's a good man," ordered Hughie.

"Mankad, if you will be so kind as to assign a few of your men to help me, we shall carry out the Major's wishes," said Tom.

After two hours or so, all animals and humans were ready to turn about and head north. The evening was descending quickly upon the travelers as they set off and the murmur of suppressed cursing provided counterpoint to the clanging, squeaking, and flatulence of the camels. The night wore on and Tom and Harry tried to make themselves as inconspicuous as possible, falling somewhat behind the mighty gun cart.

"Sir, is that bastard really your brother?" asked Harry.

"I am afraid so, Harry. He's not much like his namesake, alas."

"And what was his namesake like?"

"Wild as David and as wise as Solomon, Harry. I miss him every day."

"All right, you lot, we'll halt here!" shouted Hughie.

Tom rode up to his brother and asked, "Why are we stopping?"

"We've covered ten miles. We'll place the gun here. When Mankind and his Indians get here, we'll start out for Kantara to procure the proper materials. How long will it take the Indians to reach us?"

"A couple of days after packing up."

"Very well." In the bright moonlight, Hughie watched as his men began to array the tents, secure the animals, and post guards for the night.

Tom went back to Harry and described the current state of affairs, recommending that they pitch their tents well behind the gun.

Two days came and went with no sign of Indians. Finally, Hughie ordered a party of four to return to Mankad's position and find out what was delaying them.

Hughie's men drove their camels hard through the morning and entered the position's walls before noon. "What the hell?" asked Sergeant Spoon, as he discovered that he and his men were alone.

"Sergeant, I think I hear something coming from the direction of the canal," shouted one of Spoon's party.

The tiny party rode the half-mile to the edge of the canal embankment where they beheld Mankad's entire company running about the steep dune and swimming, their naked bodies glistening in the sun.

"I say, there!" shouted Spoon.

Sitting atop the dune bank nearby, Mankad answered, "Yes, Sergeant?"

"My Major is bloody hopping mad! Where have you lot been?"

"Swimming. Why don't you try it?"

Spoon turned to his group, and in a cockney voice said, "Well, we're here; might as well cool it off, right gents?"

The search party had nearly stripped off before settling their camels. They hit the Suez Canal with the velocity of falcons smashing into pigeons. The men enjoyed the water, and soon enough, bottles of secreted rum were being passed from one hand to another. As the afternoon was forgotten, the men reveled in the hospitality of Mankad's soldiers, who offered each a small clutch of khat to chew. As the dinner hour approached, Mankad had a few quiet words with the company's cook, and when the British sat down to their meal of porridge and flat bread, they found themselves getting hungrier and happier. Eventually, Mankad asked the cook, "How many balls of hashish *did* you cook into their food?"

The cook replied, "Enough" as their guests began falling off of their seats.

At least one more day of peace, Mankad thought.

38

David was on the desert sand again, his cap in the mouth of the camel. He looked at the brute chewing his cap, and knew he'd been lucky, unlike a few Arabs he'd seen with scarred, twisted cheeks and horribly mangled chins from camel bites. He was ready to give it up, just walk the beast the rest of the way into camp. *Just walk the beast into the camp*: it seemed to sum up his entire experience of the Ottoman Empire, perhaps even his own country's adventure. He knew the camel would never accept his authority, and the German wanted to confront the Turkish sergeant in Gaza who requisitioned the animal for his use in the Sinai. But that might never happen. Things were going to change in this war, and one way or another, so would Germany's relationship to the Turks, *young* and old. He stood up.

David collected the various objects that had fallen with him, cursed the animal, and brushed as much sand as he could from his thick hair. He needed a barber. Retrieving the bridle, he pulled the camel toward the black tents of the Bedouins, a group collected from outcasts from the Negev tribes and others and paid to support the Turks in Sinai. "Is there anything redeeming about these *Arschlocher,* assholes?" he thought.

The Arabs inhabited the north side of the encampment, a rambling cluster of small dusty tents pushed up against one large tent, apart from the Turkish army's neat rows of white tents. The men were laughing at his misfortune, bowing and clapping as he moved in their direction. Two young men ran up to him and asked him to honor them by accepting tea and a bit of bread from their master. He kept the reins and went with them toward the largest tent to meet the *sheikh,* the leader of this dubious band. He would beg off, needing to secure his equipment before leaving the camel, but before he reached the tent, a young Turkish officer approached, saluted, and asked that the *Hauptmann* accompany him to the commander's quarters, located amongst a group of twenty or so tents sheltered in the shadow of a high dune nearby. David put his hands out, meaning, "what can I do," and making his apologies to the Bedouins, left with the Turk.

"Sahin *Bey*, how may I help you, sir?" the German said in English, after entering the round tent.

The Turkish major was sitting behind a large work table with his back to the entrance flaps, writing at a small desk positioned against the fabric of the tent. English, mixed with some Italian and Arabic, was their agreed *lingua franca,* although David spoke passable Turkish. Two young Arab boys were moving sticks to push broad fans strung along a metal shaft above the commander. He stopped writing and turned around. The Turk was short and fat, with a broad, incongruously pale face set into a hidden neck, signs of Balkan heritage, which the German knew in his experience, meant slave and rather common. His uniform was tight. The khaki serge darkened under his armpits and a moist ring along the bottom of his round *Serpuş* cap, which he never seemed inclined to remove. He pointed to a chair near his map table, set away from and perpendicular to the writing desk and the worktable in front of him.

David sat.

"Captain," the commander began in English, "you have new orders from a Lieutenant Schneider, someone on *Oberst* Kress' staff." He handed the folded documents to David. "We will give you whatever assistance we can."

"Sahin *Bey*, a more cooperative camel would be appreciated," David read over the orders. "It appears that I cannot escape the worst of these beasts."

"Ah, those worthless cavalry *Çavuş* sergeants back in Gaza are still passing off their more temperamental animals to our allies, I see. It isn't enough that the magnificent soldiers of Europe's greatest nation should have to stoop to help the humble Turk in this hellish land, but that the Turk should abuse him! Bek, *Buraya gel!*"

A sullen lieutenant appeared through the tent flaps, and the Major addressed him in rapid Turkish. The officer disappeared immediately.

"I have ordered that you be given my camel; her name is Hasnae, Rožmberk *Effendi*. I will use my horse," said Sahin. "As you may have heard, we are being held in reserve and will not follow the units moving toward the Canal attack. We leave tomorrow night to form part of a rear guard, God willing."

"I had not heard, sir, but from my station I could see dust being thrown up, moving west toward us, here. Advance units should begin arriving in two or three hours."

"You leave as soon as you can develop plans. I don't know what you will be doing, but take whatever maps and supplies you need, if you do not already have them. *My* orders have me giving you three additional camels. Were you briefed on this new mission before you left Gaza?" asked Sahin.

"I was told to expect changes in orders, Sahin *Bey*," said David. This was all he would tell the Turk. In fact, he had developed the mission and trained the Indian squad Padolsky had met and recruited two days before David arrived, having found them near Jaffa, languishing in the corner of a Turkish fort.

David and Padolsky had arranged to transport the Indians on a submarine, allowing plenty of time should adjustments to the plan need to be made. They set the timetable, which unfortunately left the Indians for a few days in the desert. All planned, Gerd was instructed to send the orders to Sahin in two days' time. This did not wholly account for his appearance in the camp today, after several days spent along the coast preparing for the new task. He regretted deceiving the major, he in fact liked him, but unless information needed to be shared, his particular variety of duty and the new request from Ruth's husband forbade revealing anything. It was a way of life, of preservation, complicated and foul in reality, precluding relationships within and without the army.

Sahin stood and offered his hand, and David shook it. The German looked down at the Turkish officer and said, "Thank you, sir, for your kindness and help. Best of luck to you, Sahin *Bey*."

The Turk nodded and said, "And to you, also, *Hauptmann*."

David left the camp later that evening, after transferring his equipment from his camel to the Major's gentler beast. Hasnae was indeed sweet natured and held herself with a kind of noble poise. He also added provisions for ten days and as much water as he could fit on the camels. He would need to sustain several people for as much as a week. He set out toward the north, somewhat east of the path that had led him into the camp, planning to turn northwest toward the swamps lying south of Lake Bardawil unobserved during the night.

David had been in the Ottoman Empire for over two years, and as he left realized that, when the time came, he would not regret never seeing another Turkish soldier again. His primary task now was to establish relationships within the Ottoman intelligence bureau, especially relationships that could yield information concerning British activities in Egypt and of course, Egyptians who disapproved of the heavy hand of British influence in their homeland. Technically, the army accepted that David was a member of the staff of the German ambassador, Hans Von Wangenheim, but it was understood that he only be required to fulfill that role in the most pedestrian sense, such as occasionally being asked to join the ambassador's entourage on appointments at the *Sublime Porte,* the former seat of the Grand Vizier at Topkapi Palace, when numbers were called for.

In some ways, he had found the diplomatic routine as unsatisfying as spending hours with Turkish army officers, but as during his first posting there, he found himself fascinated by the interest of certain Turkish officials, mostly mid-level bureaucrats but even some ministers, in esoteric matters and their associated and *unusual* personalities. As he lay in the sun on the deck of the destroyer, he had thought of, *International Illuminati, Hermetic Orders, Masonic Rites, Templars,* and *Rosicrucians*: the entire range of secret societies and brotherhoods that seemed to find some level of interest amongst many of the men laboring for the *Sultan*, the leader of the Moslem world. Much less surprisingly, signs of Persian and Turkish *Sufism* were much more prevalent, everywhere in government, but none had really reminded him of old Rasheed. He dismissed most of these things as preoccupations of misfits and neurotics, but the puzzling blending of faith the centuries wove through Central Asia and the Levant seemed to petition his efforts to organize his time and thoughts.

It wasn't a life he'd known in Lübeck or Berlin. Prior experience had taught him how impenetrable the workings of the *Sultan's* government could be at any level, how truly twisted the paths to scraps of useful information always were and he knew his interest in the strange religious life so common amongst the Turkish governing class gave his engagement with them a sincerity he couldn't have contrived. And now, for all useful purposes, the *Sultan* was gone, leaving Witt fuming evermore at the chaos.

After he left Constantinople, travelling down the arc of the Levant with Olivia and spending four wonderful days with her in Haifa to visit the German Colony, he had looked up an old school friend living there, Hermann Brandt. He enjoyed hiking the slopes of Mount Carmel with Padolsky, who ventured down to him, and for a time, he could look out on the Mediterranean and almost forget his profession, breathe freely, sense the fundamental entelechy of his heart, and remember the world before military service to the homeland, his boyhood dream, pushed down upon him. Though he hadn't realized it, these adventures had been rehearsals for the journeys he would make soon. Perhaps these journeys would be the culmination of his odyssey as a soldier, if some goddess didn't hold something back for him, as was done for the great tactician himself. But in planning with Padolsky whatever his life's potential could realize for him, he feared he might be cut short in this lonely desert.

Before he had left Jerusalem, and the German command, there, he had received a note from Ephraim Yoffey, asking for a brief meeting. Ephraim explained that he had information that his niece, Hulda, was in Kantana, working as a nurse. She wished to escape to Palestine and Ephraim asked David to help him determine how it could be done. A Zionist organization had somehow inserted her there in a field hospital, but she had earlier deserted her post in western Egypt to try to make her way to Palestine and felt trapped, there. Could he help?

"Perhaps," David replied.

As he traveled, the recollection of the conversation with Ephraim reminded him that he hadn't seen Olivia for a couple of weeks, and he worried that his attempts to enquire about her father would continue to come to nothing. Isaac must be saved. The old man had promised to make his way to Italy, but nothing had come from Witt regarding Isaac's status. Now, movement would be much more difficult, since the war had begun to really bear on much of the Mediterranean world. He allowed himself to remember his lover, to let the memories of this woman dominate his consciousness. Again, he wondered what force had *really* brought them together. "Destiny" and "fate," was too simple to describe the path to this woman. It was grinding, inexorable, rough, and stumbling. It was *Tante* Kathe. He laughed, remembering his wily, adopted mother.

As he turned toward the swamps, he knew that his rendezvous with the Indians would be dangerous, but if Witt's intelligence was correct that the British planned to move the naval gun in place near Kantana, its presence would almost nullify any attempt to capture the east side of the canal. He must be successful in disproving this information or destroying the gun, David thought. After four hours of traveling, he settled his train of camels and rested until dawn, when he would make navigational observations and care for the animals. The rest of the day would involve constant vigilance and water.

As dusk returned, he roused the animals and saddled them for the evening. He started toward the designated point and expected to find the Indians waiting for him within five hours. David had considered how to get Ephraim's niece out of Kantana, but short of just walking in and taking her from under the noses of the British, he was at a loss.

David continued his journey amongst the dunes—alone, tired, wishing for some of ancient Helen's magic Egyptian potion he remembered from one of Schlarp's tales to help him forget the pains of his journey. He drank a mouthful of water, pretending Helen had slipped a drop from Polydamna's Egyptian garden. He awoke from his reverie of Schlarp's Homer and glanced about to make certain that his wits had not betrayed him. He was alone, thank god.

Soon, however, vegetation began appearing, and he turned west, below the lake now, toward the meeting point. He saw a short flash of light and stilled his animals for a moment. Dismounting, he tied Hasnae to the saddle that he'd placed on the sand, stroked the other camels, and then crouching, made his way toward the source of the light. As he approached, he heard low voices speaking a combination of English and an unfamiliar language. He crawled into position that brought the animated shadows into view and listened.

After a while, he became convinced that these were his men, and he said the password, "China."

The shadows froze, and one of them replied, "Lion."

David rose and walked over to the group, who assumed that this was Padolsky's man. *Havildar* Vinay Prakash said, "We are all here, *Hauptmann.*"

"Good work, men. We have a little traveling to do this evening. We will head southeast, and as dawn approaches, dig in using the netting I have brought. Everyone all right?"

"Yes, *Hauptmann*. I must say that after days dug in here, we are most ready," said Prakash.

"Follow me to the camels then," said David.

Once the group had secured their equipment on the camels, they set off. The moon was bright and the stars were brilliant as they traversed the dunes. David consulted his compass often, and almost soundlessly, the party moved towards its objective.

"*Havildar* Prakash, have you been able to contact your family, since leaving Aden?" asked David.

"No sir. We are well aware of the British intrusion into the private communications of their Indian Army. We choose silence. It's the only way."

"This particular duty is very dangerous; the fact that you and your men are wearing your British-issue uniforms puts all of you at risk as spies. If captured, you'll be executed," said David.

"The British put on uniforms every day to oppress my people. Using one of theirs is a particular irony we are most happy to risk, sir."

"This part of the *Sīnai ash-Shamāliyah* will be nothing but dunes, but the reputed gun placement is situated on a fairly level area, south, we believe, of Kantana. I'm afraid that it will be rough going for another day, my friend. These beasts are useful, but unforgiving."

As dawn approached, David halted the troop and settled them into a wallow between dunes. He herded the camels some distance away, to keep their rasping groans from giving his position away to a passing Bedouin or, worse, a British patrol. Netting was spread out along the back of the dune and David built a tiny lookout to observe the broad expanse of sand he'd selected as an element of his site. He bade all to drink, regularly.

By David's calculations, the party was southeast of Kantana and likely well away from probing British. As he gave the order to observe silence, he heard a camel give a long roar. He looked back toward his animals, but realized that the sound had come from in front of him, to his left. He summoned Prakash, who had also heard the camel, with hand signals to join him at the observation point. "There," David whispered. "Listen."

The men heard snatches of "bloody hell" and "read compass" and "I told you."

Prakash said, "British. What are they doing way out here?"

David said, "They're lost, my friend. We'll need to capture them. Bring everyone here, quickly."

The men gathered around and decided to drive one of their camels ahead of the intruders to distract them, then quickly surround them, moving up from behind. This was done, and as the British moved toward the lone camel, David and the Indians surrounded them, pulling them off their saddles and warning them not to resist. The sun was above the dunes, and the light was clear.

"What are you fucking Wogs doing? Can't you see that we're British officers!" said one of the men.

"They would like to kill you, Hughie, and I'm of a mind to let them," said David.

"David!" said another of the party. He stood almost as tall as David, with a freckled nose and strawberry hair showing form under his pith helmet.

"Good morning, Tom! Shall we be civilized and dispense with the bloodshed?" said David. "Hands behind your backs, gentlemen." The Indians tied them up. David had Prakash's party collect the weapons and led the captives back around their dune. David looked at Nance-Minnis and said, "How's the buggering, Minnis?"

While David wanted to catch up with Tom, he knew that the British might be looking for his friend and his brother. He ordered all to keep quiet while he inspected the new camels for provisions, finally asking Tom to join him. "How is your grandfather, Tom?"

"Dead at sea in July. Hughie is now Earl."

"I'm very sorry to hear of this loss, my friend. I also regret having to keep you and your party as captives."

"It's fucking Hughie's fault. The ass couldn't read a compass if his life depended on it!"

"Where the hell were you going?" asked David.

"Kantana."

"It's twenty miles west of here!"

"Christ!"

David took Tom back to the captured party and warned them not to make a sound. The men were put into a circle, tied together under the netting, and offered water. As the day wore on, David began to consider the plight of Hulda Yoffey, as well as the destruction of the naval gun. At length, he called Prakash over and asked, "Do you think you could lead the men to the gun and destroy it, if I have one of these British officers get you into the camp?"

"Who are these people, *Hauptmann*?"

"An old friend and his brother. My friend is the Lieutenant, and his brother is the Major. I plan to use the Major, and for me to do so, you'll have to spare one of your men for my use. We'll plan to set off after nightfall and meet back here tomorrow night. I'm going to ask

Tom, the Lieutenant, to lead you to the gun. In exchange, you will give him and his men their freedom. I plan to use the Major for another purpose. Tom hates the British Raj, and his grandfather served as one of my godfathers, so there is no need to harm him. The others will be warned, and you have free rein to deal with them as you must. Just do not harm Tom."

"I agree, *Hauptmann*. Let us not forget to take our bearings before setting off."

David untied Tom and moved him away from the group. He explained the plan and found Tom agreeable.

Tom asked, "What do you plan to do with Hughie?"

"No harm, unless he provokes it. He will, however, be my prisoner."

"Grandfather would appreciate the irony."

As night fell, the plan unfolded, and Prakash set off with his party and Minnis, Eccles and the Indian brought along to pretend to be a servant.

David walked up to Hughie and said, "Remove your uniform, Major."

"You can fuck yourself, Jew," Hughie said.

David nodded, and the Indian left to assist him hit the newest Earl of Boardcroft in the face with his rifle butt, knocking his Lordship completely unconscious. The nobleman's clothes were removed and exchanged with David's uniform. The fit was nearly perfect. As Hughie began to regain consciousness, David warned him that he was to remain silent, that he was a prisoner of the German Federation, and that the gentlemen left to guard him disliked the British somewhat intensely. "Don't provoke the guard on pain of death" were David's parting words.

David set off due west toward Kantana on Hasnae, with Hughie's camel in tow. The trip would take most of the night, and without a map to locate the hospital, he knew he'd have to practice his English and the mannerisms he'd learned in Lincolnshire. He also knew the difference between a "Home" accent and a "Midlands" accent. As he approached the small city, he could see a small wall, and in the medium distance, a waving Red Cross flag. A sentry stopped him and asked for identification and the password.

David produced the papers and imperiously shouted, "There is no password, private!" This did the trick, and the private allowed "His Lordship" through the town gates. David headed straight for the hospital, harassed by dogs and begging children. Very few soldiers were present, but occasionally, sentries in front of named buildings would salute and David would return with a lift of his riding stick. Eventually, he reached the hospital.

"Private!" yelled David, "I wish to visit one of my relations working as a sister. Be kind enough to have someone to take me through to Sister Yoffey, please."

The private who had been standing at the main doorway disappeared for a brief moment and marched out a Lieutenant Cotton. David gave the reins of the two camels to the sentry and told him not to move.

"Sir, may I assist?" said Cotton with an accent that could only have been instilled by wealthy breeding.

"You may, Cotton," replied David, using his most stilted Home Counties accent. "Take me to Sister Yoffey, at once."

"My Lord, may I have tea brought out for you?" asked Cotton. David looked at poor Cotton as if he were insane and said, "Why, of course! This is a British installation, is it not Cotton?"

Cotton told an orderly to fetch tea, and when the orderly asked where they would be, Cotton hissed, "Just look, man, just bloody look!"

As the men walked through the hallways, David began to worry that the desert scent of his uniform might begin to give him away, but as he was a Major and an Earl as most of the hospital had been quickly advised, personnel were scarce. Finally, he beheld a nurse with beautiful eyes, mid-twenties, and taking some risk, he addressed her by saying, "Hulda, my dear." It *was* Hulda Yoffey, and David breathed a sigh of relief. He hugged her and whispered, "I've been sent by your Uncle Ephraim to fetch you. You must walk out with me now!"

"It is so good to see you, Major!' said Hulda. As they walked out of the ward, she noticed the effects of a doctor recently succumbed to a heart ailment lying on a table. She took a pith helmet and a pair of binoculars that were, interestingly, of German origin.

"Cotton, thank you. Tour services will no longer be needed, there's a good man," said David.

Cotton saluted smartly, turned on his heel, and strode correctly through the open hallway doors. Someone was heard to whisper, "Bloody arse-kisser Cotton."

David and Hulda left arm in arm, proceeding out of the hospital and mounting the camels being held by the private. As the two left, David said to the private, "You'll keep this quiet, soldier!"

"Yes, sir!" shouted the sentry.

David and Hulda rode through the gate and into the desert. Meanwhile, the orderly carrying a serving tray of tea was still looking for the "Major."

After five minutes or so, David consulted his compass and ordered Hulda to stay at his side and pick up the stride. He glanced over and saw Hulda smiling and shaking her head.

She said, "I can't wait to tell my father about this!"

"Wrap your face with something, Hulda. It's going to get dusty. By the way, my name is David Samuel von Petersruhe-Rožmberk, and I am a *Hauptmann*, a Captain, in the German Army. Your Uncle Ephraim is married to my fiancée's cousin. I am taking you to Palestine."

After riding for several hours with short breaks, David and Hulda endured a fierce sandstorm and had to dismount for several hours. They resumed their journey, and at dusk, came upon the camp he'd left the evening before. David's heart was racing as they climbed the last dune.

A shout, "Identify yourselves!" came from the top of the sand.

David replied, "China. It's *Hauptmann* Rožmberk, with a guest."

Prakash ran down the dunes shouting, "We did it! *Hauptmann*, we destroyed the gun!"

"Any casualties?" asked David.

"Just one, a Captain Minnis. We don't know how, but someone strangled him while we were about setting the charges. Couldn't have been the Lieutenant. We think Eccles, the big fellow, caught him as they were all standing in a tight group, and held him up until we were about to leave them."

"The Lieutenant alright, Prakash?"

"Yes, and he asked me to tell you that Rasheed would be most pleased with this outcome."

"Dear old Rasheed," said David and laughed.

39

After David and his party, including Major Hugh Twinge-Kitchen and Hulda, arrived in Gaza, David gave over Hughie to the Turkish Army. Hughie began weeping and screaming at David, "You bastard! You killed my KoKo, you fucking Jew German bastard!"

The Turkish commander said in English, "Can't you Germans take this one?"

"I am sorry, sir, but I have no orders to retain prisoners. Perhaps he would be valuable in a prisoner exchange. He was certainly useful to us. Why not give him back, if the occasion arises?"

David looked at poor Hughie standing with Turkish guards nudging him backwards with their rifles. He said, "Don't provoke these gents, Hughie, or get too friendly. They tend to take sodomy to the extreme, I understand."

"Go to Hell."

David immediately found a staff vehicle, and driving through throngs of excited, almost panicked people, he took Hulda the four uncomfortable hours to Ephraim, Ruth, and Olivia at the *moshav*. They arrived to hysteria gripping the settlement, as people ran about and were leaving in large, terrified groups. Miles before, they had noticed heavily laden men and women walking down the oblique roadsides with children darting in and out of the lines being grabbed and scolded by frantic adults.

"What is happening?" asked David, when he and Hulda stepped into Ephraim and Ruth's little house.

Olivia ran up to him with tears about to fall from her eyes and said, "The Turks are killing and deporting us! We must get to Jaffa. The Americans are there to take us on one of their warships!"

"This is true, David" said Ephraim. He hugged and kissed his niece.

"The Turks are running wild under orders of Hassan *Bey*. If we don't go, the trouble spreading north will envelop us." Ephraim looked worried and continually fiddled with his spectacles, taking them off for a few moments and then putting them back onto his face. His black hair seemed shaggier than usual. His curls fell around his head as he looked through the front window, minding David's vehicle.

David had to sit. He had exhausted himself, and at this point, he could barely keep his eyes open. He had had trouble staying alert to drive the Daimler he had requisitioned to take Hulda to the *moshav*, and now he must turn around and take everyone to Jaffa. First, he asked if they had finally gotten telephone service in the settlement.

"Yes, there is a telephone in the meeting hall. I don't know if anyone knows how to use it, however," said Ruth.

"Oh, hell, I can use it!" said Ephraim, instantly putting his sex life into the context of that favorite of Greek words: stasis.

"Let me use it," said David. The whole group marched down to the meeting hall, where a crowd was gathered around the telephone desk, standing mute and mystified. David walked up, and putting the receiver to his ear, asked the operator in German to put him through to his headquarters. "Yes, this is *Hauptmann* David von Petersruhe-Rožmberk. Can you tell as to whether there is an American warship anchored in Jaffa?"

The duty officer answered, "Yes, the cruiser *North Carolina*."

David said, "Thank you," and hung up the telephone.

"Gather only what you can carry, and we'll go to Jaffa! But I must have some civilian clothes," said David. "May I borrow something from you, Ephraim?"

"So you are going, too? Deserting your army?" asked Ruth.

"Listen to me, Ruth. I will not leave Olivia. There are no clear choices. The Turks are mad beasts, the Germans are helping them, and this war is going to destroy Europe and God knows what other continent. *My* choice is to stay with Olivia and act as the most important people in my life would wish: to protect her. Let us hurry!"

After some bickering, the group finally succeeded in packing the automobile and set off. David had not yet changed clothes and drove as fast as was safe on the unpaved and increasingly crowded roads. He followed the coast, and as he had on the way north, encountered checkpoints on the way south. The Turkish soldiers respected his uniform and after several hours, David's group found the ship lying at anchor in Jaffa. David requisitioned a boat to ferry everyone to the ship, and changing clothes, looked the refugee, head to toe.

"Now understand, everyone," said David, "we are all American Jews, otherwise we might not be taken aboard. Let me and Ephraim do the talking—especially Ephraim."

The second and fourth stacks of the ship were belching smoke, and the crew had turned out in white and khaki. An officer walked down from the bridge as the group boarded and were being questioned and said, "Who is from the South amongst you people?"

Ephraim offered, "I'm as Southern as you can get, from Charleston, Cap."

The officer said, "I'm Commander Cuthbert Hawes, refugee coordinator for our Captain, Joseph W. Oman, and I'm pleased to meet an American, even in these circumstances. We'll accommodate you folks as best we can and return you to our shores as soon as orders allow."

"Captain, I'm David Rosenberg, from New York. The ladies are quite shy, so you'll have to forgive them if they are a little quiet."

"Well, speak for yourself, Mr. Rosenberg," said Hulda. "Commander, I'm Hulda Yoffey from Florida." The Mobile accent lilted off her tongue like a true Southern Belle.

"Well, you are mighty handsome women," said the Commander, having also noticed Olivia and Ruth, flashing gray eyes. "Another officer will show you to your quarters, which I must apologize for in advance. He will instruct you as to the routine the ship will require. Pleasure to meet you, you all." With that, the Commander tipped his hat and scrambled back up the stairs leading to the ship's flying bridge.

"Why, he sounds like one of those men those girls in Pensacola are marrying off with," Hulda said. "Those girls don't love 'you,' they love 'you all,' and they"ll snap up the one that bites!" observed Hulda.

"You better hush, Hulda, before you find yourself thrown into the wine-dark sea, young lady," said Ephraim.

"Oh, my goodness, it's my dear old Uncle Ephraim, the classist. I declare, if it hadn't been for our beautiful Ruth's good education, you'd just be a dull old engineer for the rest of your life, hanging around the Hill, looking for something to build or some old pipe to bury to move rainwater to the Bayou," said Hulda in impeccable *Mobileese*.

"*Please*, will you people quiet?" said David, slipping a little on English syntax.

A young officer approached and led them through a starboard hatch and down two flights of steps. They finally arrived near the stern and were shown a stateroom next to a Junior Officer's cabin on the portside.

"What's your name, young man?" asked Ephraim.

"I am Ensign Jonathan Marks, sir, from Savannah, Georgia."

"You're a Jewish boy, then."

"No sir, it's spelled with a 'K', sir."

"Well, my mistake. We want you to know how much we appreciate your help, Ensign."

"That's okay, sir. The Commander probably assumed I was Jewish and asked for me to conduct you through. Please notice the showers and the head—I mean the washroom—across the way. You'll need to be cautious when the ladies wish to use them and warn us, so we can keep the crew out. We'll come get you at mess, mealtime, and take you to the Junior Officers' Mess Room. In the meantime, here's some fresh bread and preserves to keep you until mess." The Ensign unwrapped the bread from some reddish paper and took a jar of peach preserves out of a pocket and gave the food to Ephraim.

"How old are you, Ensign, if you don't mind my asking?" asked Ephraim.

"I'm twenty-four, sir."

"That's a mighty good age to be, son" said Ephraim. He looked at Hulda, who immediately stuck her nose up and found a bunk to take down from the stateroom bulkhead.

"I'll excuse myself, now, but if you need anything, just ask one of the crew to find me, and I'll get back to you as soon as I can," said Marks.

David had found a top bunk and pulled it down from the bulk-head. He crawled into the bunk and relaxed into a deep sleep.

Olivia sat on the side of the bunk below David, and Hulda was opposite, falling to sleep, also. Ruth and Ephraim took the other top bunk, and in spite of her displeasure with him, she allowed them to snuggle together until she became restless and sat up and looked down out of the porthole. She wondered where her parents were now, and worried that no amount of planning could entirely protect them and the wealth they had accumulated for themselves and Uncle Isaac. She would contact a Zionist organization as soon as she reached the United States and ask them to contact her relations. In the meantime, she thought of the new life she would have to build with Ephraim, her husband. She had also discovered that she was pregnant. She kept remembering Ephraim's strange stories of "The Hill" and his eccentric brother the doctor, and she wondered how she would adapt. Finally, she eased back gently beside her husband and lay back to find sleep also.

David awakened to the ship underway, swaying gently, and apparently, under full steam. He could see wisps of coal smoke blow by the porthole, and with the assistance of a member of a passing crewman, found his way on deck, where a warm sun was beating down and a steady breeze, generated by the ship's movement, blew along the length of the vessel. He finally found Ensign Marks and asked about their destination.

"Beirut sir, and then Alexandria to assist more stranded Americans."

"Ah well, thank you, Mr. Marks. May I stay on deck?'

"You may, sir. Just make certain to alert me when you come up," replied Marks.

"Thank you, sir."

Marks had noticed a slight English accent in David's speech and wondered if his passenger had immigrated to the United States before going to Palestine. The man didn't really look Jewish, at least like the Jews Marks had known in Savannah and at Annapolis, but the thought didn't quite inspire suspicion. The height, the thick, blond hair, and the lean, well-structured, tanned face reminded him of an American college athlete. The young man appreciated David's somewhat martial bearing, his tendency to bow his head. The man appeared to *belong* in the military.

The two men separated, and David stood alongside the rail and watched as the ship moved past the Levantine coast. He eventually returned to the stateroom and saw that everyone was awake and chatting.

"I have news," David said. We are going to Beirut and then to Alexandria. Beyond that, I do not know."

"That's wonderful," said Ephraim, "I feel like Agamemnon trying to get home."

"*Oy*," said Ruth, rolling her eyes.

"So, what does that make me, Uncle? Electra?" said Hulda.

"It might make you Iphigenia, young lady, if you don't behave!" replied Ephraim.

The cruise continued taking on more passengers. The little group found ways of making themselves useful. Ruth and Olivia helped with the refugee children, and Hulda worked in the sick bay. Ephraim helped the engineer and David did odd jobs about the cruiser. At last, after many weeks, the ship gained port in Boston, and the refugees had to disembark at the Navy Yard and be taken to an immigration office for processing.

They all entered a building crowded with people rushing about and speaking all manner of tongues. Ruth, Olivia, and David declared themselves Palestine Jews and were recorded as new immigrants. Ephraim and Hulda cleared their identities as Americans to the satisfaction of the authorities, and after health examinations, all were allowed to leave. Hulda was able to send a telegram to her father, who responded several hours later with instructions to visit the Boston branch of Chemical Bank, where funds would be available to pay for traveling expenses and rail transportation to the Bay, via Mobile, Alabama.

After this had been achieved, David and Olivia returned to the Navy Yard in search of Ensign Jonathan Marks and Captain Oman.

They managed to find Ensign Marks and were able to express their gratitude and to give him their address of destination. The Ensign thanked them and David saluted, clicking his heels for the first time since deserting the German Army.

"If fate should bring you our way, please pay us a visit, Ensign" said David. "I can offer German lessons, if you need them."

Marks smiled. Someday, you'll tell me an interesting story, my friend, he thought.

The train was scheduled to leave later that evening: Boston to New York to Richmond to Atlanta to Mobile with a transfer to the Bay. Before the group departed, Hulda, Ruth, and Ephraim took David and Olivia to the Cambridge courthouse, Boston's being too busy, and with their new immigration papers, they were married.

Hulda wondered what Savannah boys were really like.

40

Isaac stood on the balcony of the red house near the head of the inlet at Riomaggiore, holding a letter he had received at Corconio. He had escaped to Italy with Mentes, prepared following the note from his dear friend Cohen with the English. He'd received a further warning, after what was meant to be a final warning from his friends in government, that the Turks were becoming less organized and suspicious. Most of his assets had been kept in Italy: The Villa Elena, with its acres, rich flocks, vines, and thick rows of chestnuts, its income and the untouched inherited wealth that had always been safely banked in Milan. Now, smuggled from Turkey, thin gold bars that had been concealed in the sub-floor, pillars, and roof of his Mercedes Phaeton were unloaded by Mentes and stored in the wine cellar of the Villa. The business in Constantinople had been turned over to Iacob Benetar *Bey*, long his trusted general manager. His household staff had been placed with other families, and his house was left empty and looked after by Iacob Bey. Only Mentes was retained.

Isaac was worried, his face more lined and crossed with wrinkles than even a few months ago, but his heart was consoled that Olivia had escaped from Palestine, according to sources, at least reliable to his brother, Binyamin. Binyamin and his wife were in hiding now that the Turks had instigated anti-Semitic hostility against every Palestinian Jew—native or settler. November had been a trying month for Isaac with little sleep. A few days by the sea, he thought, would help clear his head, and perhaps, allow him to find some welcome rest. He sat on the veranda and waited for his housekeeper Marina, brought from the Villa, to serve lunch. He slapped the plain envelope into his palm, repeatedly, trying to guess what it held. It had been post stamped in Germany and received, Marina claimed, at the Villa a week ago. He was surprised that the Italian authorities had not opened the letter, but until the country's leadership made a decision to support the Germans or the French, life would probably go on with the usual native *laissez-faire* informality. Finally, he opened the envelope and unfolded the letter, taking in the perfumed scent he'd come to know so well.

3 November 1914
Gräfin Claramond Kathe von Petersruhe-Matthäus
Vogelgesangstein
Baden
Signore Isaac Becouche-Albukerk
Villa Elena
Corconio, Italy

My Dearest Isaac:

It is with a hopeful heart that I inform you that your dear Olivia and my son, David, have escaped Palestine, courtesy of the American battleship, North Carolina. I came by this information, yesterday, via an American diplomatic consul, which I've agreed not to identify. They are en route to the United States, but I have no information on their port of debarkation. As we both have known, our dear children had given the impression of some regard toward each other before they left Constantinople, and now, with David forsaking his military career, I believe that our old friend Eros has, perhaps, aimed correctly.

I would like to suggest that you notify the Yafey family, whose American roots run deep (as deep as American Jews can!), and inform them that Olivia is due to arrive. I will ask my American to endeavor to gain knowledge of their destination and inform you as soon as I possibly can.

Needless to say, Sigi is heartbroken by David's actions, but is trying very diligently to understand how the boy could have come to his decision. David is a thoughtful, circumspect, young man and I trust that protecting your Olivia provided the circumstances that persuaded him to abandon his military duty.

I hope to see you again in spite of our agreement; I long for you.

Your

Kathe

Isaac sat still. Tears welled up in his eyes and looking up at the late fall sun moving west, he thought of man's history of decisions and sacrifices for love. He wondered: Are there gods, as represented by the manuscripts and relics he'd combed through, to push along mankind with the consequences of their own loves, hatreds and jealousies? Did Dido have to be abandoned? Was Nietzsche correct by playing with us like the ancients? He thought of his daughter with her shining, almond-shaped eyes and intelligence. Where is she now? Is she moving across the back of the ocean, waving up the flying fish and dolphins and anchoring the heart of Kathe's young son? Where do I go?

Marina served lunch and quickly disappeared. As Isaac dined, the sea continued to kick up, dashing the rocks and the tiny harbor's facilities. Marina appeared below, going to the market, walking down the cobbled street duck-like, avoiding the few people moving around the town. She found the shops she needed before the piles of multicolored fishing boats that were stacked haphazardly but secured against the foaming waves.

Isaac thought of the many fishermen locked indoors, unable to launch their boats and working on nets, repairing sails, or niggling or making love to their women. He realized that none of these things was of any importance to him, but he knew that the various and random acts of anyone in Riomaggiore could affect him, somehow. He felt defiant, ready to face the universe and dodge the thunderbolts.

He spent the night listening to the waves, feeling the cool air flow through the house, and resting well. His dreams were haunted by traveling, movement, and sudden jolts, but they were not peopled or anxious. He awoke only once, arose from his bed, and looked out upon the harbor, at the dim light and the wandering dogs. As he slid back into bed, he thought of the American ship carrying Olivia and the young man who would take her from him. He fell asleep quickly.

41

David helped Ephraim Yoffey hang the small sign reading "Bay Engineering" off one of the porch posts outside of their modest office located on South Reed Street in Belmont Bay. David had been able to obtain his engineering license partly on the basis of his claim of attendance at the *Universität Karlsruhe* before, as he characterized it, emigrating to Palestine. His success on the engineering licensing examination offered by the State of Florida sealed the effort. He had fretted that, even though he had attended the school after his graduation from the *Kriegsschule* in Berlin, he had no way to obtain a copy of his degree, for now, at least.

The two men were helped by Ephraim's friends in the Bay and soon found their talents in structural work in demand. David and Olivia rented a two-bedroom, wood frame, shotgun-style house located next door to the new office, and David placed his letter from Captain Twinge in the bottom of their only chest of drawers. Olivia caused a stir when she began involving herself in the Jewish community, finding it an interesting mix of Ashkenazim and Sephardim, with most of the women well-to-do, and speaking with a particularly Southern type of accent that their new patron, Sam, referred to as "Mobileese."

Rabbi Fischer fell in love with her, of course, even though he had married one of the doyens of the congregation ten years before. Olivia's lithe frame and almond-shaped eyes captured the attention of all, and when she spoke with her soft Mediterranean accent, she pulled a throng of listeners around her, all wishing to touch the exotic embellishments she had incorporated into her new Western clothes. She longed for her father, but she knew their plan had been well conceived, and she trusted that he was safely back in Italy, hopefully in touch with Kathe.

Eventually, after nearly a year, Olivia re-established a connection with Isaac, posting to and receiving letters from his Villa in Corconio. He often sent photographs of the lakes and vineyards and an occasional image of himself, usually with friends, and recently with a beautiful blonde woman whose eyes shone from the sepia-toned or black and white images. Isaac had written that Kathe had joined him. There was also a gaunt figure wearing a broad straw hat sitting in profile in the background. His right arm was held up into the air before him and his hand, fanned out, appeared to have just released something, his fingers fading into the tones of the Villa behind him. The name on the back of the photo: Dieter Schlarp.

Through the Red Cross, David had been able to contact Kathe in Baden to explain his circumstances, altering his desertion of the German army to a kidnapping exploit, since he knew the German censors would read their correspondence. At any rate, he felt it important that she knew he was safe and had married Olivia. He learned that Sigi and his grandmother, Elisabeth, had both died before he had left Palestine, and that Kathe had moved to Italy as confirmed by Isaac's letters. He soon discovered that her new address matched that of Olivia's father.

Ephraim, Ruth, and their baby Leah had found a small bungalow on the Hill directly across the Bayou from his office, and they enjoyed a quiet life off the Bayfront, on the opposite side of the neighborhood from Sam's home, where the old doctor had persuaded Hulda to return.

Ruth enjoyed life in the Bay, dropping most of her sarcasm and absorbing the affection of her husband and the wonder of her new baby. Her speech did not soften, however, and she commanded the rhythms of her family life, keeping her "Yoffey" circling around the ineluctable dip in space her presence brought. She and the baby walked by the hospital most days and down the Hill to the Bay, where she collected shards of pottery, unusual rocks, and parts of the regular combination of ships ballast dumped in the area. She learned to crab, stopping by the local butchers to haggle with them for scraps of unsellable meat, and dangling it from sticks she drove into the Bay bottom to entice the creatures. She built little shelters for the baby and tied string onto her tiny leg when it was time to wade out to check her lines, but she still could not resist looking back on the child.

Hulda renewed her acquaintance with the sisters and regularly visited the hospital on behalf of Sam and Anna Jane, who, despite purchasing and learning to drive an automobile to ease their labors, did not enjoy contact with the nuns. They reminded him of his *abduction* of Sister James, as the sisters liked to term it. Hulda liked walking up and down the great Hill, finding the places where she could see both the shimmering Bayou and the Bay and keenly feel the winds of the changing seasons. The old rutted highway had finally been nicely paved, causing Hill residents to begin muttering that most dreaded of phrases: City Annexation. Hulda managed her father's practice, but rarely acted in a nursing capacity. She very effectively, supervised the young lady Sam had employed who replaced the nurse who had been supervised by Anna Jane. Hulda was now approaching her mid-twenties, and Linny began a campaign of "wedin' off that girl." She told Sam and Anna Jane that they needed to bring his younger colleagues, or as Linny called them, "Hoo-Do's," around for dinner on the weekends. Gomey based *her* campaign on sending the girl off to the *rarified*, as she put it, well-connected, Mobile relations.

Temple had gotten into the ferry business after Willard had run off with Old Jones' son's *un-rarified* wife to Mobile, leaving Willard's, newer, larger-capacity, blunt-nosed bay boat to Temple. Temple didn't expect him to return, so he painted the craft yellow with paint he had borrowed from the County's paving crew while they took a break from striping the new Second Street Hill road. He had found love with the young assistant pastor, Brother Solomon, at the church he and Gomey attended every Monday evening, Wednesday evening, Friday evening, and

Sunday morning and evening. The men shared a small shotgun house that they had altered to a *faux* duplex, installing two doors on one of the long sides for the sake of appearances. Solomon had contributed a camelback sofa, and Temple brought the remains of a hurricane-wreaked dining set he'd salvaged from a large old house owned by the county tax collector and temporarily abandoned on the Bay. They enlarged the kitchen to accommodate a bed, placed opposite an old wood stove. Temple, being Temple, threatened to withhold passage over the Bayou from Ephraim and David if they continued "carrying on with that talk about a bridge" connecting the town and the Hill.

Gomey continued ironing Sam's clothes and supervising Linny. Linny finally admitted that her grown son was the product of her "helpfulness" to one of the white attendants who worked at the hospital. He also sneaked into town weekly to procure Sam's chewing tobacco. The boy, "Cuz," as he was known, had the same tall frame of his mother, but he spoke quietly if he needed to speak at all. Temple called him, "Creepin' Cuz" and employed him as a bay man. He took Willard's place on one of their older boats.

Near the end of October, 1915, a nicely uniformed young navy man walked up the worn limestone and brick walkway leading to Sam's house and took the three steps onto the porch in one bound. He had a "mouth full of teeth" as Linny later described and hair as blond as a "bowl of Gulf sand." He was sturdily built and spoke with an accent Sam later said he had heard but could not place. He was sure it was "not Floridian South or Mobileese." His woolen Navy blues appeared starched and correct, and he would have instinctively placed his hands behind his back after he knocked determinedly on Sam's mezuzah thinking it some kind of amplifier of sound, but given the pain he'd inflicted on himself, he decided to examine his skinned knuckles instead, and then try the bare doorframe with the other set of knuckles— below the tarnished metal object.

Linny appeared quickly, cracking open the worn edges of the

black screen door, and the young man asked her if "a Miss Hulda Yoffey lived here." Linny looked at the man and decided that he was "smart looking" and had to be some kind of police, being a white man and dressed up "all certified-looking."

"You needs to see Dr. Sam. His office is at 11 Second Street, just up the Hill." She shut the heavy wooden door. The man didn't know how to find that address, so he knocked again and asked Linny to give him directions. She came outside, eyeing him suspiciously, and with a rolling pin in one hand, used an oak stick in the other to draw directions in the bare, oak-shaded sand of the front yard.

"Thank you, ma'am." The man moved off with purpose. His black shoes were dusty, and he was beginning to perspire under his Lieutenant's uniform, but his determination to find Hulda rendered these usually enormous concerns almost forgotten. He trudged up the Hill and finally arrived at the picket fence just outside Sam's office. He squared himself away, went through the gate, and knocked at the door, which just eased quietly open before him. The room was almost bare, except for a large oak desk and four cane-bottomed chairs. The man called, "Is anyone here?"

A reddish-gray haired man with what resembled a cloth bowl on his head stuck his head around a panel next to the desk and said, "What's the Navy doing here? I'm Rabbi Fischer."

Hulda, the attractive, raven-haired young woman the young man remembered came through a doorway carrying a worn, brown folio and wearing a white nurse's pinafore apron and nurse's cap. Her light eyes became wider, and she said, "Ensign Marks!"

The handsome officer said, "Well, ma'am, it's now Lieutenant Marks. I've come to ask you to marry me, ma'am."

This announcement brought Fischer out of his seat and scrambling for the door, his cane bumping along the linoleum beside him. After he'd gotten outside, he began calling, "Sam!"

Hulda's hands rose immediately to her mouth, and her eyes

began to moisten. She hadn't seen Marks since Boston and had one letter from him informing her that he would be arriving at the neighboring town's Navy Station with the *North Carolina* in the coming months. Hulda walked over to a chair and sat, keeping her hands over her mouth. She looked up at the tall officer and said, "You're over in Pensacola, now?"

"Yes, ma'am. The ship is there, fitted with a long platform to launch aeroplanes while underway. You may have noticed all the crash boats this far over in the Bay. Miss Hulda, I have to get back to the ship before eight bells at dusk, and I know this must be a shock, but it would most convenient if you could give me an answer in a hurry."

"Yes."

CPSIA information can be obtained
at www.ICGtesting.com
Printed in the USA
LVOW12*0831241017
552919LV00001BA/4/P

9 781614 935247